panic-button

THE ORDER OF RAVENS AND WOLVES

To Becky and Brooklyn. You have been with me since Logan took over my thoughts. You've listened to my crazy, seen me argue with all the boys in the Order and contemplate murder (Naomi). My writing journey started with Aftereffect and this one was bittersweet for me. While I have other projects I'm looking forward to diving into, I'm sad that this series is coming to an end. But that pain is a lot less because I know I have you two in my corner. Your smiles brighten my day.

AUTHOR WARNING

This book contains themes and subject matter that is intended for a mature audience. The story may contain but is not limited to, violence, murder, death, profanity, tobacco use, drug use, kidnapping, choking, knife play, bondage, extreme sexual situations, a girl that is not happy about the extreme sexual situations, (don't worry she comes around), a very snappy turtle, suspense, crime, and Whitley family dinner. Reader discretion is advised.

Name Pronunciation

- Micha: Mike - ah
- Ryker: Rye - cur
- Silas: Sye - lass
- Riley: Rye - lee
- Paisley: Pase - lee
- Derek: Dare - ick
- Marnie: Mar - knee
- Trina: Tree - nah
- Logan: Low - gan
- Mason: Mase - on
- Preston: Press - ton
- Parker: Park - er
- Finn: Finn
- Junior: June - your
- Shelby: Shell - bee
- Naomi: Nay - oh - me (bitch)
- Chase: Chase
- Tanner: Tan - er
- Amy: A - me
- Ava: A - va
- Whitley: Witt - lee
- Kessler: Kess - ler
- Creswell: Cress - well
- Mathers: Ma - th - ers
- Grier: Gr - ear
- Harper: Har - per
- Louis: Lou - is
- Lana: La - na
- Sean: Sha - awn

The Order Of Ravens And Wolves Titles

KINGS:

- Louis Kessler (King go Kings)
- Dean Whitley
- Sebastian Creswell
- Dr. Martin Creswell
- Ryker Hudson

KNIGHTS:

- Micha Kessler (Future king of kings)
- Mason Kessler
- Logan Hudson
- Parker Whitley
- Preston Whitley
- Silas Creswell
- Finn Creswell

Playlist

'Fisher King And Traitor Down' by Felix Erskine
'Play With Fire' by Sam Tinnesz
'Choke' by I Don't Know How But They Found Me
'Take Me To Church' by Hozier
'Sail' by Awolnation
'Devil's Playground' by The Rigs
'River' by Bishop Briggs
'Centuries' by Fall Out Boy
'Enemy' by Imagine Dragons
'Bodies' by Drowning Pool
'Lovely' by Billie Eilish
'Darkside' by Neoni
'Uh Oh' by Sub Urban
'I Feel Like I'm Drowning' by Two Feet
'Dolls' by Bella Poarch
'Heaven Knows' by The Pretty Reckless
'Vigilante Shit' by Taylor Swift
'Devil Devil' by Milck
'Demons' by Hayley Kiyoko
'Panic Room' by Au/Ra

NOTE FROM PRESTON

Before we begin, I'd like to clear up a few things. This won't be another tale where the villain finds his heart. I'm not some damaged soul that does things because someone hurt me. I do them because I want to. So, get rid of any romanticized ideas you have of a dark prince falling in love. This isn't that story.

This is my story.

There will be no moment of tenderness where I pet your head and call you "Good Girl." So get rid of that hopeful sparkle in your eyes. The only thing you have to be hopeful for is a quick end.

I will fuck you.

I will break you.

Then, when I'm bored, I will kill you.

Now, take a few moments and reflect on the decisions that brought you here. Once we begin, there is no going back. I will not relent, I will not back down, and I will not feel sorry for anything I do. There is no heart beating in my chest or soul to be damned. The only thing you'll find here in this dark abyss is pain and suffering I feed on.

I am the Devil of Death.

And you are my next victim.

Prologue

Marnie

TWO YEARS AGO,

*J*ostling someone awake had the same effect as if they were forced to walk down a dark alley at night in a city with an active serial killer. A person's heart leaped forward, trying to break through their ribs, caging them in while every single nerve ending lit up with alertness.

Thanks to my sister, this was a feeling I'd become used to over the years. Since our parents nailed her window shut, Trina used mine as her secret escape.

Two or three times a week, I'd be woken up by the sound of her feet landing on my floor. I used to get mad at her but quickly realized that was a wasted effort. Trina was going to do what Trina wanted to do.

So when that feeling pulled me out of dreamland, my first thought was, 'What did Trina do now?' Except there was no light thud from the other side *of my room or whispered apology. Just a sense of unease and icy shivers that pulsed down my spine, causing my skin to prick up in goosebumps.*

The alarm tickling at the back of my brain wasn't caused by my sister sneaking into my room. It was something else—an intense sensation of eyes on me.

I was being watched.

The oppressive stare weighed me down, pressing my body into the mattress.

No...that wasn't what it was.

Someone was sitting on me! Someone a lot heavier than my sister.

This was the part where I should be panicking. My body was responding properly. My heart beat wildly in my chest as my lungs struggled to work. Riley and Shelby would be screaming by now. Even Trina would've thrashed about, but the only thing my brain would let me do was slowly flutter my eyelids open.

A million things flew through my mind in that short time. What was happening? Who was in my room? Should I turn the light on? Should I grab a weapon? Or was I in trouble again? My knees were still raw from the last pile of rice I was forced to kneel on.

The face I saw staring down at me sucked all the oxygen out of the room.

"Hello, Little Bird."

Preston Whitley!

A quick piercing squeak vibrated through my ears, followed by muffled incoherent whines. It took a second for me to realize that the sound wasn't just ringing through my ears. It was vibrating up my throat. I was the one screaming.

Not that it was doing any good, considering Preston had his hand clamped over my mouth. His fingers dug into my cheeks, grinding my tender inner flesh against my teeth. My mouth was parched, and the dull ache caused by his grip made me whimper.

But I didn't stop.

I couldn't.

Preston Whitley wasn't just some guy. He was the guy the boogeyman hid from. My only hope was to keep emptying my lungs into his palm while I prayed that my parents would hear me. Why I thought that would help, I wasn't sure. All the intelligence in the world didn't matter when instinct took over.

Preston gave my head a firm shake. "Quiet down, Little Bird."

My mind snapped back. I knew this man and the things his little society did. The fact that he thought he could order me around was nothing short of cute. Part of me wanted to smile when I opened my mouth and let out another muffled scream.

That was my first mistake. While I'd dealt with threats before—consequences of revealing people's secrets—Preston Whitley wasn't like other men.

I didn't think he was a man at all. He was every parent's worst nightmare. He was the monster hiding in your closet, the dark temptations my father preached about to his flock—kind of ironic, considering my lack of compassion. Then again, my father didn't know about my non-existent empathy.

No one did.

"I see we have a communication problem. So, I'll make this real simple for you. Shut. The. Fuck. Up." Preston tsked while pulling a pistol out from behind him. "Or, I'll go in the next room and fuck your mother with this."

Was it wrong that I was curious how that would work? A woman's vagina was meant to stretch, but the barrel of a gun didn't have any give. Would it hurt? Would it tear?

"Tell me, Little Bird, why don't you seem scared?" Preston tipped his head and cocked a brow down at me. "You know I'll do it."

Oh, I was scared, just not of his threat.

"Maybe I should visit your sister's room instead?"

That worked.

My heart stopped as I sucked back my scream so fast that I choked on it.

I may not like the things my sister did, but Trina was innocent. Suddenly, the barrel of his pistol wasn't intriguing anymore. It was the most daunting thing in the world. I could see the abyss in that tiny hole cut into the black metal.

How many people had Preston killed with that pistol? Was their last sight a bullet traveling down a tube, like I was imagining? Or was it a quick and easy 'lights out?' No, someone like him wouldn't let anything be quick or easy.

Preston's eyes narrowed, daring me to make another peep. Once he was sure I would stay quiet, he removed his hand from my mouth and sat up, pressing his weight down on my hips.

I thought about trying to wriggle away, but even if I did manage to get out from under him, I'd never be able to outrun him.

Then again, I did have options.

I slid my gaze over to the black stone lamp on my bedside table. Smacking him on the head with that might give me the advantage I needed.

"Go ahead," Preston challenged. "Pick it up."

My eyes snapped back to his. There was no way he could know what I was thinking. It was too dark for him to see anything. My window only let in a sliver of moonlight.

Unless...

I tipped my head to study the cold gray orbs staring down at me. Surely even someone like him would be a touch uncomfortable in an unfamiliar place. Yet, he was completely relaxed.

"You've been in my room before?"

"I have."

He'd invaded my personal space. Why was that more terrifying than the gun?

I remained quiet and waited for him to do something. Kill me, beat me, slap me, or give me some hint as to why he was here.

Preston didn't do anything. He just sat there staring at me, which was so much worse.

The hairs on the back of my neck rose, and my body tensed as the silence continued. Not because he wasn't doing anything, but because I could feel him on me.

His weight pressed down on my legs, preventing me from kicking. The muscles in his thighs flexed against my hips, reminding me how useless it would be to fight. He was made of stone, and I was the weak material he could smash to bits.

Why wasn't he smashing me to bits?

Preston didn't feel bad for any of the countless evil acts he'd committed or sympathize with other people. He did what he wanted and damn everyone else.

I knew this because I'd been watching The Order Of Ravens And Wolves for years. The only thing that made a secret society full of rich and powerful men worse was someone like him.

Was that why he was here? Because I'd researched the founding families and uncovered some of their secrets.

I knew I shouldn't have confronted them at Chase's parlor, but I couldn't control myself. Riley was suddenly dating Micha Kessler, whom she hated with every fiber of her being, then she disappeared. I knew The Order had something to do with it. I should've kept my mouth shut. Now Preston was going to torture me, kill me, or both.

So, why hadn't he?

I rolled my eyes over the jean jacket wrapped around his shoulders, then up to his lips, framed by the five o'clock shadow coating his angular jaw. If he'd come to kill me, then why was I still alive?

Sure, Preston looked like a dreamboat, the guy that every girl wanted with his tousled sandy hair, but he was ruthless. If he didn't want me breathing, then I wouldn't be.

"Why are you here?"

His brow arched. "Why do you think I'm here?"

If I didn't know any better, I'd say he was trying to outsmart me. That was a game I could win.

"You're not here to kill me." At least, I hoped he wasn't. I was rather fond of breathing.

I swear I saw a smirk tug on the corner of his mouth. "How sure are you about that?"

If I had any chance of surviving this, then I had to use my best weapon. My only weapon, actually. The mind was a powerful thing, and mine was more powerful than most.

"If you wanted me dead, then I would be."

"Clever girl." He nodded.

He had no idea.

My heart pounded as he leaned back and trickled his gaze down my body. Every fiber of my being told me to hit him and run away. It wasn't impulse or instinct that allowed people to survive. It was intelligence, knowing when it was time to take a chance. Now wasn't the right moment.

"The truth is, Little Bird, I had every intention of killing you." Preston leaned down, folding his large body over mine, and whispered, "Could you feel my gun at the back of your head in Daddy's church?"

My body went on full alert, tensing every muscle. Before I knew what was happening, my arm swung through the air. One word swam through my head as my palm struck the side of his face.

Stupid.

Dread settled in my bones when Preston twisted his neck to glare back down at me. The red mark on his cheek and the stinging on my palm were enough to tell me I got him good. So, why did he look pleased? A disturbing expression on someone like him. There was a twinkle in his gray eyes that wasn't there before, and now I couldn't stop staring at it.

Logan Hudson was an asshole who charmed people with a similar look. But on Preston...

The ramifications of making him feel anything were utterly terrifying. I'd heard the stories. Trina knew someone who'd spent a night with him. Let's just say she was never the same. Had she seen the same twinkle? Or was this something reserved for his darker intents? And trust me, no one, including the devil himself, was in a hurry to see the dark side of Preston Whitley.

"I'm trying really hard to follow my own moral guidelines here."

I snorted. "You don't have any moral guidelines."

"Oh, but I do, Marnie."

He brushed his hand over my forehead, sweeping my hair to the side and making me retreat into the pillow.

"For instance, I could take you now instead of waiting for you to graduate."

What the hell did that mean? Take me for what?

"But..." Preston sighed and rolled his gaze back up to mine. "I don't fuck little girls."

I couldn't breathe or make my mouth move. My mind screamed at me to do something, but I just lay there, staring back at him.

"Not very fond of that idea, I see." He pressed the barrel of his gun to my temple. "If you prefer, I could shoot right now?"

The coolness of the heavy metal bored into my skull. Then something *strange happened. I'd seen shows where survivors talked about how their life flashed before their eyes.*

My father even spoke about things like that at church. I never put much stock into it. There was no reason. Why should I worry about heaven and hell when there were so many real-world problems?

Images flashed before my eyes: Trina and I at the beach, Sundays at church with our parents, and the day we met Shelby and Riley. They were quick glimpses, yet every image was so vivid I could smell them.

Maybe there was a heaven after all?

"Or," Preston said while pulling the pistol away from my face. "I could slit your family's throats and take you regardless."

My eyes widened as one word slipped through my lips. "Don't."

I'd rather die a thousand times than watch someone I cared about suffer. There was a reason I spent my time trying to expose people like him.

Seemingly satisfied with my response, Preston tucked the gun into the back of his jeans. "I knew you'd see things my way."

I could feel tears burning my eyes every time I blinked, but I refused to let them fall. Preston didn't deserve them. He could do whatever he wanted, and I would die without giving him a single drop of my misery.

"Aww, Little Bird, look on the bright side." Preston leaned forward and braced his palms on the bed beside my head. "Maybe you'll bore me, and I'll kill you quickly." The smile that washed across his face sent a chill through my bones. "But your family will be alive."

I no longer cared that he was straddling me or that he had a gun. The only thing I cared about was getting away. I swung my arms, smacking Preston in the face and chest while wriggling with all my might to get out from under his heavy body.

My fight lasted point two seconds.

Preston's large palm cracked off the side of my face, bringing my struggles to a grinding halt with one stinging blow. A loud ringing stilled my entire body. My cheek was on fire, and my sight was hazy, but I still held back my tears.

"That was for your own good." He waved his finger in front of my face as if he was scolding a child. "If you kept that shit up, your parents would've

come in here, and I'd have had to kill them. And you don't want that, do you?"

Didn't I?

I lay there, tasting the coppery tinge of my blood while staring at the teddy bears on my faded wallpaper. My father put that wallpaper up when I was five and obsessed with Teddy Ruxpin. I hated coming in here and seeing it. It was like the walls decorating my bedroom were a constant reminder that my parents thought I was a naïve child.

I wasn't that naïve. I knew the truth about who my parents were. Just like I knew if Preston did kill them, they'd deserve it. So, why was I wondering if that wallpaper would be the last thing I had of my father?

"Answer me, Marnie," Preston demanded. "Do you want that?"

"No," I whispered because my sister loved them.

"That's a good girl."

The next thing I knew, he was folded over me, petting my head. It was weird laying there in the moonlight while the devil stroked my hair. I could hear his fingers dragging through my brown locks. It mingled with the sound of his breaths in this odd rhythmic chorus that, despite my fear, had my body relaxing.

Then he spoke again.

"You are a good girl, aren't you, Marnie? Not a slut like your sister." His lips grazed across the shell of my ear, sending a cold chill down my spine. "If you've so much as touched another cock our deal ends here."

I knew what he meant. Just like I knew if I lied, the deal wouldn't end with him simply walking out and leaving me alone.

"I'm a virgin." I'd never been so happy to say those words in my life.

"Good."

Preston speared his fingers into my hair and yanked my head back, dragging his nose up the side of my neck. I closed my eyes as he inhaled deeply, then released a feral growl.

"You have no idea how hard it is not to fuck you right now. Tell me, Little Bird, will you lie down and take my cock?" His tongue reached out, pulling my earlobe between his teeth. "Or will you fight me?"

I twisted my neck to glare back at him and winced at the burn tearing *across my scalp. "Don't worry. I'll have lots of experience by the time I graduate."*

My sister made me shake my head at least twice a day. But if acting like her saved me from the clutches of darkness, I'd date every guy in school.

All hint of amusement washed off Preston's face.

"Wrong answer." His grip slid from my hair to my neck in the blink of an eye. "Consider yourself in a cage Little Bird, and if your finger so much as peeks through the bars, I'll punish your sister."

Fear welled up in my throat, forming a lump of dread I couldn't swallow past his tightening grip. Trina and I might not always see eye to eye, but I'd do anything to keep her safe.

Last year, some guy raped her while she was passed out at a party. If I could've traded places with her, I would've. Even when she told me to drop it, I exposed the asshole in the school paper. She still hadn't forgiven me for that.

She probably wouldn't forgive me for this either.

"I'll be good," I croaked out through my constricted airway.

"Prove it." Preston eased his grip and sat up. "Kiss me."

Time stopped, and I was unable to move.

"Right here." He clarified by tapping his cheek.

There was scruff on the spot he was touching.

A kiss wouldn't be so bad, and his request could've been worse than a quick peck. At least, that was what I told myself.

Preston stopped me when I moved to sit up.

"I want a sweet kiss, Little Bird, not a quick peck." He cocked his head and smirked at me. "Pretend you actually like me."

I glared up at him and gritted my teeth. Then I did the only thing I could. Leaning forward, I pressed my mouth to his cheek. The way his stubble abraded my lips was something I'd never forget. It pricked my skin like tiny little razor blades of death, reminding me of the deal I'd just made.

Preston groaned and jumped off the bed. "Be good, Marnie."

I watched him head over to my window. This wasn't the first time I traded my dignity to save Trina's. This time though, it wouldn't be an unwanted day of detention or lecture from our parents that I got. It'd be my soul that was taken. And I'd happily hand it over.

Before he slipped out the window, Preston paused and looked back at me. "I'll be watching."

I smiled back at him. He could have me, but he'd never touch her. Trina would stay safe while I plunged headfirst into hell to beat the devil at his own game.

Chapter 1

Preston

There were many milestones in a child's life—first steps, learning to talk, riding a bike...first punishment. Events that steered them in the right direction—unless that child was me. I didn't care about my father's lectures, the disappointment on his face, or the heavy swats to my ass. Those weren't what brought tears to my eyes.

It was anger.

Why should I clean up the nanny's blood? She was the one that spilled it. I just stuck the knife in her, which wouldn't have happened if she hadn't hit Parker. So, the mess was her fault. Not mine.

Life was a series of decisions that brought you to an end. Whether that end involved me or not...well, that would depend on the choices one made.

For example, the head I was staring at currently. Some decision or action had brought him and me to this place. What it was, I had no idea and didn't really give a shit. The only thing that mattered to me was the blood I'd spill all over the pew he was sitting on.

I'd been standing back here, tucked in the shadows of this old church, for about fifteen minutes. It wouldn't take much for this guy to notice me, a simple glance over his shoulder, yet he continued to sit where he was. Staring up at the empty altar, oblivious to the danger behind him.

It wouldn't save him even if he knew I was here. This night would end with my bullet in his skull. That was what happened when someone asked me for a favor. The someone, in this case, was Chase Mathers. That one surprised me a little.

Don't get me wrong, even I was envious of the body count he'd racked up over the past couple of months, but his time in hiding made the guy soft. If Riley were my niece...that fact alone would've signed Micha Kessler's death warrant.

Lillianna used to complain that her son was an emotionless void. That wasn't true. I felt things. In third grade, one of my classmates was hit by a car, and I was disappointed that I didn't get to see it.

I also felt great joy every time my parents took Parker to the hospital because he wasn't eating. He was eating. They just weren't the ones feeding him. My baby brother was too precious to suck off the vile teat of our mother.

So despite what everyone thought, I enjoyed life's pleasures.

Right now, I was trying to decide if I'd have steak or chicken while I fingered the hilt of my Desert Eagle. It'd been a while since I had a decent steak. However, there were some pretty good chicken places in Miami.

Lou would argue that my thought process was fucked up. When I was a kid, he wasted his time asking me useless questions. How would I feel if my parents died? Or what if someone made fun of me? My answer was always a simple shrug because, aside from my siblings, I didn't give a shit about anything.

Then I stuck that blade into the nanny's leg.

That was my milestone moment.

Sometimes, I could still see her bright red blood coating my tiny hand. The way the thick sticky fluid warmed my skin stuck with me. That was the first time I got hard.

I was eleven at the time and didn't understand my reaction. Was it the blood that got me off or how she looked at me when I stabbed her? Now, I knew the answer wasn't as simple as picking one choice or the other.

Lindsay Manheim helped me figure that out. She was the first girl I took out on a date. Perfect little Lindsay, with a sweet smile. My parents even approved of her. I'd never forget the desperate gasps that left her pretty pink lips when I wrapped my hand around her neck and choked the life out of her. I came so hard that my knees buckled.

That was a good night. My father disagreed but still helped me get rid of the body. Did I feel guilty about what I'd done?

No.

As my father and I watched Lindsay's body burn to ash, I had only one regret...

That I didn't drag out that panicked spark in her bright eyes a little longer.

Too bad I didn't have a knife on me now. I would have liked to watch this guy's blood pool on the floor.

Oh well.

I sighed internally and quietly rolled a suppressor on the barrel of my pistol. Chase wanted quick and clean, so that was what he'd get. At least he didn't ask any questions.

Lou, on the other hand...

After Lindsay, he really took an interest. For weeks I was pulled into his office and badgered with questions. Most of which I had no problem answering. I got it. Lou made his living understanding people's minds, so talking with him didn't bother me. Unfortunately, I couldn't answer his biggest question.

Why?

I had no idea why, but I did have a theory.

Every species on the planet had a predator, except for humans.

Wolves were reintroduced to Yellow Stone National Park because prey had taken over, putting the ecosystem at risk. Men like me were the equivalent of those wolves with one major exception.

We didn't clear the population out of need or hunger. We enjoyed doing it, and the prey came right to us. Take Bundy, for example. All he had to do to get his toy for the night was flash a smile.

I couldn't be bothered playing pretend, yet the girls kept coming, which was a prime example of the stupidity of the human race. They were the lemmings diving off a cliff, worthless in every way other than the slight satisfaction their death might bring.

Like the asshole currently in my sights—there was no need to kill him. I knew nothing about him other than that his name was Ricky, and Chase wanted him dead. Didn't care to know anything else.

Ricky was just another life I got the privilege of ending. He was nothing more than another number to add to my book, a foil flower to add to my collection. If anything, he was more of an annoyance.

I couldn't even take my time and enjoy his end. Slice him up and torture him a bit like I wanted. Doing that would be a lot better than this shit. Maybe I'd shoot Chase when I was done here for wasting my time.

Might as well get this done.

I stepped forward and paused when moonlight glinted off one of the candle sticks on the altar. The way it slid down the clean silver edge reminded me of another church I'd been to two years ago. That building was in much better shape than this one.

Actually, this church was one step above a hole in the ground, which was saying a lot considering the neighborhood around it. Pretty sure the house across the street was a crack den, and the one next to that was abandoned. On the upside, I couldn't ask for a better place to off someone.

My vision blurred as a girl with her head delicately bowed appeared on the pew next to Ricky. My gaze trickled over the long dark locks flowing down her back like the softest waterfall as I was brought back to that day.

I even had the same pistol in my hand.

Held it up to the back of her head with my finger on the trigger. Then I saw the book Marnie Dupire had tucked into the Bible she was pretending to read.

16

Ulysses was a hard book to get through—I had to read that shit for school—and there she was reading it for fun. Who the fuck did that?

It was that intrigue that saved her life that day.

I ducked back into the shadows and followed her around. I needed to find out what else she was hiding. Oh, and my Little Bird was hiding a lot. Shit that no one would really care about, but still.

I'd get it if she were jacking cars in her spare time or something like that...but superior intelligence? Hiding that, I didn't understand.

The girl could've given Finn a run for his money. I knew this because I'd found an IQ test she'd taken tucked away in her desk drawer, but she was wasting her potential in a public school. What possible gain could she get from doing that?

Marnie Dupire had every advantage right there, just waiting for her to reach out and take it. Yet she stayed tucked in the shadow of her slut sister.

There had to be a reason, and I was going to find out what it was. At least, that was my intent until the night I stood outside her bedroom window and watched her touch herself.

That was when my plan changed.

I'd fucked with many people in my time. I watched them crack as I tortured them or someone they loved and heard their pleas for mercy, their cries to end it and put them out of their misery. I even bent over a couple of straight guys so I could listen to them cry like little bitches while I fucked them. But it had all become too easy.

Bringing someone like Marnie Dupire to heel...now, that would be fun. My blood got pumping just thinking about it. She was the perfect toy, timid and shy on the outside but not nearly as meek on the inside. My Little Bird had claws, and I couldn't wait to feel her bite back.

No one in Ashen Springs dared to get in my face like she did.

"I know who you are, Preston Whitley."

Even now, I could see her bright aqua eyes shooting daggers at me. They were right there in front of me, glimmering with anger and hatred. I could almost reach out and touch...

Fuck.

I dropped my hand and suppressed the growl threatening to

rumble from my chest. Wouldn't exactly be a quick and easy job if Ricky turned around and saw me here. Not that I'd have an issue with that, but that wasn't what I was hired to do. And I was nothing if not professional.

The problem was, when I raised my gun, I could only see the cherrywood stand Jacques Dupire used to hold his Bible. While I didn't like the guy, I did have to give him props. Ashen Springs was a Catholic town, and he still managed to draw a decent-sized flock to his Baptist church.

Wonder how they'd feel about the skeletons in his closet? They came in handy for me. When I brought him the contract, he didn't even argue.

Did Marnie ever wonder why her sister was Daddy's favorite? Did she know what was going on behind closed doors? Maybe I'd let her in on the family secret and then make her kill him? Now, that was an image I could jerk off to tonight, shy little Marnie Dupire covered in her father's blood.

First, I had to take care of this situation.

I looked back at the brown hair on the back of the head in front of me. Ricky was taking all the fun out of this. He just sat there with his head bowed in some fake-ass prayer he was muttering. A small part of me wondered why he was bothering with the charade.

Why did she?

In the public eye, my Little Bird played the good girl, but when she was in her room, all alone...

If I hadn't been there to see her slip her hand in her panties, I might've killed her. Instead, I stood outside and stroked my cock while her moans vibrated through my bones. She was too young. Otherwise, I'd have fucked her right then and there. Not to mention she was untouched. Virgins weren't my thing.

Lindsay was the only one I'd been with. I couldn't be bothered with that gentle, nice bullshit. Marnie, however...I kind of liked the idea of not tasting another cock when I feasted on her cunt. Once I'd fucked her out of my system, I could slit her throat and toss her body off the bluffs.

I closed my eyes and inhaled the enticing aroma of her ecstasy. The image of Marnie writhing on her bed was so real that I could almost hear the soft moans echoing in my ears.

Fuck sakes, Preston, get your head in the game.

Shaking away the image, I tried to refocus on my target. It didn't help. When I raised my gun, a head with thicker, longer hair was still there in the pew. The sweet scent of peaches filled my nostrils, and I almost reached out to touch the ghostly girl before looking back at Ricky.

This wasn't the first time I'd had this problem. Marnie was fucking everything up. The closer it got to spring break, the more her face taunted me. That was when I planned to put my Bird in her cage.

Then again, why wait?

I could head up to her school when I was done here and rip her from her safe little sanctuary. She was eighteen now. There was no reason to hold back. Besides, it might be a good idea to get this settled. Distractions weren't an option in my line of work.

I just had to deal with Ricky first, boring Ricky with a simple shot to the head.

Fucking Chase.

I must've sighed because the next thing I knew, Ricky was slowly turning around. I stood there with the barrel aimed at him and waited until his eyes met mine. As soon as I saw a spark of fear light up in those dark depths, I squeezed the trigger.

Even with the suppressor on, the sound of my bullet leaving the chamber was loud enough to echo around the room. No one outside would hear it, but I enjoyed the *boom* tickling my ears almost as much as I enjoyed how his eyes dulled as his brains splattered across the pews behind him.

I think I'll have steak.

Stepping up to Ricky's hunched-over form, I reached into my jacket pocket, plucked out a small foil flower, and whispered, "Mors est permanens."

I glanced down at the flower I was twirling in my fingers. This was a ritual I'd done many times. Everyone in my line of work had one. For some, it was a simple calling card.

Like an ace of spades.

Ten years ago, I met someone who marked his work with that particular playing card, but he was dead. Shot him myself. The elusive Ace of Spades killer was one of my first jobs. I still had the five-dollar bill Micha paid me for the job hanging in a frame above my bed. Now, it appeared as if someone had picked up his calling card.

Either that or...

"No." I snorted.

That wasn't possible.

I didn't make mistakes.

Dropping the flower on Ricky's body, I spun around, ready to twist the suppressor off my Desert Eagle, but stopped dead.

Standing just inside the door was a woman with her mouth open in shock. My eyes swung from her to the little boy, tightly clutching her hand.

Well, shit.

Without a second thought, I raised my gun and pumped another round into her head. Not my fault she happened to walk into the wrong place at the wrong time. Again, life was all about choices.

The little boy stared at me as the woman dropped down to the ground.

I wasn't a fan of killing kids. It didn't bother me. It was more of an 'eh' situation. Had I done it before? Yeah. When the Cartel said they wanted the whole family taken out, they weren't kidding. But, I required a large sum to take those jobs.

The kid sniffed and looked up at me. "Are you going to kill me?"

My brow arched. That wasn't the response I was expecting.

"Do I need to?"

"I won't tell anyone."

I rolled my eyes. If I had a dollar for every time someone told me that, I'd be richer than Lou. Death paid well, but not 'Kessler well.'

"Listen, kid. You'll have to come up with something better than that."

His forehead furrowed in contemplation. The kid couldn't be more than eight or nine, but anyone could see the signs of neglect. He was obviously malnourished. I wouldn't be surprised if his ribs were poking out under that dirty shirt. Maybe I did him a favor? Meaning I wouldn't have to kill him.

There were other options. I was in Miami, and so was Ava. My sister would clutch onto this little shit and never let him go. But did I really want to do that to him? Killing him seemed like the more humane option.

Ava's smile flashed across my vision when my finger twitched on the trigger.

Goddamnit. Fucking Chase Mathers and his quick and easy bullshit. I was definitely going to shoot that asshole.

"All right," I sighed, rolling the suppressor off my gun. "I won't kill you, but I'm gonna take you somewhere you can be watched."

This was a favor for Chase. He could clean up the mess.

The kid looked up at me with tears streaming down his cheeks. "Will they kill me?"

I shrugged. How the fuck should I know what a bunch of bikers would do with a kid?

"It's your choice. I can kill you now." I slipped my gun back into the shoulder holster and held my hand out. "Or you can take your chances with them."

His answer was to place his small palm in mine. Personally, I'd have opted to eat a bullet. But hey, maybe the kid made a smart choice. It wasn't my problem. Chase could feed him to the gators for all I cared. I had better things to do.

Like head off to Loftry University and catch my little bird that flew away.

Chapter 2
Marnie

The scientific community was cutthroat and competitive. Everyone wanted to be the first to cure cancer or find proof of extra-terrestrial life. Out of all the possible breakthroughs waiting to be discovered, there was one I didn't understand—the race to create a human clone.

Nature already crossed that finish line. My sister and I were living proof of that victory. Essentially, that was what identical twins were— a physical and genetic copy of one another. Allergies, freckles, and birthmarks were all the same. We were clones in almost every aspect except for one.

The mind.

There weren't two people more different than my sister and me. Trina considered being appointed cheerleading squad captain 'the peak of her high school career.' She valued popularity over everything else. Whereas I focused on more important things, like bringing down the asshole jocks she threw herself at every five minutes.

I placed my hand over my eyes to shield the afternoon sun.

This campus was full of blissfully ignorant people. I referred to them as programmable robots for men in power to puppeteer. If any of them had bothered to inspect the green grass under their feet, they'd see that the field wasn't as perfectly cut as one might think.

There was a slight deviation in the third mower line. Telling me that the landscaper was either distracted or interrupted. It could be nothing. Then again, it could be everything. But did any of these people care? Of course not because—like my sister—they made their way through life wearing blinders.

Sometimes I wondered if Trina chose to be ignorant of the realities of the world. It was incredibly frustrating to watch her flitter about carelessly. My sister acted like all she needed to get through life was styled hair and a pretty smile. Unfortunately, there was a time when I used to think the same way.

"Marnie, wait up."

The arm waving at me caused a sigh to heave in my chest.

Ashleigh, great.

I didn't necessarily have anything against my new editor. She was nice and probably the only friend I had in this place. But she was one of *those* girls. The ones that did their hair and make-up every morning and flashed a sweet smile to everyone they saw.

Shelby was the same way, and look where that got her—tied to Logan Hudson. The most unstable human I'd ever met, and I was using the term 'human' lightly. I loved Shelby and even understood her choices. If my hometown had a most eligible bachelor prize, it would've gone to Logan Hudson.

I wasn't surprised that he'd set his sights on her. Shelby, however, I thought she was more intelligent than that. Then again, I couldn't talk. Once upon a time, I was an eager participant in the dress-me-like-a-princess train until one church picnic when I received a little too much attention.

Mom had gotten Trina and me cute little jumpers, but they were blue, and I wanted to wear my fancy red dress with the frills and sparkles. It would be prettier, and it was. At least, that was what Sheriff Nash said when he cornered me in the bathroom.

I never told anyone about that encounter or the places he made me touch him. I never explained why I refused to wear a dress again.

In a way, I was thankful to the former sheriff. He taught me a valuable lesson. Monsters didn't notice the girl that hid behind the crowd. A motto I managed to live by for nine years. I even wore armor in the form of glasses I didn't need.

Not that anyone knew that. Forgery was one of the many skills I'd managed to master. A simple letter from a supposed 'optometrist' convinced my parents. My life was going exactly as planned. Trina was the shining star, and I was the shadow in the background.

Then I walked into Chase's tattoo parlor, and another monster took notice.

"Hey." Ashleigh rushed across the cut green grass and skipped up beside me. "I'm glad I found you."

Considering she knew my schedule, finding me shouldn't have been an arduous task. A fact that I was tempted to point out.

Instead, I smiled. "Here I am."

Right where I should be. On the little brick path to building C and my next class.

She tipped a brow down at the book in my arm. "I thought Professor Richards didn't start the American Revolution until the second semester?"

He didn't, but I found some mistakes in the textbook. I wanted to let him know.

"Nothing wrong with getting a head start." I shrugged.

Ashleigh eyed me. "Has anyone ever told you to loosen up?"

"Yes," I stated flatly.

"Riiight." She gave me a slow eye roll, then continued, "Anyway, we need a good investigative piece for the first edition."

Ashleigh reminded me of Trina. My sister had the same naïve spark in her eyes. How many times had Ashleigh brushed off something she shouldn't have? Did she turn a blind eye to people's actions because it might affect her status if she said something?

Don't get me wrong, as far as editors go, Ashleigh wasn't that bad.

She was a little overzealous, but at least she kept her hands to herself, which was more than I could say for some.

"We need something thrilling and real."

I couldn't help but snicker as intensity balled her hands.

Ashleigh had no idea how many *real* stories I had. My former editor, for instance…

When I left Ashen Springs, people were still looking for Collin. They wouldn't find him, just like they wouldn't find the five other people that went missing last year.

People didn't get lost in Ashen Springs. They vanished off the face of the earth. My hometown might appear quaint and cute, but it was founded on lies and corruption. The same corruption still infested the town's hierarchy to this day.

"So?" Ashleigh swung her amber gaze my way. "Got any ideas?"

Oh, I had ideas, three notebooks full of them. None of which panned out. The key word in secret society was 'secret.' This meant that after almost five years of research, I had next to no evidence. But there were a few things I'd found, like the mysterious disappearance of Lindsay Manheim and the golden rose keychain hanging on the rear-view mirror of Preston Whitley's BMW.

Lindsay had one just like it.

I knew this because Trina kept begging our parents to get her one.

Unfortunately, one little keychain wasn't enough, and I'd handed over any other evidence I had to Derek Adams. He was the current sheriff and my friend Riley's dad, a vital ally to have. That was until The Order of Ravens and Wolves sunk their claws into his daughter.

I didn't hold it against him. I'd made my own deal with the devil.

"Well…" I squinted against the sun and followed Ashleigh down the path toward the brick building where my next class was held. "We could always do something about the dark side of cafeteria food."

"Really?" she snorted. "I thought you were a journalism major? That is *so* high school."

A part of me wanted to argue that I did just graduate, but she was right. It was a lame story.

I'd only been at Loftry for three weeks. That wasn't nearly enough time to get to know my professors, let alone the secrets this place held. As far as I could tell, it was like any other college campus with prestigious buildings, well-manicured lawns, landscaped flowerbeds, and winding paths.

Dean Anderson, however…

That guy gave me the creeps. Every scholarship student was required to have a meeting with him. The way he looked at me felt like he was sizing me up for something. I'd seen some of the other professors doing the same thing with other girls in their class. Then again, it could just be my paranoia kicking in. The last two years certainly hadn't helped my nerves any.

Ashleigh's head dropped back with a disgruntled groan. "I guess we'll have to stick to the stupid campus stalker."

Campus stalker?

The hairs on the back of my neck rose as a cold shiver raced up my spine. What did she mean by stalker? "I didn't hear anything about that?"

Logic told me it couldn't be Preston. I hadn't seen him in months, but that didn't stop me from glancing over my shoulder. A few students were on the path behind us, nothing out of the ordinary, but my heart dropped when I spotted denim on a set of shoulders. Thankfully they were the denim straps of a dress, but still…

"It's just some sorority girls complaining about panty raids and stuff," Ashleigh said, twirling her hand in the air.

Relief washed over me, and I sucked oxygen back into my lungs.

Preston's gone, Marnie. He lost interest. That's why you haven't seen him.

But was it?

I tried to tell myself he wasn't lurking in the shadows around every corner. That didn't stop the sensation of his eyes constantly watching. Trina would tell me to stop being paranoid. In most cases, I would've agreed with her. But there was a big difference between paranoia and alarm. One was the illusion of danger, while the other warned you of a real threat.

A threat didn't get more real than Preston Whitley.

No one in town would help me, and even if I did go to someone for help, I risked putting my sister in danger. So, I did the only thing I could and turned Preston's tactics around on him. He followed me, so I followed him and noted everything he did.

I knew what he ate, where he went for a jog every morning at five a.m., and every single item he had delivered to Whitley Manor. After all, we were playing a long game, and a war wasn't won with one battle. It took time and strategy.

Plus, people with power had a lot more to lose than someone like me. The trick was making them think that you had the means to pull their perfect rug out from under them. There was a reason Louis Kessler left me alone.

"So," Ashleigh said. "What do you think?"

What did I think? "Panty raids are hardly a good investigative piece."

"I know." She sighed as I pulled open the glass door. "But..."

I paused when she didn't finish speaking. Then cocked a brow when I noticed uncertainty toying with her features.

"What?"

"Have you seen that movie *The Skulls*?"

It took everything in me not to let my eyes narrow. "Yeah?"

I watched that movie when I was thirteen and began my delve into The Order. At the time, I considered it research. Now, I knew how idiotic that was. The movie romanticized the mystery of powerful men. The truth was so much darker.

A furrow tugged at my brow when Ashleigh leaned in and softly whispered, "Do you think organizations like that exist?"

"No," I said, blowing out the best fake disgruntled snort I could. I shook my head. "Don't be silly."

Unfortunately for me, I was not a good actor, a fact proven by the side-eye she gave me in return.

"Maybe it's not as silly as you think."

"Maybe it is," I argued.

Her brow rose. "Do you think it is?"

"I don't know," I responded. "Do you?"

"Maybe I don't."

"Maybe I don't, either."

Ashleigh's chin lifted as her eyes narrowed. "What do you know?"

"What do *you* know?"

We stood in the breeze with the door open staring each other down. For all I knew, Ashleigh was one of The Order's lackeys sent to spy on me. Or worse…she could be working for Preston.

It was awfully convenient how quickly I got that scholarship. My grades were a little above average, where I'd purposely kept them, and my only extracurricular activity was the school paper. Trina's cheer-leading got her a free ride to the University of Miami, and even that I could understand. As painful as it was to admit, cheerleading was a sport.

My eyes trickled over Ashleigh's pink shirt and jeans. Was she actually this casual, or was she trying to appear nonchalant?

"Does the name Whitley mean anything to you?"

Her brow arched. "Like the brewery?"

Ah ha! I knew she was up to something.

"They have this great vanilla ale. It's fantastic with apple pie."

Or she wasn't up to anything.

Her hip cocked as her hand pressed against it. "What does a brewery have to do with secret societies?"

"I didn't say anything about secret societies?"

"Neither did I," she insisted.

"Good."

"Good."

We both nodded and then walked into the building.

Rumors flew around every college campus about societies and organizations. It wasn't entirely out of the realm of possibility for Ashleigh to mention it.

"Say I did say something about them—which I didn't—but say I did…." Ashleigh's gaze swung my way. "Would you be the person to talk to?"

"I don't know." I eyed her back. "Would you?"

"Maybe I would."

Alright, I could roll with this. It couldn't hurt to see what she had to say. "Maybe I would too."

"Oh, my god." Excitement filled her eyes as she clutched onto my shoulders. "I've been dying to talk to someone about the robed figures going into that sorority house."

Now, I was officially confused. "Sorority house?"

"We are talking about the same thing, aren't we?" Her gaze once again filled with suspicion.

"Of course we are." I scoffed. "I was just testing you."

I had no freaking idea what she was talking about, but I was intrigued. Hell, I was downright excited, which considering what happened back home, probably wasn't the best reaction. That didn't stop my stomach from fluttering. My blood was practically singing at the thought of another mystery to unravel. For the first time in months, I felt like smiling.

That was until I entered my lecture hall.

"We'll talk about this later," Ashleigh whispered, then skipped away.

I waved and curled my lip at the familiar blue eyes glittering my way.

"Hi, Marnie."

Ugh, Chase Ackerman. The sound of his voice made me want to hurl. Not only was he a jock, but he was an arrogant pretty boy who thought girls should fall at his feet. For some reason, he had set his sights on me.

Little did he know, I'd been watching him too. I knew what skeletons were in his closet.

Chase leaned back and flashed me a smile. "Missed you at the party last night."

I just bet he did.

"I don't party."

That wasn't entirely true. My sister dragged me around with her all the time. One thing I learned about alcohol was that it didn't just make people stupid. It gave them loose lips. Star Chadwick and I used a few high school parties to investigate our friend Tico's murder. Ned

Callaghan wasn't anywhere on my list of suspects. He seemed so normal.

"Come on, Marnie." He reached down to blatantly cup his groin. "I know you want this."

Did this barbarian bullshit actually work? I'd like to think that girls were more intelligent than that, but given the number of times I'd seen Chase walk down the quad with someone new on his arm, I'd have to go with the opposite. Either that or they just didn't pay attention.

"What do you say, sweetheart? My dick's ready and waiting."

Clearly, this guy was a moron. How did no one see this?

"I'm not sure I'm your type." I tsked, rolling my eyes over his toned frame. "I'm a little too conscious for that."

His face dropped. "Are you accusing me of something?"

"I don't know, am I?" I shot back.

"You should be careful throwing around accusations without proof." He leaned forward and growled. "It might land you in a tight spot."

Oh, I had proof.

When a man had his dick in a girl—whether she was conscious or not—he didn't exactly pay attention to who was watching. I'd managed to get a nice little photograph of Mr. Popular on top of a passed-out freshman. My next move was figuring out what to do with it. I could plaster it all over campus or write a story in the paper exposing him, but none of those options seemed fitting to the crime.

Chase's palm flattened on the empty seat beside him. "Saved you a spot."

"I'd rather choke to death on my own eyeball juice."

"Damn girl, That was graphic." His lip curled in a grimace for a split second before morphing into a smirk. "I like it."

"I'll be sure to tell Charlie that."

Charlie was the girl in the picture. I had no idea if she knew what happened to her., I'd never spoken a word to the girl, but if she were anything like my sister, she wouldn't care.

So, I'd care for her.

31

"See you later, Marnie," Chase sang as I walked up the steps and took my seat.

Not if I could help it.

Thankfully, Professor Richards strutted in just as I pulled out my books. He was the kind of man one couldn't help but watch. The way he moved with his shoulders straight, and head high oozed confidence. There was no doubt in my mind that the professor knew how to take charge. I supposed most teachers did.

"Don't mind, Chase."

My gaze shifted over to the guy sitting next to me. I hadn't noticed him before. Had he always sat there?

"He's all bark and no bite."

My brow knit. "What?"

"Chase," he explained with a sparkle in his dark eyes. "He's harmless."

Harmless, my ass. I'd like to see him tell Charlie that.

"Whatever you say." I rolled my eyes back to the professor.

The guy—whomever he was—wasn't going to let me focus on class.

"I'm Brian." He leaned in and held out his hand.

My lip curled as I stared at his hand. "Okay."

"And your name is?" He snickered.

Why was he talking to me? There were plenty of other girls to talk to. Most of which looked much better than I did. My hair was in a ponytail, glasses were on my face, and I didn't have on a stitch of makeup. I was wearing black leggings, an old T-shirt that covered my ass, and a long sweater that covered both the shirt and pants. Approachable was not the word I'd use to describe myself.

My silence didn't deter him any. The guy just sat there with his hand outstretched and a stupid smirk on his face.

"You gotta have a name, Hunny."

Ugh, fine.

"Marnie," I replied gruffly.

As if he won some kind of victory, his smile spread, showing a flash of his perfect white teeth. "Pleased to meet you, Marnie."

"Whatever," I grumbled and tried to listen to the lesson. Tried being the operative word. 'Mr. Pleased To Meet You' apparently wasn't done.

"Has anyone ever told you how cute you look when you hyper-focus?"

My face dropped. Cute? Really? Was that the best he could come up with?

I sighed and looked him dead in the eyes. "No. No one has ever referred to me as *cute*."

Or pretty, hot, or any of the other things girls like Shelby and my sister heard all the time.

"Well, you are." Brian leaned back against his chair and tipped his head. "And if you go out to dinner with me, I'll happily explain all the ways your cuteness shines."

Color me confused. "You're asking me out?"

"Yeah." Brian nodded. "That's kind of what I meant by dinner."

Was I being punked? Trina was hiding somewhere, right? I didn't get asked out. Ever. And now this guy with his charming smile and styled blonde hair was interested? Something didn't seem right.

"Why?"

He paused and gave me a weird look. "What do you mean why?"

"I mean, why are you asking me out?"

The expression on his face twisted, deepening the lines of befuddlement. "Why wouldn't I?"

He seemed genuinely confused. Maybe he really wanted to go out with me? Then again….

It was more likely that some asshole set this up as a prank. My gaze fell down to Chase, who was whispering to the guy next to him. However, I was more interested in the small bag being passed.

Was Mr. Popular planning on another private party?

"It's just dinner, I promise," Brian said. "I won't even shake your hand."

And just like that, I knew what to do with the picture in my pocket.

The corner of my mouth lifted. "How about a party?"

Chapter 3
Marnie

*E*veryone, at some point in their life, experienced that sinking sensation in their stomach that something just wasn't right. Like at the zoo when the lion stared at you while licking his lips. These were things I passed off as basic survival instincts. Let's face it. If that lion broke free from his cage, the human wouldn't be the one that came out on top.

Most of the odd sensations people felt could be explained away with the same logic, except for when twins were involved.

I was on my way out the door to meet Brian when my phone rang. Normally, I would've ignored it and continued about my business, but something made me answer. The second I heard my sister's voice, I knew why.

"Oh my god, Marnie, you should see the guys in Miami. It's man-candy central."

"Hello, Trina." I sighed. "Hungry as ever, I see."

Why was I talking to my sister instead of hanging up? Because, for some reason, I couldn't refrain from talking to her. I also knew when she was hurt, sick, or sad. Shelby called it freaky twin ESP. I called it fucked up. She had no idea how annoying it was to have a perfectly normal day ruined by the sudden onset of nerves for absolutely no reason.

"My apologies," Trina groaned. "For a second there, I thought I was talking to an actual human girl with raging hormones instead of a robot focused on her next story."

Focusing on something productive was a much better use of my time.

"Let me guess, one of your professors looked at you a little too long, and now, he's a pervert that needs to be exposed? Or maybe it was the dean? Cause God forbid a man would ever be interested in a woman."

"There's a difference between interest and predatory aspects," I said while tucking my phone between my ear and shoulder.

"Not every guy is a predator, Marnie," Trina argued.

"You would know," I spat back at her. "You've dated enough of them."

My sister's ability to chew up men and spit them out didn't bother me. It was the way she devalued herself as nothing more than a toy for them to play with. However, Trina would argue that they were her toys.

"Just because our dad's a pastor doesn't mean you have to join a convent."

"Religion has nothing to do with this." Sex wasn't off the table. I'd touched myself and knew how pleasurable things could be. Had I found guys attractive? Sure. There were even a couple of girls that I wouldn't mind kissing. It was just...

"I'm not going to give myself to someone who isn't worthy."

"Oh, my god." Trina snorted. "Tell me you're a virgin without telling me you're a virgin."

My face dropped. "Was there a reason for your call, or did you just want to lecture me about my dating life?"

We could've had this conversation back home. Trina loved bringing up my single status.

"I just wanted to remind you that we have the dress fitting for Rye's wedding in six weeks."

"How could I forget." She reminded me every other day.

"I know how you are." I could feel Trina's aqua eyes narrowing. "There's no getting out of this one, my sweet baby sister."

"First off, you're only fifteen minutes older than me," I pointed out. "And secondly, I'd never miss Riley's wedding."

I might have disagreed with whom she was marrying, but she was my friend, and I loved her. Riley's happiness was all I cared about in this scenario. That was precisely why I intended to have a word with Micha before the ceremony.

There were a few little tidbits of information I'd found. Should my friend ever stop smiling, I'd happily use said information to wipe the smile off his face as well.

"Are you gonna bring a date?"

Oh, for the love of....

"No, and I have to go." I sighed.

"I'm sure the local meeting of Women United can wait."

What? "That's not a real group."

"It could be," Trina sang back.

"But it's not."

"But it could be. Maybe I'll start one here just to prove you wrong."

"You do that." I shook my head and scooped my purse off my desk.

God help the women that joined my sister's group. She'd probably have pink cupcakes, rainbows, and shirtless men at every meeting. It would be the place where feminism went to die.

"I have to go. Brian's waiting."

That was when I froze.

"Brian?"

Damnit. Me and my big mouth.

Instead of responding, I stood there praying my sister would think Brian was a lab partner. Lying to Trina never worked. She seemed to know when I was hiding something. It didn't exactly make the past two years easy. Thankfully I could pass off most of her questions with a simple, 'it feels like I'm being watched,' which I was. But Trina just took that as me being paranoid at a new school.

I wasn't that lucky this time.

"You have a date!" She squealed so loudly that I had to pull the phone away from my ear. "Okay, okay, don't freak out."

Why was she telling me not to freak out? I wasn't the one losing my mind.

"The first thing you'll do is take off that ratty brown sweater."

I glanced down at the comfortable cloth covering my arm. "How did you...."

"And put some damn sandals on your feet. Sneakers are not date material."

What was wrong with sneakers? Sure, they were a little run down, but they looked fine with my leggings.

"Marnie?"

"What?"

"Are you wearing leggings?"

"No." I lied, and not well.

"Oh my god! Put some jeans on."

Why should I? "Who cares what I'm wearing?"

"Who cares?" The exasperation in her tone vibrated through my ear. "Okay, where are you going?"

"Just to a party," I answered.

It wasn't a big deal. It wasn't even an actual date. Brian was more of an excuse to go somewhere I normally wouldn't. So it didn't matter how I looked.

Trina's next words made me rethink that.

"Do you want to stick out like a sore thumb?"

Hmm...

I fingered the small vial I had tucked in my pocket. Standing out might be a tad counter-productive.

"All right." I sighed. "Tell me what to wear."

When Trina hung up to video call me, I learned three things: never ask someone like her for fashion advice unless trying on five hundred different outfits was the goal, mascara was a pain in the ass to put on, and my roommate had way too much make-up.

Given that she had a bright pink comforter on her bed with stuffed animals pilled near the pillows, I shouldn't be surprised. My side of the room was much more organized and simple. I brought what I needed and nothing more. The only touch of home I had was the quilt grandma made me and a family picture on the bedside table.

"Oh, Marnie." I swear a tear rolled down Trina's cheeks as she clapped her hands together. "You look perfect."

"I feel ridiculous." These jeans were too tight, and the white tank top she made me put on barely reached the top of my ass. "Can I at least put my hair up?"

"No." Trina snaked her hands through the air, adding, "You have to let it flow down your back."

Whatever.

I pushed my glasses up my nose and said, "Can I go now? I'm late."

"That depends. How late are you?"

Oh my god. My eyes slowly rolled as I lifted a finger to hang up. "Goodbye, Trina."

"You better call and tell me how it went." That was the last thing I heard before ending the call.

Brian wanted to meet me at my dorm. That was too personal. So we agreed to meet at the party. The football team's house was clear across campus. It wasn't that long of a walk, but it was an eternity when I had to come up with small talk.

Don't get Brian wrong, he seemed like a decent guy, but I had a hard enough time hanging out with Ashleigh. Who, for the most part, did all the talking.

It was a pleasant night, warm with a slight breeze. There were so few peaceful moments in life that avoiding this one seemed a shame. If I weren't already late, I would've taken a second to enjoy the moon's bright glow. Or the empty pathways around me. Seeing the campus so desolate was a touch unnerving.

I was used to pushing my way through other students, not hearing my footsteps thundering through the air. What was it about sandals that girls liked? The straps dug into my skin every time I took a step. Then there was the ridiculous slapping click sound they made. Almost as if the shoes themselves were taunting me.

Click.

Everyone can see you, Marnie.

Clack.

All your curves are on display.

Click.

If you tempt a beast, he'll poke back.

Clack.

And you'll have no one to blame but yourself, just like when you had to wear that dress.

I rubbed my arms, attempting to shake away the shiver of a long faded touch. Nash was gone, and I wasn't seven years old anymore. Yet I could still hear his voice.

"That's such a pretty dress, Marnie. Did you wear it just for me?"

"No." I shook my head and balled my fists.

It'd been years since that ghost haunted my mind, and I'd be damned if I would let him come back. Nash Hunter didn't own me then and wouldn't own me now.

I rolled my shoulders back, lifted my chin, and cut through a dimly lit field. At least the grass dampened my footsteps. It was more of a swishing now than the sharp echoing that had invaded my ears.

Wait...

I stopped and glanced over my shoulder at the shadows behind me.

Was someone following me? I could've sworn I heard a soft click followed by a flash of something.

There was nothing there except me and the breeze toying with my hair.

Still...

"Is someone there?"

No answer.

The grass swayed as I scoured the empty pathways and lit up

windows. I couldn't see anything, but I could feel it. I could feel him and those cold gray eyes watching me.

"Have you been a good girl Little Bird?"

That was the last thing he said to me almost six months ago. I hadn't seen him since. That didn't mean...

Stop being paranoid, Marnie. Preston's gone.

Sighing, I shook off the eerie sensation and ducked down a path to the right. Preston was gone. I was pretty sure he had left town because I couldn't find him. And I tried. I had to be sure I wasn't being watched before I left for college. No one knew where I was going. I kept that information to myself until the last second. So there was no possible way I could be followed.

That knowledge didn't help calm my fluttering pulse. However, the music that soon assailed my ears did. I never thought I'd be happy to see a crowd. I didn't even care that most of them were stumbling around. Like it or not, there was safety in numbers.

One girl tripped over her own feet, scraping her knees on the cement while giggling. That was one of the many reasons I'd never touch a drop of alcohol. I'd never understand why anyone would want to dull their senses to that extreme.

I waded deeper into the crowd.

The house was lit up, with music blaring through the open doors and windows. People stood outside laughing and shouting at each other while a group of guys cheered about some game they had set up on a table.

Maybe this wasn't such a good idea. There were a lot of people here. What if someone saw?

Any hesitation I had vanished when Brian spotted me.

I couldn't help but notice how his entire face lit up with a smile. He seemed genuinely happy to see me. Why?

"Hey," He rushed up and gave me a charming smirk. "I was beginning to think you stood me up."

I wrapped my arms around my waist as his eyes dropped to my cleavage. I should've kept the sweater.

"Hi." That was all I could think of to say.

41

The smile on his face spread. "That right there is one of the many ways your cuteness shines."

I arched a brow. Was he still on the cute thing?

"More like awkward."

Let's call a cow a cow. There was no need to beat around the bush. I knew I was awkward. He knew I was awkward. Hell, the people in the house probably knew it.

"Come on."

Brian moved to grab my hand, but I jerked away from him. This would be the point when most guys moved on to easier prey.

Not him. He just chuckled and said, "Sorry, I forgot about the no-handshaking rule."

"It's not really a rule." I pointed out.

He was the one who added that clause. Not me.

"Okay, well, how about we start with a drink?"

I eyed him for a second. "I don't drink."

"They have soda."

"Is it in a can?" I was not about to accept an open drink from anyone.

"You're a suspicious one." His eyes lit up with amusement. "Do I need to add an 'I won't drug you' clause to our date?"

Maybe? It wouldn't be a bad clause to have.

"Hey." He held his hands up. Palms displayed defensively. "I'm happy to stay here all night and talk to you."

That would defeat the purpose of me coming to this thing in the first place. If I had to guess, I'd say that Chase Ackerman was inside. Somewhere near the alcohol. Why would he hunt his prey when he could wait for them to come to him?

"I could use a drink," I said, then followed Brian into the house.

It was even more crowded inside. All I could smell was stale alcohol and smoke. It was so thick that I almost choked on it. On the upside, spotting Mr. Ackerman and his stupid smile wasn't too hard. He was right where I thought he'd be—standing next to the keg, hitting on an obviously drunk girl.

I had to hand it to Trina. She was right about me sticking out.

Chase didn't notice when I bumped into him and dumped the contents of my vial in his cup. He didn't look my way as I walked by. His entire focus was on the girl giggling next to him.

Brian pulled me over to a corner of the room and started discussing his major. I think he said something about...pre-law? I was only half paying attention. My eyes were glued to the red solo cup across the room. Would Chase know something was off? Probably not. Fentanyl didn't have a taste or much of a smell, for that matter, but it packed one hell of a punch.

I was almost disappointed at the lack of reaction when Chase lifted the cup to his mouth. A part of me longed for a lip curl as he swallowed the rest of his drink. I wanted him to feel the same fear he'd invoked in others. I wanted him to know what was happening and that I was responsible for it. But that moment would come. And it did.

Fifteen minutes later, Chase's body seized. For a brief moment, his eyes met mine. It wasn't more than a fraction of a second, but it was long enough for him to see the smirk tugging at the corner of my mouth.

Then he collapsed in convulsions.

Everyone panicked, running this way and that while Brian grabbed my hand and pulled me outside. We weren't the only ones fleeing either. People darted out, ducking behind bushes and tearing down pathways like their feet were on fire.

It seemed like no one wanted to help poor Chase. What a shame.

I couldn't help but smile as I glanced back at the fading house. Maybe if he'd been nicer, he'd have a friend or two that would be more concerned with him than they were about being caught.

Welcome to karma, Chase Ackerman. This was the place where you reap what you sow.

Even Brian—a supposed decent guy—didn't stop to call nine-one-one. He pulled me across campus until we were safely tucked into the hedge maze behind the dean's office.

"Holy shit." I watched him hunch over and suck in a few deep breaths. "That was crazy."

"Yeah," I snorted. "Crazy."

Or retributive, but we could go with his word.

"Can you believe that just happened? I didn't know Chase was into drugs."

"Well," I shrugged. "You learn something new every day."

By the way that Brian's wide eyes were darting around, one might think a bomb went off or something. Chase's foaming mouth wasn't that bad. If he wanted to see something really fucked up, he should watch what happened when someone's brakes didn't work as they sped around a corner, sending their car careening off the bluffs.

Now that was a mess. But Steven Hamilton wouldn't be risking anyone's life by speeding again.

Brian took a few minutes to collect himself, after which I thought we'd go our separate ways. Apparently, I was wrong.

My brows knit as he grabbed my hands and looked deep into my eyes.

"Look, Marnie. I know this wasn't the best date...."

It wasn't a date at all.

"But if you give me another chance—"

His voice was cut off by a loud gurgle and spray of warm fluid that washed over my face. It took a second for my brain to register the coppery tint filling my mouth and the blade being dragged across Brian's throat.

I couldn't move or talk. I just stood there while his skin was sliced apart as easily as butter spread on toast. The sleeve of a jean jacket had my feet stuck to the ground.

The last thing I saw before darkness took me was the horror in Brian's eyes and the cold gray stare of the man who killed him.

Chapter 4
Preston

One of the greatest masks people wore was the façade of innocence. No one was truly innocent, not even children. There wasn't anyone more selfish than a toddler who wanted what someone else had. That didn't stop people, especially men, from searching for that sense of purity.

There was something built into men that filled them with the desire to taint the untainted. They enjoyed marking their territory, hence the attractive factor of virgins, which I never understood. Why the fuck would I want to train some bitch to suck my cock when I could easily find someone who knew what they were doing? Seemed like a waste of time to me.

Then Marnie Dupire came along, and the thought of someone else touching her...

Let's just say there were a few men lining the bottom of the bluffs and one coating them. Geysers really fucked a body up. It took me a week to get all the bits of bone out of my hair.

My Little Bird didn't know about that one. I wonder if she ever thought about her chemistry teacher. Guess he shouldn't have paid her so much attention.

"Isn't that right, Marnie?" I looked over at my beautiful little captive, passed out with her head flopped back against the passenger seat of my rental.

Damn, she looked good, covered in blood. My eyes trickled over the now stained fabric of her white shirt to the jeans hugging her hips. The outfit pissed me off. When she first came prancing out of her dormitory, I didn't mind the view. I enjoyed watching her ass sway.

The best part was her look over her shoulder when I clicked my lighter open. The fear sparkling in her bright eyes damn near made me bust a nut. Stalking her was one thing. But toying with her...there wasn't a high out there better than that.

Then she ruined my good time by walking up to that asshole.

Marnie was fucking lucky I didn't slap the shit out of her right then and there.

"You haven't been good, Little Bird." I tsked while sweeping back the hair that had fallen over her face. "Let's hope, for your sake, that all you did was hold his hand."

Did I care if her virginity was intact? Yes, but not because I wanted her innocence. Marnie wasn't innocent at all. She was dark and twisted. A killer the same as me. I never understood my fascination with this girl. Not until she slipped drugs in that frat boy's drink.

As that idiot collapsed on the ground foaming at the mouth, I knew why she was placed in my path. All the answers I needed were in the smirk tugging on the corner of her mouth.

Marnie Dupire was my soulmate.

She just didn't know it yet. But that was why I was here. I'd not only help her understand the beast inside her. I'd make her fucking embrace it.

"No more hiding, Little Bird," I said while turning onto the airstrip.

Monsters like us didn't hide. We walked headfirst into the depths of hell and played with demons. That was the only place where genuine desire could be found. Would she accept the blood her soul craved, or would she make me shove it down her throat? I was excited to find out. Nothing was quite as exhilarating as fucking with someone who thought they had it all figured out.

Adrenaline coursed through my veins as I drove into hanger number five, then died when I pulled to a stop.

A familiar face with glittering green eyes caused me to groan.

"Hey, man." Logan waved as I opened the door and stepped out.

"What the fuck are you doing here?"

The last time Logan just showed up, I shot him in the foot. And what did the asshole do? He laughed and said he probably deserved it.

"Did you honestly think you could commandeer one of my jets, and I wouldn't know?"

Sighing, I crossed my arms. "I'd be more worried about the big mouths at your company if I were you."

I knew I should've shot that receptionist.

"Well," Logan's brow rose. "When you pull a gun on a pilot, the CEO tends to hear about it."

Okay, he may have a valid point there. But in my defense, I'd just spent forty minutes listening to some kid recite lines from his favorite video game. I was slightly frustrated.

That still didn't explain why he was here.

"You could've called."

"I could've, but where's the fun in that?"

Asshole.

Shouldn't be surprised, I guess. Micha, Mason, and Silas didn't want to know what I was doing. Neither did my brother, for that matter. They couldn't stomach my version of fun, which was more than fine with me. I liked my privacy. Something Parker learned at a young age. Logan, however, got off on sticking his nose in my business. If I thought it would work, I'd threaten the bastard with something.

Everyone had proverbial lines drawn in the sand. Lou, for instance, didn't like getting his hands dirty. Logan Hudson was a different breed of crazy. You couldn't threaten someone who'd charge headfirst into the afterlife and take on the reaper. His only weakness was Shelby Grace and the fallout from that wouldn't be worth the hassle.

"Speaking of fun." Logan leaned over to eye my passenger. "Looks like you had some."

I shifted over to block his view. If he didn't wipe that mischievous glint off his face, I might reconsider paying his girl a visit.

"Shouldn't you be getting back?" I rolled my cold stare up to Logan's twinkling gaze. "Wouldn't want your girl worrying."

"If I didn't know any better...." He wagged his finger. "I'd say that was a threat."

I sighed and walked around the hood to open the passenger door. "Never said you were stupid."

There was no point in waiting for the idiot to leave. We both knew that wouldn't happen until he was good and ready. Asshole was lucky I had a soft spot for him. Lou could blame himself for that bond. Personally, I'd have opted to keep us far apart. Insane and sociopathic weren't exactly a safe combination, but hey...to each their own.

At least I knew I could trust him. Logan might be a tad unstable, but he was utterly devoted to Shelby. He wouldn't touch my Little Bird with a ten-foot pole, which he proved when I ducked into the car, and Marnie freaked out.

"Get away from me," she screamed while throwing her arms about wildly.

Goddamnit. I blamed Logan for this shit. I'd have been paying attention if he hadn't shown up. And what was he doing while I fought to get a hold of Marnie's flailing limbs? He was laughing. Son of a bitch was hunched over, clutching his side like this was the funniest fucking thing he'd ever seen.

Not that I was complaining. If the roles were reversed, I'd find it amusing too. Plus, I was nothing if not prepared. One jab from the needle I had stashed in my jacket was all it took for Marnie's attack to die down.

I would've used it earlier, even had it in my hand ready to go when she fainted. Now that shit I didn't see coming.

"Get away," Marnie whispered while trying to lift her hand.

I watched her fingers twitch against the seat.

"What's wrong, can't move your hand?"

She was trying. I could see the frustration in her expression as she ground out, "Fuck you."

I admired her conviction. It was a useless fight, of course. There was no staving off the drugs pumping through her veins, but she still tried.

"Don't you worry, Little Bird." I cupped her face and grazed my thumb across her cheek. "We'll play that game soon enough."

Even though her eyelids drooped shut, she still managed quietly to mumble, "Never."

There was nothing more beautiful than the way she looked right now. Perfect skin streaked with blood while beads of sweat trickled down her supple cleavage. I was half tempted to fuck her right there and then, but...

"That was fucking great," Logan cackled.

Why the fuck hadn't I killed this prick yet?

Grumbling out my dissatisfaction, I scooped Marnie's limp form up and headed for the jet. I was anxious to get my Bird locked in her cage, away from prying eyes.

The only thing that made me pause was the look on Logan's face.

"Jesus, Preston." His eyes roamed over the girl in my arms. "I get that you have particular tastes...."

"What?" One quick glance down told me what he was talking about. "It's not her blood."

"Oh." He shrugged.

And that was why I liked the guy. Anybody else would've asked a million questions. What did you do? Where's the body? And so on. Not Logan. I could've come back drenched in blood carrying two heads, and he wouldn't give a shit.

His sense of boundaries was another matter altogether.

When I moved to climb the stairs into the jet, I had to stop and look back at him. Prick was getting ready to follow me in.

"Can I help you?"

"Nah." He shook his head. "I'm good."

This mother...

"Don't you have your own ride?"

His brows knit. "And?"

"And, go home the way you got here."

Logan's head fell back with a groan. "But there's no one to talk to."

"Like I give a shit." That was his problem. I didn't tell him to fly out here.

"Come on," he whined.

It was time to try a different tactic.

I shrugged and walked up the steps. "Your funeral."

That made him stop.

"What do you mean my funeral?"

"You're about to get on a plane with a guy that kidnapped a girl."

"So?"

Idiot wasn't getting it.

"A girl that just so happens to be your girl's friend," I explained. "I don't think Shelby would take too kindly to that."

"Who says she has to know?"

I looked him dead in the eyes and said, "If you get on this plane, then I do."

"You wouldn't."

Yes, I would. He knew I would. I didn't give a shit about Shelby. Besides, what the fuck was she going to do? Pretty sure her boyfriend wouldn't have a problem if I put her in a cage. Which would be the only way he'd get a piece of ass if she found out about this shit. Fuck it. I'd throw Riley in the mix as well. The girl might learn some manners if she were locked up for a while.

Logan eyed me for a second before holding up his finger and said, "You win this round."

I won every round.

Satisfied, I climbed the last few steps and nodded at the attendant to close the door. When his eyes dropped to the girl in my arms, I thought I might have an issue. But he kept his mouth shut and did what he was told.

Smart man. Wouldn't stop me from taking him out when we

landed. Or the pilot. Rule number one for people in my line of work…
no loose ends.

I wove through the seats, heading for the small bed in the room in
the back. Where I carefully placed my pretty little captive. She seemed
to like it. Marnie sighed and snuggled into the pillow.

I couldn't stop staring at the way her eyes fluttered under her
closed lids. Did she have the same fluffy rainbow dreams as other
girls, or were hers filled with darkness and death like mine?

My entire life was spent getting sideways glances from people. I
could smell the fear when I walked into a room. No one truly knew
what I was capable of, yet they were all afraid of it. Well, everyone
except for Logan. Perhaps that was why the thought of ending his life
had never crossed my mind because, on some level, he understood
me.

I sat down on the edge of the bed and traced my finger along my
Bird's delicate jawline. She was so small and sweet. The type of girl
any man would kill to taste, but she was mine to feast on. Mine to
fuck, mold, and lead into the depths of depravity.

Did she know what she was? Could she feel the need to feed
clawing inside her? I saw it there, hiding under the glimmer of satisfaction on her face. She got off watching that guy overdose.

Parker had the same beast, but my brother wasn't willing to accept
it. Marnie was on the precipice. All it would take to send her off the
edge was the right push.

"Should I set you free, Little Bird?" That was the real question.

Should I help her soar or keep her in a cage, all for myself?

Seeing her dose that guy was so fucking hot. I'd never been more
turned on in my life. The look on her face was permanently burned in
my mind. I'd be jerking off to that image for years. Then again, why
would I use a memory when I could fuck the real thing?

My eyes trickled over the dried blood staining her cheek to a spot
dotting her bottom lip.

I bent over, sucking her lip into my mouth before I could stop
myself. An intoxicating concoction of blood and sweetness made my

dick twitch. I groaned as the flavor flowed across my tongue. Nothing had ever tasted better.

For two years, I'd waited to touch this girl.

Popping her lip out of my mouth, I ran my tongue up the side of her face and crawled over her prone form.

"Should I fuck you now?" I whispered in her ear while sliding my hand down her side and under her shirt. "Or wait until you can look at me?"

Marnie's eyes fluttered under her closed lids as her face screwed up. Somewhere in her drug-hazed mind, she knew what was coming. She'd known for a long time, and I was done waiting.

I swept my finger along the underside of her breast and bit down on her neck. The small whimper she released in response shot straight down to my dick.

"Feel that, Little Bird. That's the first of many marks I will give you."

And what a good mark it was. Bright and red, not enough to draw blood, but enough that she would feel it every time she twisted her neck. She'd feel me.

I pushed myself up and looked down at her outfit. The same outfit she wore for that fucking asshole was now covered in his blood. Served him right. Motherfucker thought he could touch what belonged to me, and Marnie let him.

My eyes snapped back up to her face as my hand wrapped around her chin. "You've been a bad girl, Marnie."

Her brows once again knit as my fingers dug into her flesh. She didn't like that. Good. I didn't like the way she held that guy's hand.

If I could, I'd kill that asshole all over again. I might still kill her. That would all depend on just how much she let him touch.

Only one way to find out.

My knife popped open before I took my next breath. Her shirt was the first to go, followed by her jeans. My fury increased with every slice and tear of the fabric until nothing was left but scraps. Marnie wouldn't be wearing that shit ever again.

If she wanted to dress up, that was fine, but she could wear clothes she put on for me. Though I did have to admit, I enjoyed the under-wear. They were a simple pair of blue cotton boyshorts and a matching bra. Nothing like what her sister would wear, but a sensible set that didn't show off parts of her body meant for my eyes only.

The most delectable quiver raced across her stomach as I slid my palm over her skin. How many nights had I jerked off to this very image? Sometimes it was so real I could almost taste her on the tip of my tongue. And now, I had my hands on the prize, the soft, supple, and tempting prize.

My mouth was practically watering by the time I slipped my hand under the waistband of her panties. So long as no one else had seen what was under here, I could forgive Marnie's infraction. We'd call it a lapse in judgment and move on.

The hardest thing I'd ever had to do was to deny the urge to slam my cock inside her. But I did it. I gritted my teeth and pushed my finger into her warm, wet walls. Almost immediately, I was met with resistance that made my anger melt away.

She was still untouched.

"Good girl." I breathed out, sliding my hand out of her panties and sucking my finger into my mouth.

Satisfaction filled my chest as her flavor hit my tongue. There was no other cock in that sweetness, just her and me. My dick begged to claim her, and I was tempted to give in.

But when I looked down at her face, I knew I wanted more. I wanted to feel her fight, then watch defeat spark in her eyes when I tore through her virginity. Sure, I could fuck her now, but then she'd have no memory of what it felt like to be conquered. And that would be a shame.

I sat up and let out a breath.

"I suppose I should clean you up." Her clothes were gone, but there was still a fair amount of blood. "Wouldn't be much fun if you passed out on me again, now would it, Little Bird?"

Besides, cleaning her up would give me something else to focus on other than how she looked lying there, all vulnerable and tempting.

So, I set to work.

I got a cloth, and a warm bowl of water from the bathroom, then began wiping her skin clean. It was cathartic in a way. Every streak and speck I washed away erased a little more of that asshole. Once his taint no longer stained her skin, it would be almost as if he never existed. Marnie would be my pure and clean Little Bird again.

That was until I rolled her over.

All my anger came crashing back in a tidal wave of marks that scared her flesh.

They were all over Marnie's back. Crooked lines and slashes. Some were so old they'd faded with age.

I gritted my teeth and pulled my thumb along one of the jagged white lines marring her complexion. Someone whipped her. My guess was with a belt with a cross on the buckle. There was only one person I knew with a belt like that. The mark on her lower back was unmistakable.

I knew exactly who my Little Bird's next kill would be.

Daddy Dearest.

Chapter 5
Marnie

The beds in my dorm weren't what I'd call top quality. They were stiff, lumpy, and smelled like mothballs. Kind of what I imagine a prison cot felt like. Not that I was complaining. A bed was a bed. Besides, the need to stretch was my cue that it was time to get up. That was just how every morning started.

Except for today.

Instead, I nuzzled into the cloud under me. My bed was never this soft before. Come to think of it, nothing I owned was this silky. And since when did my room smell this good?

Usually, I was choking on the overwhelming stench of my room-mate's perfume, but there wasn't so much as a hint of that floral scent in the air. It actually smelled fresh with a slightly familiar undertone.

My brows knit as I tipped my head. Distant sounds were hitting my ears.

What was that?

It was like a soft, lapping echo. Was that…water? That didn't make sense. There were no lakes or beaches near Loftry. Why the hell would I hear water?

Oh my god!

My heart lurched forward, banging against my ribs.

It wasn't just any body of water. It was the ocean. I was back in Ashen Springs!

I shot up and clutched my chest. All I could see was the look in Brian's eyes. A nice, normal guy whose only infraction was talking to me. And now he was dead. I could still taste that coppery tinge on the back of my tongue. It was right there, getting thicker with every swallow I forced down my dry throat.

His blood was everywhere. I had to get it off me.

My hands frantically pawed at my body, trying to eliminate the red tinting my vision, but my fingers weren't clawing at fabric. They were dragging along skin. My skin. The jeans and shirt I was wearing before were gone. All I had covering me was my underwear.

One thought rang through my mind as I stared down at the dried brown spots dotting the top of my bra. Someone stripped me.

No, not someone. Preston. And he didn't just remove my clothes. He touched me. There was no blood on my skin, not one single speck of transfer from my stained bra. Preston Whitley had put his hands on me.

I was going to be sick.

My body hunched over as I gagged. I couldn't chase away the images making my stomach churn. What else did he do to me? Everything felt normal, but that didn't mean I wasn't violated.

"It's okay," I whispered to myself.

He wouldn't have raped me. Not yet. Preston would want me awake for something like that. So he could watch me struggle. As uncomforting of a thought as that was, it allowed me to breathe and calm down enough to get my bearings.

Giving into panic wouldn't do me any good. I needed to figure out my situation and what I had at my disposal to devise a plan. Everything from this point on relied on one moment of opportunity. If I acted brash and missed my chance, I was as good as dead.

"One moment," I reiterated while sitting back to take in my surroundings.

The first thing that slapped me in the face was the thick metal bars circling me. My eyes followed their path up to a domed roof above. The raven perched at the top sent a chill through my bones. I'd seen it before on the person-sized birdcage Preston moved into Whitley Manor.

If I had my days correct, that was eight months, three weeks, and two days ago. I spent the entire afternoon watching various boxes and furniture arrive. A year before that, construction started. I didn't dare get close enough to see what Preston was fixing, but the sound of power tools and hammers echoed long into the night.

Meaning he'd put a lot of planning into this. The birdcage I was locked in was an indicator of that. My guess was that this room was one of the ones I'd heard him working on. The open beam roof screamed attic, while the dark cherrywood walls and floor appeared shiny and new. Then there was the open door to my left, though I wouldn't call it that since there wasn't an actual door—just an empty frame displaying the clean white tiled floor on the other side.

It was a bathroom. I could see the edge of what I thought was a toilet. There wasn't much else in here. The large bed, whose platform frame appeared to be built into the floor, dominated the room. A dresser with a single lit-up lamp was next to a large metal door. I was, however, curious about the contents of the black steamer trunk beside the bed.

Maybe I could find a weapon in there? I sure as hell wasn't going to find one in here. The cage was amazingly empty. I didn't even have a blanket. Just the large plush purple pillow I was sitting on.

I ran my hand along the material and sighed. At least it was soft. There was always the option of smothering him with it, though I wasn't sure I could handle something this size, let alone lift it. It was almost as big as the bed.

A shiver ran up my spine as my eyes landed on the mattress across the room. The implications of that piece of furniture were terrifying. Preston even gave me a warning two years ago.

'I don't fuck little girls.'

I didn't put much stock in his threat before. Now, those words were all I could hear. I had to get out of here. But how?

Kicking the bars didn't do any good. They didn't so much as budge when the twang of my hell vibrated up to the dome roof. I tried the door, but that was securely locked. There was a keyhole, and I still had my glasses, but I couldn't bring myself to break them. The feel of them sitting against my temple was the only thing comforting me. As long as I had those, I had something.

My vulnerability and fear were protected by those lenses. They gave me the power of anonymity. When I wore them, I was never truly seen. Not by my friends or parents. Not even my sister. They were my shield. The safe place I could retreat to. My sanctuary from the rest of the world. I couldn't destroy them.

Unfortunately, that left me with few options. *Unless...*

I cocked a brow at the golden cord wrapped around the edge of my makeshift bed. It was a thick braided rope, definitely strong enough to strangle someone. I looked over my shoulder to ensure no one was hiding in here and reached for the one piece of salvation I had.

It was harder than I thought it would be to dig my fingers between the rope and the pillow, but I did it. After that, all I had to do was pull, pull, and pull some more. Whoever made this thing did a good job. It was really sewn on there. If I kept at it, I'd exert all of my energy, which I needed to conserve.

So, I bent down to gnaw at the stitches, which was not fun with a mouth drier than the desert. My lips kept sticking to my gums, and every swallow grated down my throat like sandpaper. But my dedication paid off. My teeth cut through the last stitch, allowing me to pull the rope free.

I shuffled to the back of my cage and tucked my weapon between the bars and the pillow. Not so far down, I couldn't get to it quickly, but enough that it wouldn't be easily seen.

Now I just had to wait.

I sat down, pressed my back against the bars, and glued my eyes to the large metal door.

Preston should be here any second.

'Any second' turned into minutes and then hours. At least that was what it felt like, not that I had anything to guesstimate the timeframe. There was no clock or windows in this place of darkness, and counting didn't help. I got bored with that after the first thirty minutes.

My mind began to wander. First, over the happy things. Shelby's smile, Riley's art, and Trina's laugh. Then my thoughts turned to my captor. I went over all the encounters we had, searching for something.

Was there some hint or clue hidden in his actions that I'd missed? Why did he start following me? Was it the tattoo parlor that triggered him, or something else? The answer to that might be the key I needed. But where did I start?

That was when another smile flashed through my mind. A bright, happy grin that brought a tear to my eye...

My knees sunk into the soft earth as I reached out and swept some dirt off the headstone. The name etched on the stone broke my heart. Tico, my beloved friend, was gone, torn away by a monster no one saw. Well, one person did.

Harper knew what her father was and didn't say anything. Lord knows I understood the trauma an abusive parent could cause. My back was still stinging with it, but my father wouldn't punish anyone else. That would ruin his perfect God-fearing image.

My fingers dug into the grass under me.

If Harper had just spoken up, then Tico would still be here. But she didn't. She kept her secret behind her closed lips, and now all I wanted to do when I saw her was cut her mouth open. Riley, Shelby, and Star were quick to defend her. They said I shouldn't blame her. Harper was beaten into submission and was afraid of her father.

I say fuck her fear. She and her family were the cause of my pain.

All I wanted was my friend back.

I was so lost in sorrow that I didn't hear the footsteps coming up behind me.

Preston tipped his head down at me. "Don't cry, Little Bird."

Why was he here? "Leave me alone."

"That's not going to happen. But I'll tell you what I will do."

I didn't care what he was going to do. I didn't care about anything right now. Not even the hand that reached out to sweep a wet streak off my cheek.

"I'll find whoever did this and make him pay."

A snort shook my chest. "We already know who did this."

And trust me. He didn't pay nearly enough.

Preston arched a brow. "Do we?"

THAT WAS the last time I saw Preston until last night. If it was last night? I wish I could see if the sun was up. And was it too much to ask for a glass of water? My tongue was starting to stick to the roof of my mouth.

Huffing, I slumped back and crossed my arms.

That was when a hiss echoed, and the metal door started to open.

Chapter 6
Preston

The faint thrum and screech of Ozzy Osborne tickled my ears as I pulled a black T-shirt over my head and rounded the corner. I didn't believe in such a thing as a perfect day, but this was pretty damn close.

It started the same as every other day. Woke up, had something to eat, did a couple of chores, had a shower, then headed down to the basement—nothing out of the ordinary. What put the cherry on top was the time I spent watching my Bird scuttle around her cage.

Sweet little Marnie, with her determined mind, was like crack. For three hours, I sat in that chair, transfixed by the monitor. The look on her face when she realized what was happening was priceless.

Even after she stashed her weapon away, fear still tugged at her features. My guess was she was planning on choking me with that rope or something along those lines. I'd let her have her little security net. If anything, I looked forward to the fight.

I kept waiting for her to give up, but she never did. She just sat there waiting. Every once in a while, her eyes would dull, like she was drifting off somewhere in her mind. Then that spark of defiance would reignite. It was her internal struggle that got me hard.

I jerked off twice while zooming in on her face. Solitude wasn't an easy thing to handle. Stronger men than her would've broken by now. Like the man behind the large metal door at the end of the hall.

My eyes dropped down to the watch on my wrist.

I counted the seconds, slowly ticking away to the minute when the endless loop of Crazy Train would get cut. Sure enough, as that hand moved up to mark the hour, silence cascaded into the darkness. Everyone had their place of serenity. Micha found solace in the water, and Logan had Shelby. For me, that place happened to be a basement dug under the east wing.

Some might call it a dungeon, I suppose. Then again, they didn't know this place existed. No one did. That would defeat the purpose of building it myself. Bet my old man never expected this when he passed Whitley Manor down to me. If only he knew who I had in this room.

I leaned over to look in the retinal scanner and unlock the door. The metal pane swung inwards, pushing a gust of air past me. The scent of blood and sweat wasn't one I found distasteful. I rather enjoyed it. There was something about desperation and fear that called to me. However, the stench from this room made my lip curl.

It was time to hose this prick down again. Eh, I'd do it tomorrow. I wasn't in the mood to drag out the firehose. Plus, I had stuff to do today. Should shower again before I did that, though.

Shrugging, I stepped into the darkness.

I didn't have to turn on the light to see the figure huddled in the corner. The sconces out in the hall cast enough of a glow to outline his naked form. He was pressed into the corner, shivering. The cement encasing this place didn't offer much warmth, nor did the metal table in the center. Not that I gave a shit. I was nice and toasty, even had a cup of coffee in my hand.

Lifting the drink up to my lips, I took my time and reveled in the way he watched me slowly sipping the hot liquid. He was practically salivating over the steam rising from my mug. If he wasn't so dehydrated, I might've seen some drool form in the corner of his mouth. I was thoroughly enjoying the show. I especially liked how his wide eyes seemed to light up against the dirt on his face.

Oh, how the mighty have fallen.

Once upon a time, he was at the top of his game. He was a leader in his chosen career, with a position that gave him power and arrogance. He was respected and feared. Now, look at him, curled up in the shadows like a scared bunny. No one in his past would recognize the man he'd become. If one could even call what he was a man? I suppose he did still have a dick. Hadn't taken that yet. I figured it'd be a fitting way to end his miserable life finally and let him bleed out.

"Hmm," I hummed while lifting my gaze to the panel of fluorescent bulbs on the ceiling. "I think we need some light."

My prisoner didn't like that. He ducked under his arms and grumbled out an inhumane wail. Over the years, I've learned a lot of things about people. Given the right circumstances, anyone could switch from talking to sounding like an animal. Civility was but a myth. Strip away everything that polite society deemed acceptable, add in a lot of desperation, with a dash of basic survival needs, and that was when you really saw what someone was made of.

My friend here was down to one-word sentences, like when he croaked out, "Thirsty."

He didn't need to worry. He'd get all the hydration he needed when I hosed his ass down tomorrow. I was more concerned with the untouched gruel still sitting by the door.

I tapped the plastic bowl with the toe of my boot and shook my head. "You didn't eat your food."

"Thirsty," was his only response.

"I don't give a shit if you're thirsty," I barked loud enough to make him jar back.

I took precious time out of my day to make sure he had something to eat, and he ignored my efforts. That would not do. I suppose I shouldn't be surprised. It wouldn't be the first time he tried to kill himself.

That happened five years ago after I removed his testicles. Then there was the Pear of Anguish incident. An ass was not meant to stretch like that. I thought he was done for, but the fucker pulled through. Now he was too weak to bash his head against the wall. His ribs were visible through his skin.

I gave him a year, maybe two tops, before his organs failed. That didn't mean he could stop eating. I decided when he died. Besides, if he didn't eat, the LSD wouldn't have time to kick in before the next round of *Crazy Train* started.

"Do you want the IV again?"

He quickly shook his head, but he still didn't move.

"Well, what the fuck are you waiting for?"

That got him going. He crawled across the floor and picked up the bowl.

I held up my finger, stopping him. "No hands."

If he wanted to whine like a little bitch, he could eat like one.

Like the good dog he was, he bowed his head and dropped his face into the bowl.

"That's it, Nash," I said while walking back out into the light. "Now, you make sure you eat every last bite."

I didn't want to waste any more time on him. There was someone else who needed my attention. A pretty little bird tucked away in her cage. I couldn't even wait to get back upstairs to see her. Marnie's face was displayed on my phone before I rounded the corner to the stairs.

She looked so sweet, tucked up against the bars, with her dark hair flowing down her back. I couldn't stop pulling my eyes along her creamy complexion. Perfect porcelain skin, just begging to be bitten into. The red mark on the side of her neck called to me. Could she feel it like I could? All night long, my teeth yearned for the softness of her flesh while her tantalizing taste taunted the tip of my tongue.

What I wanted most was to see that strong will of hers crumble. One day it would, but not today. Today was the day she got a taste of her future. Marnie Dupire could be as fierce and defiant as she wanted. Hell, I'd help her burn the world down if that was what she wished. But I would be the only person she bowed to.

It would take time, of course. People like her didn't bend easily.

You had to pick away at their walls. But once those fortresses came down, they didn't just break.

They completely collapsed.

I couldn't wait to watch her fall. Only then would I be able to push her past her self-erected boundaries. And I'd start by taking those glasses.

There was a reason I left them on her face. They were a tool. One that I wanted to see if she'd utilize. She'd have to break them to do that, though, and at one point, I thought that was precisely what she would do. I held my breath while she pawed at the frames in contemplation until she dropped her hand. That was when I knew my suspicions were correct. The only purpose those brown frames had, was to give her a shield.

Too bad. I was looking forward to her trying to run. It had been a while since I had a good game of cat and mouse. The adrenaline coursing through my veins as I chased some scared bitch was exhilarating. Throw a little blood and hardcore choking into the mix, and I was hooked.

My thumb brushed over the curve of my Bird's delicate neck. The need to feel her pulse flutter under my grip was literally twitching my fingers. Would she scream for me? Would she gasp and claw at my face? Those were questions I'd have to answer another day. Marnie's virgin mind was nowhere near ready for that.

Something told me I wouldn't be able to stop once I got a taste of her hot cunt. Meaning I had to take it easy on her. That was the purpose of taking my piercings out. Tearing her up would accomplish nothing more than extra healing time. As disappointing as that was. The six barbells running up the top of my shaft didn't exactly do well with tight unused holes. After the first time, though, all bets were off.

I cocked a brow as Marnie's bright aqua eyes once again dipped down.

"Oh, Little Bird," I tsked. "You shouldn't give away your secrets so easily."

She kept looking at the spot where she tucked the rope. It was kind of comical. Did she think it was going to disappear? Maybe she was as eager to use her weapon as I was to use her.

Guess I'd find out.

"Are you ready for me, Little Bird?"

She couldn't hear me, of course. But I could hear her. I listened to every single huff and wispy breath as I made my way through the house toward the west wing tower. A prisoner held at the top of a tower, how cliché was that? What else should one use that for, if not to house a beautiful girl? Every single childhood story I'd been told dictated exactly that. Not that I believed in fairy tales, but I did appreciate the irony.

My very own captured princess. "I like the sound of that, Little Bird."

I'd never been more aroused than I was when her pink lips parted with a grumbled, "I'll show him."

Ah, the searing venomous bite of hatred.

Was there anything sweeter?

Need ached through my balls, making my cock twitch. I reached down and squeezed my shaft through the denim of my jeans.

It was time to greet my tempting little houseguest.

Chapter 7
Marnie

The swish of the door opening was soft, yet it sucked all the air out of the room as seconds ticked by like hours. Each individual hair on the back of my neck spiked with alarm while my stomach flipped and turned, weightless in an endless void of uncertainty.

He was here.

The man Riley called Death walked into the room.

His cold gray eyes met mine, and I couldn't help but wonder if he could hear the rapid hammering shaking my ribcage. Could he smell the desire behind my fear, making me slip my hand down to finger my stashed contraband?

Preston Whitley wasn't the only one who dreamt about ending a life. I'd killed him three hundred and seventy-five different ways in my dreams.

"Good morning, Little Bird."

Was it morning? I couldn't tell. There were no windows in here or clock to look at. Time displacement was a good tactic. I may have used it once or twice myself.

Every sensation suddenly lit up as he stepped past the threshold. Sweat coated my palms while my hand twitched to snatch my weapon. A heaviness crept in as a booted foot lifted off the floor, then the echoing vibrations when that same foot landed.

I felt every emotion that rolled through me.

Dread, fear, panic, and finally, when I saw the twinkle in his cold stare...hate.

"I trust you slept well."

"You mean after you killed Brian?" I shot back. "Sure. There's nothing like waking up covered in blood."

He gave me a slight shrug and waltzed further into the room. "I cleaned you up."

"What else did you do?" Not sure I wanted to know the answer to that.

"Sorry, Little Bird, I'm not into necrophilia. I prefer my prey a little more...." A lock of sandy hair flopped to the side as he tipped his head. "Feisty."

I'd give him feisty.

"Your first mistake was considering my prey." I shifted over to peek out the door as it swung shut.

The hiss of it clicking closed rang through the room, but I did manage to spot what looked like stairs before my view was cut off. At least I knew I wasn't on the main floor. That was more information than I had seconds ago.

"And what's my other mistake?"

My eyes rolled back over to Preston. "What?"

"You said my first mistake." He explained while running his hand over the dresser. "I assume you meant I made more than one."

I didn't say anything, just fingered the velvety fabric hiding my secret. The second he walked into this cage, I'd grab the rope and show him what his other mistake was.

Preston's response to my silence was a smirk. A small, simple expression that should not be at all ominous. But on him, that slight tug at the corner of his mouth sent a chill up my spine.

I pressed my back against the bars behind me and focused on more important things, like the lit-up panel next to the door and the fact that it closed independently. Meaning it wasn't a lock and key device. I needed to find a remote or something more drastic, like cutting Preston's hand off. Considering I didn't see anything sharp around, that would pose a problem. Of course, there was always the possibility that Preston himself had a knife.

My eyes returned to the man slowly stalking across the room. I didn't see anything sticking out of his pockets, but that didn't mean he didn't have something.

Hmm, how easy would it be to take it from him?

Preston took his time closing the distance. It was a game that predators in the wild played. A lion crept through the grass. Wolves circled their prey. Even the insect kingdom had its own version. It was a dance meant to instill fear and hopelessness. That was what the gentle tapping of his fingers against the wall was meant to do. Just like the subtle way he glanced back at the bed. It was all part of the dance.

The glimmer that sparkled through his eyes was unnerving, to say the least, but that didn't mean I'd give in to my fear. I was not the gazelle standing alone in a field or the deer that was circled in the forest. I was the praying mantis hiding in the leaves. My judgment would not be impeded.

"You think you're pretty smart, don't you, Little Bird?"

I knew I was smart. That didn't stop intimidation from seeping into my bones.

Each long graceful stride Preston took was more daunting than the next. He moved across the floor without making a sound as if silence itself followed him. Even the corded muscles under his black shirt tensed smoothly in his shoulders. I'd seen well-oiled machines that didn't perform half as well as he walked. It was sickening and disturbing though something did seem...off.

My eyes narrowed as I searched for the source.

It wasn't something. It was him. He was different.

At first, I thought maybe it was the dampness glistening on his disheveled sandy hair. Did he shower and use a scent that would throw me off? I'd been around him so much for the past two years that the faint woodsy tone had become part of me. That scent was in here. On the pillow where I sat and in the air. Places I assumed he'd been or touched.

It could be the way he moved. There was a little extra confidence in his step, but not enough for it to be perceived as different. So what was it?

My eyes rolled up to his chest, and that was when it hit me. Preston was missing something—the denim jacket he always wore. I'd never seen him without it. I didn't know if anyone had. It was odd. That also meant he had fewer pockets and fewer places to stash a weapon for me to grab.

Damnit.

Preston cocked a brow, "I know what you're doing."

He had no idea what I was doing, but I was more than happy to let him think he did.

"I'm doing the same thing anyone in my predicament would."

"If that were true, you'd be pleading with me to let you go." He stopped a few feet away from my prison and crossed his arms. "And I don't hear any begging."

I snorted.

That would never happen. If I'd been trapped in the desert for a thousand days, and he had the only bottle of water, I'd drink my own blood before ever accepting a drop from him.

"Arrogance won't win you any favors, Little Bird."

"I think you're confusing arrogance with determination." I pointed out, and I was very determined.

Preston hummed and continued his stroll in my direction. "Do you know what people with those personality traits have in common?"

I didn't really care, but he decided to enlighten me anyway.

"When they break, they don't just crack. They crumble."

He thought he was going to break me. That was laughable. I had to hold back a chuckle. "Good luck with that."

"I'd be careful if I were you." The arch in his brow deepened. "You already have two strikes."

Did I care what the strikes were for? No. This was Preston Whitley. For all I knew, I stepped on the wrong blade of grass. There was no winning with him. Just beating him at his own game.

However, I was curious about one thing.

"What happens when I get to three?"

"Who said anything about three? Maybe my magic number is two, or maybe it's five." He wrapped his fingers around one of the bars and tipped his head to peer in at me. "Or maybe I keep track of all your infractions for when I'm feeling extra sadistic."

My throat bobbed with a heavy swallow. Not sure I wanted to find out what his idea of sadistic was. Death and misery were the only things someone like him understood. Fortunately for me, I also understood the icy touch of the reaper.

Tightening my grip on the stolen piece of rope, I shuffled backward. The press of fabric against my palm was the only thing that comforted me when Preston slowly began to circle my cage.

"What are you going to do?" I had a good idea of what his intentions were, but I needed to keep him distracted.

"Don't ask stupid questions, Marnie." He paused his stalking long enough to roll his stare my way. "You know what's coming."

I felt my heart drop as the need to hide my body and hug my knees rolled through me. That would put me at a disadvantage, though, and I already had so many—strength for one. I never questioned my carefully laid out plans more than I did when Preston raised his arm and began clinking his fingers along the bars.

The firmness of his forearm tensing made me miss the denim usually wrapped around his form. Guys like Micha and Mason openly displayed their capabilities, but Preston was deceptive. The power contained in those chiseled grooves and bulges wasn't obvious. Was that why he wore that jean jacket? So people would underestimate him?

Was I underestimating him?

"You're not doubting yourself now, are you, Little Bird?"

His ability to seemingly sense what I was thinking was more disturbing than the disappointment in his tone.

"I'd have to consider you a formidable foe for that to happen."

"Formidable foe?" His lips pursed together as he gave a slight nod. "I like that."

My pulse picked up pace as Preston took one last, long step around the cage. It wouldn't be long now. Any second now, he'd unlock the door and come in here, and I had to be ready. My entire body tensed when his hand dropped down to finger the lock.

"I'll tell you what...there's a knife in my back pocket."

My gaze instantly snapped back to his.

"If you can get it, then I might let you take a swing."

Why would he tell me that? This seemed like a trick. Still...a knife would be more effective. I took a second to calculate the length of my arm versus the visual width of his hip. It was possible, but was it worth the risk? I could always use the rope first and then go for the blade. He couldn't fight back if he were unconscious.

It wouldn't be the first time I had to do something like that. My dad still didn't know who put that tattoo on his stomach. Maybe if he had practiced what he preached, he wouldn't have been branded a deceiver.

"It's right here." Preston reached around to pat his right back pocket.

He wanted me to take it? "That's your second mistake."

"You think I'm underestimating you?"

"Aren't you?"

"I've watched you for two years Little Bird." His brow rose. "I know you're patterns."

Not all of my patterns. "I guess we'll find out."

For some reason, my comment made Preston smirk. "Welcome to my parlor said the spider to the fly."

Seriously? I knew that poem well. If he thought that was how this was going to go, then he was dead wrong. This was my parlor, not his.

"You do realize that ninety percent of male spiders are eaten by the females they mate with."

"There's only one problem with that Little Bird." Both his hands wrapped around the bars as he brought his face in closer to growl, "You're the fly in this scenario."

My eyes once again shifted back to the lock.

We'll see about that.

My first hint that something was wrong was when Preston stepped back instead of unlocking the door. Then came the gleam heating up his otherwise cold stare. I didn't even notice the small object in his hand until a hollow click rang out, and the cage began to rise.

I jerked away from the bars sliding up my back.

What the hell?

That I was not expecting, all my nerves lit up as panic dug its roots deep into my gut. In the cage, I had a barrier. There was something between us. My safety net was dwindling by the second.

This wasn't how things were supposed to go. Preston should've come in the door.

Was it even a door? I'd never seen it open, nor did I think to look for hinges. If I was wrong about that, what else was I wrong about? Were we in Ashen Springs? Did the pillow I was sitting on have a pit under it? Was the bathroom even a bathroom, and was that drip echoing from inside always there? I wasn't sure about anything anymore.

Well, there was one thing I was sure about.

Preston Whitley was having fun.

The predatory look on his face caused my heart to stop. I couldn't breathe. All I could do was sit here while he stretched his neck from one side to the other as if he was getting ready for something.

He *was* getting ready for something.

Preston Whitley was preparing to attack.

This was bad.

All logic went out the window. The only important thing now was getting away.

Before I could form a coherent thought, I slipped under the rising metal and knocked my glasses off. Not even that overrode the frenzy of hysteria tearing through me. While my hand twitched to grab my comfortable brown frames, my legs took off, carrying me as fast as possible.

Where I was going, I had no idea. I just had to go. The only thought floating through my mind as my feet furiously pounded against the wooden floor was, '*Thank God, I didn't actually need those lenses to see.*'

"Where are you going?" Preston called out. "There's nowhere to fly away to, Little Bird."

The air swept over me, cooling my skin. That was when I realized how little clothing I had on. The only thing protecting me were scraps of fabric called underwear. Suddenly that felt like the most important thing.

Blankets!

My eyes sought out the bed as I turned and headed in that direction. But there was nothing on the mattress for me to use—no pillows or soft comforter, only a sewn-on fitted sheet that refused to come off. And to make matters worse, my chest was already heaving for air.

I crouched down at the side of the bed to catch my breath and cursed my sister's name.

Trina wouldn't have this problem. While I was chasing down my next story, she was at pep rallies and playing volleyball at the beach. Who'd have thought something like cheerleading would ever be useful? Now, I kind of wished I signed up for that stuff instead of panting for air while trapped in a room with the man who stalked me for two years.

The man who was still stalking me.

Preston was barely exerting any energy. He simply turned in my direction and casually made his way over. And why not? I wasn't going anywhere, and this wasn't a chase. It was pathetic.

No, goddamnit. I am not this meek!

If Preston Whitley wanted to come at me, I'd fight him tooth and nail.

"What are you going to do with that rope?"

My eyes widened.

The rope!

I still had it in my hand. It was a makeshift attempt at a weapon but still a weapon. Besides, it wasn't as if I had anything better.

Or did I?

My attention twisted to the other side of the bed and the shiny black lamp on the dresser. The rope slipped from my grip as I jumped up to roll over the mattress.

Preston's deep voice boomed through the room as my feet touched down on the ground. "You sure you want to do that?"

Hell yes, I was sure.

My hands shot out, snatching up the lamp. It was heavier than I thought—not at all easy to wield. Plus, I had to jerk the cord out of the wall. The weird thing was that the bulb stayed lit. But I had bigger things to worry about.

I turned around to face the predator approaching.

A grin curled the corner of his mouth when he saw me, but it was the condescending tsk that really pissed me off.

"You'd have been better off with the rope."

"You better leave me alone!"

His eyes rolled as a disgruntled snort huffed from his chest. "Put that thing down before you hurt yourself."

"Oh, I'm not worried about hurting myself." I was going to crack this lamp off his head and then stab him in the neck with the pieces.

"This will go one of two ways," he said while casually strolling in my direction. "You can get on the bed, do what I say, and maybe you'll have some fun."

It was my turn to snort.

"Or," he drawled out while locking his glare directly on mine. "I can have some fun."

His brow arched in a silent challenge when I firmed my stance, refusing to back down.

"Okay." That was all the warning I got before Preston charged.

Let me just say he was a lot faster than I was. Preston cleared that space faster than I could blink. I was surprised my reflexes kicked in, allowing me to swing the lamp in time. My aim, however, wasn't great.

Instead of smacking the base off his head, he twisted to the side and took it in the shoulder. The only indication I hit him was the grunt he let out and the sound of breaking ceramic. Everything else happened too fast.

One minute my feet were on the ground. The next, I sailed through the air and slammed down on the bed. All the oxygen in my body was forced out in one violent huff. I felt my lungs deflate when my back hit the mattress. They burned in my chest, dulling the ache crawling across my tailbone.

"Fuck me, that was fun."

If I could see beyond the blackness seeping into my vision or breathe without coughing, I might've slapped him. This was the worst feeling in the world. Even when I rolled onto my side, I couldn't get rid of the tightness in my chest.

"You can do it." Something patted my back.

If this was what it felt like to get tackled, then I had a new respect for football players. Parker Whitley deserved props for not only surviving his siblings but going on that field every day. How the hell did he do it?

"Come on, Little Bird."

The first gasp down my throat was gargled and harsh. Thankfully the second flowed considerably smoother.

"That's it. Breathe."

Preston's hand was the thing patting my back. Not only that, but he was behind me, whispering in a soothing tone. And my lungs were giving into the rhythm of his hand.

I was wrong. This was the worst feeling in the world.

"Get away from me," I hissed, throwing my elbow back into his ribs.

That action probably hurt me more than it did him. I was pretty sure I heard him snicker when I tried to crawl away—*tried* being the operative word. I managed to pull my head and shoulders off the side before a large palm clamped down around my ankle. One thing caught my attention as I was pulled back—the rope.

It was still lying on the floor.

My arm slapped down, and my foot kicked out, jarring the hold Preston had on me long enough to grab the coil. The next thing I knew, my belly was rubbing against the sheet as I was pulled back. If there was any chance of this working, I had to catch him off guard. So, I did everything I could to act defeated.

When Preston's palm smacked off my ass, I gritted my teeth against the sting and stayed still. I tried not to shiver when his lips swept over the small of my back on my skin and then again when he laved a hot trail up my spine.

"I'm going to eat you up, Little Bird."

I didn't respond to the deep sound that vibrated through his chest or wince when his fingers twisted in my hair.

"You don't really think I'll fall for this docile kitten routine, do you?" He growled in my ear.

I could smell the minty scent of his breath, but still, I waited because this wouldn't be good enough for him. Preston didn't just want to overpower me. He wanted to look me in the eyes while he did it.

"If that's how you want to play it, all right," he tsked while tracing his finger over my shoulder blade. "Why don't you tell me who put these marks on your back."

That made me twitch as the crack of leather rang out in the back of my mind.

"Pray for salvation Marnie, and hope the good Lord hears you this time."

"Oh," Preston purred. "You didn't like that."

If it was the last thing I did, I'd make sure Preston Whitley tasted every single ounce of my hatred.

"What's wrong, Marnie?" He bent down and pressed his lips to the back of my head. "Weren't you daddy's good girl?"

Oh, fuck him!

Driven purely by anger, I flipped over and wound the rope around his neck. Using all my strength, I pulled and twisted my hands. All I could see was the swing of a brown belt, followed by the crack of it hitting my back.

Fuck Preston Whitley. Fuck my Father and fuck my mother for letting it happen. They could all go straight to hell, and I'd happily send each and every one of them there.

My wrath and vengeance were broken by a single sound, the taunting mockery of a laugh.

Chapter 8

Preston

Watching my Bird plot was the single most erotic experience of my life. Survival instilled the fight-or-flight instinct in almost everyone, but Marnie thought about every choice she made. Panicked or not, she still ran through possible actions and outcomes.

Her mind was fascinating and sexy as hell. Power came in forms. Making someone kneel before you, holding another's life in the palm of your hand, and demanding respect from those around you. But a man who could control a woman like that…he was a god.

Every time her perfect plans failed, and she got that look on her face, my dick got harder. Of all the people I'd toyed with in my life, Marnie Dupire was the most amusing. I might even say I was enjoying myself. When she hit me with that lamp, I damn near busted a nut. Then to top it all off, the little minx wrapped that cord around my neck.

There was nothing hotter than blood lust. And she wanted mine bad.

So I played along for a bit. Faked a couple of gags and such. Poor thing was so blinded by hate that she didn't see my hand tucked under her strangulation device. The only damage she was doing was exhausting her own strength. My lungs were nice and full of air. A fact that made me chuckle at the satisfaction in her expression.

Then I laughed when her big eyes rounded.

The confusion sparkling in those bright aqua orbs was breathtaking, but it was the storm brewing underneath that I could get lost in. That was something I had in common with Micha. We both enjoyed the rage of a wrathful woman, except I didn't want to break it.

I wanted to harness it.

Marnie's grip on the rope loosened as her brows knit, "You're not...."

"No, Little Bird." I shook my head.

Did she really think she could get one over on me?

"B-but...I-I..."

Aww, she did. Isn't that cute?

"Consider this your first lesson, Little Bird," I tugged at the rope so she could see my hand tucked between her strangulation device and my neck. "I always get what I want."

How hard that would be on her was entirely up to Marnie.

I held back a chuckle when her eyes dropped to the fingers preventing her from constricting my airway. That was when doubt really set in. It was funny how fast the mighty could fall. I was sure enjoying the show.

"You tricked me," she whispered.

"Now, now, Little Bird," I tsked. "Don't put your failure on me."

We were going to have to work on her situational awareness. Were all virgins this naïve? Because I was thoroughly enjoying the spark glimmering across her face.

"Failure," she muttered. "I didn't...did I?"

That wavering tone that wisped out of her mouth was so fucking sexy that I couldn't stop myself from crashing my lips down on hers. The shocked gasp she let out floated down my throat like fucking candy.

That wasn't anywhere near as good as the wince when I tore the cord out of her grasp. Rope burn hurt like a bitch. That didn't stop her from trying to push me away. Groaning, I pushed in on her so that I could feel her wriggle around. She bucked and jerked, struggling to get my weight off her. The only thing that accomplished was me throwing two years of patience out the window. Marnie would be lucky if she made it the next five minutes with her panties intact.

She slapped my back and twisted her neck, "Get off."

Not a fucking chance. I was just getting started, and I needed more. But every time I tried to slip my tongue in her mouth, my stubborn Little Bird clamped her lips shut. I would not be denied.

Yanking on her hair, I deepened the kiss and growled, "Open your fucking mouth."

I needed to taste her anger.

Marnie's jaw clenched as she tightened the seal on her lips. The only thing defiance would get her was a sore ass after I threw her over my knee. Her pain and fear were mine to feast on.

I let go of her hair, grabbed her chin, and dug my fingers in to pry her jaw open.

The instant my tongue dipped into her hot little mouth, I knew I was fucked. I'd never get enough of her sweet flavor. The hint of copper lingering from that asshole that dared to touch her only added to it. Fuck me. I wanted to slit someone else's throat just so I could lick the blood off her.

That would have to wait for another day. I had other things to do. Like, contain the hands clawing me. I felt that last rake of her nails down my arm.

Begrudgingly, I released her jaw and lifted off of her to pull away. Until Marnie's hand slapped down my ass and stilled, her palm was right over my pocket knife. I wasn't lying when I told her I had one.

"Go on," I coaxed. "Take it."

I could feel her hand twitching as her eyes snapped up to mine. But she didn't trust me.

Smart girl.

"What are you waiting for, Little Bird? Your salvation is right there."

All she had to do was reach out and take it. It wouldn't get her anywhere, but I was game to let her try.

"I don't believe in salvation," she hissed back at me.

Kind of ironic coming from a preacher's daughter, but I got it. However, I was curious about when exactly she decided to give up on her faith. Was it the first whipping or one of the many after? Maybe it was when her sister started acting differently, which, according to Marnie's diary, was around the age of thirteen. Apparently, the good pastor had a thing for teenagers. Wonder if Shelby ever told Logan about the last night she spent at the Dupire household.

"Don't say that." I pushed myself up on my hands so I could slide my eyes over the top of her breasts. "Maybe God will hear you this time."

I should've taken her bra off.

"There is no God."

That one she got wrong. "I am your God."

I watched her jaw clench and smiled inside when her hand darted into my pocket.

So easy to bait. That was the thing about temptation. It was predictable. What wasn't predictable was what Marnie did with my knife. I thought she'd fumble around trying to open the locked blade, and then I'd take it from her like a petulant child.

That was not what happened.

Marnie didn't even look at the weapon before cracking it off the side of my head.

"Goddamnit." Fuck me, that shit hurt.

It'd been a long time since someone hit me hard enough to see stars. It was also kind of hot. If Marnie kept this shit up, gentle was the last thing she was going to get.

"Give me that."

I reached out for her hand, but she threw it back, then twisted to the side and thrust her hips up, knocking me off balance for half a second.

"You're starting to piss me off," I warned.

That didn't stop her. If anything, Marnie amped up her struggle. Ever tried to hold onto a wriggly worm when your head was ringing? It didn't work so well.

"Give me that fucking knife!"

"Eat shit," she grunted while slipping out from under me enough to swing her fist back.

This time I was ready.

I snatched her wrist before she could strike and slammed her arm down while crawling back over her to sit on her hips.

She thrashed about and yelled, "Get off me."

But it was the way she spat in my face that made me stop and glare down at her.

Taking a deep breath, I wiped the wet spot off my cheek with the back of my hand and said, "That's strike three."

There were a lot of things I'd put up with. Disrespect was not one.

"Take your strikes and shove them up your ass!"

If she wanted to shove things up asses...

"Well, seeing as you already gave me some lube...." I paused long enough to lick her spit off the back of my hand.

Her throat bobbed in the most enticing way. "You wouldn't."

"Oh, I would." And she knew it.

There were two choices she could make in this situation. Poking the beast was not the right one, which was exactly what she did. One second she was a fun little game to play. The next, she was fucking annoying. Throwing her arms and kicking her legs while screaming, "Fuck you. I hate you."

Fuck nice. She was getting it hard and rough, and if she were lucky, I'd leave her ass alone.

First, I had to get my knife away from her. She kept swinging her fist to hit me with it and even managed to land a couple of strikes. Thankfully, they weren't on the side of my head again, but I still felt it.

Little bitch had a tight hold on it, though. I was having trouble prying her fingers apart. The twisting about wasn't helping. Every time I got somewhere, Marnie would jerk and retighten her grip.

"You better give me that shit."

Marnie answered by turning her hip to bring her knee up into my back.

All right, where the fuck was that rope?

One glance over my shoulder was all it took to spot the golden cord. I snatched her wrist and stretched my other arm to grab it.

Binding someone was a pretty simple task to accomplish. A quick arbor knot after winding the rope around her wrists and bam, done. Quick and easy. At least it should've been. But just like the knife, every time I got somewhere, she'd pull a hand free.

That problem was solved with a firm slap to her face. A crack rang through the air, stilling Marnie's fight. After that, she opted to grit her teeth while giving me the look of death.

"There. Now, isn't that easier?" I twisted the fabric around one wrist before looping it over the other.

"You'll get what's coming to you."

"Sure," I snorted. She wasn't the first person to say that, and I still had yet to meet this divine retribution. "And who's going to give it to me, you?"

Marnie lifted her head up to hiss in my face, "You're not the only one people should be afraid of."

Now we were getting somewhere. I was tempted to bring up the frat boy she drugged, but that little tidbit of information might be useful later.

So instead, I sighed and pointed out the flaw in her statement. "I'm incapable of feeling fear."

Or regret, remorse, or sadness. I used to wonder why people cried. Now I didn't care.

"I'll never stop fighting you."

I gave the rope one last twist in between her arms and said, "You just did."

The daggers in her eyes sharpened.

Marnie could hate me all she wanted. Eventually, she'd give in. She wouldn't be able to help it, just like Nash couldn't help but ask me for a drink. I was the cause of his years of torment, yet he still sought comfort from me. That was how things like this worked. Someone always caved, and it wasn't the one without a conscience.

"Careful." Marnie twisted, attempting to yank her hands out of my grip. "You're close to making another mistake Preston Whitley."

Fuck me. It was hot when she used my full name. I might make her call me Mr. Whitley from now on.

"The only mistake I made," I dug my fingers into her fist to snatch my knife away. "Was letting you have this."

Marnie snorted, "Let?"

I could've kissed the sneer she shot me.

Then again, why would I waste my efforts on that when there were so many other parts of her I had yet to explore? The tiny beads of sweat glistening on her skin called to me almost as much as the flushed hue tinting her fair complexion. I wanted to run my tongue over every inch of her body. Take my time to enjoy every quiver and wince of objection while I made her come.

First, I needed to secure her. So I could take my time.

"I hate you."

"Good for you," I muttered while dragging her up to the head of the bed. There I attached her bound arms to one of the metal loops on the frame.

Unless it was her pussy wrapped around my cock, I didn't give a shit how she felt.

Marnie's eyes grew as they darted to the hooks, loops, and binds attached to the frame. That was when things really started to sink in. Her muscles twitched while her voice softened into a whisper.

"This isn't a bed, is it?"

Oh, it was a bed. Just not one necessarily meant for sleeping. "Don't worry. We'll play with those later."

After she was broken in.

"You don't have to do this."

And there was the fear I'd been waiting for.

I moved my hand over her hip and up to the underside of her breast. "Don't tell me you're giving up this easy, Little Bird."

She was so soft and smooth, and I enjoyed the nervous tremor quaking her stomach. My cock was aching to stretch her open. Would she scream? I was slightly disappointed that I had to tie her hands. I would've liked to feel her claws dig into my back, but we had plenty of time for that.

For the first time, I heard a fearful tremor vibrate her tone. "You're sick."

"So they tell me."

If she wanted to see sick, I could've shown her what was in the trunk. See, I could be nice.

The loop clacked as she gave her hands a firm yank. "If you do this, I'll never forgive you."

"You mistake me for someone who cares." The only thing I cared about was getting her clothes off.

It suddenly bothered me that there was fabric in my way. I wanted to sink my teeth into those full round breasts and hear her squeal while her blood touched my tongue. I could always start with the sweet spot between her thighs or knead my way down her chest while I buried my nose in her neck.

There were so many options that I didn't know where to start.

Every inch was more tantalizing than the last. From the way Marnie's legs clenched tightly shut to the slight tremor in her chest when she breathed. I couldn't stop touching her. My hands moved over her soft skin, soaking up the warmth, but that wasn't enough. I needed everything. Every last sweet note in her scent and spark of fear in her eyes were mine.

She was mine, and she let that motherfucker touch her.

"You've been a bad girl, Marnie."

Her eyes met mine as she hissed through her teeth, "I wish I'd been worse."

There was that feisty little thing I wanted to take over my knee. It was official, Marnie Dupire was my favorite game.

"Hold still." I smiled at her and flicked open my knife. "Or don't. You look good in red."

Chapter 9
Marnie

One flick was all it took to shift my entire being to a single point in time. I could still feel Brian's blood dripping off my skin. I saw him die and watched the light fade from his eyes. That should bother me, but it didn't, not nearly as much as the sharp tip of the black blade in Preston's hand.

It was the same knife that ended Brian's life.

'You look good in red.'

The slight coppery tinge in the back of my throat reminded me just how dangerous that blade was. In anyone else's hands, it was just a weapon. In Preston's, it was an instrument held by a masterful surgeon. He'd even branded the side of the hilt with what looked like a flower. A carved line of what appeared to be a petal was curving out from under his fingers.

Huh?

"This is the part where you plead for mercy."

"Why?" I rolled my eyes up at the crooked smile on Preston's face. "You're not going to kill me."

He tipped his head and cocked a brow. "There are worse things than death."

"Such as?"

"Depends on who you ask," he said while raking his gaze down my torso.

I swallowed back the lump threatening to bubble up my throat. There was no denying the look in Preston's eyes. I'd seen it countless times on the boys watching my sister. Lust had a very distinctive spark, even in someone like him.

My stomach churned as Preston's armed hand dipped closer to my skin.

The reality of my situation set in while everything else faded away. The rope biting into my wrists, the man sitting on top of me, and the bed underneath all fell back. One thought flew through my mind as a shadow closed in through the thickening air.

I left my glasses.

My only shield sat on a cushion across the room, and I couldn't even see it. Nothing existed beyond the light slicing off that sharp metal edge and my naked face.

I needed my glasses. Those lenses were the only thing that prevented fear from taking over. Without them, I was vulnerable. Even the hatred burning through my veins chilled to an icy spark.

"Wouldn't it be better if I could see you?" I tried to peek around his large body, hoping to at least spot the edge of my brown frames.

I couldn't, which was so much worse because I knew they were right there, waiting for me to grab them.

"Aw." Preston's lips pursed in a fake frown. "What's wrong, Little Bird, feeling naked without your glasses?"

Yes.

"If you don't want me to see, that's fine," I sneered. "Personally, I'd rather stay in oblivion."

Reverse psychology was a good tactic. I'd used it many times on my parents. Even my sister fell for it a couple of times.

"Let's drop the charade, shall we," he sighed. "We both know you don't need glasses."

He didn't know that. No one did.

"Yes, I do," I insisted.

"Then why doesn't your sister have any?" He shot back. "Identical twins means identical genetics."

That was a hard point to argue. It took a few seconds for me to come up with a plausible excuse. "Not that it's any of your business, but I was injured as a kid."

"Now that I believe." Preston lifted his hand and pointed the tip of the knife at me. "But it wasn't your eyes that were injured. Was it, Little Bird?"

That made me roll my eyes. His mind games wouldn't work on me.

At least, that was what I thought until he folded over me and whispered, "My sister has that same look in her eyes."

My heart stopped. Everyone in Ashen Springs knew what had happened to Ava. While I felt sorry for her, it didn't excuse Ava's behavior. Besides...

"I'm not your sister."

"No, you're not." Preston pushed himself up and trailed the knife slowly down my side. "But someone did break you."

'That's a pretty dress, Marnie. Did you wear it for me?'

I pushed the distant voice into the back of my mind and rolled my eyes away. Nash Hunter had no dominion over me. Those memories were dead. I killed them years ago. Preston Whitley sure as hell wasn't going to be the one to bring them forward.

"Did I touch a nerve?"

"Don't flatter yourself," I snarled back.

"You shouldn't lie, Little Bird," Preston tsked. "Don't worry. We'll talk about that later."

Like hell, we would.

"Right now, I'm curious about something else." The way his fingers swept over my stomach sent a shiver up my spine. "Do you moisturize?"

What kind of question was that? One second he was trying to pull on old wounds, and the next, he was asking about moisturizer.

Preston must be trying to throw me off my game. Well, that wasn't going to happen. I refused to answer his meaningless questions.

"Dry skin takes longer to heal."

I didn't think it was possible to feel a heart stop, yet mine did. The quick pattering thrumming through my veins died away when he pulled the blade over my ribs and up my chest. Nerves tingled across my skin, making my stomach flip. I didn't like this feeling, and I wasn't weak or pathetic. If my childhood prepared me for anything, it was survival.

Okay, Marnie, think. You've researched things like this.

Every problem had a solution, meaning there had to be a way out of this. Escape was the obvious answer. I tried wriggling my hands to see if I could slip out of my binds. That didn't work. Preston not only wound the rope around my wrists, but he looped it between them as well. And since I couldn't see the knot when I peeked up, untying myself was out of the question.

My motion was too restricted to search around the fabric. I could barely stretch my finger down enough to feel the edge of the rope.

I was stuck on the bed with my hands in a praying pose, the irony of which wasn't lost on me.

My father's voice practically screamed in my mind, telling me to pray for salvation. The only salvation I'd get was one I claimed for myself.

Taking the knife from Preston wasn't an option, nor was overpowering or attacking him. There wasn't much I could do. Maybe if he wasn't sitting on my hips, I could kick out, not that it would've done me a lot of good.

There was only one choice left.

Reason with the devil.

Most survivors had one thing in common. They made their attacker see them as a person instead of a thing. There was only one issue with that. Preston Whitley didn't have a soul to tug at.

"I see the wheels turning in your head, Little Bird." He swept the blade down my stomach and lazily dragged it up my torso. "You won't be able to think your way out of this one."

I shivered against the coolness scraping across my skin and whispered the only thing I could think of, "Think about your sister, Preston."

There were only two people I'd seen him show any sort of compassion. Parker and Ava. Ava had her problems—like being completely crazy—but she was his twin. And twins had a different bond than other siblings.

It wasn't something I could explain, but it was there. Trina felt it too. It was a force that made us sneak into each other's room at night or pick up the phone. We just knew when we needed each other. If there was anything capable of reaching Preston's humanity, it should be his sister. It was worth a shot, at the very least.

What did I have to lose?

"What would Ava say?"

"Are you trying to humanize me? Come on now, Marnie." He shook his head. "I thought you were smarter than that."

There had to be something he cared about. "What about Parker?"

"What about him?"

"What would he say if he knew what you were doing?"

Preston swirled the knife around my belly button and sighed, "You're going to have to be more specific. My brother has a lot of opinions."

Attempting to escape the tingles pouring up my body, I sucked back a breath and hallowed in my stomach. "You kidnapped me. I doubt Parker would be okay with that."

"Probably not." He shrugged. "Now, ask me if I care."

That was the question.

Preston grazed the knife around my hip and up my side, causing goosebumps to travel up my arms.

Concentrating was becoming problematic, but I still managed to say, "You have to care about something."

"Do I?" He didn't even look up at me. His eyes were fixed on the knife, lazily gliding up my body.

"Yes." Even Ted Bundy had a heart. Otherwise, he would've killed his girlfriend. I just had to get Preston to feel it.

"Preston..."

"I'm going to stop you right there." He cut me off. "Bringing up my family and saying my name won't make me see you any different than I do right now. So you can stop wasting your time."

My mouth opened before I could stop it, "How do you see me?"

The answer was displayed in the playful glimmer darkening his eyes. For the first time, I saw a touch of blue in those gray orbs. Tiny flecks that sparkled with depravity. The worst part was that I let it seep in. I could feel defeat edging its way into my veins.

I hated it, and I hated myself for letting it press down on me. A long time ago, I swore no one would have that kind of power again. That vulnerable little girl cornered in the bathroom was gone. I shoved her into the swirling pit in my stomach and closed the door. Fear was a weak emotion used by weaker men. I was better than that.

I was better than them.

So why couldn't I move?

Why didn't I jerk away when Preston dragged the knife up my side? Why did I lay there praying the metal didn't pierce my skin? Why didn't I do something?

Adrenaline made me feel everything. Every inch, the blade moved. The warmth from his hand soaking into me. I was starved for something.

I tried to shut it out and focus on more important things. But no matter what I did, I couldn't stop the sound of blood whooshing through my ears as little tingles and sparks funneled straight into my core.

This was so fucked up. I should've yelled or lashed out. Anything would've been better than staring up at Preston. But I couldn't tear my eyes away. The way he looked at me like he wanted to bathe in my blood and devour me whole wasn't as terrifying as my thighs squeezing together when his tongue darted out to moisten his bottom lip.

There was something wrong with me. Maybe there were still some drugs in my system. Who knows what he gave me? Some of that stuff stayed around for days. It was the only thing that made sense because I would never react this way. Not to something like this.

"There's nothing quite as enticing as the scent of fear." Preston slipped the blade under my bra between my breasts and tipped his head. "Except for maybe the taste of blood."

The fabric gave way with one flick of his wrist, and all I could do was grit my teeth as cool air wafted over my exposed flesh. My nipples hardened, making me swallow the gasp threatening to break through my lips.

"I'm not afraid of you."

"Yes, you are." A curl tugged at the corner of his mouth. "And you're getting off on it."

"No, I'm not." I was just trying to figure out my next move, which I almost had until he moved the blade up to my shoulder.

Suddenly I was back in my room, staring down the barrel of a gun.

I had two years to prepare for this moment.

I told myself that Preston had his fun and moved on, but there was always a twitch in the back of my mind. Deep down, I knew this was coming. I didn't want to accept it.

I brought this on myself.

Preston sliced through one strap, then moved over to the other, and all I could think about was how close the tip was to my face.

My neck stretched in an attempt to keep my head out of danger. Not that it helped any. The second I moved, I was pricked.

I winced, and Preston tsked.

"I told you to stay still."

Bastard was waiting for a reason to cut me.

A sting burned over my collarbone and down my chest, making me hate myself more. Because Preston was right, some part of me was getting off on this. As much as I wanted to deny it, the evidence dampened my panties.

I told myself that this was normal. The subconscious did all kinds of things to ease trauma. This was just my body's way of preparing for my impending violation and nothing more.

Then his mouth clamped down around the cut on my shoulder.

Everything heated up.

The air filling the room, my breath, the sweat coating my palms, and even the mattress underneath me felt like it was on fire.

"So fucking sweet," Preston growled while licking the blood off my skin.

A hot tongue slithering over my skin should not feel that good. Combine that with how his feral tone vibrated through me, and I was convinced this was definitely the result of residual drugs. Either way, Preston sure seemed to be enjoying himself.

I half expected to be cut again. Maybe a part of me wanted it? But it wasn't the knife that dug into me. It was Preston's teeth.

He pinched one nipple and bit down on the other. And it wasn't a nice playful nip. It was hard, firm, and painful enough to make my back arch off the bed. Or at least I thought it was pain that did it. The humming buzz vibrating through my core would disagree.

I never thought I'd want to be cut or stabbed. But the longer Preston's mouth was on me, the more I longed for the sting of his blade. Then my body might remember the danger we were in instead of giving in to a monster who toyed with lives for fun.

Despite the sensations clouding my mind, I still managed to keep some modicum of control.

My jaw clenched as I clamped my lips shut, turning whatever sound was trying to come out into a garbled muffle.

Preston didn't like that.

He lifted up and glared down at me. "You're holding back, Little Bird."

I returned the challenge on his face with a challenge of my own. "Untie my hands, and we'll see how little I am."

"Tempting," The corner of his mouth lifted in an almost smirk. "But I have another game in mind."

Half a second later, my panties were gone. I wasn't even sure how he did it. The knife was still in my view, and yet Preston managed to strip me completely. And all I had to mull over was the sound of tearing fabric and a brief snap.

"How did you do that?"

Preston's brow rose. "Do what?"

I opened my mouth to explain, then quickly thought better. While I wanted to know how he ripped cotton fabric—women's underwear was well made—I wasn't willing to admit my curiosity or any other weakness that could be used against me.

Unfortunately, it appeared I could not hide my inner thoughts. One quick scan of my face was all Preston needed.

"Your nose crinkles up when you're confused."

My acting skills, however.... "I think you're misconstruing anger with confusion."

"Do you really think that straight-laced, calm-voice bullshit is going to work on me?"

Why not? It worked on everyone else.

"Let me give you a tip."

That made me snort.

"The little things will *always* give you away." His tongue darted out to flick my nipple.

I cursed the gasp that came out in response. Especially when a victory smile tugged on the corner of Preston's mouth. If it were possible to kill someone with a single look, my glare would've stopped his heart cold.

"Don't worry, Little Bird." Preston rolled his eyes over my bare breast and licked his lips. "I'll teach you everything you need to know."

"I don't want to learn anything from you." Unless it was how fast he'd bleed out after his jugular was sliced. All I had to do was get my hands on that knife. Sooner or later, he'd have to untie me, and when he did, I'd be ready.

A chuckle whispered past his lips as his gaze shifted to the blade, cooling my skin. "You want this, Little Bird?"

That was the dumbest question I'd ever heard.

"How many times have you thought about stabbing me?"

"Are you talking about the past ten seconds or from the day I met you?"

That was a valid question. I'd killed Preston Whitley about five hundred and fifty-three ways in my head. Right now, I was imagining what he'd look like choking on his own blood.

The way his mouth curled made me think he was pleased by my response. *Let's see how pleased he is when I'm on the other end of that knife.*

All I had to do was bide my time until that moment. I learned a few things from my sister, including how to toy with men.

With an exaggerated sigh, I rolled my eyes, "Can we get this over with? I'm bored."

Unfortunately, Trina never dated someone like him.

"Well, we can't have that." He snickered and lifted off my hips.

I thought this was my chance for a brief second until he forced a hand between my thighs. Then all I could think about was crossing my legs to keep him out. It didn't matter how tightly I pressed them together. Preston still wedged his way in.

When his hand cupped my mound, I tried to focus on other things. The cool air wafting across my skin and the bite of the rope digging into my wrists. None of it worked. Instead of shivering uncomfortably, my body zeroed in on the warmth emanating from the man touching me.

I gritted my teeth and hissed, "This isn't going to work."

"We'll see about that." Preston slid a finger through my folds and pressed down on my clit.

The satisfied glimmer that sparked across his face was almost as gutwrenching as the moan that broke through my lips. It was as if the universe itself was working against me. Every swipe and swirl sent a zing of pleasure up my spine.

All I could do was clench my jaw and grumble, "I won't give you what you want."

He could play my body against me all he wanted. I refused to budge. I would not let the cloud of bliss fogging my mind win. If I had to bite my tongue off, then so be it.

"Yes, you will." Preston pulled his hand away, allowing me to breathe a sigh of relief.

My pussy, on the other hand, did not agree. It pulsed at the loss of his touch. Luckily for me, I wasn't ruled by needless urges.

"You'll fight it, and you might even hold off for a bit, but you won't be able to stop it." His eyes rolled up to mine as his lips pressed against my hipbone. "Like it or not, you were meant to be owned."

I never wanted to hurt anyone more than I did him. The bitter taste of wrath tainted my thoughts.

"I hate you."

"I'm sure you do." Preston dug his fingers into my thighs, forcing them apart. "But not as much as you're about to hate yourself."

That was all the warning I got before he bent down and clamped his mouth around my clit.

All logical thought fled as his tongue laved over me. Lust took over, drowning out the need for revenge. Nothing had ever felt this good. I couldn't stop my hips from moving. My body begged for more while a voice in the back of my mind screamed at me to stop it.

I tried to fight it. Told myself I was better than this and jerked my hands. All that did was tighten the knot binding me, which sent a burning sensation down my arms, adding to the coil tightening in my core. Every muscle in my body tensed while beads of needy sweat trickled down my face.

I would not give in. I refused. Preston Whitley would not break me.

My head shook, denying the pleasure lighting up my nerves as I swallowed down every last moan. Sheer determination was the only asset I had.

"Be as stubborn as you want, Little Bird," Preston's breath warmed my delicate flesh as his tongue swirled around my opening. "One way or another, you'll be screaming my name."

"Never." I ground out.

Then he pushed a finger inside my opening.

I snapped.

My back bowed off the bed as euphoria surged through my very soul. White hot blinding light took over my mind. I couldn't see past it or even breathe. All I could do was ride the wave tearing through my body. It was an unbridled, intense pleasure, and I hated every second of it.

I hated the satisfaction pouring through me and the pattering in my chest almost as much as I hated myself. Because somewhere deep down, past the anger and loathing, I craved more.

"So much for never."

Asshole.

I closed my eyes and focused on steadying my breath. "I didn't say your name."

Yes, he forced me to orgasm, but I wasn't so delighted that I misheard the inhuman sound that came out of my mouth.

"No, but you did scream." To add insult to injury, Preston gave me one last, long lick, causing my body to convulse.

"When I get out of here." *And I would get out of here.* I rolled my eyes open and glared at him, "I'll enjoy watching you take your last breath."

Yes, I may have caused some misfortunes for a few deserving people, but I never enjoyed their end. That wasn't my goal. I was teaching them a lesson. If they happened to die during that lesson, then that was on them. They shouldn't have been shitty people. But Preston...him I'd take my time with, might even record it.

His next words caused my heart to stop.

"Is that what you told that frat boy before you drugged him?"

Chapter 10
Preston

There were a few things that got my blood pumping. Most came with the challenge of the hunt or the tears, pain, and terror of others. But none of that got me as hard as the look Marnie gave me. Complete and utter shock. Now that was a great aphrodisiac.

"Y-you can't...I didn't...."

Every time her pink lips parted with a stutter, my dick twitched.

My Little Bird wasn't so superior now, was she? I liked this raw version of the perfectly flawed person she pretended to be: mediocre grades, a mediocre family, and mediocre life. Marnie Dupire was anything but mediocre. Her secrets were the only place she lacked substance. Or was it pure arrogance? That shit was a motherfucker that would bite you in the ass.

"What's wrong, Little Bird?" I grabbed her chin and twisted her head to stare right into those beautiful aqua orbs. "Don't like it when someone can see past your mask of mediocrity?"

That cool and calm expression snapped back on her face. "Are you actually going to do something or bore me to death with your theories?"

Even now, she was trying to take control of the situation. How cute.

"Sorry, Little Bird, you don't call the shots."

That wasn't how this game worked. She'd learn that. In the meantime, I could have a little fun.

"But who knows." I let go of her chin and sat up. "Maybe you'll get lucky."

"Luck has nothing to do with it."

I'm sure that was what she thought. "The fact that you drugged some idiot in a room full of people would say otherwise."

"I don't know what you're talking about." She added a defiant chin lift with that statement.

It was so fucking adorable I couldn't help but chuckle.

"Are you really trying to play the innocent game with me?"

Her lids narrowed as a spark of anger flashed through her eyes. "You're hardly the person to talk about innocence."

"Touché," I said while wagging my finger.

"Besides, it's not my fault some random guy decided to take drugs."

Decided? That made me laugh. "That's an interesting word choice, though I suppose it's not completely inaccurate."

He did decide to chug back the drink she dosed. The random remark, however, was a flat-out lie. Marnie went to that party with a goal in mind. The smirk on her face when he collapsed told me that. Not that I particularly cared about her motives.

I had much better things to occupy myself with, like the sweet tinge of her honey in the back of my throat. The flavor was so intoxicating that I couldn't help but dart my tongue out to lick my lips. My cock ached with need, yet I stayed where I was and pulled my eyes down her flushed face to the lovely red bite mark next to her pert nipple.

Something was nagging at the back of my brain. A question that wouldn't go away. What made Marnie Dupire tick? It was fucking annoying. My prey was strung up, ready to be used. I should be enjoying the way her pussy squeezed my cock. Not sitting here searching for answers. What the fuck?

"Who looks confused now," Marnie sang, drawing my attention to the snarl on her face.

"Well, aren't we the observant one? Careful, Little Bird," I leaned down and whispered, "curiosity killed the cat."

"I'm curious, which of us is the cat in this analogy?"

I couldn't help but smirk at that one. There was a reason I let her follow me around town. I liked knowing she was watching. It was amusing when the prey thought they could become the predator.

"You think you have me pegged, Little Bird."

"I know what you're capable of."

"Is that so?" I snickered.

While I was sure she thought she knew what I was capable of, she had no idea. The problem with that word was the limits. Capable implied guilt or empathy. A conscience that would stop someone before they went too far.

I didn't have that problem.

"Lindsay Manheim." She shot back.

There was a name I hadn't heard in a while. My interest was officially piqued.

"What about her?"

"She was last seen at prom."

"And?" If she wanted the answer, she would have to ask the question.

There was that spark of uncertainty again. "You were her date."

"Come on now, Little Bird." I lifted my finger and lazily traced a path down between her breasts. "If you want to impress me, you'll have to do better than that."

"She was last seen with you."

"We've established that." *Ask the question.*

A part of her didn't want to know the answer, while another part reeked of morbid curiosity. The anticipation of which part would win was killing me.

Marnie's chest shook with a shuttered breath, then the words finally left her lips, "You...killed her."

There it is.

"I did."

It wasn't my blunt answer that caused her eyes to widen. It was something else.

"Do you want to know how I did it?"

"No." Her brows knit in a tight scowl. "I don't want the sick details."

Oh, but she did. My Little Bird wasn't as good of an actress as she thought she was. No good girl smile or hate-filled glare could hide that spark flashing across her face.

"I wrapped my hands around her neck." I reached out and curled my fingers around Marnie's throat. "And choked the life out of her."

My grip tightened, making her breath shallow. Lindsay had the same mix of fear and bewilderment on her face. As if she couldn't believe that her date did this to her, but that wasn't why Marnie was surprised or why her thighs squished together.

"Strangling someone isn't as easy as movies make it look. You have to hold on for about four minutes."

Marnie's face paled as I dug my fingers and thumb into the sides of her neck, cutting off more of her oxygen.

"And they fight the entire time."

I was almost disappointed when her hands jerked on the rope. Lindsay slapped and clawed at me so frantically that I had scratches on my face for a week.

"Of course, all the fighting in the world doesn't matter once oxygen deprivation kicks in."

Marnie was trying to remain calm, but I could feel the beat of her pulse. That wild and erratic rhythm told me that despite her bravado, she was scared.

"Do you know what oxygen deprivation does to you, Little Bird?" My nostrils flared with the desire to soak up her fear as I leaned in closer. "Your body goes limp before your brain shuts off, so you know exactly what's happening to you. And there's fuck all you can do about it."

Like right now. Her eyes glimmered with hatred, yet her arms were unmoving and hanging from the rope binding her. I could do whatever I wanted. Marnie was completely at my mercy.

"Lindsay took her last breath with my cock buried inside her." I grazed my cheek off hers and whispered, "I never came so hard."

The swallow that bobbed under my palm vibrated down my arm, but it was the raspy "Fuck you." That snapped the last of my resolve.

"You know what?" I pressed my lips against her and growled, "That sounds like a great fucking idea."

All my Little Bird could do when I removed my hand from her neck was cough air back into her lungs. That didn't stop her from glaring at me when I climbed off the bed. She really hated me. I wanted to loosen her binds and go for another round, but not as much as I wanted to sink deep inside her hot little cunt.

When I reached over my shoulder to grab my shirt, Marnie sang, "don't you want to know how I knew?"

"Knew about what?" I asked while pulling the black cloth over my head.

"Lindsay."

What exactly was she asking? Did I want to know how she knew I went out with Lindsay or that I killed her? It didn't matter. I didn't give a shit about either of those answers. Besides…

I sighed and reached down to unbuckle my belt. "No more stalling, Little Bird."

While the conversational war we having was intriguing, I was done talking.

I looked over at my strung strung-up victim and unbuttoned my jeans.

That was when she started to panic.

There was a moment when fear took hold of people. It was fleeting and fast but unmistakable. Every muscle in their body would tense, and they'd get this expression on their face. This was the time I referred to as judgment hour. Once the masks and self-deluded facades of 'everything will be okay if' were ripped away, nothing was left but raw instinct. That was when the real person showed their face, and only two options were left.

Fight or flight.

Unfortunately for my Little Bird, flight wasn't available. The rope around her wrists clipped her wings. That didn't stop her from flipping over to inspect the knot binding her to the bed.

I wasn't worried. Hell, it might be fun if she did get free. I could chase her down, push her face on the floor and fuck her hard. And then there was the view.

My jeans dropped to the floor as I rolled my eyes over the firm globes of her ass.

From this angle, I could see everything. The little arch in her back, the way her hips shifted, and that perfect pink pussy just waiting to be used. None of that was as erotic as the desperation quaking her petite form.

I grabbed my shaft and sucked in a breath. "Need some help Little Bird?"

"Fuck you," she hissed without so much as darting her gaze my way.

Marnie didn't want to look at me. It would shatter her illusions f she saw me standing here, stroking my length. Was she afraid of what was coming or that she'd like it? It was time to find out.

My knee pressed down on the bed, and she dropped face-first into the mattress. I almost laughed when her legs clamped shut and her ankles crossed. Only a virgin would think something like that would work.

"You'd have been better off flipping over." I straddled her legs and slapped her ass. "There's a reason most animals take it from behind. No matter how tightly you close your legs...." I swept my dick down between her shut thighs. "Can't hide your pussy."

The muscles in her back tensed as I brought my palm down on the other side of her ass. I had to hand it to her. Most people would've flinched. That hit was hard enough to send a resounding smack through the room.

"I'm not gonna lie, Marnie…." I pressed my cock against her opening. "This next part's going to hurt." And pushed in.

Fuck me. Her pussy fought against my grith and tried to force me back out. But I kept going, pushing past her tight muscles until I bumped up against resistance. It felt like it took forever to work the head inside her. I could already feel the need for release tingling up my spine.

My eyes were stuck on the delicate pink flesh squeezing my cock. It was just the tip, and she was stretched wide. All I wanted to do was slam in balls deep.

It took everything I had not to give in. Strain vibrated through my body while sweat dripped down my brow. Marnie was stiff as a board and needed to relax. If she didn't, then I would tear her in half.

"Shhh," I soothed while dragging my hand down her back. "You need to relax, Little Bird."

I couldn't stop as the head of my cock slid in and out of her. A primal need raged through my veins every time I bumped against that virginal barrier. I was barely hanging on. Then Marnie opened her big fucking mouth.

"I want you to remember this moment," her glaring aqua eyes rolled her her shoulders. "Because my smile will be the last thing you ever see."

Fuck control.

My resolve shattered with a hard thrust that had Marnie gritting her teeth to hold back a scream. I speared my fingers in her hair, yanked her head back, and snapped my hips forward. As hard as she fought to hold back her pain, a single tear still dripped from the corner of her eye.

"I want *you* to remember *this* moment." I pulled her back, stretched her arms to the limit, and licked the tear off her cheek before whispering in her ear, "This is what it feels like to lose."

There was no holding back after that.

I smashed her face into the mattress and fucked her with no remorse. I used her like my personal fucktoy, and didn't give a shit about her cries to stop. If anything, they spurred me on. Every time she spewed a hateful remark my way, her hot little cunt fluttered and clenched. But the best part came with a soft, almost inaudible sound.

A moan.

The sexiest moan I'd ever heard broke through Marnie's lips, and I damn near came. The sweet sound of victory was followed by a wiggle of her hips. Marnie could hate me all she wanted, but her body begged for more. And I was more than happy to give it to her.

I thrust deep and groaned at the way she wrapped around my length like a glove.

"You like it rough, Little Bird." I grabbed her neck and pulled her back against me.

Her eyes locked onto mine as she snarled, "I hate it."

I could've given her another warning about lying, but why waste my time? When I could prove her wrong and shatter that ego.

One shift of my hips and I was slamming against a spot that made Marnie's eyes roll in the back of her head. She couldn't stop the scream that came two pumps later when her cunt convulsed, and her body seized.

"Feel that," I hissed in her ear. "That's you coming on my cock."

Even through her orgasm, she managed to get out a garbled, "Fuck you."

"No, no, no, Little Bird, it's me who's fucking you." I tsked and drove into her fluttering walls. "And this is just the beginning. I'm going to fuck you in ways you didn't know were possible and when you think you can't take anymore." I grunted as my balls pulled up and held back my orgasm long enough to growl, "I'll show you just how sick and depraved I am."

The roar from my chest rippled through my veins as I sunk my teeth into her shoulder and shot my seed inside her. I came so hard that it felt like my heart stopped.

Lindsay Manheim didn't have shit on Marnie Dupire.

Chapter 11
Marnie

$\mathcal{I}$ don't know how long I was left alone in the dark.

Preston put me back in the cage when he was done with me. Not that I was complaining. I'd take this stupid purple cushion over the other option. Which involved Preston lying on top of me while kissing the back of my neck. It was bad enough that my body responded to him, but I'd be damned if I was going to cuddle.

An unwanted orgasm or two I could forgive. It was a natural reaction to my violation, like pain or hunger. I didn't blame myself for deriving pleasure from it. The mind did all kinds of things to survive. After all, did people blame the road for their skinned knee or hate themselves because it hurt?

Of course not. Pain was your body's way of telling you that you were injured. What happened with Preston was no different than that. A coping mechanism and nothing else.

So why couldn't I stop thinking about it?

It wasn't like I wanted it to happen again. The second I caught my breath, I threatened to cut his balls off and shove them down his throat—hence my current position in the birdcage. And I stood by that threat. But I couldn't stop my mind from returning to him as if Preston Whitley was some inescapable force. I could feel his hands on my skin and smell him everywhere I turned. This room was permeated with him.

"Desire is the fruit of Satan."

And there was that.

My father had been spouting off random bible quotes for I don't know how long. I even argued with him a few times, despite knowing that my father wasn't actually here. Perhaps I was going insane? It wasn't that bad. At least I had my glasses again. That was a plus.

I also had a blanket, an apparent reward for my ability to please a narcissistic sociopath. There was a skill I should've put on my college applications.

Not only have I dedicated many hours to the school newspaper and many other academic programs, but I can put a satisfied smile on a cold-hearted murderer.

If that wasn't Ivy League material, I don't know what was.

Instead of Harvard, I got a thin, itchy blanket. On the upside, it did give me something to cover up with. Considering I was just dumped in here without even being cleaned up, I'd take whatever I could. No one could accuse Preston Whitley of being a gentleman.

As soon as I figured out a game plan, they could call him a murder victim, though. And I meant murder—none of that homicide bullshit.

There was a profound difference between those two words. One was the ending of another's life. Whether purposeful or accidental didn't matter, the result was the same. The other was when someone not only took joy from another's demise but wanted to watch the light fade from their eyes. And trust me. I would watch that man's life drain away.

Preston might be death incarnate. Hell, he could be the devil himself. It didn't matter. One way or another, I would destroy him.

I shifted to the side, then flopped to the left, searching for a more comfortable position.

Nothing seemed to work. Everywhere I moved, that damn ache in my core followed. Was it supposed to hurt this much? It didn't seem right to me. Losing your virginity wasn't an easy experience, but that was hours ago. I don't know exactly how many hours. I did sleep, though. Surely the pain should've eased up by now? So why did it feel like he was still inside me?

I pounded a fist off the pillow under me and muttered, "Stupid lumpy cushion."

All I wanted to do was get comfortable. I couldn't think like this. It was too quiet in here. My breathing echoed through my ears, and every little move I made was amplified.

'All you have to do is ask for salvation.'

Ugh, why couldn't he shut up? I didn't ask for his company. I was perfectly happy being forgotten in this dark place.

'You must invite the Lord's light in.'

I rolled my eyes.

My father had some holy message for every situation. If I didn't like the food I was given, then I was ungrateful and full of pride. Not wanting to go to church meant the devil was whispering in my ear. Questioning his rules...well, that warranted a full-on purge. Hence the scars on my back.

Out in the real world, Trina was the one that ran around doing things she shouldn't. At home, I was the sinful child. All because I dared to question his religious morals. When I pointed out the flaws in the story of Noah's Ark, I was made to kneel on rice until the 'Good Lord' decided to forgive me. And by 'Good Lord,' I meant my father.

Honor thy mother and father. What a load of crap. I hated him, and I hated my mother for letting it happen. But mostly, I hated this goddamn room.

My foot shot out, kicking one of the bars. "Let me out!"

'Refrain from anger and forsake wrath.'

"Oh, you would like that wouldn't you?" My father needed a dose of wrath with a splash of vengeance. I'd even sprinkle on a side of, 'you reap what you sow' just for him.

'If you open the door, the devil will walk in.'

What kind of bullshit was that? I didn't ask Preston to take me.

There were no doors open. All I did was confront some assholes because I was worried about my friend. Riley was missing, and they were conveniently in Chase's tattoo parlor. Call me crazy, but I didn't believe in coincidences.

'The road to hell is paved with good intentions.'

That one made me snort, though I couldn't really argue it. Look where I was.

If hell did exist, it was probably a lot like this room. Dark, cold, and with no one to talk to but the voice in your head. It was suffocating. I couldn't see the walls through the darkness, but I could feel them moving in. Every inhale brought them a little closer. The scent of dust and sweat was so thick I could taste it.

"Is it too much to ask for some water!"

The unending void of blackness didn't answer. Not that I expected it too. There was no one here.

'Blessed are those who hunger and thirst for righteousness.'

Except for that goddamn voice.

It figures that the person I waited years to escape would be the one to follow me into a pit of misery. The only thing missing was the overwhelming smell of my father's cologne. That spicy stench followed me around like a constant reminder of how I sinned or failed to prevent Trina from sinning…

The drops falling around me thundered through my ears. I could hear each distinct sound the rain made. The way it tinkled off the house behind me, the plops into the grass under my knees, and the tiny splashes in the puddles.

I made myself hear it all. It was the only way I could stop my soaked body from shivering.

"I hope you've had time to think about your actions."

Every fiber of my being wanted to glare at my father as he circled around me. It wasn't my actions that dragged me out here in the middle of the night to kneel in the rain.

The birth control was in Trina's purse, but that didn't matter to him.

Trina already tried arguing and was now locked in her room where she couldn't interfere with his correction. Not that I wanted her to.

I'd kneel for a thousand days in the rain before I allowed my sister to endure one second of our father's torment.

A pair of shiny black shoes stopped in front of me. I hated those shoes and the pristine image they represented.

"Because of you, your sister steered off the righteous path."

I balled my hands, digging my fingers into the wet earth. What did he know about righteousness? The grand Pastor Dupire was nothing but an illusion. His flock had no idea who their beloved leader really was.

"I will not have you taint this family."

Pfft, taint.

"You can hide behind that mask of purity all you want." I lifted my chin and rolled my eyes up to my father's cold stare. "I see your real face."

"You will not speak to me that way. You will respect me." He ran his fingers through my wet hair. "Honor thy mother and thy father."

There were so many things I could've said in response to that, but I chose to throw his holy words back at him.

"The devil wears many masks. Your smile is just one of them."

Next thing I knew, I was lying on the ground with a sharp burn radiating across my cheek. It happened so fast that I didn't even hear the slap. Either that or I was too numb to register it. My body gave into the cold hours ago.

My clothes were so wet that they'd become a part of me, a second skin molded to my frame. I couldn't help but think of Shelby at that moment and the sweet smile she wore when she gave me this sweater. She thought I would look pretty in purple, and now I was lying in the dirt with her birthday present weighing down my shoulders.

"Get up," my father demanded.

I knew what was coming next. I could hear the fire crackling in the bin to my left.

When I didn't move, his shoe connected with my hip, jarring me while I lay in the dirt. "I said get up."

I did as I was told and pressed my palms into the ground to push myself up.

"Kneel before the Lord, Marnie, and pray for salvation."

My jaw was already clenched when he grabbed my wrist. Salvation never came to this place.

A flash of lightning lit up my mother's face as she passed the hot iron to my father. A crack of thunder followed from above as if the sky itself agreed with me.

I couldn't stop the words from coming out. "Mother is God in the eyes of a child."

She didn't say anything. I didn't expect her to. My mother did what she always did and stepped silently into the background.

My father, on the other hand, had a lot to say.

"The devil has his grip on you, child, and it's my duty as your father to cleanse you."

I looked over at the bright red cross on the end of the poker.

"Purge me all you want, Father." My eyes rolled up to lock on his, "It won't make you clean...."

MY THUMB MOVED over the cross, scorched into my palm. This was the third brand he'd given me, and I promised myself it'd be the last. Guess I didn't have to worry about that now. Unless I killed Preston, I was never leaving this room.

Sighing, I pushed myself up and flopped my head back against the bars of my prison. The loud twang that rang through the air snapped realization into my mind. There was a reason for leaving me in the dark. Getting mad at inanimate objects, talking to myself, and even the voice in my head were all symptoms of sensory deprivation. This was part of Preston's plan, and I fell for it.

Son of a bitch.

Touché, Mr. Whitley.

It was an effective tactic and one that I should've seen coming. Naturally, Preston would do things to mess with my head. It was the only way he could beat me. That much I knew. What his end goal was, I wasn't too sure. Actually, I had no idea what he wanted.

I thought I did, but if that assumption was true...Why was I still breathing? He should've killed me after he raped me. So why didn't he? One thing was for sure. I'd have to be more careful in the future. The biggest mistake I could make would be underestimating my opponent.

'The Devil's greatest trick was convincing the world he didn't exist.'

I sighed. "Are you still here."

'Spare the rod, spoil the....'

The voice was cut off by a sudden burst of light.

While I was thankful for the silence, my eyes burned, making me duck under the blanket.

One lamp should not be that bright, especially broken on the floor. All that was left intact was the shade and somehow a still working bulb, which considering the base was in pieces, didn't make sense.

If my retinas weren't being scorched out of my head, I might have inspected it to see how it was on. Thankfully the thin fabric helped filter out some brightness long enough for my eyes to adjust.

When I could finally come out from under my shelter, my eyes weren't drawn to the click of the opening door. They were pulled over to the bed.

I could've sworn the sheet on it was white, not blue. And where did those two pillows come from?

"Good morning Marnie."

The way Preston's deep tone wrapped around those syllables made me hate him a little more. No one's name should sound that enticing, especially when it came from someone like him.

"I trust you got enough sleep?"

I huffed out a snort. There was the understatement of the year. "Not much else to do in here."

"Aww." His bottom lip popped out in a mocking frown. "Are you bored, Little Bird?"

Was a glare a good enough answer because that was all he was going to get?

"I can find something for you to do."

I just bet he could. "I think I'll pass."

"You sure about that?"

I opened my mouth to tell him to fuck off, but that was quickly forgotten when Preston lifted his hand to display a bottle of water.

Suddenly that was all I could see. Nothing in the world seemed more important than that clear fluid. It sloshed and swayed off the sides with every step he took. And the closer he got, the more my throat felt like sandpaper.

"Is that for me?" *Was my voice always that hoarse?*

"Maybe?" Preston stopped a few feet away from the bars and tipped his head. "But this is a tit-for-tat situation."

Of course, it was. "If you think I'm going to dance like some pet monkey, you're sorely mistaken."

I wasn't that desperate. Okay, maybe I was. I couldn't tear my eyes off that bottle, but I wasn't going to let him know that.

"Dancing wasn't what I had in mind, Little Bird. But I would like to see you crawl."

I snorted. "That's not going to happen."

I'd die of thirst first.

"All right." Preston tipped his head to the side. "Maybe two more days will make you reevaluate that statement."

It hadn't been that long. Had it? I was talking to myself, so it was possible. Damnit, I wish there was a clock in here.

"You're bluffing."

"I'm a lot of things, Little Bird. A liar isn't one of them."

As much as I wanted to argue, I couldn't think of a single point in time when he had lied. I couldn't think at all. My entire focus was centered on the possibility of a drink. I didn't think I could survive another two hours, let alone two days.

"Will you let me out of this room?" If I had any hope of escaping, it wouldn't be found within these four walls.

"That privilege will have to be earned."

Lovely. I could just imagine what that would entail.

"But...if you're good, I will let you have a shower."

How honorable of him.

"I'll even make you something to eat while you clean up."

That did sound intriguing. My stomach was already rumbling at the thought of food, but was it worth my dignity?

"So, what's it going to be, Little Bird?"

One look at the smirk on his face told me the answer to that question.

"Go to hell."

Preston let out an exasperated breath. "Have it your way."

I thought he'd walk away and leave me alone, but I forgot one crucial factor. Preston liked to torment people.

My heart dropped when he twisted the cap off and dumped the contents. I smelled the water as it hit the floor. Then to add insult to injury, he placed the empty bottle in the puddle then walked out. Leaving me alone to stare in desperation.

Chapter 12
Preston

My Little Bird was a stubborn one. She was so intent on fighting me that she wouldn't even contemplate demeaning herself long enough for a drink. Her determination was admirable, but it wouldn't last. Sooner or later, she'd give in. Her body would demand it. Basic human needs were a hard thing to resist.

There was always the possibility that her stubborn streak would hold up, forcing me to hook her up to an IV and start our ritual all over again, but I doubted it. The desperation on her face when I dumped out that water was evident. If I were a betting man, she'd break when I returned.

I glanced over my shoulder at the closed door. "See you soon, Little Bird."

My feet moved down the stairs, but my mind stayed in that room. I could see Marnie sitting in the same spot, with that thin wool blanket draped over her shoulders, while she stared longingly at the puddle on the ground. A large part of me was tempted to go back in there and watch her. Video only did so much.

I couldn't smell her through the screen or listen to her tiny whining mewls. But it wouldn't be as much fun now as when the lights were off. Night vision goggles were a fantastic invention. I wonder if she heard me jerking off? A couple of times, she looked my way but didn't say anything. Marnie just crawled around, trying to feel through the dark while I stroked my cock.

I'd done it so much that my dick begged to be inside her again.

Unfortunately, I'd neglected some of my duties. While I didn't enjoy falling behind, it did give me something to do to kill some time.

It turned out to be around three hours. I cut Nash up a bit and fed him, stopped in to see my other guest, and did some general maintenance. There was a leak in one of the pipes that required patching, and a shelf in one of the closets needed to be replaced. After that, I cleaned Timothy's cage while he attacked my shoe, then had a shower. There was only one thing left to do.

I took a pull of my cigarette and sighed at the door.

It was awfully tempting to stay outside and watch the trees sway in the breeze. Not that I found nature relaxing, but I could learn to like it if it meant I didn't have to listen to him talk. And that little fucker liked to talk. How's so and so? What's happening here? Who's doing this? Can I make a phone call? It was insufferable.

May as well get it over with.

Sucking one last pull of smoke down my throat, I stubbed my cigarette out and walked inside.

Hopefully, the food I made would keep his yap shut long enough for me to get away.

I grabbed one of the trays off the island counter and headed for the west wing.

When I first unlocked the door, it was quiet, and I thought my wish for a quick in and out had been granted. Then I heard the toilet flush. There wasn't enough time to put the tray on the table and leave. Then again, the bed was an option, and it was much closer to the door.

"Preston?"

Damnit.

"You're late."

Not as late as I'd like to be.

With a sigh, I accepted my fate and walked across the room. "I was preoccupied."

Tico's brow arched. "You never get preoccupied."

"These were special circumstances."

I could've slapped myself when a smile spread across his face.

"Like girl special circumstances?"

"Do you really want to know about my sex life?"

As I expected he would, Tico thought about it for a second, then shook his head.

"No, I don't think so."

I passed him the tray, said, "Good call," and turned to leave.

"But out of curiosity...."

Goddamnit.

When I paid off the doctor to pronounce him dead, it wasn't because I wanted someone to hang out with and shoot the breeze. The kid's family had ties to the cartel, and I was having some trouble finding a mark. I even promised him protection in return for helping me. Had I known that promise would've resulted in this—I would've shot him.

I could still shoot him...

"Do you even enjoy sex?"

What kind of stupid question was that? "Of course I enjoy it."

What wasn't there to enjoy about fucking. It felt good, and I got to make people cry. I suppose there was that one girl. She kept touching me and kissing my neck like we were in love or some shit. Things picked up after I smacked her around. Live and learn. Everyone made mistakes in the beginning. Like the chick I knocked up. My father took care of that problem.

"Of course you like it, but do you *enjoy* it?"

My brows pulled together as Tico approached the table and sat down. "I don't understand the difference?"

Was he drunk again? I was damn sure I removed all the alcohol after the last time. He spent four hours throwing up and crying over his friends. I should've shot him then.

"How do I explain this?" Tico hummed and lifted the silver lid off his food.

I didn't know what he had to think about. There was nothing to explain because there was no difference. Though I was curious about the point he was trying to get across. Or the point he thought he had. I'd learned a few things about Tico. He didn't have the best education, but he was intelligent, and he didn't like pussy.

I found that out when I brought a girl home for him. The kid was pretty hard up, but he didn't want her. I still got my money's worth, even used some of her bones as fertilizer in the garden. Was that what all this was about?

"Do you want me to get you some dick?"

"What?" Tico's brows knit. "No."

He may have said no, but he was thinking about it. His eyes looked up while his fork absently shifted through his eggs until he eventually looked back at me.

"Why? Do you know someone?"

Parker would be the ideal candidate, but he would want to bring his wife, which would cause a whole bunch of shit. People would find out Tico was alive, and the Cartel would come looking for him, putting Micha and Logan's girls in danger. They'd start bitching at me, and it was a cluster fuck I didn't want to deal with.

There was another option.

"I could call my dad."

Tico's eyes widened. "Your dad?"

"Yes."

"Wasn't he married to your mom?"

Don't remind me. "So?"

"So he fucked men while he was married?"

"Yeah." I shrugged. "He fucked women too."

Sometimes at the same time. Try and explain that to an eight-year-old that walked in on their parent. Parker left my room more confused than he was when he got there. His first mistake was coming to a twelve-year-old. All my sexual knowledge at that point had come from the shit I'd seen. And Ryker.

"Did he fuck your mom?"

Why did he ask something if he already knew the answer? "They had three kids."

It nauseated me that I came from that cunt's vagina.

A glimmer flashed across Tico's face as he tipped his head and rolled his eyes over me.

"Do you fuck guys?"

My brow arched. "Do you really want to go down that road?"

His mouth opened, then quickly shut.

That was what I thought.

"Do you want me to call my dad or not?"

"You're serious?"

Of course, I was serious.

"You do realize how fucked up this is?" He shoveled a forkful of eggs in his mouth and shook his head. "You're basically pimping out your old man."

"Trust me. He'd be into it."

A small guy with a head of thick dark hair that he could bend to his will. My dad would be all over that shit. Tico even had some bulk now. Sometimes I'd make him work out with me just to get him to shut up.

"Your dad's hot and all but…I don't know."

Fuck it. I was calling him. Maybe my dad could fuck some sense into him.

"Enjoy your food." I waved at him and headed for the door. "I'll see you tonight."

I was just about out when Tico called out, "wait…you didn't answer my question."

My hand tightened on the doorknob.

Marnie was waiting upstairs, and this little prick was getting in the way.

"Do you enjoy sex?"

Yes, I enjoyed it and would very much like to get back to it.

"And by enjoy, I mean have you ever made love to someone?" He clarified.

"I'd have to love someone for that to happen." And even if I did, I doubt I'd make love to them.

There was no blood, pain, or screaming. Why the fuck would I waste my time on that shit?

"But what if you did? Would you try it if they asked you to?"

No.

"Why are you asking this shit?"

Why did he care? What I did in my private life made no difference to him. I could fuck a hundred bitches in this room while he watched, then slit their throats, and it wouldn't change anything about the course of his life.

Tico sighed, "I'm just trying to understand you."

That statement made me turn around and look at him. "Why do you want to understand me?"

"I don't know…It's just…You…." He dropped his fork on the tray and swiveled in the chair. "When I first woke up and saw you, I thought I was dead. Whatever was about to happen would end with a bullet in my head."

That was a fair assumption.

"But you cared for me and nursed me back to health."

"I hired someone." I had to when I went to Canada. Their bones were also fertilizing my garden—I always tied up loose ends—but I still hired help.

"Yeah." Tico nodded. "But the rest of the time, it was just you and me."

"I don't like strangers in my house." I didn't even like people I knew in my house.

"Okay, but I'd like to think we've become friends."

My face dropped. Friends? Really?

"Some part of you must think so too." Tico looked over at me and waved his finger through the air. "I am still alive."

"I could still kill you."

It wouldn't take much. There was a gun in the other room, and I had a knife in my pocket. The garden could always use more fertilizer.

"Or, you could admit that a part of you likes me, just a little bit." To emphasize this, Tico held up his hand and moved his fingers together.

"Let's get one thing straight. You were a means to an end—a way to reach my target. I don't like you. In fact, I find you whiny and annoying. The only reason you're still breathing is that I promised to protect you, and I always keep my word."

Tico sat back and crossed his arms. "Sounds like an excuse to me."

"Do you want to know what I've been doing the past few days?" It was time to knock that delusion out of his head. I wasn't his friend. I wasn't even his ally. He was a nuisance.

"I have a girl locked up in my tower. A pretty little thing that I raped the first day." I stepped back into the room and slowly stalked toward the table. "The way her cunt squeezed my cock…." I sucked in a long breath at the memory of Marnie's sweet pussy. "Now that was fucking divine."

Tico's eyes got wider with every step I took.

"Since then, I've left her alone and naked in the dark with nothing but a thin blanket to cover up with. Now and then, I sneak in there and watch her shiver while I jerk off and think about what I will do to her next. Maybe I'll cut her. Maybe I'll choke her. Or maybe I'll take her ass and whip her back until it bleeds."

I slammed my hands down on the table, making Tico jar back. "The options are endless."

His face paled as he stared at me with his mouth open.

I tipped my head and cocked a brow. "Still want to know if I *enjoy* sex?"

He didn't utter a word as he sat there and stared at me with this look on his face like he was trying to figure out what to say. But there wasn't anything to say. People like him could never understand people like me. The sooner he figured that out, the better off he'd be.

When Tico finally spoke, it wasn't what I thought it would be.

"So you have another person locked up in the walls?" He braced his arms on the table and leaned in, "Are you that lonely?"

I shook my head and pushed off the table, walking back to the door.

"It's okay to need a friend, Preston."

He just didn't get it, which was exactly why the world would eat him alive.

I stopped with my hand on the door and looked over my shoulder. "By the way, the girl I was talking about is Marnie Dupire."

Chapter 13

Marnie

Desire, need, anger, and happiness had various effects on the body. The threat of incoming danger was no different, though the signs were harder to recognize. Most people didn't pick up on a quick stomach flip or the shiver that shot up their spine. But for those that paid attention, that silent alarm was unmistakable.

A shift in the air or a drop in temperature as the hairs on the back of the neck rose were all warning signs. My survival growing up depended on listening to my body's signals. Unfortunately, the option to avoid it wasn't always there. In this instance, my captive role prevented that.

I knew something terrible was coming. I could feel it in the heavy footsteps I shouldn't hear. My pulse picked up on the dark cloud floating in, and everything inside me told me to run. But there was nowhere to go—no place to hide in this gilded cage.

The only thing I could do when the door hissed and clicked open was press my back against the bars and try not to panic when a booted foot stepped into the room.

This wasn't the same as when I went home and knew what was coming. The weight of the world followed my captor through the door. Every breath I took pressed down on my lungs like the air had grown heavier. This was the oppressing depth of dread.

One look at Preston and I knew survival was the best outcome I could hope for in this scenario. The usual void in his gray stare was replaced by a flickering black flame of anger. I needed to watch my footing. One wrong move could be the difference between life and death.

I could adjust his mood somehow...maybe. I'd never tried seduction or playing docile. Trina did it all the time. I'd even seen Shelby turn Logan from full-on insanity to sweet as pie.

I forgot one crucial factor when I touched my ear to my shoulder and shot him a smile...I wasn't Shelby or my sister.

Preston stopped and curled his lip. "Don't do that. You look like your fucking sister."

Considering I was the other half of a set of identical twins, that was an odd thing to get mad about. Not that I would point that out. It was safer to stay cautious. Especially when Preston's eyes slowly trickled over my huddled form.

The man watching me wasn't the one I was used to. It wasn't the killer version of him either. This was something else. Something I don't think many people saw. And if they did, they sure as hell didn't live to tell about it.

Preston took one long, purposeful stride, and I swear every shadow in the room flooded into the scowl on his face.

I didn't know what to do.

Did I say something? Did I move? Or should I stay completely still and pray that he didn't notice me despite the fact that he was looking right at me? For the first time, I was genuinely scared for myself. Preston was close to snapping. I could feel the tension tightening his string of control with every step he took.

Then, he stopped, and I was even more unsure what to do. Anxiety bubbled up inside me, which only churned my stomach more.

Preston tipped his head, and I held my breath waiting for him to say something.

His voice never came. All I got was a pair of rolled-back shoulders and the shadows darkening his expression.

This was bad. I didn't need the hairs on the back of my neck to tell me that.

"Did you bring more water?"

I wasn't sure why I said that. I don't know why I spoke at all. Maybe I was delirious from thirst? Or maybe my panicked heart was trying to placate him? Either way, it was a bad choice on my part. That much I knew the second his eyes fell on the empty bottle still sitting upright on the floor.

I never wanted to disappear more than I did when the muscle in his jaw twitched.

"*Now*, you want a drink?"

The venom in his tone burned down my throat as I forced down a heavy swallow.

If there were any kind of benevolent force out there, he would cast me back into darkness and cause the bulb on the floor to burst.

That didn't happen. Despite what my father and all the other preachers out there said, no one was watching over us. There was nothing in this room except for Preston and me. A monster...

Preston's cold eyes snapped up to mine.

And his prey.

"You want some water?"

I really, really didn't. Judging by the look on his face, I didn't want anything. I'd stay right here and happily starve to death. The cage wasn't so bad. I had a nice soft cushion, blanket, and a bucket in the corner. I didn't need anything else. Freedom and food were overrated anyway.

"Speak up, Little Bird. I'm not a mind reader."

"Go fuck yourself."

Me and my big mouth. Riley was the one who suffered from word vomit, not me. Then again, I wouldn't complain if I suddenly found a fork in here. Maybe she was on to something with that.

"You want to play Little Bird?" Preston tipped his head in a slight nod and pursed his lips. "All right."

And that was how she died, your honor.

Two seconds later, he reached out for the door.

That was when panic really took hold. I jumped back, completely forgetting about the bars behind me, then tried to wriggle and squirm through them. Ever seen those gifs with animals stretching their paws between bars? Well, that was me.

I reached out, desperately searching for a gap large enough to squeeze through. I didn't find one, of course, but that didn't matter. My mind had given up all forms of logic. Escape was all I could think about until Preston grabbed a fistful of my hair and pulled me onto my feet.

Then I did something really stupid.

I spun around and slapped him across the face.

The pain tearing across my scalp was nothing compared to the look on Preston's face.

Until that point, he'd managed to maintain some modicum of control. It wasn't much, but I saw that string tensing up just like I saw when it broke.

Preston's head twisted to the side, and that string snapped. His typically cold eyes filled with lava so hot I could feel the burn when he slowly turned my way.

One swallow.

That was all I got before my neck was grabbed, and my feet were off the ground.

The fact that he could lift me with one hand was terrifying enough. Add in my quickly depleting oxygen supply, and I was in full panic mode.

The only thing that stopped me from flailing around like a mad woman was the ringing in my ears from being slammed violently back into the bars. It took a second for the ache to follow. When it did, it crawled up my spine with hooked claws that dug into my nerves. Not even that could dull the threatening tone of Preston's voice.

"Did you just fucking slap me?"

This was it. I was going to die in this cage, and no one would ever find me.

Mustering all the courage I could, I peeked up through my glasses and croaked out, "I didn't mean to."

"Uh-huh." That was all I got before he snatched the glasses off my face.

"No," I cried out as they fell to the ground.

My entire world shattered when the heel of Preston's boot slammed down on them. As if that wasn't enough, he twisted his leg, grinding his heel against my fragile frames. The crunch that floated up broke my heart.

My shield, the one protection I had, was gone. My vulnerability was laid bare for the entire world to see.

"Ooops," he hissed. "I didn't mean to."

I didn't care about the tears trickling down my face or the constriction in my throat. All I wanted to do was hurt him.

I kicked my feet and swung my arms, striking Preston anywhere I could. He responded to my attack by dropping me on the ground and backhanding me across the face.

That was enough to make me stop.

Blood trickled from my split lip as I rolled my eyes up. "I hate you."

"You think I give a fuck?" Preston bent over, grabbed my chin, and dug his fingers into my cheeks. "I want you to hate me."

This was different than all the other times. Usually, he was calculated, calm, and cold. But now, Preston was pissed, and not because I hit him. Something else irritated him before he came into the room. As intriguing as that was, it was something I could figure out later.

Right now, I had to calm him down. Otherwise, I really would die in this cage.

The only question was, how in the hell did I do that?

I don't know where the words came from or why I even thought of that moment, but when Preston started to lean in, I quickly spouted out, "You said you were going to teach me."

He paused and knitted his brow. "What?"

147

Was this working?

"You said you would teach me everything I needed to know." I pushed myself to sit. "So, teach me."

I assumed he meant sexually, but given the other choice, that was the lesser of two evils.

Preston stared down at me as if searching for something, but his shoulders relaxed slightly, so I decided to keep going.

I got on my knees, sat down on my calves, and peeked up at him through my lashes.

"Is this what you want?"

There was a second where I held my breath and waited for everything to blow up in my face. That moment didn't come.

"Put your hands on your thighs," Preston ordered. "Palms up."

I did what he said.

"Bow your head."

I did that too.

Playing docile kitten was a small price to pay. I would humiliate myself if that was what it took. My problem came when Preston stroked the back of my head. I had to remind myself not to flinch while my scalp tingled and fear pumped through my heart. It was a strange yet somehow enticing contradiction. A soft, tender touch coated in rage. It was also disturbing how much I liked it.

"I know what you're doing."

That wasn't exactly hard to figure out. "Is it working?"

"Yes."

"Do you still want to hurt me?" I shivered at that question.

Then again, with his answer.

"Yes."

"Are you going to?"

Preston continued to pet my head. Forever seemed to pass while I sat there waiting. The feel of his fingers combing through my hair was oddly relaxing, so much so that I'd almost forgotten about my question.

"Yes, Little Bird." I heard him let out a heavy sigh. "I'm going to hurt you."

This time, I lifted my chin to look up at him before saying, "Why?"

"Because your pain feeds the beast inside me."

The beast inside him? Was that why he was so cold all the time? Because he was trying to control something clawing at the back of his mind? Strangely I understood that. Some days it felt like all I did was fight off the thoughts rolling through my head.

"What happens when you can't feed it?" I was genuinely curious.

Preston's gray eyes trickled over my face. "You don't want to find out."

Why did that feel more like advice than a warning?

He dropped his hand and sighed. "Go have a shower while I clean up."

I didn't need to be told twice. I jumped up and scurried out of the cage. It didn't matter that the bathroom had no door or that Preston might stay in here and watch. The distance was more than welcome. Still, I couldn't stop thinking about what he said.

Why would he say it in that tone? Just because I drugged Chase didn't mean anything. He was a bad person who needed to be taught a lesson. I didn't need his advice. I didn't want it.

I looked over at Preston as he picked up the bucket in the corner of the birdcage. "I'm nothing like you."

He didn't even look my way when he answered.

"The only difference between you and me, Marnie, is I accepted who I was a long time ago."

Chapter 14
Marnie

There wasn't much to the bathroom. Actually, it was annoyingly plain for someone of Preston's status. Not that I expected a captive's lavatory to be anything special, but I thought there'd be a little more to it. There was a toilet, a single sink, and a shower. No pictures or cupboards to stash things. Just the bare necessities and nothing more.

I'd settle for a soap dish or toilet paper holder. Something that I could use as a weapon. There wasn't even a door or curtain around the shower. Just crisp with tiles with a drain in the middle of the floor.

Even the lightbulbs were gone, replaced by an LED strip circling the roof. I had to hand it to Preston. He nailed the locked-up-in-prison atmosphere.

There was always the possibility of using shampoo or body wash as a weapon. I wasn't sure how that would work, but there had to be a way.

"I don't hear any water running!"

My eyes peeked over my shoulder to where Preston was pulling the cushion out of my cage. The way he cleaned up like I was some kind of pet was degrading. Was this how animals felt? Did I just compare myself to a pet?

God, how far down the rabbit hole did I fall?

Preston lifted his head and shot me a look.

Yeah, yeah, I'm going.

Huffing out a sigh, I turned around and headed for the shower. Not because he told me to, but because I wanted to. After two days locked up with nothing but a bucket to use, a shower sounded like nirvana. Plus, I could finally wash his smell off me, which was the biggest bonus as far as I was concerned.

The spray was quite relaxing.

The situation was not.

Warm water cascaded down my back, massaging my tired muscles, which was counterproductive to the tension that wound through me whenever I turned around and saw the open doorway. Granted, Preston wasn't currently watching me, but it wouldn't take much. The shower was in clear view of the doorway. Most likely, it was a purposeful placement by him.

I was tempted to snatch the blanket I'd left draped over the sink and cover myself. Instead, I focused on the one thing I could control—getting clean.

'Cleanliness is next to godliness.'

Once that rag started moving over my body, I couldn't stop. My father's voice played in my mind as I ferociously swiped over every inch of my skin.

'Remove evil from your deeds, consecrate yourself, and be holy.'

That was what he said after the church picnic. I tried to tell him about Sheriff Nash but only got as far as 'he was in the bathroom' before being dubbed a sinner because I shouldn't have gone into a man's domain.

I didn't get a chance to tell him about the other stuff or point out that he followed me in. I was on my knees, praying for forgiveness before another word left my mouth.

That was when I decided God wouldn't punish the wicked because he didn't exist. So, I would do God's job for him. I'd redeemed seven men so far and one woman. Lillianna Whitley was next on my list, but fate found her first. Too bad. I had a good plan for that witch.

But now I was faced with her son, a man who kept polluting my thoughts by making me hear my father's lessons.

'Consecrate yourself' gave way to 'do not share the sins of others.'

I tried to quiet the voice and rid myself of Preston's touch, but I could still feel him no matter how hard I scrubbed or how much soap I used. His scent mingled with the vanilla aroma of the body wash. His hands remained on my skin, and every time my hips shifted, a dull ache radiated up my core.

I could hose myself down in bleach and still not be pure. Preston took that from me, and some sick twisted part of me liked it. My body tingled at the thought of him stretching me. No matter what I did, I couldn't be cleansed.

That was the worst part because I wasn't sure I wanted to be purified. Every reaction my body gave to Preston's violation was a silent fuck you to my father and his holy daughter's image. For years, I dreamed about defiling the clean persona of Pastor Dupire. He was the one person I couldn't devise a punishment for because nothing seemed fitting enough. How did I make someone like that see the error of his ways?

"How do I make someone like Preston?"

"Depends." I shrieked at the sound of Preston's voice. "What are you trying to make me do?"

I quickly hugged the front of my body against the tiled wall and grumbled, "Get out."

"You didn't answer my question."

And I wasn't going to. I didn't like having conversations with Preston when I was clothed, let alone naked in the shower.

"Get. Out," I reiterated.

Preston snickered. "What about this situation makes you think you have any control?"

One could hope. Though now that he pointed it out, I could see the idiocy in my demand. I wasn't a guest in this place. I was a prisoner. Preston could and would do whatever he wanted. Who was going to stop him? Me? I'd need more than liquid soap for that. That didn't mean I had to make it easy for him. At the very least, I could cover myself up.

I glanced back at the blanket lying across the sink.

That was my mistake.

As I glanced over my shoulder, Preston pulled his shirt over his head. The strength I'd seen in his arms was nothing compared to the hard ridges on his abdomen. I didn't even know a guy could have an eight-pack. How extreme was his exercise regimen for him to have those two extra muscles? That was a terrifying thought all on its own. When I considered his beauty, it would be easy to dub him the perfect predator.

Everything about the man drew you in: the disheveled appearance of his sandy hair, the heat in his eyes, and the detailed tattoo of a black and red Asian dragon crawling up his torso. Even his scent was enticing. Masculine yet crisp and clean. I think I hated him more now. If that was even possible?

My eyes trickled over the scales of the dragon that seemed to move whenever he shifted. The beast stared back as if daring me to look away. And trust me, I was trying. Every time I moved to tear my gaze away, another muscle would tense under his tanned skin, and I'd be stuck gawking like a hormone-driven teen. Technically eighteen was a teen, but still. I wasn't Trina. Boys didn't rule my life.

But he sure is pretty.

I tipped my head to the side as my gaze trickled down his chest. I'd admit he was nice to look at—okay, maybe a little more than nice, but that didn't erase who he was. Preston Whitley had a lot of innocent blood on his hands, like Lindsay's and countless others. They deserved justice too.

"You're staring at me, Little Bird."

That snapped my attention away from his physique.

I turned my head back to the tiles I was squished up against and grumbled, "I was thinking."

"Oh yeah?" There was a soft rustle, followed by what I was pretty sure were his jeans hitting the floor. "What were you thinking about?"

"I'm plotting your murder," I snarled into the wall.

When two hands flattened against the wall beside my head, I audibly gulped.

"I love it when you talk dirty to me," he purred in my ear.

I shirked away, or at least tried to, but the tiles prevented that. A very distinct part of him was digging into the small of my back—a large and way too hard part.

"I'm curious, Little Bird." Preston leaned in, swallowing my shivering form with his large body. "Are you going to fight me this time?"

Twisting my neck, I snarled, "That's what you want me to do."

I didn't know which was worse, the way his dick jumped or the smirk that curled the corner of his mouth.

"And people say I'm hard to understand."

Oh, I understood him quite well. I spent my life researching men like him. Preston Whitley wasn't the kind of man who would take his time and court a girl. The fight is what got him off. He wanted to overpower them and watch defeat bleed into their eyes. Well, I wasn't going to feed into his fantasy. If he wanted someone to struggle with, he'd have to find someone else.

As hard as it was, I forced myself to remain still and not react.

That was easier said than done. I managed to maintain my composure for a while. Preston moved around, pawing at my flesh, and I stayed right where I was.

When his palms smoothed down my sides, I sucked in and zeroed in on the sound of my breathing. When his tongue slid up the side of my neck, I balled my fists and dropped my forehead on the wall. And when his fingers dug into my ass and scratched a hot path across my skin, I gritted my teeth.

It was the groan that rumbled from his chest that broke me. That deep sound echoed through the room, and I turned to run. Not from him but from the way his groan vibrated through my core. Unfortunately, I neglected to remember that Preston was physically superior in every way, including speed.

My foot was barely off the ground before he grabbed my neck and slammed me back.

"Where the fuck do you think you're going?"

Not only had I epically failed in my attempt, but I was now in a more precarious situation. Face to face with the beast himself.

Don't fight him, Marnie. That was what he wanted.

Taking a deep calming breath, I looked into his eyes and smiled. "Why would I be going anywhere?"

"Ah, we're playing good girl now, are we?"

It took everything I had to keep my eyes from narrowing at his condescending statement.

"All right, good girl." His brow arched. "Why don't you reach down and stroke my cock?"

I could feel the challenge coming off him. Every fiber of my being wanted to punch him in the nuts, but that would give him exactly what he wanted. I wasn't about to lose this game. So I did the only thing I could and wrapped my hand around him.

That was my first mistake.

The second my fingers made contact, my entire body lit up. I'd seen porn and pictures before, but a man's penis didn't feel at all like I thought it would. It was hard and hot, yet soft and silky at the same time.

My second mistake came when I felt something metallic and looked down. A small ring was pierced through the head of Preston's cock while six bars decorated the top of his shaft. But it was the size that made fear twitch through my heart. He was so thick that my hand couldn't wrap around the girth. I doubted that his could.

I'd never understand how he fit it inside me in the first place, but it explained why I was so sore afterward. One thing was for sure, that thing was not going anywhere near me. I was officially tapping out.

I dropped my hand and jerked away, which would've worked a lot better without the grip on my neck. I moved right and was pulled left.

My entire plan went out the window after that. I screamed and swung my arms.

"That's it, Little Bird," Preston growled. "Fucking fight me."

And I did. I fought hard with everything I had. Got him good a couple of times too. My nails clawed into his shoulder, and Preston's grip loosened for a fraction of a second. Not enough for me to slip away, but enough that it gave me hope.

Then my feet left the ground, and suddenly all I cared about was my ability to breathe. My lungs burned while I kicked my dangling feet and slapped at the strong arm holding me.

"Here's the thing Little Bird." Preston's knee wedged between my thighs, taking off some of the weight choking me. "I know more about you than you do."

I highly doubted that. Not that I could argue my point. I was having trouble sucking little bits of oxygen back into my body, let alone trying to speak.

Then something weird happened.

Preston lifted his knee into my core, and my pussy clenched.

"Feel that?" He breathed while sliding his hand over his knee to cup my mound. "That's your pussy asking for what it needs."

I was about to open my mouth and spew curses his way when a finger pressed inside me. All words were lost as my inner walls clamped down. My skin tingled more and more with each stroke Preston gave. The truly humiliating part was being unable to hide my reaction from him. I could hear the way my juices were coating him. There was no way he couldn't feel it.

Proof of which came in the long feral growl that erupted from Preston's lips. "You're such a fucking hypocrite. I love it."

I tried to shut the feelings he was igniting out, but the world was against me. The dull ache from him adding a second finger only heightened the hot desire burning through me, especially when he hooked his fingers and hit a spot that had me biting my lip to hold back my moan.

"Poor little Marnie Dupire." Even Preston's mocking tone pushed me closer to the edge of bliss. "That's what you want everyone to think. That you're a sweet innocent church girl?"

God, I wanted to hurt him. Reach over and claw his eyes out. But I also didn't want him to stop. His hand felt so good I couldn't stop my hips from gyrating.

"You pray to the same god I do, Little Bird." He picked up the pace, fucking me hard with his fingers. "Look at you getting off on fear and pain."

A twang of guilt pinged through my chest. I wasn't getting off on it. He just knew what he was doing. At least, that was what I told myself when a white-hot wave of pleasure started to crest up my spine.

"My masochistic little bitch," Preston purred as my back bowed and vision blurred.

There was a sensation of a gush of liquid as my entire body jerked into orgasmic spasms. I barely heard Preston groan, "Fuuuuck," before a hard slap to my pussy threw me right back into the cloud, hazing my mind.

I was snapped back into reality when something much larger than a finger pressed against my opening. Somehow my leg had wrapped around Preston's hips, and he was lining himself up.

Oh, hell no.

My legs dropped faster than he could blink.

Preston didn't like that. He shot me an unimpressed look, sighed, tightened his grip on my neck, and lifted my feet back off the ground.

I gasped and clawed at his hand, but he just tsked like I was a petulant child in need of scolding.

"You have two choices here, Little Bird. Put your legs back where I fucking had them. Or choke to death." He leaned in, bringing his face a breath away from mine, and hissed, "I'll fuck you either way."

What other choice did I have? There was no such thing as an idle threat when it came to Preston. So, I did the only thing I could and swallowed my pride before hooking my legs back around his waist.

I don't know why I stared into his eyes when he lined himself up. Maybe I was looking for something to hold onto? A small piece of humanity he kept hidden. Some sign of compassion or goodness that would help me sleep at night. Because as much as I tried to deny it, I liked the way he felt.

Preston thrust inside me, and I moaned at the stretch in my core. That feeling got more intense the more of his length he pushed in. I was almost disappointed that he couldn't slam all the way in. Apparently, so was he.

Strain pulled on his brows as he muttered, "I hate this shit. You're too goddamn tight."

Trust me. I hated it too. I would rather get it over with, so I could hate myself for enjoying it. Every slow aching inch was a reminder of how much I enjoyed it.

"I'm going to have to work you in."

By the time his pelvis smacked against me, I was teetering on the edge. Lost to everything but the sensations pouring through me. Desperation had my hands clinging to Preston's shoulders while mewling whines slipped through my lips. Honestly, I was amazed that I stopped my hips from moving. Not that it made any difference.

He still noticed everything.

"That's it, Marnie." His first thrust rippled through my body. "Whine for my cock."

The second made my toes curl, and the third completely cut off my air.

Wait...that wasn't his thrust.

Preston dug his fingers and thumb into the sides of my neck. I couldn't breathe at all. Panicked, I choked and pried at his hand. And what did Preston do? He fucked me harder. He plowed into my pussy while I fought for my basic human need. When blackness began to seep into my vision, he'd let me cough and catch my breath. Then it started all over again.

At some point, the two needs combined. The burning in my lungs became euphoric while desperate need clamped my walls down around his length. But it was the look on Preston's face that put the final nail in my coffin.

When he sucked my bottom lip between his teeth, desire, unlike any I'd seen before, sparkled in his eyes. It was as if he stole the very air around us. Passion, need, and desperation had mingled into a supercharged electric pulse. And when that pulse shot into me, it tore my atoms apart. I came so hard that I wouldn't have been able to scream if I could. I heard it. Every syllable of my pleasure rang through my ears like a siren.

The last thing I heard before oblivion finally took me was a masculine grunt followed by, "Never forget who your real god is."

Chapter 15
Preston

When I was a kid, people said one of two things about me. 'There's something wrong with him,' and 'He shouldn't be around other kids.' Playdates weren't a thing because other parents feared me. Everyone was afraid of me. My own mother thought I should be locked up.

The only person I had in my corner was my father. Whenever someone suggested I take an extended vacation in a padded cell, he'd respond, 'Every kid has their issues.' If I were honest, then I'd have to agree with everyone else. I was out of control.

If I wasn't hurting someone, then I was dreaming about it. The only time I felt anything was when someone else was screaming. Perhaps that was why Logan and I got along. We both had the same beast. His was created by a sick fuck for a father, whereas mine was always there. I didn't have darkness tainting my actions. I was the darkness.

Death was in my soul from the moment I was born. My mother almost died. It took three doctors and hours of surgery to save her.

Ava came nice and quick, but I tore her apart. Blood and misery were what I was born into, and there was no doubt in my mind that was how I'd go out.

I was the child every parent prayed they wouldn't get. There wasn't a single time I could think of where I smiled because something was *nice*.

Yet here I was, running my fingers through my sleeping Bird's hair, with a smile on my lips. I couldn't stop watching her chest rise and fall.

She looked so peaceful, with her eyes fluttering under closed lids. I could hear every breath that slipped past her parted pink lips. They wisped through the air like delicate, soft feathers that had my cock hardening. But it was the purple bruises on her neck that drove my hand to start stroking my length.

Marnie Dupire was not what I expected.

A couple of hours ago, I was ready to kill her. I'd already snapped her neck in my mind. And what did she do when I reached out? Marnie rolled those big aqua eyes up and said, 'You said you'd teach me.'

"Fuck." I grunted and twisted my wrist, smearing precum over my tip.

The hot wetness wasn't near as enticing as the sweet nectar between her legs. Just the thought of that flavor was enough to make my mouth water.

My eyes locked on her perfect pink lips.

Why should I be the only one who gets to have a taste?

Seeing my come glistening on her mouth made me damn near bust a nut. Then she grumbled and licked her lips. My hand was between her legs before the next breath could leave her body.

She was already slick and ready for me.

"You might not like me, Little Bird." I dipped my finger in her entrance and licked a path up the side of her neck. "But your pussy fucking loves me."

And it loved the rough treatment I gave her. The harder I finger-fucked her, the wetter she got. She needed to be dominated and used hard. Her body was practically begging for it. Proof of this came when a whispered moan left her unconscious form.

"That's it Little Bird." I shuffled in and pressed my dick against her ass. I wanted to feel the little movements her hips were making.

Right now, her body was in control. Marnie was a perfectly docile toy. I could do whatever I wanted, and she'd love every second of it. It was her mind that got in the way. Morals were a son of a bitch, but eventually, I'd knock those down too. I'd teach her to embrace who she really was.

'You said you'd teach me.'

I knew those words didn't mean anything. Marnie didn't want me to teach her shit—her arrogance wouldn't allow that—but she still said it. And that was the part I couldn't get out of my head. Everyone else would've written me off and accepted their fate. I was the monster who brought the end. But not her.

My Little Bird used her intelligence and cunning to do what no one else could. She pushed past the beast and reached the man.

Marnie Dupire, with her sweet voice and big eyes, pulled me back from the edge of darkness. She was my anchor, which was essential for someone like me to have. It was easy to get lost in blood lust.

Or her sweet little cunt.

Her entire body shuddered when I hooked my fingers to stroke her g-spot. She was so fucking responsive. I loved it.

"I'm going to fucking eat you up."

That was how I'd keep myself grounded.

My grandfather gave me that piece of advice. Lou sent me to stay with him when I was thirteen. Let's just say the Whitleys weren't exactly normal. Serial killers tended to run in the family. Lou thought I could learn some control from my grandfather. If Micha knew that his old man was in contact with the older generation of kings this entire time, he'd lose his shit.

I couldn't complain. There were some things my grandfather deserved credit for. My control and understanding of who I was, were a few. The whole anchor thing, though, I always thought that was bullshit.

Until I watched Shelby redirect Logan's attention mid-fight. I may not see the world the same as other people, but Logan Hudson redefined the term 'unstable.' And Shelby Grace pulled him out of bloodlust with a few simple words.

Now, I couldn't help but wonder if I could have the same thing.

"You want to be my outlet, Little Bird?"

Could Marnie Dupire take all my sick desires and ask for more? Could she be the mother of my children and slut in the bedroom?

My dick liked that idea. Especially the mother part. How sweet would she look, belly swollen, strung up, and freshly whipped with blood dripping down her skin? There was an image I wanted to live out.

I slid my hand out from between her legs and traced my wet fingers over the curve of her hip. "I'm going to pump you so full of my come."

Marnie whimpered and shifted her shoulder.

That was when I got pissed.

The scar slicing across her shoulder blade was right there in plain sight. A thin white line cutting through her perfect complexion that I didn't put there. It was her fucking father's mark. He'd pay for that.

In the meantime, I'd transform those scars and make them mine. If that meant slicing through each and every one, so be it. In fact, I looked forward to erasing every trace of him.

And I'd start with this one.

Flattening my tongue on her skin, I licked along her shoulder blade.

Fuck me, she tasted good.

My cock throbbed with need as I growled and yanked her hip back, tucking her ass back up against me.

Marnie grumbled and wriggled her hips.

Even in her sleep, she fought me. It was so fucking hot I couldn't stop myself from sinking my teeth into the soft flesh on the back of her neck.

That woke her up.

The sexiest whine I'd ever heard left her lips as her eyes shot open, and she tried to pull away. But like the feral animal I was, I hung on. This was my fucking female, and she wasn't going anywhere.

I slipped my hand under her head and grabbed her neck while my other snaked around her waist to the sweet spot between her thighs.

"Preston...Stop." Her arms swung back to swat at my face.

But I just growled and sunk my teeth in deeper.

The scream that erupted from her chest was pure and utter euphoria. Marnie could say she didn't want this as much as she liked. The wetness coating her thighs said otherwise. Another growl rolled through me as I moved in and finger-fucked her hard.

There was nothing more beautiful than the way her pert pink nipples popped out when her back bowed. I loved watching the struggle on her face as she tried to hold back her orgasm, almost as much as the flavor of her blood permeating my mouth.

"Preston...please."

Yeah fucking beg me.

"Let go. It hurts."

Her whimpering cry shot straight into my dick, but it was the tear that slid across her cheek, down her neck, and into my mouth that did it.

I threw her left leg over my hip and thrust violently into her tight little cunt.

Marnie screamed and jerked, scraping her skin against my teeth, which made her scream louder.

I didn't give a shit that her pussy was too small to take my length in one go. I'd never been so fucking hard in my life.

I clamped my bite down and forced my way inside her.

Nirvana didn't have shit on how it felt to be balls deep, finally. Her pussy fluttered around me while I groaned and soaked up every spark that tingled up my spine.

Three pumps...

That was all I got before a loud alarm went off.

I rolled my eyes up to the red light flashing in the corner of the room, then took my mouth off the back of her neck.

"Fuck."

Someone was here.

"What was that?" Marnie asked while looking around.

"Nothing." I slowly slid my length out and then power drove back in. "You just worry about taking my cock."

"Fuck you." She snarled while slapping her hand back to push on my hip.

And there was that fucking mind getting in the way again.

"Get off me!"

Technically I was beside her, but that could be fixed real quick. I rolled us over so Marnie was on her stomach, then lifted her hips off the bed and sunk deep inside her.

"Fuck yeah," I growled when my cock slammed into her cervix.

Marnie didn't like that. She whined out a whimper and tried to scramble away.

I clamped my hand around her hip and brought the other one down on her ass so hard that I could feel the vibrations of the strike in my dick.

"If you move again, I swear to fucking God, whatever whipping your Daddy gave you will be a walk in the park compared to what I'll do."

She was pissed—I may have thrown the daddy comment in there to get under her skin—but she stopped trying to get away. And just in time, because the alarm went off again.

I sighed and bent down to grab my phone from my jeans on the floor.

"What is that?" Marnie asked again.

"Shut the fuck up," I growled while smashing her face into the pillow. "Now ride my cock."

Just because someone was here didn't mean I was going to stop. Fucking her felt way too good for that. That was if she did what I told her to.

I stopped scrolling through my phone and cocked a brow down at her. "What the fuck did I just say? Get that pussy moving."

It took a second, but Marnie complied and slowly started moving. Too slow for my liking.

"I said ride my cock." My palm cracked down on her ass. "Now get fucking going."

My victory came with a tight squeeze around my girth. My Little Bird was stubborn, but a part of her liked being told what to do. While she didn't exactly pick up the pace, Marnie did move enough for me to watch her delicate flesh swallowing my cock.

I scrolled through my phone while enjoying the way her wetness glistened off my Jacob's Ladder piercings. Six barbells had never looked so mouth-watering. Unfortunately, whoever was at my door wouldn't go away.

Sighing, I clicked on my security app.

My brow rose when the outside camera view was displayed. What the fuck was Micha doing here? He was the last person I expected to see standing at my door.

"What?" I said, pressing the intercom button.

Micha's eyes rolled up to the camera. "We need to talk."

His voice caused Marnie to take notice. Her eyes widened as her head lifted. I knew what was coming when she sucked back a breath.

My hand clamped down over her mouth before the scream could break free.

"You want to scream, Little Bird? I can make you scream." To reiterate my point, I drove my cock into her, hard and deep.

This time it wasn't a scream that my hand muffled, which only made me fuck her harder. I held her head against my shoulder and plowed into her hot little cunt, groaning at how she tightened around me.

"Preston!"

Shit.

I pressed in deep and rolled my hips before returning my attention to the screen display.

"I'm busy."

"I don't give a shit," Micha growled back.

"We don't give a shit either, do we, Little Bird," I whispered in Marnie's ear.

Nothing could make me stop. The world could be burning down around us, and I'd still keep fucking her.

"Open the fucking door, Preston, or I'm coming in."

Except for that.

I considered letting Micha kick the door in, but the gunshot to the head might be kind of hard to explain to Lou.

Goddamnit.

Sighing, I pressed the intercom button. "Give me a minute."

I gave Marnie's ass a hard slap, then begrudgingly pulled my cock out.

"We'll pick this up later."

I'd barely pulled my jeans over my hips before she asked, "Who's here?"

She was probably hoping to get some help, but hope was for the weak. No one was coming to help her. And if they did, I'd kill them.

"Micha, why do you want me to see if he'll join us?" I looked back at her. "He likes it rough too."

Her neck bobbed with a swallow that made me want to shove my cock down her throat. I'd slit Micha's throat before I let him even look at her. But she didn't need to know that. I was curious though.

"Could be fun." Snaping the top button on my jeans closed, I turned around and dropped my palms down on the bed. "Maybe I'll like watching you take another cock. What do you think, Little Bird? You want to be the filling in our sandwich?"

Marnie scuttled back as I crawled over her and grazed my cheek off hers.

"Micha knows how to fuck. I bet he'd ride you real good."

That part was true. Micha had a touch of exhibitionist in him. I'd seen him fuck a couple of girls. Never joined in. We didn't exactly have the same tastes. Or should I say, Micha couldn't handle my tastes. Though lately, I was starting to see the appeal of fucking in front of someone. That was one hell of a way to claim a girl.

Marnie licked her lips and shook her head. "I'll be good."

Out of all of the things I'd threatened her with, it was another cock that turned her docile. Now that made me smile.

"Remember, Little Bird," I kissed her lips and growled, "Good girls get rewards." Then I left.

The good girl act lasted about point two seconds. As soon as I had the door open, she started screaming for help. There was no doubt in my mind that she'd have made a play to run out if I didn't have her ankle chained to the bed. Too bad for her, the room was soundproof.

Not a peep could be heard once the door was closed. Not that it would've mattered. Micha was the last person that would help her. The son of a bitch was almost as cold as I was. A man in his position had to be. That didn't mean I wanted him knowing my personal business.

I strutted down the stairs, grabbed a shirt out of the closet then headed around the corner to open the door, where I was met with Micha's unimpressed glare.

"Where the fuck is she?"

My brow rose. "Where is who?"

He was going to have to be a lot more specific than she. In the last month alone, I'd had a hand in five disappearances.

"Don't play dumb with me. I know she's here." He shouldered past me. "Logan's got a big mouth."

Fucking Logan.

Micha spun around and crossed his arms. "Did you kill her?"

"Why?" I said while shutting the door and walking past him to get a drink. "Who the fuck is she to you?"

"No one. But my pregnant fiancé has been bitching about her missing friend for two goddamn days."

Yeah, I could see how that would be annoying. On a good day, Riley Adams was a pain in the ass. Micha should've just let me shoot her.

I took a drink of my whiskey and shrugged. "So?"

"So?" His face dropped. "Did you not hear what I said?"

"Oh, I heard it. I just don't care." His problems with Riley were his. I didn't give a shit about what happened in their relationship.

"I could make you care."

I snorted. Good luck with that.

Micha closed his eyes and sucked in a deep breath. The fact that I did shit without informing him pissed him off. I didn't care about that either. He was our leader, but that didn't mean he knew everything that happened. That was the entire purpose of guys like me. We handled the dirty shit no one else wanted to.

My brow once again arched when Micha tipped his head and narrowed his eyes. "Is that blood on your mouth?"

I lifted my finger and wiped my bottom lip. "So it is."

The red streak on my fingertip called to me. I couldn't resist popping it in my mouth and sucking off every last drop.

Micha stood there with his mouth open. "Did you fucking eat her?"

"No." I wasn't a fucking cannibal. "But I would be coming inside her right now if you hadn't shown up."

I was still pissed about that.

"Fuck sakes. I didn't need that image in my head." He dropped his head and pinched the bridge of his nose. "Are you going to keep her?"

This time it was my eyes that narrowed.

"You took out a contract, didn't you?"

How the fuck did he know about that?

"All right," he sighed. "I want to talk to her."

That was not happening. "I don't need your help, Micha."

"I wasn't asking your fucking permission, Preston."

Normally I'd kill someone for talking to me like that, but I liked this change in attitude. For years I'd waited for Micha to step up to the plate and earn the throne he would inherit. And I was curious about what exactly he planned to say.

"Alight." I shrugged. "I'll go and get her."

Chapter 16
Marnie

When screaming didn't work, I figured I'd try something else. Not that I thought Micha Kessler would help me, but there was a chance he wasn't alone. Riley wouldn't turn a blind eye. All I had to do was get her attention. That was a task much easier said than done.

Either this room was soundproofed, or I was too far away to be heard. I assumed it wasn't the latter. Preston was nothing if not prepared. It was disgusting how prepared he was. I wouldn't be surprised if he had a contingency plan in case I did get out of this room.

Meaning I needed to pay more attention when he walked into the room for patterns in footsteps or movements. Before any of that came into play, I needed a way out of here. This was the first time I'd been alone without being surrounded by bars, and I planned on taking full advantage of that opportunity. I just had to be careful about how I did it.

My eyes narrowed in on Preston's black T-shirt crumpled on the ground. Why would he leave that in here? It seemed too convenient. Then again, there was a high chance I was simply being paranoid. Still...

I slid to the edge of the bed and dipped my foot down to carefully toe the fabric. It felt like a normal shirt, but that didn't mean anything. I'd learned not to trust my senses lately, like the push in my mind telling me to melt into Preston's strong form. There was nothing enticing about being used by a monster. Not that my pussy would agree.

I was still wet, and there was this ache that kept clutching at my core as if my walls were trying to grab onto something that wasn't there. It was annoying and starting to piss me off. Which in turn made the idea of clothing myself in any kind of fabric appealing.

Huffing out a sigh, I dropped my eyes to the floor. What damage could a T-shirt possibly do? It wasn't like he could booby-trap it. Besides, it was better than nothing.

I snatched it up and pulled the cloth over my head before I could change my mind. It was big and warm, and I hated how much I liked the way it smelled, but it offered more protection than I had. So I sucked it up and moved on to the next task—the chain around my ankle.

Or should I say fur-lined, leather cuff? It was well made, hugging my ankle tightly and locked in place. At least it wasn't digging into my skin. That was something, right? Bastard probably expected me to thank him for taking my comfort into account.

"I'll get right on that." I snorted while crawling across the bed toward the trunk on the left side.

Surprisingly that wasn't locked. It was just latched shut, which didn't help my paranoia any. I eyed the golden buckles and tipped my head. Why wouldn't he lock that? It didn't make sense. There was nothing in this room I could use. No blankets or heavy objects I could hit him with. Yet that I was free to look inside? Why? What was the catch?

That question was answered when I pushed my nerves down and flipped the lid open.

I couldn't move. My eyes were stuck on the contents. Crops, whips, floggers, strange little clamps, and various other devices lay inside like a sexual torture treasure trove. I was scared to touch anything in there, let alone think about what he planned to do with it —especially that purple dildo. The thing was thicker than my fist.

A thought tugged at my brow.

That thing had to be heavy. It might make a good weapon. Sex toys were usually well crafted so they wouldn't break like the lamp. But did I really want to lunge at him with a giant dick? There's an idea I never thought I'd have. Imagine explaining that to the *Time Life* people making a movie about your heroizing escape.

'Would you say it was your faith that got you through.'

'No, Jon, it was the giant purple dildo I found in his tickle trunk.'

Somehow I doubted that part of the story would make it into the movie. But hey, the best parts were usually left out. And beggars couldn't be choosers.

I swear a strained 'oof' came out when I lifted that thing. It turned out it had a name. Scrawled across the handle was Bubba. Go figure, my first friend in this hell was a dick named Bubba.

"All right, Bubba," I sighed and looked around. "Where the hell are we going to hide you?"

That was a good question. I couldn't hide by the door and wait for Preston to come back. My chained ankle prevented that. There were pillows on the bed, though. Tucking it underneath one of those and waiting seemed the best option. So that was what I did.

I sat on the bed, gripping the silicone dildo, while my heart pounded in my chest.

Whether or not this was going to work, I had no idea. But I had to try.

The most disturbing thing wasn't the silence or the way the hairs on the back of my neck rose—which, by the way, hurt like a son of a bitch. Every time I twisted my head, I was reminded of Preston's teeth digging into my flesh. That I could handle. Pain was easy. It was the thoughts going through my head, comparing how a fake dick felt to a real one…Now, that was mortifying, mainly because the real one was winning.

The hardness and silky smooth heat were nothing like what I was currently touching. This thing felt…wrong somehow.

I didn't have time to ponder that.

A click to my right caused my heart to lurch forward.

The door was opening. He was here.

Every second ticked by with the length of an hour. I saw the dust dancing in the light. Preston's fingers came around the door, followed by his knee, hip, and finally, his cold gray stare.

I waited for his 'Hello Little Bird' greeting.

Instead, I got a sharp tsk. "Did I say you could get dressed?"

"I didn't ask," I said while shifting my eyes to the black fabric on my shoulder.

"I should punish you." He wagged his finger and took a few steps forward. "But I like the way you look in my shirt."

Suddenly, I didn't miss clothes anymore. I was tempted to rip the shirt off my body, but like it or not, it did give me some form of shield. A flimsy and easily torn one, but it was still better than nothing.

A charge sparked through the air when Preston tipped his head and licked his lips. Those cold gray orbs heated up the lower they dipped, and as much as I hated myself for it, my thighs yearned to part for him. Give him just a peek at what was underneath.

Maybe that wasn't a bad idea. I did need to lure him over here. So it wouldn't be like I was giving in to desire. In the right hands, seduction was just like any other tool.

My hands were not the right ones.

I slowly parted my thighs while sliding the shirt over my knees. I was doing it all, giving him that sultry look I'd seen my sister do countless times while silently coaxing him to come to me. The scene was set.

At least, that was how it played out in my head.

What actually happened was I wound up fighting with the shirt because it was trapped under my ass. Then I yanked it free, which pulled the shirt up over my breasts as I smacked myself in the face. Seduction was not my forte.

"Son of a bitch." Jesus, that hurt.

I rubbed my face while Preston snickered, which only pissed me off more than my failed attempt.

"It's not funny!"

"It's a little funny."

Two things stunned me. The amusement that sparkled in his eyes, causing them to brighten up like polished silver. "Are you...laughing?"

That was the end of that. Preston's face fell flat quicker than a five-gallon barrel rolling down a hill.

"No." He crossed his arms. "I don't laugh."

"But you just—"

"That was a chuckle," he explained. "There's a difference."

I rolled my eyes.

Forgive me, oh Lord of Definitions.

"Did you just roll your eyes at me?"

"I don't know." I stuck my chin up. "Did you just laugh?"

He sighed and cocked his hip against the dresser. "That lasted longer than I thought."

"What lasted longer?" Was he speaking in code now?

"The good girl bullshit."

We both knew I didn't mean that. Don't get me wrong. If he brought Micha up here and they started undressing, I'd play the good girl role. I'd be so obedient that my father would praise my behavior. But that would never happen. I couldn't speak for Micha, but Riley would murder him if he so much as looked at another girl.

He cocked a brow at me. "You try too hard."

What the hell did that mean?

"I do not."

"Then what the hell was that shit you just pulled."

I assumed he was referring to my graceful attempt at being sultry.

"It's called seduction." Why I told him that, I had no clue.

I may as well have invited him to have his way with me, which I didn't want, despite the heat rolling through my body. I was nervous, that was all. It was perfectly normal to experience a few butterflies when one was in danger.

"Hmm." Preston studied me briefly before pushing off the dresser and sauntering closer.

"You want to know how to seduce me, Marnie?"

No.

Maybe.

I don't know.

It could be helpful information. Preston wasn't exactly forth-coming with his wants and desires. He just did it. Beyond choking myself, I didn't really know what got him off. And given my situation, that could be a valuable asset to have.

Preston's knee pressed down on the bed, and my hand tightened around the silicone. He made his way across the mattress, and all I could think was, 'Just a little more,' as tension poured into my muscles. Then he said something that made me stop cold.

"All you have to do to get me hard is exist."

My eyes snapped up to his as he crawled over me.

"You have no idea how many times I've jerked off to the sound of you breathing." He lifted his hand and tucked a lock of hair behind my ear, causing a shiver to race up my spine. "I've come more in the past two years than I have in my entire life. I can't go more than an hour without seeing your face, hearing your voice, or smelling the stash of your panties I have in my room."

I may have whispered, "You have my underwear." But my mind was thinking of something else. Dark, sick thoughts tingled across my skin with the minty smell of his breath.

"I took them after you got yourself off. Every single time you laid down at night and fingered your sweet little pussy, I took your panties. Then jerked off on your bed."

Something that dirty should not sound that good.

Preston swept his thumb across my mouth and tugged on my bottom lip. "And thus my problem."

I gazed back at him as my brows knit. It looked as if he was contemplating something.

"Men like me can't afford to have weaknesses, and you, Little Bird." His chest expanded with a long breath. "Are a big fucking weakness."

I didn't know how to take that. Was it a compliment? A distraction? Some new way to fuck with me?

Preston slid his hand over my cheek and down to wrap around my neck. "I should kill you now."

The truth in that statement made me swallow. He wanted to do it. I could feel it twitching in his fingers.

"So why don't you?"

That was the question. Death was nothing to him. It was like breathing or waking up in the morning. Blood and pain were a typical Tuesday afternoon. So why was I still alive?

But Preston didn't answer me. Instead, he leaned in and growled in my ear, "Are you going to hit me with that thing, or just hang on to it."

My heart dropped.

Shit.

I huffed and slapped the dick in his open palm. "It's not my fault you left the trunk unlocked."

"That, right there." Preston smirked down at me. "That's how you seduce me, Little Bird. I'd fuck you right now if Micha weren't waiting."

I'd scratch his eyes out if he tried. I was not...

Wait.

"Did you say Micha was waiting?"

"That's right." Preston nodded.

"And he wants to see me?"

"Guess it's a good thing you put a shirt on."

Why the hell did Micha Kessler want to see me? I hadn't spoken more than three words to the man, so I doubted he was here to save me. But there was an upside to this. Mainly the leaving this room part, which I assumed was the plan when Preston unlocked my ankle.

Excitement poured through me. I was ready to jump up and run to the door, but Preston stopped me. He pushed me back and pulled my thighs apart. I didn't fight him for fear that he would change his mind and bring Micha up here. It was odd how violating the thought of that was. In some weird way, this gilded cage had become my space. Not necessarily safe, but mine, nonetheless.

"Look at that freshly fucked pussy."

Mortification heated my cheeks as air cooled my delicate flesh. I wanted nothing more than to tug the shirt over my knees and had to remind myself not to move. A feat that became impossible when Preston bent down and bit into my inner thigh. His teeth pierced my skin, and I screamed and slapped at his head.

The sharp stab radiating around my hip morphed into a spark of pleasure with one long lick up my slit. Preston latched onto my clit, and my brain barely had time to register the sensation before his mouth was on mine. It took a second for me to realize that it wasn't just blood I tasted on his tongue but my own arousal. Then it was gone.

I was left with nothing but heated gray eyes staring down at me. "I should make Micha hold you down for me."

He had my head spinning so much that all I could utter was, "My neck hurts."

It was true. The man practically tore a chunk out of me, which wasn't at all pertinent to this situation, but it was still valid. And now my thigh had joined in on it.

"Aww...." I wanted to slap the fake frown Preston gave me in response. "Is the poor Little Bird injured?"

Asshole.

"Now, come on." He held his hand out for me. "Let's get this shit over with. I have a pussy to break in."

Chapter 17

Marnie

*P*reston chained himself to me, which took running away out of the equation. I highly doubted I'd be able to dart past him and out the door without being caught. But I still would've liked the option.

The cuff attached to my ankle had a chain a couple of feet long, nowhere near enough room to get a reasonable distance away. If I could have hidden around a corner or something, I might have been able to get free of my bind. I'd need more than a few feet for that, though.

On the upside, I was leaving this place, which might mean an actual bathroom. I was getting tired of using a bucket. God forbid I be allowed the common courtesy of a toilet. Or privacy.

The last time I said I had to pee, Preston watched. I thought I'd been in uncomfortable positions before. I was wrong. Ever tried to relieve yourself while someone was staring at you? It wasn't fun. I didn't even like using the bathrooms at school when someone was in there.

Now I was chained to the cause of my discomfort, and he'd stolen more from me than the simple act of privacy.

Grumbling curses, I got off the bed and resisted the urge to squeeze my thighs together. I was all wound up, achy, and sweaty. It was a horrible feeling that I hoped would go away soon. And it was all his fault. Bastard. Who did he think he was? Telling me what to do and touching me in ways I didn't want to be touched.

My eyes dropped down to the chain as it slithered and slinked on the floor.

Maybe I could choke him?

It was long enough and made of metal. I'd like to see him get his stupid fingers under that.

"You look upset, Little Bird." The glimmer in Preston's eyes did not help my mood any. "You didn't think I was going to let you walk out of here, did you?"

I was definitely going to strangle him.

Let's face it—a leash seemed fitting. I'd called a giant birdcage home for god knows how long now. The fact that he hadn't started calling me 'pet' was astounding.

"What next?" I hissed. "Are you going to feed me blueberries if I do tricks?"

He smirked back at me. "Depends on what kind of tricks you do."

Asshole.

I wouldn't be shocked if Preston had a bag of treats tucked away somewhere.

"Besides, you don't like blueberries," he said while punching in a code on the panel by the door.

The blueberry comment was disturbing. I didn't want to know how Preston came across that piece of information, but the code he used to open the door was worse: 0423. April twenty-third was my birthday, and I'd never wanted to slap myself more. I should've seen that coming. Of course, he used something personal to lock me away.

"Ready, Little Bird?"

Ready to get stabbed in the eye with the first sharp object I find?

"Why yes, Master. I'm so ready to meet your asshole friend. Please, lead the way."

"Keep talking like that." He pressed a button on the screen, causing my pulse to jump as the door clicked. "And Micha might have to wait."

I didn't have time to analyze the fire burning darkly in his stare. Nor did I care because this was it. I was finally leaving my prison.

Excitement made me want to bounce around and jump from one foot to another. Despite my insides screaming, I managed to stay still and act like I was waiting patiently. Only the sound of whooshing blood in my veins gave away the anxiety raging through my system.

Did the door always open this slowly? Why was it taking so long?

I practically squealed at my first peek of the stairway.

Preston paused to eye me. "Before you get any ideas, the code changes immediately after I use it."

Uh-huh.

"So you can try and leave." He stepped across the threshold. "But I'll know if you enter the wrong code."

Whatever, can we just go now?

Besides, who cared about the code changing? All that meant was that I had to figure out the right one, which shouldn't be too hard. If Preston used my birthday, then he probably used others. Riley dragged me to a party Lana had for Parker, so I knew his birthday was March 10th. I'd done enough research on the Order to know that Louis was born in March, Dean in October, and Martin in August. I was pretty sure I knew them all except for Silas and….

"Your birthday's in May, right?"

The corner of Preston's mouth lifted. "No, Silas's is in May."

Well, that was one down.

"I'm a New Year's baby." He leaned in and whispered, "Wanna try that code?"

It was entirely possible that he was trying to throw me off track. One thing I'd learned about Preston Whitley, he liked fucking with people. Or at least he liked fucking with me. But not this time. This time, I would hold my head high and march out the door.

I said, "I don't know what you're talking about," and walked out of the hell hole I'd been trapped in.

That first step was heavy, but the second lifted all the weight off my shoulders. I could smell what I thought was cinnamon and see the sun at the bottom of the stairs. It was so bright and inviting that all I wanted to do was feel it on my skin. I may have even smiled a bit until Preston snickered from behind me.

"Will you smile like that when my come is dripping down your thigh?"

I shot him a glare before walking down the stairs. It wasn't until we reached the bottom that a thought occurred to me, and I stopped cold.

His come, meaning he didn't use protection and I wasn't on birth control. Suddenly, I was terrified for an entirely different reason.

Preston tugged on my arm. "Come on, Little Bird, pick up the pace. I'm still hard, and Micha likes to talk."

I reluctantly let him pull me down a hallway. Did I say something to Micha? Did I want to know the answer? Maybe Preston didn't care because I wouldn't be around long enough. Either way, I had to know.

"Are you going to kill me?"

"Are you going to keep pissing me off?"

Probably.

Anyway, that wasn't the point. "If you're not planning on killing me, don't you think you should be taking precautions?"

"What's wrong, Little Bird? Afraid you'll give birth to a monster?"

"I'm not giving birth to anything." That was so not happening.

"Is that so?" He paused long enough to arch a brow down at me. "According to my calculations, you started ovulating yesterday."

What?

I stopped. "You're trying to get me pregnant?"

"Why not?" He shrugged. "Your intelligence alone makes you a prime candidate for reproduction."

Prime candidate? Talk about being romantic. Though, I did understand his logic. Speaking from a strictly genetic standpoint, I could attest that the human race had gone down as a species. Inbreeding, among many other things, warped our gene pool. Taking Preston's sociopathy out of the equation, he would also be an ideal candidate. I could imagine how intelligent our children would be. But that did not mean I wanted to have a kid with him. I didn't want kids with anyone, let alone him.

"I'm not having your baby!"

"Don't worry, Little Bird." He steered me around a corner. "When the baby is born, you'll love it."

The need to bolt grew with each step. I could feel my heart pounding and wouldn't be surprised if Preston could hear it. My mouth was dry, my palms sweaty, and I no longer cared about the annoying ache in my core. I only cared about one thing—getting the hell away from him.

I had to be smart about it, which was easier said than done.

It was difficult to maintain my composure. Even if I could somehow break free of the chain connecting us, it would do no good to run around when I had absolutely no idea where I was going. I still didn't know the layout of this place. So, I did the only thing I could and paid attention to where he was taking me.

I studied the hall, taking note of every door—six on the left and four on the right. The second one on the left was open, and I saw the edge of a desk on the other side. But it was the last door on the right that intrigued me. It had a panel and no knob.

Then there were the pictures, most of which were of various land-scapes, including one of Manning Keep. It was smaller and unbal-anced compared to the others, yet it stood out because the frame was more ornate. Golden feathers were carved into the wood, with a raven in each corner. Interesting.

Another thing I noticed was the general ambiance. Preston's house was warm and inviting, with a neutral color scheme and plush, comfortable-looking furniture. Not at all what I imagined a man like him would call home. He didn't wear designer clothes, but the Persian rug we walked on likely cost more than my parent's house. It didn't add up. Why present yourself one way, but live another?

My brows knit at Preston as he steered us out of the hallway to an open-concept area with many potted plants and a huge skylight.

"Why do you wear that jean jacket?"

He didn't even look at me when he answered. "It reminds me of something."

I looked over at a cluster of flowers—poppies and lilies. Opium came from poppies, and lilies were poisonous. So were some of the other plants I saw. Leave it to Preston to have a room of floral death.

"So...the jacket is a trophy?"

It made sense. Most serial killers had them, which was how I classified him.

His shoulders lifted in a shrug. "Call it what you want."

"It's not a matter of want," I explained. "The literal definition of trophy is a cup or other decorative object awarded as a prize for victory or success."

"Victory or success." He nodded. "I like that."

I rolled my eyes. "Murder is not a victory."

Preston stopped before a set of double doors and peered down at me. "You seemed pretty pleased with yourself when that frat boy dropped."

I squared my shoulder's as I turned away. I was not talking about that with him. He would never understand. Besides...

"He could still be alive for all we know."

"You're not that stupid, Marnie." Preston bent down to whisper in my ear. "You knew exactly what would happen when you dumped that vial into his drink."

"I'm not like you, Preston." Just because I gave him more than four times what a man his size could safely handle didn't mean Chase would die. There was a chance he could've been saved.

"No, you're not." Preston sighed. "I don't hide my kills behind divine retribution."

I didn't hide behind anything divine. The very thought of that made me nauseous. There was nothing divine about justice.

"Death is never my intent."

He cocked a brow. "Yet you don't feel bad about it."

I opened my mouth to argue, but nothing came out. Because Preston was right. I didn't feel bad. Not a single twang of guilt flowed through my veins for Chase or any of the others. I told myself they got what they deserved, but was I deluding myself? Did I really not care? Was I just as bad as the people I delivered justice to?

I looked up at the smirk on his face, and for the first time in my life, I questioned my moral standing.

"Welcome to my world, Little Bird."

No!

I wasn't anything like him.

Preston wanted to see the world burn. I wanted to see people like him burn. That didn't make me honorable, but it didn't make me evil, either.

"Sometimes, the only thing that can slay a monster is another monster."

The smirk on his face grew into a grin that sent a shiver down my back. "Welcome to my parlor, said the spider to the fly."

Not this again.

I huffed out a sigh. "I thought Micha was waiting."

Not that I was super excited to see him or anyone from Preston's nefarious club. It was better than getting into a moral debate with someone who had none. Talk about a waste of time.

His face fell, twisting the grin into a scowl. "Yes, he is."

Someone seemed annoyed. Perhaps that was something I could use.

Preston pushed the doors open and led me into a large kitchen. I looked around at the dark wooden floors, tan stone island, and stainless steel appliances. This room was bright and sunny, with everything anyone could want—a microwave, coffee station, and hanging pots and pans. There was even a vase of fresh flowers sitting on the table in front of a bay window.

It was the kind of kitchen Stepford housewives dreamed of owning. I, however, was more interested in the knives sitting next to a large oak butcher's block.

"Took you long enough."

Oh, and there was Micha.

I twisted my neck to glare at the dark-haired man seated at the head of the table, Micha Kessler, future king of kings. He was definitely someone in need of justice. Unfortunately, he'd attached himself to Riley, and I would never hurt her. One day, I'd find out how he managed to do that.

"Could've taken longer." Preston shot back while dragging me over and pulling out a chair.

The seat was comfortable, with its navy crushed velvet padding and oak frame. That wood was strong and could come in handy when beating someone to death.

I grabbed the side of the chair and wiggled my butt to test the weight.

Pretty sure I could lift this thing if I needed to and at least swing it once. But I'd have to make it count.

Preston gazed down at me as if he knew what I was thinking, then tipped his chin at Micha, impatiently tapping the tabletop.

"Pay attention, Little Bird. Apparently, Micha has something to say."

Annoyed wasn't the right word. Preston was downright exasperated, and Micha seemed frustrated.

Excellent.

I couldn't help but smile when Micha's dark chocolate glare rolled, and he let out a long breath.

Welcome to my parlor, indeed.

"Marnie," Micha growled.

I smirked back at him. "Micha."

Could I pit them against each other, and if so, who would win? Micha was bigger, but Preston was lethal. Could be interesting.

"You seem to be in good spirits."

"Oh, yeah," I grumbled. "Getting kidnapped and raped repeatedly was at the top of my bucket list."

Good times.

Micha's brow rose. "So, right to the point, then?"

"I guess that depends on what your point is. Personally, I don't really care, but you can talk if it makes you feel better."

He sighed at Preston. "Can I hit her?"

"I got it."

That was the only warning I received before Preston's hand speared into my hair and yanked my head back. The burn across my scalp was outweighed by the searing pain reigniting from the bite on my neck.

"Remember what I said about good girls?"

I locked my glare on Preston's and gritted against the pain. "Remember when I said go fuck yourself?"

He stared at me.

I stared at him.

Then he smirked. I should've seen what was coming next. One hand snapped his jeans open while the other smashed my face down into his crotch, giving me an intimate, way up-close look at his dick. Let me just say that thing was scary before, but feeling the hardness pressed against my cheek was downright terrifying.

"Smell that, Little Bird?" The ball on the piercing right next to my eye was mocking me along with his words. "That's your sweet pussy on my cock."

I hadn't noticed anything until he said that. Now, it was all I could smell. It was sweet with husky undertones and a tad enticing. Self-hatred poured through me as my mouth watered. Deep down, a part of me wanted to lick him.

Thankfully that didn't last long. Preston pulled my head back up and looked me dead in the eye. "Keep mouthing off, and you'll get a taste of it."

"You sure you want to stick that in my mouth?" I challenged. "You might not get it back."

I'd bite his dick off so fast...

"Enough." Micha's palm slammed down on the table, making the vase wobble. "God-damnit, I do not need to see your fucked up version of foreplay."

Preston shifted his gaze to Micha. "Fucked up version? And what exactly is it that gets you off?"

Micha's face dropped for a second before he shook his head. "That's not why I'm here."

What did he mean by that comment? Did Riley need help? What exactly was Micha doing with my friend?

Preston let go of my hair as I narrowed my glare on Micha.

"Listen up, Marnie." Micha's eyes rolled back to me. "As you know, Riley is pregnant and trying to plan a wedding. So you can imagine my home life is less than desirable."

I could see that. Honestly, I was surprised Micha wasn't limping around. Riley was vicious on a good day. I was kind of disappointed he was walking at all. Micha Kessler didn't deserve her.

"And?"

"And…" He braced his forearms on the table and leaned forward. "I need to know if you're going to be a problem."

It disgusted me how much he reminded me of his father. I'd taught a lesson to a few deserving people. But Louis Kessler…he was my title match. A hatred that I might've been able to hold onto if the arm beside me didn't start moving. Heat flooded into my cheeks as realization hit me. Preston was jerking off. Right there in front of Micha. I didn't want to see that.

Did I?

My eyes slowly slid to the side before I stopped myself and snapped my attention back to the man who didn't have his hand on his genitals.

"I'll repeat the question," Micha said when I didn't respond. "Are you going to be a problem?"

Know what was a problem? The soft grunts that were invading my ears.

I cleared my throat while shifting to a more comfortable position. "Does the phrase 'thorn in my side' ring any bells?"

Micha tipped his head as I followed his lead and leaned in.

"The second I get out of here," I started. "You'll learn the true meaning behind that saying."

The arch in his brow deepened like he was shocked I dared to say anything like that to him. No one talked to a Kessler that way. They ruled this town, but they didn't rule me. And I meant every word I said.

"I don't think you understand the situation—"

"Oh, I understand. Don't underestimate me, Micha. I will rip that pretty little rug out from under you faster than you can blink."

He did not like that. Though, I had to say the tick in his jaw filled me with satisfaction, which I would've enjoyed more with fewer distractions.

"Is she always this difficult?"

I tugged on the collar of my stolen shirt and rolled my neck.

Did someone turn up the heat?

"She's just practicing the art of seduction." Preston's gray eyes swung my way. "Isn't that right, Little Bird?"

Did Preston always sound that gravelly?

While Micha was confused, I caught onto Preston's jab.

"Ha, ha. Very funny."

I hated how good he looked right now with his soft hair and wicked smirk. Asshole. I should punch him in the face, though he'd probably like that.

"I'm not the one that smacked myself in the face."

I shot him a dirty look and snarled, "Still felt better than anything you've done."

Next thing I knew, I was pulled onto Preston's lap. I struggled to get away, but that came to a stop with a firm pinch on my thigh. It stunned me long enough for Preston to grab my neck and pull my head back against his shoulder.

"Careful, Little Bird." He pressed his fingers tighter into my neck. Not enough to cut off my oxygen, but enough to let me know he could if he wanted to. "I will fuck you in front of Micha."

To prove his point, Preston snaked his hand under the shirt and up my thigh, pushing a finger into my opening.

I gasped and swallowed back a moan while Micha tipped his head.

"She's responsive."

That was all he could say?

Mister, 'I didn't want to see your fucked up foreplay' didn't have a problem now. And what did Preston do? He pumped his finger and purred into my ear.

"That's it, grind your ass against my cock."

This was so messed up.

I was trapped on a monster's lap while another asshole watched him finger me, and I was getting off on it. My hips begged to move and grind in on the hardness under me. But I couldn't let them win.

I glared my hatred at Micha and hissed, "How are you going to explain this to Riley? I doubt she'll be too happy that you let her friend get kidnapped and violated."

"First off..." Micha held up a finger. "No one lets Preston do shit."

Preston, the sick bastard, was enjoying my anger. He shoved another finger inside me and traced his tongue over the shell of my ear. And my sick, twisted response was to bite back a moan while my pussy clamped down around him.

"And secondly..." Micha popped up another finger. "Riley will never know."

That made me snort. "She will if I tell her."

That was now my first task once I got free.

"You can't say shit if you're dead."

Preston stopped and slowly turned Micha's way. I wasn't the only one that felt the threat coming from him. A spark of fear flashed across Micha's face for a brief second.

"Relax. She has a twin that would be a great body double."

What!

"No!"

Forgetting about Preston's grip on my throat, I tried to spring forward and scratch Micha's eyes. Instead, I found myself slammed back into Preston's muscular body.

"Leave Trina alone," I croaked out, then realized my mistake.

Micha's eyes narrowed as a slow grin curled his lips. "You're more like my mouse than I thought. You know what self-sacrifice gets you, Marnie?"

As if his words were some type of cue, Preston stood up and smashed my face into the table.

Before I could do anything to fight him off, Micha grabbed my wrists and stretched my arms out. I heard a soft rustle and then felt Micha's hot breath brush across my ear as something large pressed against my opening.

"It gets you fucked." Micha whispered, "Every. Single. Time."

A scream tore from my lips when Preston grunted and thrust into me. He was too big. I couldn't handle his girth, but he didn't care. Preston continued to stretch my pussy beyond its limits while Micha swept my hair off the side of my face.

"Here's the thing, Marnie. I would rather help Riley get over your death than explain this shit to her."

My mind yelled at me to tell him to fuck off, but my body sang with the enticing concoction of pleasure and pain. I was afraid, and my fear would come out if I opened my mouth. So I lay there, silently groaning every time Preston sank into me as I was jarred across the table.

"So here's what's going to happen. I'm going to come back in three weeks." Micha leaned in and hissed, "If you can't convince me you're in love with Preston, I'll gut your sister."

Trina may annoy me, but she was the person I went to when I was hurt. She was the one who held my hand through our nightmare childhood. I endured our father for her so that she could be happy and pure. Trina wasn't just my sister. She was the other half of my soul. I couldn't survive without her, let alone feed her to the beast.

"Enjoy your self-sacrifice, Marnie." Micha stood up, smoothed his shirt, and turned to walk away. "I hope you survive it."

My heart sank as an orgasm tore through me, ripping every atom I had apart.

Chapter 18
Preston

Logan and I were the only ones who understood the dark hunger that consumed our thoughts. I didn't fault the others for it. Micha tried, Parker hid from it, and Mase...well, he had his own problems.

Out of everyone, Louis was the worst. Psychiatrists always were. But I could put up with his constant poking because someone got it. Logan Hudson and I were two sides of the same coin.

Then Shelby Grace came along.

I was happy that he found someone who could calm his chaos, but a part of me wanted to gut her alive. That girl had no idea how many times I held a knife to her throat while she slept. I didn't like to share, and in a matter of weeks, Logan and I went from enjoying someone else's torment to me watching Logan fawn over a chick. The only thing that saved her life was the peace he found being with her.

That didn't stop me from wanting to throw up whenever I saw them sucking face in public or cuddling. Logan didn't have balls anymore because Shelby took them. It was pathetic how he pampered her.

So why was I brushing Marnie's hair like she was a fucking doll? Even worse, I was enjoying it. Every time I smoothed out a section of those beautiful dark locks, I couldn't stop myself from touching her. My palm felt empty without the warmth of her soft skin. If I killed her now, I could rid myself of the sweet tinge of her scent in the back of my throat.

"Ouch!" Marnie jarred her head to the side. "That hurt."

Good. It should hurt. Everything I did to her should hurt.

"Shut the fuck up." I jerked my wrist, tearing the brush through another knot. "You're the one that let it get this tangled."

Snideness curled her lip. "I must've missed the comb in my cage."

"You have fingers."

If I wasn't busy trying to straighten this mess, I might've admired the hatred etching deep lines in her brow.

"I hate to point this out to you, but I'm going to need more than my fingers to get rid of the 'I just got fucked' look."

"I like that look."

"Then stop complaining, or better yet...." Her bright eyes shot daggers at me over her shoulder. "Someone could keep their dick in their pants."

She had a point. I'd fucked her while Micha was here, then again in the bath, and I was already hard again. I couldn't get enough of her. All I could think about was sinking back into that sweet little pussy. The mirror in front of her wasn't helping. Her calves were tied to the legs of the chair, spreading her thighs just enough to get a peek of her delicate pink flesh that made my mouth water.

Marnie was my toy to use. So why the fuck was I wasting my time brushing her hair when I could be fucking her? Then again, why not kill two birds with one stone?

My eyes darted over to the silver handle on my bedside table.

A couple of knives were in there, one of which had a serrated edge that would make a nice mess of her throat. I could already hear her choking on her blood.

"I don't need you to do anything for me."

Ungrateful little...

"You have no idea what you need."

My head tipped as dark locks wrapped around the brush's teeth, and I pulled the handle down. But it wasn't her hair that caught my interest. It was the slow pulse beating on the side of her neck. One nick, right there, was all it would take.

"You suck at this."

Grab the knife. It's right there.

I didn't know why she was complaining about. Most of the knots were taken out in the bath with conditioner.

Grab the knife. It's right there.

"If I wasn't tied up—" She tugged on her arm, rattling the chain around her wrist. "I could do it myself."

"We could always get back in the bath?"

Or, you could cut her throat.

I wouldn't mind a bath, either. Usually, I was a shower guy, but the way she felt, wet, naked, and pressed up against me...I liked it.

Damnit.

"No thanks," Marnie huffed. "I've exceeded my drowning quota for the day."

Okay, that was fun and entirely her fault. One would think she'd have learned not to talk back after the first time. However, I enjoyed how her eyes widened as she fought for air. And oh, did she fight.

My cock stirred as I glanced down at the fresh scratches on my forearms.

"Sick bastard," she muttered.

I smacked the brush off the top of her head. "Stay still."

"Oww," Marnie cried out, dropping her head away.

Instead of responding, I sucked in a deep breath and yanked her head back. How hard was it to follow a straightforward direction? I liked her argumentative side, but this was getting ridiculous. There were worse things I could be doing to her. If Marnie had any idea what was going through my head right now...

The things I wanted to do to her in this chair would make the devil blush. It wouldn't be hard to spin her around and slam into her. I wouldn't even have to remove the towel from around my waist.

Marnie could say she didn't want it, but I saw her looking at my reflection. Right now, her aqua eyes were rolling over my chest. For anyone else, this would be considered a tender moment, a man caring for his woman. Bathing her, then drying her off and brushing her hair. I even took the time to put lotion on her soft skin.

This wasn't a romantic gesture or loving action. It was a continuation of the twisted game we'd been playing for two years. Neither of us said anything about it, but we knew the rules. Stay hidden in the shadows and watch. There was something satisfying about knowing that Marnie's eyes were on me.

"Keep looking at me like that, Little Bird, and I might find other uses for this brush."

It was also extremely satisfying to fuck with her.

Her big eyes widened. "You wouldn't?"

Oh, I would.

I wanted to work the handle in her ass while I plowed into her pussy, but not as much as I wanted to be the one to take that hole for the first time. All of her virginities were mine to pluck away. I'd bathe myself in her innocence while pulling the demon out and making her embrace who she really was. There were worse things than death. Marnie would learn that.

Then we'd have some fun.

Unfortunately, some things needed to be coaxed. That was why butt plugs were invented, and I just so happened to have some in the drawer next to her left knee.

But before that happened, we had obligations that I wasn't looking forward to dealing with.

May as well get it over with.

Sighing, I set the brush on the dresser next to us and opened the top drawer, where I had her phone stashed.

"Now, I want you to listen to me very carefully, Little Bird. You're going to do something, and you need to have a clear head when you do it."

I knew what her question would be before the words left her lips.

"Why would I do anything for you?"

"I think you'll want to do this."

The snide snort I got made me seriously reconsider the knife.

How quickly she seemed to forget our conversation with Micha. She was about to get a harsh reality check.

"You're going to call your sister," I said, dropping the phone on the vanity in front of her.

The curl in Marnie's lip fell away.

I couldn't tell if she was worried or planning to cry for help. A bit of both, I assumed. Anyone in her position might have considered this an opportunity. Some might say panic drove people to act irrationally, but hope was the real enemy. One spark of that, and before they knew what was happening, they said or did the wrong thing.

I'd seen it over and over again, pleading with someone who got off on desperation—grabbing an unloaded gun or a mother telling her child to run, only to find out that there were men outside. The end result was much worse than what would've happened. Marnie needed to understand the repercussions of the choices she made.

I crouched down to her eye level and grabbed her chin. "I don't like problems, Marnie. Don't make your sister a problem for me."

Trina texted her numerous times and talked to Micha's girl about calling the cops. A bit of an overreaction as far as I was concerned. It'd only been a couple of days, but chicks tended to react emotionally. Ava once cried for three days because I ripped the head off her doll.

There was a second of silence where Marnie searched my face, but she already knew I didn't make idle threats.

"How am I supposed to explain not answering her?"

Shrugging, I let go of her chin. "That's up to you."

I didn't care. Marnie knew her sister well enough to realize she'd try to contact her.

"She's going to know I'm lying."

Sounded like a personal problem to me.

"I could always put a bullet in her head."

That was my personal choice. I'd even make it quick. Trina wouldn't see it coming.

"No." Marnie shook her head. "I'll call her."

The fact that she thought she had a choice was adorable.

"Uncuff my hand, and I'll do it."

My mistake. That was adorable.

"No, no, Little Bird," I tsked. "I'll be listening in on this one."

For the first time, I saw fear visibly quake through her body.

Interesting. When her safety was threatened, Marnie held back and put up a strong front. But not when it was Trina's. When did her sense of self-preservation take a back seat? Micha wasn't lying when he said self-sacrifice got you fucked. Men like me were more than happy to pull on that thread, except for this time. This time I was just pissed off.

Maybe I'll get lucky, and she'll fuck up?

Panic tugged on Marnie's expression when I reached out to dial her sister's number.

"I-I can't be calm if you're hovering over me?"

Ring.

"You better figure it out. Your sister's life depends on it."

Ring.

Part of me hoped Trina didn't answer. The other part was praying Marnie would say something. I'd been dreaming about slitting her sister's throat from the day I started stalking her.

My hopes died when Trina answered on the third ring.

"Marnie! Oh my god, are you okay?"

If she only knew how not okay her sister was.

My Bird took a deep breath and said, "I'm fine, Trina."

I couldn't help but admire how steady her tone was because her body was anything but calm. Shivering and pale as a ghost, the stench of fear was so thick in the air I could taste it.

Sparks shot up my spine as I pressed my mouth down on her shoulder, and the panic coursing through her tingled on my lips.

So, fucking good.

The only thing ruining this moment was the voice on the other end of the phone.

"Do you have any idea how worried I was?" Trina barked out. "Where the hell were you?"

Her pitch grated on my nerves.

'Where the hell were you?' What right did Trina have to demand shit from my Little Bird? Marnie was mine! The only person she had to answer to was me, not some weaker carbon copy.

"Sorry," Marnie uttered while I grazed my hand up her arm and sauntered around behind her. "I was sick."

"Bullshit! Being sick doesn't mean you don't answer your phone, Marnie. Now, what the hell is going on?"

It appeared Trina wasn't as stupid as people thought she was. Given her sister's intelligence, I wasn't surprised—two peas in a pod, as they say. The Dupires had a knack for being underestimated.

"Sorry, I left my phone at Andrew's."

That was when Trina's tone changed, and so did mine.

"Did you say, Andrew?"

Marnie thought she was sly, but I caught that spark in her eyes. I was a twin, too. We all had our own language. There would be no secret messages on my watch.

"Careful, Little Bird," I whispered, then leaned down, bringing my mouth next to her ear. "I'd hate for something to be misconstrued."

That was the first time I lied to her.

I was begging for a reason to make a trip to Miami. The thought of fucking Marnie while I had her sister's blood on my hands had me ready to rip her out of that chair. Instead, I slid my palm down her chest to the sweet spot between her thighs.

"Relax, Trina." Marnie cleared her throat and shot me a dirty look as I swept my finger over her clit. "Andrew's in my class. I told you about him."

"No, you didn't."

"Yes, I did," Marnie insisted with so much conviction that I almost believed her. "He's the same one that helped me go through textbooks."

"Okay?"

My heart flittered at the skepticism in Trina's tone, then again when Marnie whispered, "You're not helping."

I smirked and dipped my finger in her tight channel.

Didn't she get it? I wanted her to fuck up. Trina Dupire's mere existence pissed me off. Her long brown locks, the sparkle she had in her eyes, and her smile all matched my Bird's.

She was another Marnie.

Meaning countless guys knew what my girl tasted like and how it felt to be buried deep inside her. They'd heard her moan and call out their name while she came on their cocks. Even their father was in the line-up of men who'd been with my Bird without ever touching her. And I wanted to kill every single one of them. But mostly, I wanted to kill her.

Trina let them have what was mine to take.

"Oh wait…I remember that guy." Trina let out a loud sigh. "What kind of guy gets excited about finding mistakes in a textbook?"

What kind of guy, indeed.

"Someone didn't pay attention to the rules," I breathed while thrusting my finger into her hot little cunt.

Whomever this guy was, he was a dead man. The name was obviously fake, but I'd find him. Let's see how excited he got about textbooks when one was shoved up his ass.

Marnie gasped and quietly snarled, "Stop it, Preston."

Not a fucking chance.

Her attention was quickly diverted when her sister asked, "Who are you talking to?"

Mistake number one.

"No one."

"That's it, Little Bird," I softly growled, lifting my hand to smear her juices over her stomach. "I fucking love watching lies slip through these pretty lips."

"Are you sure?" Trina didn't sound so convinced. "I could've sworn you said, 'Preston.' "

Mistake number two.

But my Bird was wise.

"Why would I say, Preston?"

"I don't know—"

Marnie cut her sister off. "Just because you're obsessed with everyone in Ashen Springs doesn't mean I am."

Oooh, she really let her anger pour out in that one. It was hot.

"I am not obsessed with them," Trina snarled back. "College guys are so much more mature."

Marnie rolled her eyes at that one while I couldn't help but smirk.

What would her sister say about the college guy she was with right now? I'd moved my last year to online courses, but I was still technically a student.

"I just got a beautiful bouquet of flowers that no guy back home would've sent."

Why would they waste their time when she gave the milk away for free?

"There was no name, though, just an ace of spades. But tracking him down could be fun. It's been a while since I had a secret admirer."

My eyes snapped up to the phone. Did she say ace of spades?

Marnie's glare narrowed on me. "Secret admirers are creepy."

She had no idea.

"I wasn't secret," I whispered back.

Mr. Ace of Spades, however...I couldn't say what he would do. I'd have to know what his endgame was for that. Everyone assumed Ned Callaghan was responsible for the death of my brother's nanny. I knew better. It wasn't people like Ned that left calling cards to mark their kills. It was people like me.

At first, I thought it had something to do with Nikolai. Lana was his only child, and the Bratva life wasn't safe. Trina didn't have shit to do with the mob, Russian or otherwise. Nor did she have a connection to The Order beyond being friends with Riley and Shelby. Meaning one of two things...

Mr. Ace of Spades had a bone to pick with my family or *me*. The mystery flowers leaned more toward the *me* option. Couldn't help but laugh at that.

The dumb fuck went for the wrong twin.

Maybe he'd take care of my Trina problem for me. It seemed like a win, win situation. I could fuck Marnie while her sister was gutted, and she could blame me for shit. Now there was a thought that got me hard.

I tore the towel off my waist. "Say goodbye, Little Bird."

And thank you, Mr. Ace of Spades.

Chapter 19
Marnie

TWO DAYS LATER:

I couldn't breathe or see beyond the wall of muscle surrounding me.

"No more…please."

Preston grabbed my thigh and lifted my limp leg. "I love it when you beg."

When he plowed into me, I wanted to cry. Exhaustion came hours ago, or Or maybe it was days? I didn't know anything beyond the way he felt inside me. That was all I'd gotten since I talked to Trina. Sex, sex, and more sex. Was I still my own person, or had we become one?

"I told you I was going to break this pussy in."

That he did, and I'd never take one of his threats causally again.

Desperate, I whimpered, "I need to sleep."

"You'll sleep when I fucking say you can sleep."

Chapter 20
Preston

FIVE DAYS LATER

I eyed the silver tray on the island. Everything looked good. Melon balls on the far right side, hashbrowns on the left, and the omelet centered at the top, but something was missing. Garnish maybe?

Reaching over to my right, I plucked a sprig of parsley off a potted plant and then dropped it on the omelet.

Perfect.

Cooking wasn't a skill people expected someone like me to have. As Micha would say, we have staff for that. That was the only thing Riley Adams and I had in common. She didn't like being waited on either, though I think it was more of a pride thing for her.

I simply didn't like people and never invited them into my personal space. Unless, of course, there were other reasons for bringing them here. Despite valid reasons, Tico taking over one of my suites was still agitating.

Little prick insisted on having some paintings from a local café. Insisted might be a little strong. He kept whining about them. So I broke in and took them. Now, I barely recognized that room. Would he cry if I burned them? That might be an interesting theory to test later. Maybe it would calm his ass down. I was tired of dodging shit he threw every time I went in there.

"I want to see Marnie."

We all wanted shit. Life was full of disappointments. He should be comforted by the knowledge that she was still alive. That was more than a lot of girls could say.

Why was she alive?

The past week was nothing but one long fuck fest. One would think she'd be out of my system by now. I should be bored, not getting excited every time I thought about her chained to my bed. Yet here I was, cooking her fucking breakfast with a goddamn hard-on. This shit was annoying.

Obsession didn't even begin to explain it.

I couldn't go five minutes without her bright eyes invading my thoughts. The air felt empty when she wasn't around. Food tasted bland, and sounds were muffled. Except for the thrumming in my chest—that pulled me toward the room she was locked in—the world without her was empty.

That was a new fucked up feeling. Half of my existence was empty. I didn't know what guilt or regret felt like and couldn't even explain it to someone. I didn't feel bad about anything—including the shit I'd done to her. Yet I wanted—no needed—to be around her.

Gotta say I didn't see that one coming. Never thought I'd be that guy. Then again, I never thought I was the type to take a contract out. When the time came to have an heir, I figured I'd take some bitch, knock her up, and bury her in the garden after the baby was born. Then Marnie Dupire came along.

The look on her old man's face when he walked into the church that night was fucking priceless...

· · ·

BASIC, was all I could think as my eyes swung from a simple wooden desk to the fake tree in the corner. Given the Pastor's ability to suck money from his flock, I expected more. Maybe a nice leather chair or paintings on the wall. A wrangled child's fingerpainting would be an upgrade to that peeling wallpaper. But I imagine that would dip into his 'hobby' fund.

Did his wife know about his extracurricular activities? He didn't have any pictures of her. There were pictures of Trina everywhere, but not a single one of his wife. Interesting. Maybe he had a hard time looking at her. Guilt was a bitch, or so I'd been told.

I strolled over to the desk and picked up the wooden frame beside a large black bible. The little girl smiling back at me wasn't anything like the teenager I'd been stalking. There was a sparkle in her eyes that wasn't there anymore.

My sweet Marnie. She looked so happy here.

"Who hurt you, Little Bird?" I whispered while swiping my thumb over her smile.

Someone took something from her. I knew what that looked like. Ava used to smile like this too. Marnie wasn't as broken as my sister, but she was definitely cracked. And not because of her father. His 'special treatment' seemed to be reserved for her sister. Or at least it had better be.

My ears twitched at the sound of footsteps echoing down the hall.

Right on time. Jacques Dupire was a creature of habit. Mondays were for errands. Tuesdays were yard work. On Wednesdays, he planned his next sermon and, at midnight, came here for a meeting. But his meeting tonight wouldn't be coming.

Sitting down on the edge of the good Pastor's desk, I crossed my ankles and waited.

"The door was unlocked, Gina. How many times do I–"

The words stopped the second the door swung open.

Jacques's mouth hung open as his face screwed up in confusion.

"Gina's not here," I said while sliding the picture out of the frame.

Jacques didn't seem phased by my presence. He took a second to dart his eyes around the room—probably looking for his 'meeting'—before taking a step forward.

"Why are you here? And where is Gina?"

"She's in my trunk." I took one last look at my Bird's happy face, then tucked the picture in my jacket pocket. "But don't worry, I made sure she prayed before I cut her throat."

"That's mine," he growled, without so much as flinching at my confession.

Not surprising, I suppose. My closet was full of skeletons, but the good Pastor's would make Ryker Hudson jealous.

Sighing, I rolled my eyes up to his. "You're awfully demanding."

"This is my church, son." He marched forward and held out his hand. "I'll take my picture back."

"It's not yours." Marnie was mine. "And neither is this church. The town owns this building, and I own the town, so I guess it's my church."

While I appreciated the irony of that statement, Jacques did not.

He let out a huff and crossed his arms. "This is a holy place, and I won't have you defiling it."

"Is that what you tell your daughter when you bring her here?"

For the first time, I saw concern in his expression. "What did Trina do?"

"I don't give a fuck what Trina does or what you do with her."

That got him. His throat bobbed as his eyes widened. "I don't have much money."

This idiot thought I was here to blackmail him? Well, I guess he wasn't too far off.

"I don't want your money." Nor did I need it.

"What do you want?"

I looked him dead in the eyes, "I want your daughter...."

AND SHE WAS DEFINITELY his daughter. Marnie had the same calm, cool demeanor as her father.

A vase flew past my head when I opened the door and smashed against the wall.

Well, maybe not quite the same.

"You can't keep me chained to this bed forever!"

I begged to differ. "The cage is always an option."

The look she gave me was all the answer I needed. Solitary confinement wasn't all it was cracked up to be. It didn't take much to turn someone's mind against them. Their thoughts would eat them alive every single time.

"I brought you some food."

"I'm not hungry," she snarled back.

"I didn't ask if you were hungry." Nor did I care for the attitude.

Marnie sighed and rubbed her hands over her arms. "I'm cold."

"I don't care."

She was sitting on a bed full of blankets. I wasn't giving her any more clothes to wear. My jaw was already tensed at the thin gray spaghetti straps wrapped around her shoulders. Whoever said all the fun was in unwrapping the present was a fucking idiot. Don't get me wrong, I liked how that tank top hugged her waist and how her ass looked in those gray yoga pants, but I preferred how she looked out of them.

I placed the tray on the edge of my bed and grumbled, "Just be glad I allowed you to get dressed."

"I'm not sure throwing a handful of clothes at me and saying put this shit on constitutes allowing." Her eyes rolled, causing my hand to twitch.

I warned her about that shit. She could scream and hit me all she liked—I enjoyed the challenge—but disrespect was something I would not stand for.

I'd let it go this time. Only because I knew what punishment would lead to, and she needed a break. I probably should've stopped fucking her days ago, but that was what lube was invented for.

Seven days I spent deep inside the greatest pussy ever born. Didn't even stop when she passed out. I did pause our marathon a couple of times so we could eat. Stamina was not my Bird's forte, but we'd get there.

Marnie's aqua eyes fell on the tray. "Where did you order this from?"

"I made it."

Skepticism tugged on her brow. "You made this?"

"Yes." It wasn't anything special, just a ham and cheese omelet with dill and garlic hashbrowns, balled melon, and a strawberry muffin.

"All of it?"

"Yes." Everything except the muffin. Someone else baked that.

She eyed the food and then looked back at me. "Is it drugged?"

Really? "I think we're past that part of our relationship, don't you?"

"This is hardly a relationship."

I snorted. "That's a great attitude to have when you have two weeks left on Micha's deadline. You must not like your sister that much."

Micha's threat wasn't needed. That didn't mean I wouldn't use it. Whenever I brought up her sister, Marnie's eyes would round as an enticing spark of panic flashed across her face. I got hard just thinking about it.

"Fine." She slammed her fist down on the mattress and shifted to the left. But it was the small wince I noticed that made the corner of my mouth curl. "I'll eat your stupid food, though a table and chair would be much more efficient."

Nice try.

"So would no clothes, but you don't hear me complaining."

Honestly, I gave that outfit three hours tops before it was shredded.

I should've left her clothes in her dorm room. Ah, well, it was done now, and I did enjoy going through her personal effects. She'd been sticking her nose in places where it didn't belong. If Lou knew what she had on her laptop...

"Be good, Little Bird." I gave her a small wave and turned to walk out.

"You're leaving me alone...In here?"

"I have dishes to do." How much trouble could she possibly get into?

This was my bedroom. Yes, there were weapons in here, and some were within reach of her chained ankle, but I liked having Marnie on my bed.

"What if I find something?"

The cocky clip in her tone had me tempted to say fuck it and tear those clothes off her.

Instead, I glanced over my shoulder and shot her a wicked smirk. "Remember what happened last time?"

Her face paled while my cock jumped.

Seeing her come at me with that knife was the single most erotic moment of my life. Unfortunately for her, Marnie's hand-eye coordination was shit. It took three seconds to disarm her, and she didn't even manage to scratch me. It was a tad disappointing. Some self-defense lessons might be in order.

"Are you going to watch me eat too?"

"Maybe." I'd like to slide something else between those lips.

The little minx was too good at reading my cues. I don't know what was hotter. That she knew me well enough to push my buttons or the way she sucked a melon ball out of her fingers.

"Mmmm, that's so good. You want to feed me the next one?" She even leaned forward and parted her lips.

Careful, Little Bird, you shouldn't poke the bear.

"In case you haven't figured it out yet, I like teeth play."

That dropped the seductive look off her face.

Marnie snapped her mouth shut and sat back to glare at me.

I needed to get out of here before the flush crawling across her chest led to another seven-day marathon.

"Eat your fucking food," I growled and walked out before I could change my mind.

The dishes didn't take long enough, so I occupied myself cleaning the kitchen.

Why not give my Bird more time to find something fun to play with? There was a reason I left two knives and a paddle in the top drawer of the bedside table. I didn't even turn on the camera to spy on her. The unknown would be a nice change.

It would also give me a chance to test my skills. Since Marnie got here, I'd been neglecting my workout routine. Though one could argue I still got plenty of exercise.

The surprise I got when I finished cleaning wasn't Marnie lunging at me with a weapon in hand. It was the doorbell.

God damnit. When did my house become Grand Central Station?

Grumbling, I dropped my cloth on the counter and headed for the door.

My first thought was that Micha had come for an update, which I was prepared to answer by slamming the door in his face.

But it wasn't a pair of dark eyes I was met with. It was an annoyingly chipper smile.

Fuck my life.

"Hey, son." My dad slapped his hand down on my shoulder. "The place looks good."

Pointing out that he hadn't been inside yet, seemed kind of moot when he pushed past me.

"I'm busy."

Was it too much to hope he'd take my cue and leave?

"These are nice." He tapped his foot on the floor as if he didn't hear a thing I said. "Walnut would look better."

"I'll keep that in mind." Did he come here to give me home decorating tips or waste my time? I had shit to do.

My answer came when my old man looked around and tapped his chin. "You need a darker marble slab for that island."

Waste my time, got it.

Muttering under my breath, I scrubbed a hand down my face and shut the door.

"You should probably have that oven inspected." He promptly waltzed over to stick his head in my brick pizza oven. "Gas leaks are tricky business."

I turn it on...

Parker couldn't get mad about that. Oops, my shoulder must've hit the button. Why he kept his head in there long enough to burn to death might be hard to explain.

"Are you sure you connected everything properly?"

Yes, but I would have to do it again if he kept tapping around in there.

"Is there a point to this unwanted visit?"

With his head still in the oven, my old man wagged his finger and tsked. "Now, now, son, all visits from parents are unwanted. Harassing our children is in the job description."

Sometimes I swore he took the role of dad too seriously. When I sprained my ankle, he insisted I go to the doctor, which would've been fine if it happened when I was ten and not last month.

"See, look at that. You've got something stuck back here."

That would be hard to do, considering I had yet to use the thing.

Why couldn't he bother Ava?

"I knew it." He popped out of the oven and held up a small pipe. "It's a good thing I found this."

Yeah, he found it alright, attached to the other pipes where it was supposed to be.

His eyes lit up as a smile spread across his face. "What would you do without me?"

Live a happy, less annoying life?

"That's great, Dad. Thanks for the help, and feel free to leave anytime."

"Are you trying to get rid of me?"

Yes, yes, I was.

My brow arched as he propped his elbows on the island and dropped his chin in his palms. "One might think you were trying to hide something from me."

I was hiding many things from him. If only I could figure out how to hide myself.

"You have soot on your face." There was a big smear across his left cheek. It looked a bit like a bird's wing.

What is she doing right now?

If my father weren't here, I'd know because I'd be in there instead of out here.

"Don't worry about that." My old man waved his hand dismissively. "I want to know what's new with you."

My eyes narrowed. I didn't like that stupid grin on his face. It made me want to bash his head in.

"Come on. There has to be something. Maybe you got a new TV, took a trip, oooor…Maybe you met someone?"

Son of a bitch.

My face dropped. "You talked to Micha?"

Micha just made it to the top of the list for head-bashing. Looked like Riley would be a widow before the wedding. Too bad.

"Logan may have mentioned something...."

Alright, Logan, it was. Prick would probably like it too.

"Though Micha did say you had a date for the wedding."

"Uh-huh." That was it. I was killing them both.

"When do I get to meet this cute little thing Logan was talking about."

Right after I removed Logan's balls. "She's a little tied up at the moment."

"Oh...Well, where did you meet her? What's her name? Is she nice? Do I hear possible wedding bells..."

He wouldn't stop until I gave him something, so I barked out, "Her name is Marnie, and if you shut the fuck up, I'll bring her to dinner tomorrow."

Shit.

The smile on my old man's face grew as I silently cursed myself.

Why the hell would I ever suggest some dumb shit like that? This was all Parker's fault. He had to up and move to Boston all because his wife got into Harvard, leaving me to deal with this shit instead of him. If we ended up orphans, he'd have no one to blame but himself.

My eyes slid over to the knife block on the left side of the island.

"Great." My old man clapped. "Your brother and sister will be so excited."

What? Ava, I could see. Miami was close enough to drive. But... "Why the fuck is Parker coming home?"

If Lana hurt him...

"I don't know, something to do with the wedding."

Oh, right. I forgot about that.

So now I not only subjected Marnie to a night with my father but my entire family. Fucking great. Oh well. I suppose we could look at it like a practice run—time to see how good of an actress my Little Bird was.

An alarm went off on my phone, reminding me of another problem. One that my old man could possibly help with, and it would get him out of my hair.

"Hey." I tipped my chin. "You busy today?"

He shook his head. "Why? What's up?"

"I got someone in the west wing who's a little lonely."

The little lonely part was a slight exaggeration. Tico's mood was more along the lines of fucking pissed. The last time I went in there, he kicked the TV over after demanding to see Marnie again. I had to slap him around a bit. A good hard fuck might knock some calm back into him. And my old man seemed intrigued, at least.

The curl in his mouth deepened. "Oh, yeah. Well, why don't you introduce me to this friend."

I didn't say, friend. "He's down the hall, third door on the left."

That was all he needed to hear.

My old man pushed off the island and skipped away like a kid on Christmas morning.

"The code is 1117." Lindsay's birthday.

Next thing I knew, I heard a loud crash followed by Tico's voice. "Oh, hello, sir."

"Sir? I like it. Keep calling me that," my old man said before closing the door.

I'd never been happier for soundproofing in my life.

Chapter 21

Marnie

The definition of suffocation was: the state or process of dying from being deprived of air or unable to breathe. Or a feeling of being trapped and oppressed. Both of which applied to my current state of mind. I wasn't living in a cage anymore, but the bars were still around me. Each breath I took tasted more stagnant than the last.

Don't get me wrong, compared to my other accommodations, Preston's room was an improvement. Or at least I assumed it was his room based on the familiar jean jacket draped over a black armchair, but that was the problem. That denim material sat across the room, mocking me.

Every time light glinted off one of those silver buttons, my stomach would churn. I couldn't explain why my teeth gritted whenever I looked at it. The jacket never bothered me before, but the longer I sat here, the more I hated it.

If I weren't trapped on this bed, I would've destroyed it. I told myself it was because Preston was attached to it, but it was more than that. There was something nauseatingly familiar, and I just couldn't put my finger on it. I'd been wracking my brain trying to figure it out. Had I seen that jacket before? Perhaps in a movie, I didn't care for or on someone I didn't like besides the obvious choice.

Fashion wasn't my thing, but that jacket...I loathed its very existence. The why was driving me crazy, which was precisely why I occupied myself with other things. Like snooping around Preston's room.

My chained foot restricted my free reign. That didn't stop me from inspecting what I couldn't reach. The furniture was about what I expected, based on the rest of the house: a big California king bed with silky sheets and blankets, chair, desk, laptop, and a flatscreen hung up on the far side that was perpetually playing an infomercial. For only three easy payments of $99.95, I could get a knife that cut through a soda can. Personally, I'd choose the twenty-dollar department store version, but hey, to each their own.

The color scheme was a little different. Unlike the neutral tones I'd seen in the rest of the place, this room was flooded with dark hues. Mostly navy and black, which seemed fitting given who slept in here, though I did admire the little decorative touches. Like the slight splashes of brighter colors on pillows and throw blankets. My favorite was the cream chair rail cutting across the center of the navy wall. It was so intricately carved in the shape of an ivy vine that I could see the veins on each individual leaf.

Yet the closet was full of regular clothes that could be bought at any department store. Preston Whitley was a conundrum that I didn't understand. There were no staff in the house or people to take care of things like yard work and cooking. All of that he did himself. I knew this because I watched him for years, and not once did I see someone other than delivery people come to this place.

Even the giant terrarium taking up the entire right wall confused me. It was clear and clean, filled with plants, rocks, and a little pond in the left corner. Who cleaned that, and what was it for? At first, I thought maybe the plants were unique.

Then a tiny green head poked out of a plant as a turtle charged the glass. And I meant charged. He or she came bursting out and slammed against the pane with so much force that I cringed. And he didn't stop there. His mouth continued to snap while he tried to get out.

I decided to ignore it and search through Preston's drawers. Most of the contents were mundane things like magazines and small bottles. I didn't want to think about what I found in the bottom drawer, but Bubba, the purple dildo, no longer seemed threatening. I did find two knives, one of which I tucked under a pillow for future use.

Afterward, I sat back on the bed, intent on waiting for my captor's return. What happened was a stare-down with a turtle. At first glance, the creature was cute. Stumpy legs, a colorful shell, and a tiny little body that could probably fit in the palm of my hand. It was the attitude that sucked.

The instant my eyes were on the turtle, it started throwing itself at the terrarium again. As if it thought it could break through. Animals with rabies had a better disposition than that thing.

"You know, vicious animals are usually put down."

It answered me by snapping at the glass.

"What exactly are you trying to accomplish? You're not getting through that glass, and you're way too small to do any permanent damage, so you're just wasting your time."

The stumpy feet started slowly backing up, and for half a second, I thought it would retreat into its plants. Then it took off, running full force into the glass.

"So, you're just an asshole then?" *Got it.*

The turtle's head tipped, and I swear I saw those beady little eyes narrow. Leave it to Preston to find the only sociopathic turtle on the planet. Then again, I was talking to a turtle...so who was the crazy one?

"You're losing your mind, Marnie."

Apparently, sanity wasn't the only thing that abandoned me. Luck decided to smack me in the face as well when the door opened just as I spoke.

The turtle was no longer my main focus, though I noticed it didn't calm down any when its supposed owner walked in.

"Don't fret, Little Bird, you're faring better than most."

"Fantastic," I muttered back at Preston as he strutted over to the dresser in the corner. "I'll keep that in mind the next time you rape me."

"Rape implies not wanting it."

"I didn't want it!" And I sure as hell wasn't thinking about what was under that shirt or shifting because I was suddenly hot and uncomfortable.

His gray eyes slid my way. "Do you always moan that loud for things you don't want?"

"The body's desires don't equate to the mind's." That didn't prove anything.

Anyone could make a girl orgasm if they knew what they were doing. And unfortunately for me, Preston did. I couldn't help but wonder if I could do the same. If I learned what got him off, could I turn his sick game around on him? Was that something I wanted to do? That would require me touching him and, even worse, letting him touch me.

My eyes traced down Preston's back to the fabric hugging his ass. He did look good in those jeans. It pissed me off how good he looked. What right did he have to be all dark and broody with sculpted muscles I could see pressing against his shirt? Asshole. I could look good too. Wait...since when was I concerned with my appearance?

Screw that. I was going to embrace the troll look. From this point on, hairbrushes were no longer a thing. And showers were definitely off the table. Except for at night before bed. Germs were real. But brushes...those were totally gone.

My head tilted to the side as Preston's forearm flexed when he reached out to grab something. I wasn't sure what he grabbed. Wasn't sure I cared either.

Was it always this hot in here?

"You're gawking, Little Bird. Are you looking for attention?"

No! And I wasn't gawking. Just because I watched how his shoulders firmed when he moved his arms didn't mean anything. I was studying him.

"It's good to know one's enemy."

"Is that so?"

I didn't like the underlying gravelly tone in his voice or the glint in his eyes when he spun around and stalked across the room.

"Tell me, Marnie." Preston stopped at the side of the bed and looked down at me. "What has that beautiful brain of yours told you about me?"

Why would I answer that? I wasn't going to give him tips or a forewarning of my plans. And I had a few. Most of which depended on him doing something specific—like falling asleep on the bed next to me while I had a weapon.

"I'm not giving my secrets away."

Preston's palms hit the bed, making me jump back. "I already know all your secrets."

"I highly doubt that." If he had any idea of the information I had, I wouldn't be breathing right now. Louis Kessler would've told him to put a bullet in my head.

Preston snorted. "You think I haven't been through your room or hacked your laptop?"

Fear lumped up in my throat. If he found my hidden files, then...

"That's a nice little collection of videos you have."

Shit.

That nice little collection was more than enough to sign my death warrant. So why hadn't he used it?

"What did you do with them?"

"Nothing." The chain around my ankle prevented me from moving away when he crawled onto the mattress. "Lou wouldn't be too happy."

Attempting to keep some distance between us, I pressed my back against the headboard. "Are you going to tell him?"

"No."

That confused me more than anything else he'd done. The Order Of Ravens and Wolves was built like any other corporation. While there were numerous employees and managers, there was always someone on top. In this case, it was Louis Kessler. Unless I was wrong?

"Isn't he your leader?"

"You know me, Marnie." He leaned in to growl softly, "Do you really think I take orders from anyone?"

A nervous swallow bobbed down my throat. No, no, I didn't.

"What about Micha?"

Did I need to take his threat seriously or worry about something worse?

"Let's not talk about Micha." Preston buried his nose in my neck and let out a groan that rumbled through me. "I already want to kill him. Now take your pants off."

My pussy ached at the thought of being touched. I was exhausted, sore, and wanted to be left alone for just one day. At least, that was what I told myself when Preston grabbed my hip, and tingles shot up my leg.

I needed to change the subject and divert his attention.

"Maybe I want to talk about Micha." I didn't, but Preston did say he wanted to kill him, so...

I knew my plan backfired the second Preston's mouth tipped up.

"I know what you're doing, sneaky Little Bird." He tsked, then grazed his lips against mine. "You can't hide from me."

The underlying meaning was so disturbing that I shivered.

Preston wasn't talking about things I'd done or planned to do. The hide in this scenario referred to me and who I was at my core, which was truly terrifying.

I'd never felt more seen than I did around him. My body could be covered in yards of fabric, and I'd still feel naked. That was the purpose of my glasses.

I didn't realize how much I needed them until now. Nor did I notice my hand move up to my temple until the corner of Preston's brow rose.

"Missing something?"

Asshole.

I gritted my teeth and hissed, "I'm fine."

"No, you're not."

My breath hitched as his hand slid up my side. One touch was all it took to make my body hum. The heat from his palm soaked through my shirt and flowed into my chest, where it became a white-hot flame of self-hatred.

'Desire is the fruit of all sin.'

No matter how many times I tried to rid myself of my father's infernal voice, it was always there—reminding me to be the righteous daughter he expected. But I wasn't righteous, and neither was he. Righteous people didn't beat their children. They didn't steal money from their church or manipulate their flock under the guise of religion. They didn't cheat on their wives. They looked at them like...

Like how Preston looked at me.

My brows knit as I searched the glint hidden deep in his eyes.

There was no way I saw what I thought I did. It simply wasn't possible. Preston Whitley wasn't capable of love and compassion. *Was he?*

He seemed to care about his brother. We may not have gone to the same school, but we grew up in the same town. No one messed with Parker, not on playdates, in school, or on the playground. The whispered threats traveling from kid to kid were enough to stop that.

Trina looked out for me the same way. While bullies taunted Riley, I was left alone because my sister threatened anyone who bothered me.

And now it was my turn to protect her.

"Will Micha really hurt Trina?"

It was a valid question. He was marrying our friend. Would he hurt her like that? Not that she would ever know it was him, but still. His love for Riley was something I never questioned. It was his moral standing I had a problem with.

Any hope of that being a fake threat died with one word.

"Yes."

That was that. It was me against them. Somehow I always knew this day would come. I never thought the stakes would be so high, though. My death I could live with, but Trina was innocent in all of this.

"I'll never give you what you want." I don't know why I said that.

Despite everything, I still hoped I could get Preston to listen to reason. Or maybe I was trying to reason with myself because some part of me felt...free.

For the first time in my life, I wasn't pretending to be someone else. Even my sister believed I was that meek little girl with glasses and a notebook. But not Preston. He saw past all my guises.

With a sharp exhale, Preston backed away and sat down next to my legs. "I admire your spirit Marnie, but you need to accept the loss. You can't win this fight."

"I disagree." He may have turned my body against me, but my mind remained intact. That he'd never break. All it took was one moment, and the tables would be turned.

"All right." His lips pursed together as he nodded. "I'm going to show you something."

My heart practically leaped out of my chest when he pulled a key out of his pocket and unlocked my ankle cuff. Automatically my eyes swung to the door as I calculated the probability of me making the distance before him.

"Go for it." Preston challenged. "You won't get far."

Like it or not, he was right.

Damn him and his superior build. I needed to start an exercise regimen.

"I could still try."

"You could." He nodded. "And who knows, maybe you'll luck out... but would you make it to your sister in time?"

My stomach dropped.

That was one thing I hadn't taken into account. If I ran, then Trina would be in danger, and that was too much of a risk. I'd have to make sure she was safe before I did anything.

Without another word, Preston got off the bed and held out his hand.

Resigned to my fate—for now—I sighed and placed my palm in his.

He pulled me out of the room and around a corner. I took in everything I could, placements of possible exits, where stairs and doors were, how many turns we took, and hiding places. All of it was tucked in the back of my mind for future use.

Then he opened a door, and I no longer cared about collecting information.

A whoosh of cold air and a darkened stairwell into the ground instantly brought me back to every horror movie I'd ever seen. The wooden steps even creaked as we walked down them. But it was the faint sound of music that sent a chill up my spine. Someone was down in this dark stone pit of misery.

The further we descended, the more my situation didn't seem so bad. I at least had comfort and warmth. All that was down here was a cold earthy scent draped in desperation and death.

"What is this place," I asked while looking at the sconces on the walls.

"This is where I come to relax."

"Relax?" This was hardly the place for that.

"Some people go for a walk, others paint. I come down here."

"And do what?" Why did I ask that? I didn't want to know. Then again, maybe I did.

"Piss me off, and you'll find out."

That was comforting.

What does one use a dungeon for these days anyway? That was what I'd call this place. The Dungeon of Death. All dank and sad, with no natural light or fresh air. Why would anyone need something like this? It was one thing to kill someone, but this was a whole other level of demented.

I had no idea how true that thought was until Preston typed a code into a pad, opening a door on the right.

My jaw dropped to my feet. Metaphorically, of course.

The room itself was basic. A little outdated—the couch, TV, table, and carpet were all fifties style. It was the woman in a blue floral print dress that shocked me. Her pleated skirt flowed as her blue high heels clicked off the floor.

I was so stunned that all I could get out was a quiet, "Lillianna?"

Her red-painted lips twisted into a large smile that didn't reach her eyes. "Preston, you brought a friend."

That happy, chipper tone was so out of character for the Lillianna Whitley I knew. Happiness didn't exist in her world. She was the cause of misery for so many people in this town. Riley and her mother, Tico, and even Lana Crawford, who married her son, weren't beyond her wrath. I once heard her call Riley's dad a traitor because he married a woman from Mexico.

That was Lillianna Whitley. An arrogant, self-absorbed, bigoted bitch that deserved all the miseries hell had to offer. Yet here she was with a frilly apron tied around her waist and a bun in her blonde hair. I couldn't stop staring at her.

I barely heard Preston say, "This is Marnie."

"You two are just in time. I made cookies." She sang in a sweet tone that further confused me.

Sweet was not a word to describe Lillianna Whitley. I don't think I'd ever seen her smile, let alone dance over to a cookie jar in the corner. What the hell was happening? She'd clearly been through something. Two of the fingers on her right hand were gone, so was her left ear, and she had a large scar curling up from the corner of her mouth to her forehead. Yet her eyes shone brightly.

"I thought she was dead." She looked pretty good for a dead person.

"She is."

He was not going to make me question my sanity this way. His mother was not a hallucination. Anyone could see her. "She's right there, Preston."

"But is she?"

What the hell was that supposed to mean?

"Look at her, happy as a clam baking shit." He leaned in and added, "Could you see my mother doing something like that?"

Well...no. But the evidence stated otherwise.

"Death isn't the worst thing that can happen to someone. Isn't that right, Lillianna?"

"That's right, dear." With the smile still on her face, Lillianna twirled around and set a plate of cookies on a small table. I watched her stare at the plate as if searching for something, then jumped back when she clapped her hands. "Milk! You can't have cookies without milk."

"That's not your mother." That much I was sure of.

"No," Preston agreed. "That's Ava's mother."

Preston walked over and placed his hands on the table to lean down and look into his mother's eyes.

"Mine's still in there somewhere, screaming to get out. Aren't you, you fucking cunt."

Lillianna didn't say anything. She just stood there smiling like a robot. It was eerie, to say the least. "What did you do to her?"

My blood ran cold when Preston gazed over at a small table, and sitting on the top was a long, skinny, silver spike. The same tool that was used to—

"You lobotomized your mother!"

"It's surprisingly easy to do. Slip it in behind the eye, a quick pop later, and you have someone entirely complacent."

The disturbing aura in the room became suffocating when his head tipped toward me.

"One way or another, you'll give me exactly what I want, Little bird. How that happens is completely up to you."

Chapter 22

Marnie

A heavy sigh came from the driver's side as Preston glared out the windshield. Personally, I was happy to be outside. I almost forgot how warm and rejuvenating the sun felt. There was no doubt in my mind that I was smiling like an idiot, and I didn't care one bit. The only thing that ruined my mood was the object in my ass.

When Preston forced me to bend over before we left, having some cone-shaped metal plug shoved in my ass was not what I expected. He claimed he was doing me a favor, yet he was the only one impressed with his sick, demented task.

The bastard had the gall to say how pretty the pink diamond looked with my complexion. Trina had countless necklaces, bracelets, and other trinkets given to her, and my first piece of jewelry from a boy was lodged in my rectum. How was that for irony?

I glared at Preston, who was staring out the windshield at his father's house, and muttered, "I hate you."

"Good for you," he grumbled back without glancing my way.

Asshole. "I should shove something in his ass."

"Wouldn't be the first time."

Crap, did I say that out loud? And what did he mean by it wouldn't be the first time? "Do you...like...guys, too?"

Parker did, and I'd heard stories about Dean, so that wouldn't be entirely unexpected.

"No, I fucked a few, though."

"But..." My face screwed up as I shifted to a more comfortable position. "If you don't like guys like that, why would you...."

"You know a better way to emasculate someone?"

My jaw dropped. He did that to someone for no other reason than a power trip? "How does that even work? If you're not attracted to someone, then—"

"It's a dick, Marnie." He cut me off. "Not rocket science. Touch the fucking thing, and it'll get hard."

"Well, how the hell am I supposed to know how a dick works," I growled back. "I don't have one."

"Not true, you have mine."

That was the most ridiculous thing I'd ever heard. "I hate to inform you of this, but your dick is attached to you. Hence, it can't be mine."

"Don't play dumb. It doesn't suit you. You know what I mean."

One might assume he meant metaphorically, but I was feeling argumentative. Perhaps because of the thing shoved in my ass.

"All I'm saying is a part of someone else's body is not only impossible to own but highly illegal. Aaaaand," I drawled out in the snarkiest tone I could muster. "I don't want your penis."

"I don't give a fuck what you want!"

Someone was angry, and he could join the club.

The scowl on his face was satisfying until he grabbed my neck and yanked me over the console.

"Every fucking hole you have is mine. If anyone thinks about touching you, I'll gut them alive."

I swallowed my pride and didn't say a thing.

Preston glared at me for a few seconds, then shoved me back in the passenger seat.

"I assume the same goes for you and my dick."

I should've stayed quiet. He was teetering on the edge, and that dark cloud was creeping across his face. Every fiber of my being screamed at me to shut the hell up. My mouth didn't listen.

"What if it's another girl?"

His eyes snapped back to mine. "What?"

Don't say it.

"What if it's another girl touching me?"

You said it. Congratulations. This is how you die.

To my surprise, Preston didn't appear agitated. The darkness even lifted off his expression a bit when his brow arched. "Do you want to play with another girl?"

I didn't want to play with him. Why on earth would I subject another woman to that? Some girls liked the rough stuff, and I did mention it, so I must've, at the very least, thought about it. What would it be like? Would a woman be soft where a man was hard?

Stop it, Marnie. You're letting him distract you.

Right!

"No," I scoffed. "Why would I want that?"

"Then why did you say it?"

My eyes narrowed. "Shouldn't we go inside?"

Annoyance instantly washed back over his face.

I'd ask Preston why he bothered to come if he didn't want to, but then I might end up locked inside again. I was already past my limits. Besides, anything was better than being trapped on a bed again, which was where he took me after we had cookies with his mother.

That was the most fucked up night of my life.

Never thought I'd be sitting in a room with fifties housewife Lillianna Whitley discussing the calcium content of milk. Though her entire argument was that kids needed milk for strong bones. That was it. No explanation. Just kids need milk. I almost felt sorry for her and utterly terrified that the same would happen to me.

I couldn't help myself, let alone my sister, if my mind was gone. If something did happen to Trina, I'd probably never know. Or worse, I would but would just continue baking cookies with a smile on my face.

239

Suddenly everything I did mattered. Should I play sweet or just fall asleep on the bed while silently thanking my luck that Preston didn't join me? That was what I did last night. Should I complain about this thing lodged in my backdoor? What would push him past that point?

The unknown picked at the back of my brain. I needed guidance.

Sucking in a deep breath, I forced a smile and said, "We shouldn't make them wait."

I felt the anger when Preston's head rolled back my way. "Don't do that."

"Don't do what?"

"Don't placate me."

Frustrated, I threw my hands up. "Well, what the hell do you want me to do then?"

Give me some direction!

"I want you to be yourself."

Myself? Really? That was the direction he was going with?

"You want me to stab you in the eye with that pencil?"

I'd been watching it roll around on his dash and wanted nothing more than to reach out and grab it. It was right there, just waiting to be used.

"Yes!" Preston barked, then scrubbed a hand down his face and sighed. "Look, you can play pretend when we're around Micha and others, but when you're with me, I want you to be exactly who you are."

Was it wrong that I found that kind of sweet?

"I don't want your fake fucking smiles."

That made my brow raise.

"Do you want any smiles?" Cause he wasn't going to get them.

His hand was in my hair, pulling me over to his side of the car before I could blink. My arm swung as a burn tore across my scalp.

"Let me go!"

The really fucked up part came when he sat me on his lap, and my core clenched.

"How's that butt plug?"

My face dropped. "Great, I can't wait to shove something up your ass."

Preston opened his mouth to say something but was cut off when the front door was thrown open.

Ava Whitley came rushing outside with what looked like a flipper in her hand. I cocked my head as she started smacking a thick tree trunk like she was trying to chop it down.

"What the hell is she doing?" Preston grumbled.

I shrugged. Who knew? It wasn't the strangest thing I'd seen her do.

"Hurry, get inside," she yelled over her shoulder. "I can't hold it back much longer."

Okay, that was pretty strange.

"Is she talking to us?"

Preston let out a breath and shook his head. "Don't eat the cookies."

The word cookies never sounded more ominous. I wasn't about to ask. I didn't even want to think about what that statement meant. But I sure as hell wasn't touching anything baked in that house. I may give up baked goods altogether.

Things didn't get better when we went inside.

I barely made one step through the door before I was engulfed by a pair of arms and smashed into the solid chest of Dean Whitley.

"Logan was right. You are cute."

Great, Logan Hudson referred to me as cute. All my dreams had come true, and I could die any time now.

"You found a good one, son."

Dean's hold tightened to the point where all I could cough out was, "Can't breathe."

And yet, he continued to hug me.

Desperate to escape, I did the only thing I could think of and carefully tapped his back. Finally, he let me go. My brief reprieve was squashed when Preston pulled me into his hold.

I went from being trapped by one Whitley to being held by another.

"Is everyone in your family this grabby?" God, I hoped not. Ava was small, but I didn't trust her. And she still had that flipper.

"It's usually just our dad." Parker sauntered around the corner and nodded at his brother. "I don't know what's up with him?"

Or at least I thought it was Parker. Preston had me tucked so far under his arm that I couldn't lift my head enough to see his face. My assumption was purely based on the white sneakers I was staring at. There was a small grass stain on the left side of the right one and what looked like a spot of blood....

Fantastic. This day just keeps getting better. Welcome to the psycho house, full of smiles and people who try to cut down trees with a flipper.

Preston snorted, "You hold Lana."

Yup, it was definitely Parker. Score one for me.

"I hold my wife," Parker scoffed. "I don't try and morph her body into mine."

"Fuck you," Preston growled but did release his hold a little.

"Fuck you too," Parker growled right back at him, after which Preston pulled him in for a hug.

Boys were weird.

Speaking of weird...

Two sparkling gray eyes came into view as Ava sang, "We can morph people into us?"

And that was when I started praying again. I closed my eyes and asked the good Lord above to save me from dining with the Manson family.

ANY OTHER FAMILY with status and money would have some five-course meal prepared by chefs. Micha had a cook, and so did Logan and even Parker. Star and I had gone over to hang out with Lana several times. She had the best homemade bread.

The Whitleys did not.

I wasn't even sure that the loaf on the table was bread. That mystery was solved when Ava proclaimed she had made it. The rest of the food, however…

I looked over at the large meatloaf shaped like a heart, then at the bowl of lumpy mashed potatoes. Beside that were a plate of baked Brussels sprouts and a large Caesar salad.

Dean apparently didn't have the same cooking skills as his son. Not only that, but everything here was baked except for the salad.

Guess what I ate.

"So." Dean cleared his throat and looked over at Preston and me. "How did you two meet?"

I could've ignored him, but Preston did say he wanted me to be myself. So I looked Dean dead in his eyes and said, "Your psycho son kidnapped me."

"Well, Preston did always know what he wanted."

Don't know why I expected anything else. This entire family was crazy. I was pretty sure I heard someone knocking on the floor earlier, but I wasn't about to ask. I didn't want to know about anything in this house, including the weird doll in the corner with a melted face.

"You kidnapped her?" Parker roared.

Okay, maybe he wasn't so bad.

"Let me guess." Preston rolled his eyes and popped a Brussels sprout in his mouth. "You have a problem with that?"

I had a problem with it.

"Yes, I have a problem," Parker bellowed. "Lana knows this girl."

That she did, and I didn't imagine she'd be too happy about this situation. It'd be a shame if she found out.

Preston sighed at the scowl on his brother's face. "And?"

"What the hell am I supposed to tell her? Lana's going to notice she's missing."

But would she? Don't get me wrong, I liked Lana, she was very sweet, but I didn't really know her. I tended to avoid conversations with her. The speed at which she talked scared me. Shelby was bad enough, but Lana…I'm still not entirely sure what she said the last time I saw her.

Preston shrugged. "Tell her what you want."

I never noticed the similarities between them until now, but Parker had the same two lines on his forehead when he was angry. And his mouth dipped down just a bit on the left side. Then there were the eyes. Preston had this glint deep down in those gray depths. The same glint I saw on Parker. It made me question his golden boy persona.

Was Parker Whitley the person people thought he was, or was he faking it just like me?

"I kidnapped someone."

The entire room went quiet as everyone stopped and turned toward Ava.

"Don't worry. I'll let him go." She rolled her eyes and returned to her plate as if she hadn't just blurted out a confession to a criminal offense. "Just as soon as he learns his lesson."

Dean and Parker dropped their faces in their hands while Preston didn't so much as cock a brow. I was intrigued. This was quite possibly the most fascinating dinner I'd ever had. It was also disturbing and wrong in every way possible, but I wasn't bored or locked in a room.

"Ava, sweetheart," Dean said while pinching the bridge of his nose. "Who did you kidnap?"

Dean not only sounded completely calm asking that, but he said it in a way that might lead one to think this wasn't her first time.

"Mr. Chang thought he could stop making spring rolls."

And the intrigue just took a violent turn into get me the fuck out of here.

Happy and smiling, Ava was dangerous. Being around her was like picking a lollipop out of a bunch when you knew half of them were poisoned. She burned down the west side of Ashworth because she got an A in chemistry. I did not want to find out what happened when she was agitated.

Preston leaned over and whispered, "You look nervous, Little bird. Do you not like my family?"

Fuck no.

"Do you like your family?" I whispered while Dean gave Ava a lecture on the errors of abduction.

"I fucking hate them."

"Then why are we here?" Why was anyone here? This was not a safe place for people.

"Eh." He shrugged. "They're family."

And what a family they were.

"Why? Are you uncomfortable?" Preston teased.

I glared at him and hissed, "I'm fine."

Why wouldn't I be fine? It wasn't like I was sitting with a man proudly wearing a dad of the year shirt while he sipped from his grandpa of the year mug and talked to his psycho kids about how spring rolls were not a valid reason for kidnapping. It wasn't as if there was a current captive dining at the table with them. But did I get any sympathy? No. All the lectures were saved for the spring roll guy.

Fuck you, Mr. Chang. I hope you choke on your spring rolls.

One text on Parker's phone caused an eruption of chaos. The next thing I knew, Preston shoved me violently away as Parker roared and flipped the table.

Chapter 23
Preston

My sister gave new meaning to the term unpredictable. Add in my old man's mysterious yearly trips to a cabin that didn't exist, and my mother's cunt proclivities and chaos reigned free. Parker was the only stable one, at least by outwardly appearances.

My little brother could pretend to be 'normal' all he wanted, but I knew better. I recognized that glint hidden deep in his eyes. And when that glint was thrust to the forefront of his mind...

My arm shot out, pushing Marnie out of danger before Parker snapped. Her chair screeched and then thudded backward on the floor as Parker's hands gripped the bottom of the table. Our dad managed to jump back while Ava stayed where she was and watched the large oak slab flip through the air like she was at a goddamn movie.

"I'll fucking kill him!" Parker picked up his chair and threw it against the wall.

Who he was going to kill didn't matter right now, nor did the text that set him off.

I lunged. Shot forward and dug my shoulder into my baby brother's chest while kicking his legs out from under him. Parker was a big boy, but this wasn't the first time I took him out. Football taught him to take a hit, so he wasn't winded when his back hit the ground, but he was down, and I wasn't giving him a chance to get back up.

"Fuck you, Preston," he snarled when I jumped on top of him. "I'll fucking kill you!"

I hissed back, "Do it."

His arm swung through the air, and I was reminded of when he was seven, and I caught him sneaking back into the house covered in blood. I didn't ask what happened while I cleaned him up because I understood the look in his eyes. Just like I understood this day would come.

I ducked under his strike and jabbed my knee into his ribs.

Parker grunted and punched me in the side with so much force that I was almost pushed off him. I gritted my teeth against the ache crawling across my ribs and clocked him in the jaw.

"That's all you got, fucking pussy."

A fraction of a second passed, yet I saw the snap in my brother's eyes. I sat on top of Parker and watched as the twinkle in his gray orbs twisted into something dark and hungry. One hand wrapped around my neck while the other landed in my gut.

"That's it, Parker." I choked through his grip, "Let it out."

Every beast needed to feed, and my baby brother starved his for far too long.

I'd never been more disappointed than I was when the agony of his actions knit his brow.

"You don't know what I just saw."

His hand dropped from my neck, and I sighed. "So show me."

Parker shook his head. "I can't look at it again."

My baby brother didn't get it. This urge that dug into the pit of our stomachs couldn't be held back. Eventually, that darkness inside of us broke out, and it didn't give a shit who was around. Parker needed a release before the only thing he'd have to return to was blood and guilt. I wouldn't let that happen, and luckily there was a time and place for everything.

I looked back to where my Bird should've been, only to see her sprinting for the door. Well, I couldn't blame her for being an opportunist.

"Someone wanna handle that?"

Go figure it would be my sister that jumped at the opportunity. And I meant that in the literal sense.

She sang, "On it." Then skip-hopped across the room like a kangaroo on steroids.

As unconventional as Ava was, her methods worked. She had Marnie back in the room in under a minute. That didn't stop my Bird from struggling against the way Ava was wrapped around her.

"It's okay," Ava soothed while petting Marnie's head. "We can play board games."

Fuck that. I was opting out of that one.

I left them to their thing and walked across the room to find my brother's phone. The video text he'd gotten was still open on the screen. One look at Lana's drugged face, and I knew what set him off. Ned Callaghan recorded the rape. Parker didn't get any justice, he was dead before Lana told him about it, and now he had to see it. Who the fuck sent this shit to him?

That question was answered when a large ace of spades appeared on the screen with the words: 'Tell your brother I said Hi.'

This guy was starting to piss me off. I doubted Parker saw that part because he snapped seconds after receiving the text, and I can't say I blamed him. There was a moment when I thought the good pastor had a thing for both of his daughters.

"I WANT YOUR DAUGHTER."

Most fathers would react one of two ways. They would fight tooth and nail *against it like Derek Adams, or they looked at it as a business deal like Nikolai. The Bratva weren't new to the concept of trading their daughters.*

The occasional few thought we were kidding because marriage contracts were slightly outdated. But eventually, their eyes would round when they realized there was no joke to be had. And then there was Pastor Jacques Dupire, a supposed holy man.

What did he do when the monster haunting his town came to claim his daughter? He crossed his arms and said, "You can't have Trina."

Trina.

Not stay away from my daughters, or I'd never let someone like you near my children, but you can't have Trina. Who, in my opinion, was the inferior version of her sister.

"I would say I find your extra special bond to one daughter interesting, but we both know why that is." I pushed off the desk and took a few steps closer. "Don't we, Jacques?"

The only hint that I'd struck a nerve was a slight arch in his brow. "Trina is a good girl who's evaded corruption."

"Some would define what you do to her as corruption."

"It wasn't long ago when it was considered the father's right to break in his daughter."

"Or the pastor's duty for the daughters of his flock?" I tipped my head. "That's what you tell the parents of the girls you defile in here. Isn't it? That only a holy man can bless their journey into womanhood?"

"The priest is to present it before the Lord and make atonement on her behalf."

"Leviticus 12:7."

His brow rose. "You know your bible."

"I do. And you're not the first person I've seen corrupt it for their own purposes."

That was the thing about the bible. It was open to interpretation.

Apparently, the good pastor didn't like being called out on his bullshit.

"I wouldn't expect you to understand." He let out a heavy breath and marched past me to sit behind his desk. "Now get out of my office."

I didn't want to understand, nor did I care what he did so long as he kept his hands off Marnie.

"Sign the contract I left on your desk, and I will."

He looked briefly at me before opening a drawer and pulling out a pen. That got my interest piqued.

"Tell me, Pastor." I spun around and strutted back to the desk. "Why aren't you arguing for your other daughter?"

"Marnie has the devil inside her." He paused his writing to roll his eyes up at me. "Perhaps the devil can cleanse her."

Cleansing was the last thing on my mind. However, I was tempted to cleanse this church.

Jacques returned to signing the pages in front of him. He didn't bother to read any of the print, but he had no problem talking.

"I tried to help and show her the righteous path, but she was tainted."

My fists balled. If he touched her...

"The good Lord saw fit to give me two beautiful girls to love. Children should remain innocent, and Marnie couldn't even do that." He held up the signed contract and looked me in the eyes. "I washed my hands of her a long time ago."

My hand twitched to grab my knife, but then I got to thinking. Why should I waste my time ending him now? When I could really make the prick suffer.

Tucking the contract in my inside front pocket, I nodded at him. "Have a good evening."

Let's see how much he'd washed his hands of his daughter when I turned her against him...

I ROLLED my gaze over my Bird's long dark hair to the tangle of limbs engulfing her.

A snarl curled her lip as those bright aqua eyes met mine. "I hate you."

Those were my favorite words slipping through her lips. They were dripping with so much venom that I could taste the sweet sting in the back of my throat.

"Be good, Little Bird. My brother and I are going for a ride."

"I'm not going anywhere with you," Parker argued.

"Shut the fuck up and get in the car."

"Good, go," Marnie hissed as I pushed Parker toward the door. "Don't get mad at me if I'm gone when you get back."

If I didn't know any better, I'd say she was going to miss me.

I looked at my old man, who was grabbing some bungee cords from a cupboard, then at Ava. She was still petting Marnie's head, and I snickered. "Good luck with that."

Playing the Game of Life with my old man and sister was not an experience I wished to share with her.

PARKER'S HEAD cocked at the town sign we passed. "Why the fuck are we in New Haven?"

"Because Mason is an idiot."

Unlike his brother, Mason Kessler was impulsive, rash, and constantly causing problems that needed to be cleaned up. He was in desperate need of some form of control. However, tonight I didn't mind. His decision to participate in an underground fight in the one town that didn't give a fuck who we were, provided me with the perfect place to take my brother.

For the first time, I was grateful to receive a text from Silas Creswell. Not that we'd texted much over the years, maybe five or six times. But that was why I liked the guy. He kept his nose out of my business. Though I was curious why he didn't send his SOS to Logan or Micha, both of whom would care more about their well-being than I would.

Personally, I'd leave Mason to deal with the repercussions of his actions. If people stopped sheltering him from the world, he might understand the meaning of consequences. Every time Micha bitched about his brother, I wanted to slap him. Of course, Mason rebelled. Everyone around him treated him like he was five fucking years old. I'd have acted out too.

I assumed that was why Micha no longer called me to help clean up his brother's messes. The last time he did, I showed up with Mason in tow and made him do the hard work. Why the fuck should he get to carry on with his happy day while the rest of us had to give up our plans. Fuck that.

"What the fuck did Mason do?"

A better question would've been, what the fuck didn't Mason do. "Decided to go for a celebratory drink at Gators."

"Are you fucking kidding me?" Parker sighed and shook his head. "That's Skevers territory."

"I'm aware," I said while pulling the car into the dimly lit parking lot of a run-down bar.

The Skevers was a local gang with a hard-on for anyone from Ashen Springs. If Mason wanted to get burned, this was the perfect place to find the fire.

"Please tell me he didn't bring Harper with him?"

I eyed the two jacked-up thugs standing by the door and shrugged. "Didn't ask."

Nor did I care.

"Fucking Mason," Parker muttered and got out of the car.

It didn't take long for the two bouncers to notice him. When they rolled their shoulders back and started our way, I considered staying where I was and letting my brother take care of them. He was more than capable of defending himself. However, he'd also had time to cool down, and the real show was inside.

Sighing, I followed my brother's lead and stepped out onto the parking lot. Instead of preparing to square off, I pulled out my Desert Eagle and shot them both in the head.

"What the fuck, Preston?"

"What? They're a waste of time."

Judging by the sounds echoing from the building, we didn't have time to spare.

"No more killing," Parker growled while strolling across the parking lot behind me.

Famous last words...

We stepped through the door and took in the mayhem. Mason was by the bar throwing punches at four guys, and Silas was on the other side of the room. One guy had his arms pinned behind his back while the other two were taking turns jabbing him in the gut. But the redhead being held down made the corner of my mouth twitch.

Little Harper Callaghan wasn't faring as well as her boyfriend. My gaze trickled over the arms holding her down on the ground, then up to the crooked smile on another Skever's face.

He tipped his head down at Harper and cupped his crotch, "You sure are a pretty little thing."

And just like that, my brother snapped.

Parker charged across the room and slammed his shoulder into the chest of the guy smiling at Harper. Satisfaction rolled through me as I watched his body fly through the air and crash into a nearby table. Before the sound of the table breaking could resonate in my ears, Parker picked up a chair and broke it on the face of the one holding her down. Then took the splintered piece of wood in his hand and stabbed it in his leg.

And it didn't stop there. Parker plucked him off the ground as if the fucker weighed nothing. He slammed his body into the other guy, who was just starting to pull himself up.

The sickening crunch cracked through the air and alerted the others to our presence. They all turned to look as Parker kicked a jukebox over on his victims.

Someone screamed, probably Harper, while two others made a break for the door. A bullet to the leg stopped that. They weren't going anywhere. Not until my brother was done. And he was nowhere near burned out.

I sat down and watched as Parker made his way around the room, painting the walls with blood and bone. It was beautiful, like a graceful dance of pain and rage.

Silas and Mason tried to help, but it quickly became evident they were just in Parker's way. So they grabbed Harper and joined me at the only table still standing.

Keeping my eyes on my brother, I pulled out a pack of cigarettes and lit one.

"You can't smoke in here."

All three of us turned to look at Harper as she lifted her finger to point at a sign. "It says so right there."

My brother was crushing people to death with whatever he could grab, and she was worried about a bit of smoke.

I rolled my eyes over to Mason. "Why the fuck did you bring her here?"

"This was where the fight was. A fight I won, by the way."

"Was the prize getting your girlfriend raped?"

Mason's green eyes narrowed. "I'd never let anyone touch her."

"You were doing a bang-up job of protecting her." He should've never brought her here in the first place.

"I had everything under control," Mason said. That made me snort. Control and Mason didn't go together.

Mason tipped his head at Silas. "Back me up here."

"Fuck you," he growled. "I told you we shouldn't come here."

"What's wrong with this place?" Mason looked around the bar.

"It's fucking New Haven, you idiot."

I was with Silas on that one.

"What the fuck were you trying to prove?" Silas barked.

That was the dumbest question I'd ever heard. Silas was Mason's best friend. Why, I had no idea, but he should've known better than anyone why Mason wanted to come here. It wasn't about trying to prove something to someone else. As much as everyone deluded themselves into thinking everything was fine with Mason and Harper, they weren't. Sure, they said, 'They'd figured shit out.' But that was bullshit. Mason traded hating Harper for guilt over not seeing what was really happening.

Mason didn't come here to prove anything.

He came here to punish himself and wanted Harper to see it because that was redemption for him. He wanted to suffer as much as she did.

"Look at her," I said to Mason while nodding at Harper. "How often do you think her father made her shake like that?"

Guilt washed over his face.

255

"Don't pull her out of the fire just to throw her back in it."

Mason's arms shot out and wrapped around his girl. "I'm sorry, Baby."

"It's okay," she whispered and snuggled into his chest.

No, it wasn't, but Mason would get there. As much as he annoyed me, he was still one of my boys, and I'd help him get to where he needed to be, just like I helped Parker.

My attention returned to my brother. His fists were raining down on what was left of some guy's face. Every strike sent a sickening squelch through the room. Mason was too busy sucking up to Harper to notice the destruction, but Silas did.

His lips twisted up in a grimace. "What's up with him?"

"He's good."

My baby brother had finally stopped running from his true nature.

Chapter 24
Marnie

"**D**on't even think about it," I said. True torture was being tied to a chair with bungee cords while playing the Game of Life with Ava and Dean Whitley. "I don't need any more kids."

"Yes, you do." Ava held up a tiny pink peg. "You need another girl."

"I already have three!"

"But you have four boys." Ava pointed to my little blue car on the game board.

And whose fault was that? I sure as hell wasn't the one piling crotch gremlins into my plastic car. I couldn't even spin the damn wheel—stupid Whitleys and their knot skills.

"There," Ava sang while placing the peg between two others. "That's perfect."

The pile of pegs placed in my game piece was hardly perfect. There weren't enough holes to put them in. Not that I could pick them up when they fell out because I couldn't move my hands. I tried. God, I wanted to slap that happy-go-lucky smile off Dean's face.

My jaw clenched as Dean reached out to spin the dial. The real kick to the gut came when he picked up a card that said, 'Grab another child.'

Ava slapped the peg out of his hand because he already had three. Why the hell was he being denied children when I had a frigging baseball team? That wasn't fair.

That was when it hit me. I'd fallen far, far down the rabbit hole. My first concern should've been escaping this madhouse, not being pissed off because I couldn't move my own game piece.

Was crazy contagious?

The evidence pointed that way.

"Ava, honey, don't pout." Dean looked at his daughter, who had her lips pursed and arms crossed.

Why had her mood shifted so fast?

Who knew?

The first ten minutes after Preston left, her emotions switched like a kid flipping through the pages of a book. Ava Whitley was always off, but she still had her lucid moments. However, lately, that switch between sane and insane was constantly flicking. I didn't know what had changed. I also didn't understand why she wasn't locked up. If she kept going like this, there wouldn't be a choice. It was kind of sad to see.

I remembered her as a kid before all the bad stuff happened. She was always smiling. Ava never treated other kids differently because she was happy to have playmates, and whenever we played house, it was Ava who taught us the rules.

Then she was broken.

The whole family was.

Dean stopped smiling for a year, Parker stayed inside, and Preston...well, he didn't change. At least not that I noticed, but he didn't really hang out with the rest of us. It was more like he lurked. Even as a kid, he was creepy.

"Maybe our guest would like a drink?"

What?

"No—" I was too late.

Ava was up and over here, dumping water down my throat before I could say another word. No one could swallow that fast, so most of it ended up on my shirt. Sputtering and coughing, I tried to move my head out of the way. I never thought I'd drown from a cup of water.

"What the hell are you doing?"

I never thought I'd be happy to hear Preston's voice, either. But I could've kissed him when Ava sang, "She was thirsty."

She pulled the cup away from my mouth, and I turned my head. Everything else faded away.

All I saw was the deep crimson staining every inch of Parker. Literally, I couldn't find a spot of clean skin. His face, arms, and hands were completely covered, and I could taste the coppery tinge surrounding him.

Parker looked like the personification of murder. Preston didn't have a single speck of blood or dirt on his clean clothes.

This was why Riley called Preston 'Death.'

"Son," Dean tsked. "You need a shower."

What kind of reaction was that? How about what the hell did you do? Who did you hurt? How many bodies are out there? Hell, I'd have settled for a firm, disappointed shake of the head—anything but that father-of-year smile.

I couldn't hold back anymore. "You're all crazy!"

"Hey," Ava scolded. "Crazy isn't a nice word."

"No, it's an accurate word," I stated.

I didn't think there was a more accurate word to describe this family.

"Calm down, Little Bird." Preston walked over and began untying my binds. "It's time to go home."

My anger caused my vision to narrow. "You and I have very different definitions of what home is."

Home was a place where one should feel safe to relax and unwind. The gilded cage he had for me hardly met those parameters.

"Uh-huh. What kind of home did you come from?" His cold gray eyes rolled up to mine. "Did mommy and daddy treat you well?"

My teeth gritted. "That's none of your business."

"Oh, but it is Little Bird. I don't like other people marking my property."

"I'm not your property."

"You've always been mine." He dropped his gaze back down my binds. "Despite all those scars on your back."

Everyone in the room heard that comment. Parker's face filled with sadness while Ava's eyes widened, and Dean touched my shoulder.

"Did someone hurt you?"

The pit in my stomach dropped, and I was kneeling in the rain again back at my parent's home. My father's voice tickled at the back of my mind as my thumb grazed over the cross burned into my palm. I may not have had a place where I felt safe, but I had Trina. My sister was my home. I didn't need anyone else.

"Get off me." I shrugged Dean's hand off my shoulder.

Ava stepped closer. "If someone hurt you—"

"I'm fine." I cut her off. "My father is a good man. He helps people all the time. Where was yours when you needed help?"

The look on Dean's face made me regret what I said, but I was too angry to care.

"Hey now," Parker warned.

"Fuck you, Parker. You walk around town like a good guy, but you're not. Look at you, standing there, dripping with what's left of your last victim. Did it feel good when you killed them?"

His mouth shut, but he didn't need to answer. I could see it written all over him. "Of course, it did because this is who you really are, right? A cold-hearted, murderous bastard who's just like his brother."

"Lash out all you want, Little Bird." Preston unclipped the bungee cord around my hands and looked up at me. "It won't erase your scars."

"I don't want to erase my scars." They were mine. My war wounds were meant to remind me of what men with too much authority could do. Every time I saw one of those marks, I knew I'd survived. My father didn't break me.

But Preston did.

"Those aren't the scars I'm talking about."

I lost it.

My fists swung, pounding against Preston's chest while tears streamed down my face. He took every hit. He stayed there and let me beat my frustration and anger out while my father yelled in the back of my mind.

"I will beat the devil out of you, child."

"Pray for salvation."

"Your taint is a stain on this family."

Then another voice.

"That's a pretty dress. Did you wear it for me?"

I fought against the grimy touch crawling up my spine and beat away that wretched voice by pounding my fists until I couldn't lift my arms anymore.

Exhausted, I collapsed against Preston's chest.

My father didn't believe me when I told him about the sheriff. He called me 'dirty' and said, 'It was my fault for tempting him. If I had been a proper little girl, none of it would've happened.' I was wrong in his eyes from that day forward.

I was wrong in everyone's eyes. Trina thought I was too meek. Shelby wanted me to dress up more. Even Riley said I spent too much time in the library. I was the one that needed to be protected, sheltered, or enjoy life more. Everyone found fault in who I was.

Everyone except Preston.

Chapter 25
Preston

My Bird's emotional outburst cracked straight through her carefully built-up wall. She was exposed now—raw and prime for plucking. The hard work was over. The first break always took the longest, but once it occurred, other fractures followed. I didn't expect my family to help me get there, but hey, whatever worked.

To top it all off, my brother also had a relevant breakthrough.

All in all, this was turning out to be a productive day. I might even go so far as to say I was in a good mood. But that was because of the spark in Marnie's eyes as we pulled into my driveway.

The spark of panic.

I fucking loved that look. The way her body trembled and her muscles tensed.

She'd let me hold her. Not only that, but I was the one who calmed her down, and now she was freaking out. Her mind was spinning. I could see the wheels turning every time she looked my way. Poor little thing was confused, filled with self-hatred and a little intrigue, but it was the panic that held my interest.

What a beautiful cherry on top of my almost-perfect day.

Pulling the car to a stop, I reached out and grazed my fingers down her cheek. "Do you need to cry some more?"

She'd been sniffing for most of the ride home, though her tears had dried up. Not that I particularly cared. My motives for tenderness were purely selfish.

"Don't touch me." Her blazing aqua eyes locked on mine. They held so much rage and hatred. I fucking loved it.

"It's okay, Little Bird. Come here." I held my arms out, motioning her to snuggle in. "I'll make it all better."

Then I got what I wanted. That spark in Marnie's eyes flared as she threw the door open and rushed out of the car. A smile spread across my face as she broke for the tree line.

I bent over, opened the glove compartment, and grabbed a small bottle of lube.

Let the games begin.

Chapter 26
Marnie

My heart raced, beating hard off my ribs with each resounding pound of my feet on the ground. I had to get away and escape the taunting at the back of my mind, a tiny little voice urging me to accept the devil's embrace.

Preston was a monster who kidnapped and violated me. My body's reaction to him was basic biology. But when he held his arms open...I knew I had to run before it was too late. Because when I looked at him in the car, I didn't see a monster anymore.

I saw a man.

And that thought I could not abide. I refused to be that girl. The one who saw something in their captor beyond the evil acts he committed.

I burst through the tree line bordering Preston's property and veered left. There was no logic or thought about which direction I'd run because my panic-button had been pushed. All I felt was the adrenaline and frenzy surging through my system. Not even the leaves or branches whipping my body could suppress my need to escape, but I wasn't running to save my life.

It was my soul that was at stake.

The devil had come to claim me, and a part of me wanted to give in.

So I ran.

When my lungs started to hurt, I ran harder until I couldn't move my legs one more step. Hunching over next to a thick oak tree, I leaned up against it.

While I fought to catch my breath, I tried to figure out my next move. But there were too many variables. Did I escaped? How much distance did I gained, and was it far enough to classify me as free? How long had I been running? It felt like forever.

Bracing my forearm on the tree trunk, I peeked around the rough bark. Every breath I sucked back burned coldly in my lungs. Air scratched down my throat as I scoured the foliage. I didn't see Preston, but he was out there. The devil was hidden somewhere in those thick green leaves.

I could feel him stalking me.

My ears perked at a crack echoing in the distance. Then again, when a soft breeze rustled through the trees, the hairs on the back of my neck rose as the world began to close in around me.

What was I thinking? This was not a safe place. But was anywhere safe?

'Resist the devil, and he will flee from you.'

Except Preston wasn't fleeing from me. He was hunting me down, and every fiber of my being knew that. Doom was crackling across the deadfall littering the forest floor.

Wait, that wasn't doom.

I held my breath and listened.

It was footsteps coming from the right. The causal strides were hard to pick up, but there was no mistaking that sound.

My first instinct was to rush away in the opposite direction. Then I got to thinking. Why should I be the hunted when I could be the hunter?

A quick scan of the ground gave me what I needed.

I picked up a large branch and swung it through the air to test it.

It was sturdy and strong with a nice sharp tip, perfect for stabbing. Preston couldn't hurt anyone if he were dead. As for the rest of the kings…I had more than enough information to take them down.

No one was getting close to my sister.

Another footstep rang through the air as my eyes snapped to the right. Only one of us was leaving this forest alive, and it wouldn't be Preston.

I slipped off into the trees and cautiously made my way in that direction.

Our yearly hunting trip was one of the few father-and-daughter activities I looked forward to. Trina would bitch the entire time because she didn't have a curling iron or running water. I took the opportunity to enjoy nature and learn things, like how to disguise my clothing to blend in with the surrounding area.

Mud, leaves, and a few branches were all I needed to craft a home-made camo suit. It wasn't perfect, but I wouldn't be easily spotted.

After that, I only had to worry about staying quiet. Not a simple task when moving through terrain like this, but not impossible. It all came down to timing. The closer I got to Preston's footsteps, the easier it was to match my strides with his. Soon enough, I caught a glimpse of a familiar jean jacket.

I stopped and hunched down in a bush to watch my prey. I thought he might've spotted me for half a second, but he didn't move in my direction. Preston didn't move at all. Nor could I hear his footsteps.

Something wasn't right.

Creeping slowly closer, I kept my eye on the patch of denim I could see through the leaves. An adrenaline rush tightened my grip on my makeshift weapon, but it died away. It wasn't Preston I saw standing there.

It was his jacket hung on a tree.

"Tricky, tricky Preston Whitley."

"I thought so."

I screamed at the whisper warming my ear and sprang forward. My entire body tensed, jarring something I'd completely forgotten about. The thing shoved up my ass.

My hatred grew as Preston stepped out and dropped his eyes to the stick in my hand. "You shouldn't play with sharp things, Little Bird. You might hurt yourself."

How in the hell did he sneak up on me? Oh well, he was here now.

I lunged forward, swinging the stick with all my might.

Preston ducked under my strike, then spun around and caught it when I came in for another attempt. But I refused to let go. I firmed my hold and glared up at him.

"You have shit for fighting skills."

Preston tugged on the stick, and I tugged back.

"If my fighting skills are shit, why are you trying to disarm me?"

It wasn't going to work. We pulled the stick back and forth, Preston was using only one hand, and I had two, but still. This was my weapon, and I was not giving it to him.

We stayed there silently, staring each other down while the breeze cooled my face.

"What's wrong, Preston?" I sang while giving him a mock frown. "Scared I might hurt you?"

A shiver ran up my spine when a smirk tugged at the corner of his mouth.

"I'll tell you what, Little Bird, how about you play with your weapon...." My blood ran cold when a soft click rang through my ears. "And I'll play with mine."

Fading sunlight glinted off the very sharp edge of a knife. I'm not sure what came over me, but the next thing I knew, I drove the heel of my hand up into his nose, and my knee slammed into his groin. A grunt pushed past his lips. That was all I heard or saw before spinning around and bolting back into the foliage.

All I could think as I ran was that I'd left my weapon behind. Or did I? The thing in my ass was metal, much stronger than wood. But could it be used for that?

Only one way to find out.

Let me just say taking that thing out was about as uncomfortable as having it put in. Standing in the middle of the woods with my hand down my pants certainly didn't help. But it was worth it. Not only was it pointed, but the thin stem before the diamond end fit nicely between my fingers.

I looked at the cone sticking out by my knuckles and the gem on the other side by my palm. Something formerly in my ass wouldn't be my first choice, but it would do some damage. Who needed brass knuckles? It was kind of funny. I'd been cursing this thing's existence, and now it might be my salvation. How was that for irony?

Now I just needed my target.

My eyes narrowed. The world appeared to be quiet, but…. "I know you're out there."

Something rustled to my left, and I held my breath waiting for that cold stare to emerge. But it didn't. Nothing moved except the wind. Where the hell was he?

I didn't like this. It was too quiet. Too still. I should be able to hear birds chirping or some other animals, yet there was nothing. Or my pulse was overpowering everything else. Eerie didn't even begin to cover it. Goosebumps broke out across my skin as my palms grew sweaty. The longer I stood there, the more my nerves woke up.

Was this how people in horror movies felt right before the monster jumped out? They never fared well. Why would I think I would be any different? Yet here I was, preparing to take on the devil with a butt plug.

Something snapped behind me.

Fuck this.

I took off. Just in time, too, because half a second later, I heard a voice call out, "Run, Little Bird."

And I did just that. As I moved through the forest, I suddenly understood why Shelby liked running track so much. This feeling was freeing, exhilarating, utterly terrifying, and one hundred percent addictive.

That was until something rushed out and jumped on me.

I barely had time to scream before I was knocked down, tumbling face-first into the dirt. We landed with a heavy thud that momentarily stole my breath. I didn't have to look behind me to know what had happened. Preston caught me. Was it wrong that my body recognized the weight pressing in on me?

"Tip number one, Little Bird, you shouldn't kick someone in the balls. You might just piss them off."

Good. He should be pissed off. I would've jabbed my knee in his nuts again. Instead, I coughed and fought for air while Preston flattened his palm between my shoulder blades and grabbed the waistband of my pants with his other hand.

"Or," He bent over me, bringing his mouth to the edge of my ear, and growled, "You'll turn them on."

My pants were ripped down my legs to my knees. My senses came back when I heard the jangle of a belt. That wasn't a good thing. My mind told me to get away, but my body warmed the instant his hand slipped between my thighs. Preston shoved two fingers inside me, and I couldn't stop the moan.

"You're wet, Marnie. You like this shit, don't you?"

I licked the dirt off my lips and hissed, "Never."

I didn't enjoy this. I hated everything about it—how good he made me feel, the tingling sensation that coursed through my veins, but mostly, I hated how my body purred for more. Every sense heightened—the grimy taste of the earth on my face, the breeze cooling my exposed flesh, and the warm feeling of the man behind me.

Even Preston's tsk rolled through me. "Hear that?"

I heard it. The squelching sound my body made as his fingers pumped into my pussy was mortifying. I should be fighting it, not melting into his touch. Yet, there I was, lying in the dirt, moaning like a cat in heat.

"This is wrong." But felt so right.

Every nerve I had lit up. Preston's fingers felt so good, but it wasn't enough. I wanted more, and despite how much I wanted to kill him, I groaned and ground my hips back.

"Why? Because it makes you a slut." He pulled his hand away, and I momentarily whined at the loss. Then something bigger pressed against my opening.

"Or is it because it makes you my slut," Preston growled and thrust hard, burying his entire length inside me.

I screamed at the sudden stretch. It was too much, too fast. Not that Preston cared. He didn't even slow down. He fucked me with so much force that my body was pushed across the ground. And I loved every minute of it. Sticks and dried leaves pricked my skin while his hard cock, and the little balls on the end of his piercings rubbed against my inner walls.

The wave of pleasure threatening to crash into me seemed unstoppable. I tried to hold it back. My teeth gritted as I dug my nails into the earth and refused to let desire take over. It worked at first. Then I felt the cool metal touch my back, followed by a sharp sting that traveled down my spine.

There was no stopping it after that. That wave burst forth with the power of an atomic bomb. An inhuman sound erupted from my chest as my muscles seized. I barely felt the trickle of blood, but the tongue that laved over it broke through my haze.

"So fucking sweet," Preston groaned, then cut me again, and again, and again.

A murderer was getting off on slicing me, and he wasn't the only one. Every sting brought on by his knife dragged out my orgasm. Just when I thought he was done, Preston grabbed my neck and pulled me back against him.

The next thing I knew, his lips were on mine.

He smelled like smoke and tasted like whiskey, but there was something about the coppery tinge that laced his tongue. It did something to me. Something that made me grind my hips and fuck him back. I couldn't have stopped if I wanted to. I was gone, lost to the euphoria. The only thing that pulled me back were the words he growled in my ear.

"Now, when you look at your back, you'll know Daddy doesn't own you. I do."

And that was when I remembered what was gripped in my hand.

Logic slammed back into my mind. I lurched away and hopped to my feet. However, I neglected to take into account the pants around my knees. My grand attempt at turning the tables instantly became an epic failure. I jerked away from Preston and landed face-first on the ground. Then to add insult to injury, I choked on a mouthful of gritty, crunchy earth.

The slow clap was already rolling through my head when a sadistic snicker hit my ears.

"I'm not often surprised, Little Bird, but that's a new one. How's that dirt taste?"

Asshole.

"Great," I hissed into the ground, too embarrassed to look at him.

That didn't stop me from throwing my hand back when he started to crawl over me again. I didn't know where I hit him, but I did make contact. And it was enough of a strike for him to grunt.

"Did you just hit me with a butt plug?"

Yes, indeed I did. "How's my ass taste?"

It wasn't often that I came up with a good sarcastic comment, but that one was at the top of my list. What I didn't expect was for Preston to take it literally.

He lifted my hips, and his tongue was suddenly lapping at my backdoor. Humiliation unlike I'd ever felt burned down my chest as he smacked his lips together.

"Not bad, Little Bird." I went stiff when something cold and slippery dripped down my ass. "Shall we see how it feels?"

That was all the warning I got before something that felt like his thumb or finger forced its way past that tight ring. Surprisingly, it didn't hurt, unlike when he put the plug in. It felt weird and awkward, but there was no pain. Even when he added a second finger, it wasn't bad. I might even go so far as to say oddly pleasant. That didn't stop me from trying to wriggle away when more wetness dripped down my crack. Preston just grabbed my hair and held me in place.

That was when the pain came.

It wasn't his fingers I needed to worry about. It was his cock.

I couldn't see past the burn. My legs and arms were flailing about, but I had no control over them. God, it hurt. And what did that motherfucker do? He let out a long, heady groan.

"Fuuuuck…that's good."

Good? Good! This was so far from 'good' that the word 'bad' didn't even begin to describe this pain.

"You need to relax," Preston growled.

Fuck him.

I was not doing anything he said.

"This is happening whether you like it or not. If you fight, it'll only hurt more."

Hurt more? Was that even possible? Okay, maybe it wouldn't be the worst thing to listen to his advice in this instance. As hard as I fought to make my body relax, it wasn't working. Preston would force more of his length inside, and I was right back where I started.

I shook my head and whimpered, "I can't."

"Too bad," Preston gritted out.

At some point, I think I blacked out. Either that or my mind decided to leave. When I came back, Preston was peppering kisses up the side of my neck.

"Your ass feels so fucking good."

Did it? It didn't hurt nearly as bad as I expected. I tested the waters and wriggled my butt. Preston answered my action by giving me a small thrust.

It was a different sensation that felt somehow more intimate than anything else. As if, for the first time, he was really inside me. Curiosity tugged at my thoughts.

Could he feel my heartbeat?

Did he know what I was thinking?

Did he feel me like I felt him?

My breath hitched when I twisted my neck to look at him. Preston's usually empty gray eyes were sparkling with more life than I'd ever seen. It was so mesmerizing that I couldn't look away. Not even when he began fucking me. I locked my eyes with his and watched bright, silver flecks dance around. When he slammed deep inside me and roared out his release, it hit me.

He wasn't dead inside. He'd just never had anyone breathe life into him.

Even the villain of the story had a heart, and I was starting to wonder if Preston Whitley's heart was...me.

Chapter 27

Preston

The rippling waters of Cherry Lake didn't give me the same sense of nostalgia that it did my brother. For Parker, this beach reminded him of family outings and childhood fun. I assumed that was why he'd started bringing his kids here.

Personally, I thought one was too young for picnics—they'd barely figured out how to use a fork—but he insisted and even dragged my ass out here a few times.

Don't get me wrong. I had fond memories of this place. None had anything to do with water, sand, or laughing children. For men like me, Cherry Lake was good for one thing—shopping. Tourists flooded this place in the spring, and it was a prime setting to pick someone off from the pack.

Many college girls decided they wanted to vacation in Florida to avoid bigger crowds, which made it so easy to lure one away. A couple of drinks with the promise of a good time, and they were putty in my hands. The only good time to be had was mine, of course. They made their choice. They would've been better off in Miami. Now, I wasn't saying the city was a safer place to go—I knew a couple of guys who trolled that turf—but I wasn't there.

The screaming cries of wide-eyed girls—and occasionally guys—were my nostalgic memories of Cherry Lake. There were others, though...

My eyes wandered over to a large oak tree with a dip at the base of the trunk.

Most people wouldn't notice where the bark had healed over. They wouldn't know what caused the wound either. But I did. The image of Chet covering his face was as vivid today as the night I bashed that prick's head in.

Nash wasn't Ryker's only friend. He was just the hardest to get to.

Wanna see absolute defeat. Watch a grown man's face when an eleven-year-old takes them down. The pathetic bastard never saw me coming. Who would suspect a child? It wasn't like I killed two more of his friends a year before—they were still considered missing. Not him, though. I displayed Chet's body in the middle of the town square.

That was a personal 'fuck you' to Ryker Hudson.

Logan's dad was a lot of things. An idiot wasn't one of them. He knew who did it. I think the sick fuck found it entertaining. It was his own game of 'who would be next.' I wouldn't have been surprised if the fucker took bets.

My only regret was missing the opportunity to take that mother-fucker out. Logan pulling the trigger was an easy pill to swallow. I could sleep at night knowing that the prick's son was the one to end his miserable life. Let's face it. If anyone deserved to gut him, it was Logan. But to find out that Lou was the one to put the final nail in his coffin—that shit wasn't right. Ryker got off easy.

I'd have impaled him with the same pool cue he used on my sister. But I had to settle for fucking with Nash. He didn't like the cue. Neither did his wife. His son I killed quick, a mercy killing in my eyes. Maybe I'd bring Nash here one day and impale him on that fucking tree.

But that could wait for another day. Nostalgia wasn't what brought me here.

I glanced down at the video open on my phone.

Mr. Ace of Spades decided to send me a good morning text. The familiar face lying in the sand was the only thing that stopped me from deleting it. Ned Callaghan left Tico for dead, but he didn't carve the raven into his chest.

That was someone else, someone who decided to share their handiwork with me. What he did to Tico didn't piss me off, nor did the text he sent my brother. If anything, he helped me out in that department. Parker now understood what would happen if he kept ignoring the beast clawing at his gut. But what made my fists ball was the sheer ineptitude of this asshole.

He'd been in Ashen Springs for at least a year and couldn't leave an obvious enough sign for me.

No.

He had to send me recordings of his handiwork because his crap ass hints weren't perceivable. If he were using someone else's mess to create his own, he could've at least left a distinct calling card.

My eyes fell back to my phone, following the slice of a bowie knife cutting through flesh. Why start with Tico? He had no ties to The Order or me. We had no idea the kid existed.

It didn't make sense.

If I had to guess, I'd say Tico was nothing more than convenient—wrong place, wrong time type of thing.

There was always the chance that Mr. Ace of Spades was working with Ned Callaghan, but I doubted it. Harper's old man spent years planning his revenge, and he might've succeeded if he hadn't teamed up with Ryker. That was Ned's downfall. The chances of him bringing an outsider in on his plot were highly unlikely. And that was what Mr. Ace of Spades was.

If he knew anything about this town or myself, then he'd know I wouldn't give a fuck about Tico. He was just some random kid, which led me back to my theory of Tico being convenient.

Asshole was looking for a way to get my attention subtly and stumbled across a body. Or what he thought was a body. Tico looked dead, all fucked up and beaten black and blue. Ned really did a number on him. I might've made the same mistake. It also explained why Tico never mentioned my apparent stalker. He was unconscious at the time.

I strolled down the left side of the beach and stopped near a 'No Dumping' sign to compare the view of the lake to the one in the video.

This looked like the place, though all signs of what had happened were long gone. The sand, lake, and people enjoying the afternoon all appeared normal. It was a little windier and less occupied. The incoming hurricane saw to that, but still normal.

Honestly, I don't know what I expected to find or why I came here in the first place. Mr. Ace of Spades wanted to meet on Devil's Peak at the bluffs. That wasn't going to happen. I knew a trap when I saw one. Besides, any good predator would say the first rule of the hunt was to know your prey, and I knew fuck all about this asshole.

Perhaps that was why I came? I needed to learn something about him. As much as I'd like to write him off as inept, he managed to hide under my nose for over a year. I couldn't help but wonder what he wanted. If it was my death, then why not just take me out? Sure, there'd be repercussions, and he'd never leave town alive, but the deed would be done. Why waste all this time? Those unanswered questions were starting to grate on my nerves.

Grumbling under my breath, I kicked the ground and prepared to leave. That was when something caught my eye—the tiniest glint of metal under the sand. I squatted down to sweep my hand over the buried object.

My brow instantly rose.

Hidden in the sand, under where Tico's 'body' was found, was a small foil flower.

What the fuck?

I picked it up and held it in the sunlight to examine the folds. It was definitely one of mine. I knew only one other person who could make them, and he wasn't around anymore. When I was ten, I was stuck in the principal's office. Evidently, it was wrong to smash a kid's head into the slide, but Mr. Grier thought I needed something to keep my hands occupied. So once a month, we had arts and crafts class, where he taught me how to make them.

The only difference between this flower and one of mine was that it was made from gold foil. I used silver. Or at least I did now. I was a kid the last time I made a gold one, and I never left one on a...

Shit.

A motel room flashed through my mind. One from years ago, with an old tube television in it and worn shag carpet...

"What are you doing in here, kid?"

"This..."

Bang.

I'd almost forgot about that hit. It was my first one. When I was thirteen, Micha paid me five dollars to off some asshole that slapped Mase. We discovered he was also in the business after the deed was done. Lou was pissed when he found out. Apparently, he'd gotten permission to conduct his work in town, and we'd fucked with Lou's word.

Sunlight glinted off the flower as I twirled it between my thumb and forefinger.

Mr. Ace of Spades couldn't be that prick. He was dead.

Wasn't he?

I watched him die. Or at least I thought I had. Was it possible I made a mistake? I was only thirteen at the time. There was one way to find out.

Standing up, I dialed a number and pressed the phone to my ear.

The Lost Souls Enforcer answered on the third ring.

"Hello?"

"Snake, it's Preston—"

"I'm going to stop you right there. I don't care what your crazy ass sister did or how much of a mess she left behind. Call someone else. No amount of money is worth dealing with her."

I rolled my eyes. "It wasn't that bad."

"Not that bad!" Snake growled back. "Do you have any idea how hard it is to cover up an explosion?"

"Depends on where it was."

There was a moment of silence before a long heavy sigh came from the other end, followed by a muttered, "Why do all these crazy people come to me? Do I have something written on my forehead?"

Who he attracted was his problem, but I was in a giving mood. "You have a gun. Take them out."

"Ah, to live in a world where it was that simple."

It was that simple. I didn't see the problem. "Perhaps these people aren't the crazy ones?"

It was a valid argument. Not everyone could handle the guilt that came with our work, and Snake had spent time in prison. I'd seen more formidable men crack from less.

"Have you ever found a girl tied up in your closet?"

"Yes," I said.

Why was that odd?

"One that you didn't put there," he clarified.

"I grew up with Ava." Finding random people throughout the house was a typical Saturday night. It took three days to find our nanny, who Ava declared the winner of hide and seek, despite not volunteering to play.

"So, your sister was always...." He paused for a fraction of a second, then said, "No, I don't want to know. What did you call for?"

An enforcer wasn't the same thing as a hitman. Snake fucked people up for a living. Sometimes that involved death. Often it didn't. But we ran in similar circles. He may have heard something I hadn't. Socializing wasn't something I did. Most of my clients contacted me directly.

"I'm looking for someone?"

"A mark?" Snake asked.

"No, more like my competition."

"So, your line of business."

"Correct."

"Okay, what's the name? And calling card?"

"Lucky. He used to leave four-leaf clovers?"

He didn't say anything for so long that I had to check to make sure I hadn't lost the connection.

"You there?"

"Sorry," he said. "Did you say, Lucky? What is he, a fucking leprechaun?"

Yeah, it wasn't the best name for a hitman. I never got that. I didn't see the point of picking an alias. People were going to call me what they wanted. Besides, I already had a name.

"I guess it's better than Weasel Legionnaires."

My brows knit. "Who?"

"Oh, it's just a rival club."

"Who the fuck would name their club Weasel Legionnaires?" The president of that club should be drawn and quartered.

"Listen, man, if you'd seen the shit I have…." Snake sighed, and I could picture him shaking his head. "Anyway, you got a real name?"

"Chad Brunswick."

"Of course, his name is Chad. Let me guess. He's a douche?"

"I wouldn't know. Never really talked to the guy."

People weren't particularly chatty when a gun was pointed at them. Well, most people weren't. Not that I gave him time to say anything.

"All right, I'll let you know what I find out."

"Talk to you soon," I said and hung up.

There was no point in assuming who Mr. Ace of Spades was. For all I knew, Chad Brunswick was dead, and this was his brother, or some shit was trying to exact revenge. Although, they'd have to find out who did the deed first. That'd be difficult, considering only Micha, Lou, and I had that knowledge.

The more I thought about it, the more it annoyed me. Luckily, I had something at home to occupy myself with.

Nothing like spending the day buried in my sweet Little Bird to relax my mind. She was pissed when I locked her back up in the cage. Her aqua eyes blazed with hatred while she spat promises of death. I may have left a knife in there for her to find. I wouldn't have lived up to my Devil namesake if I didn't tempt people. Whether or not she took the bait, I couldn't say, but I was excited to find out.

Chapter 28

Preston

By the time I pulled down my driveway, I was practically salivating to get my hands on Marnie. I wanted to fuck her on the soft velvet cushion, up against the bars and through them. What was the point of locking her in a cage if we didn't play with it?

How good would she look swallowing my cock? I could see those pretty pink lips wrapped around me while I shoved my length down her throat. That image needed to become a reality.

The trick was figuring out how to do it without losing my dick. That would be my next mindfuck, and I was given the means to do so when I pulled up in front of the house.

Standing by the door was a girl that looked almost identical to my Bird. Almost.

Fucking Trina.

Just looking at her caused my jaw to clench. Marnie was perfect and natural. She didn't wear her brown hair tied up like that, nor did she have a streak of purple in it.

Why the fuck was Trina here? Did she want to die? Nothing would make me happier than washing that fucking makeup off her face with sandpaper.

Trina turned around and narrowed her gaze on my BMW, making me want to pluck those bright aqua eyes out of her skull.

She looked too much like my Bird while at the same time looking nothing like her. Marnie wouldn't be caught dead in clothing that tight.

It took everything I had to remain calm and causally step out onto the driveway.

"Preston," Trina greeted.

Cunt.

"Trina," I said back, hating how my dick stirred at the similar sweet tone in her voice.

Most people probably didn't see the differences, but I did. Everything about her was a mockery of the real thing, even how she leaned her shoulder against one of the pillars bordering my front door. The confidence she tried to portray in her actions was fake. But that was all Trina was. Fake and dull. Her eyes had no bright sparkle, just the faded shadow of what used to be. I suspected that died the same night daddy snuck into her room.

I headed over, twirling my keys on my finger so I didn't automatically punch her in the face. As much as I despised the bitch, she would serve a purpose. I tapped a button on the remote in my jacket pocket, which would cause a section of the wall in Marnie's room to rise. Marnie wanted to see her sister, so now she could. She could watch the entire thing and not hear a word we said. Silence could drive a person mad.

Bet she'll use that knife now.

Trina didn't say a thing. She just stood watching and calculating every move I made. I knew that look. Her sister made the same one every time I came into the room. The wheels would turn in Marnie's head, rolling through plausible scenarios for her to play out. Trina wasn't trying to figure out her next move. No. She was trying to figure out mine.

It was almost a shame that I had no interest in toying with her.

Strutting right past her, I put my key in the door.

The second I unlocked it, she crossed her arms and huffed, "Aren't you going to ask why I'm here?"

Quite frankly, I didn't give a shit why she was here. Her perfume invaded my nostrils, tainting the sweet scent in the back of my throat.

I guess daddy's little princess didn't like being ignored because when I said nothing and rolled my eyes her way, I saw her jaw twitch.

"I want to see my sister."

Good for her.

I swung the door open and prepared to slam it in her face, but Trina stuck her foot in the way and looked me dead in the eyes. "I'm not leaving until I see Marnie."

"Maybe you should go and find her then."

"I know she's here."

Eyeing the flattened palm pressing on my door, I sighed. "Do you?"

Logan had a big mouth, but there was no way he would've said anything to her. Fucker had more secrets than Lou, and he understood their value. Ava was still in town, so she couldn't have let anything slip, leaving me to assume that Trina was calling my bluff.

Trina's eyes narrowed into angry slits. "Don't think I didn't see you following her around town."

"It's a small town." I shrugged.

For a moment, I considered breaking her foot, but I didn't see the harm in toying with her a bit. Besides, my Bird needed a show to watch.

"Not that small," she retorted.

Huh? I didn't think she saw past whatever guy she was dating, let alone notice what was happening in the world around her. The only question was, what was her goal? That thought had me intrigued.

"Say I was stalking your sister. Why didn't you tell anyone?" I leaned in to add softly, "Or haven't you heard? I'm the devil incarnate."

"I've heard the rumors."

"Maybe they aren't rumors?"

"Everything's a rumor until proven otherwise."

While she had a point... "That's an odd statement coming from a pastor's daughter."

That was all organized religion was—a worldwide rumor.

"So is arranging *'accidents'* in the name of justice."

Was it possible that Trina knew about her sister's extracurricular activities? "Nothing I do is accidental."

"I wasn't talking about you." Trina's brow arched. "But you already knew that."

Now, that was interesting. "Why don't you clarify for me."

Assumption was the mother of all fuck ups. If Trina wanted me to listen, she'd have to give me more than quasi-half answers.

Trina's chest rose with a deep breath. "A body was found in a maze on my sister's campus. I'm not sure if it was you or her, but neither would surprise me."

Okay, now she had my attention. Still... "If you know so much, then you'd know *if* I did have your sister, I'd never let you see her."

I had to hand it to Trina. She was stronger than I thought. Instead of backing down like most people would, she rolled her shoulders back and stepped closer. "First off, the only 'let' in this scenario is when I *let* you take her."

I snorted. Nobody let me do anything. "And why would you do that?"

The answer I got was not one I expected.

"I can't clean up after her anymore."

The dosing job Marnie did at the frat house was sloppy as hell. So much evidence was left behind—the vial with her fingerprints and numerous possible witnesses. All of which I took care of. Her previous victims' clean-up hadn't occurred to me, but someone must've handled it. Marnie was intelligent but not aware enough.

Could Trina have been in the background this whole time? "And by clean up, you mean...."

"Old man Farris saw Marnie cut Stephen Hamilton's brake lines."

"Old man Farris had a heart attack."

Trina's brow rose. "Did he?"

Hmm? I couldn't help but wonder how many other town tragedies were purposeful.

I stepped back and waved at Trina for her to enter. "Welcome to the devil's den."

She shot me a look, then waltzed in, and I slammed the door.

That action was a test.

I wanted to see how she would react to the resounding bang. People on edge or nervous might jerk or jump, while others would take it as an insult and glare back. None of which came from Trina.

She didn't so much as twitch while running her hand over a cherrywood bookshelf. "You have a nice house."

"Don't waste my time with pleasantries." Dropping my keys on a table by the door. "You don't give a shit what my house looks like."

Her eyes rolled. "Learn how to take a compliment."

I was starting to regret letting her inside.

"I don't want your compliments." A drink, however, sounded like a fantastic idea.

She continued to walk around and annoy me by touching everything. "You like the classics."

And there was the idle chit-chat she liked to spout.

Sighing, I uncorked a bottle of whiskey. "Not really."

"Then why do you have them?"

Why do you keep asking me meaningless questions?

"They came with the house."

"Uh-huh," she muttered.

I could feel her eyes on me, watching as I poured the amber liquid into two glasses—one of which I held out for her.

"Preston Whitley," she sang in a way that made me want to slap her. "Are you contributing to the delinquency of a minor?"

"Take the drink or don't. I don't give a fuck." I set the glass on the small table in front of me. "But if you keep flirting with me, I'll use your guts as fertilizer in my garden."

That got to her. Trina's strong demeanor broke for a second as a spark of fear flew across her face.

Her eyes dropped to the glass. "Is it poisoned?"

My shoulder lifted as I swallowed down a mouthful. "Maybe."

It wasn't, but that was her risk to take. Poison was so boring. There was no blood or tears, just vomit and mess. No one liked that shit.

Eventually, Trina sauntered over, scooped the glass, and took a tentative sip before smacking her lips together. "Is that cherry I taste?"

"I have no idea." My old man was constantly coming up with new concoctions. I gave up trying to keep up with them.

"You're not going to let me see my sister, are you?"

There was no need to say anything. We both knew the answer.

"Why invite me in? So you can kill me?"

The ironic part of that statement wasn't the teasing way she said it but that I had five different plans in place to dispose of her body.

"Curiosity," I said because that was what this conversation boiled down to.

Trina casually strolled around the room, running her fingers over each surface she passed. Each touch made my jaw clench tighter. I hated her being here, invading my personal space with her fakeness. Marnie's scent should be the only thing I could smell within these walls.

"My sister's stubborn, you know." Trina stopped and looked over her shoulder. "She'll never stop fighting."

I looked up at the camera hidden in the corner of the ceiling. "Oh, I think she'll see things my way."

"Did you fuck her?"

My brow arched. "What do you think?"

Yes, I fucked her, and I would be doing it right now if Trina weren't wasting my time.

"Did she like it?"

Why was she asking me stupid questions?

"Yeah, she did." The tiniest of smirks tugged at the corner of Trina's mouth. "Marnie's so repressed. Of course, she'd never admit it."

What was the point of this conversation?

Exasperated, I scrubbed a hand down my face. "Why are you here?"

"To see if she's safe."

"Define safe." That word had many different meanings.

She looked me in the eyes and said, "Away from our father."

So, that was what she was worried about. The prodigal daughter wasn't so 'prodigal' after all. There was a time I thought Trina actually enjoyed the extra attention from her father.

"Does Marnie know?"

"No." She shook her head.

"Does anybody?"

Whatever sparkle was glimmering in her eyes died and faded behind dullness.

"Our mother does. She gave me a big speech the first time he came into my room." Nothing but disdain emanated from her as she trickled her fingers down the side of a crystal vase. "Only a righteous daughter can keep the bloodline pure. That was her bullshit justification. He left me alone for a while...thought I was infertile. Then he found out about the abortions."

The smile on her face was filled with vindictive satisfaction. "He wasn't too happy about that."

"Why haven't you killed him?" I would've. Who the fuck cared that he was her father?

"Unlike my sister, I don't have the stomach for death." A heavy sigh left her lips. "Even for someone like him."

I could see the turmoil twisting her features. She'd thought about it and might have even tried a couple of times. Maybe she held a gun to his head but couldn't pull the trigger or something along those lines.

"Your sister would've done it."

"My sister is broken. Even when he's not there, she hears him. She's not strong enough to fight him off."

That explained why she was arguing with herself in the dark.

"You underestimate her. Marnie's stronger than you think."

"Maybe." Trina shrugged. "But she's not smart enough to get away with it."

"And you are?"

"No." She stopped and whispered, "But you are."

Oh, so that was her game. "You want me to kill your father. For what? In trade for your sister?"

"You make it sound so dirty." Trina twirled her hand through the air. "I'm sure you can take care of her and give her what she needs."

I agreed with her on that one. "I'm the only one that knows what she needs."

"There you go," she said. "It's an amicable trade. He's gone, and Marnie's safe."

There was one thing she left out.

"What about you?" I took a sip of my drink.

Selfishness was laced within everything humans did. We could survive on rainwater and bread, yet we wanted that ham sandwich because it tasted better. Big houses, well-paying jobs, power, everything people sought had a self-indulgent intent. Basic survival needs didn't drive society. Desire did. So what was Trina's desire?

"What do you get out of this?"

Her eyes rolled up to mine. "Nothing."

"I find that hard to believe."

"Believe what you want, Preston." She shrugged. "I died a long time ago."

Chapter 29
Marnie

I was starting to think that the absence of sound was my own personal hell. I could handle the dark and even the cold, but the silence…it was getting to me. There was nothing to listen to but my thoughts, and those were the last things I wanted to hear.

That sparkle in Preston's eyes was constantly replaying, turning my mind against me. The flip from 'I hate him' to 'when is he coming back' happened so fast that I couldn't say when it started.

Was it the first time he took me? One of the many after? Or was it something else? Something that made me see him differently? Preston Whitley was the last person I should miss. Yet, here I was, alone in the dark, anxiously awaiting the sound of his footsteps.

It got so bad that I sought out other sounds to concentrate on. A drip in the distance, the wind blowing against the house, anything was better than this mind-numbing silence.

My wish came true when a click rang through the air, and a panel slid back on the far wall. I clung to that sound for as long as I could.

The soft grating of wood on wood was like a miracle. Then the screen behind it came to life, and my stomach pitched.

Preston, I wasn't surprised to see. The person he was walking toward...horror filled my gut. What was Trina doing here? This wasn't a safe place.

I tried screaming and yelling, banging my fists on the bars, hoping she might hear something. She didn't, and neither could I. All I could do was sit there and helplessly watch as she entered the house. The view switched to another camera. My sister was there on the screen, but she'd never felt so far away.

Would my last memory of Trina be filled with her pain and blood? Why did Preston bring her here? I'd done everything he wanted. So why was my sister in his house? Was he trying to torment me, or had my sins come back to bite me in the ass?

'Sinners are condemned in their sin and will perish and go to hell.'

"No," I whispered. "I'm condemned."

'Your taint is a stain on this family. I will not let you drag your sister into damnation.'

I would never hurt Trina. She was innocent and unscathed by our parents. Our father purged his hatefulness on me so she could make it out clean. A normal life was all I wanted for her, and now, she was here in this hell with me.

Maybe I was a stain...

'Pray for salvation.'

My forehead rested against the cage as I dropped down to my knees. But I couldn't bring myself to clasp my hands together. My fingers were so tightly wrapped around the bars that I could feel the blood drain from my knuckles. Once upon a time, I believed in the fairy tales of a benevolent being watching over humanity. Every night, I asked him to protect my family. Those prayers were answered in a cold bathroom at a church picnic.

No one came to save me. No one cared when I told my father what happened because there was no one to care...no one but Trina. Prayer didn't do anything but fill naive minds with fantasies and illusions. The only devils people had to worry about were the ones walking the streets. That was whom I had to protect my sister from, humans like Preston.

The entire time I watched Preston and Trina interact, I was on pins and needles.

What were they saying?

I couldn't hear anything but my heart beating.

When she turned to leave, apparently unscathed, I finally let out the breath I'd been holding. Then the screen shut off seconds after her hand wrapped around the doorknob.

I wanted to scream. Did she make it out? Or did Preston grab her before she could? Was my sister another prisoner in this place?

No! I refused to let my fate determine Trina's. If Trina were here, I would get her out, no matter what it cost me.

Footsteps never sounded more menacing than the ones echoing up the stairs outside my gilded cage.

It was incredibly hard to unfurl my fingers from the bars and stand up. I missed the cool metal pressing against my palm. Somehow it grounded me because if I had something to hold onto, I wouldn't be exposed to the darkness trying to creep into my soul.

The first thing I noticed when Preston walked in was the smirk on his face. Like every other expression he wore, it was wrong and disturbing. Unfortunately, a part of me liked the crooked way his mouth lifted.

"Enjoy the show, Little Bird?"

I knew I shouldn't engage in his taunt, but I couldn't help myself. "Where's my sister?"

Trina was all that mattered now.

Preston tipped his head and said, "She left."

Bullshit. Men like Preston were all about keeping the advantage. He would never let her walk out of this house.

"If I can't lie to you, then you can't lie to me." Fair was fair, after all.

His brow rose. "So when it suits you, lying is a problem?"

"I never...you can't..." Had I lied to him? Yes, but... "You kidnaped me!"

What the hell did he expect? That I'd bare all my secrets to him.

My closest friends didn't know my secrets, a thought that suddenly made me sad. Riley and Shelby grew up with us. I loved them with all my heart, and I couldn't let them in, and Tico…he died never knowing the real me because I was too afraid of getting hurt.

If I could've trusted them just a little...

"True, I did kidnap you." Three steps. That was all it took for Preston to close the distance. "But I've never lied to you."

He just did—no more hiding. The time for fake glasses was over. If I was going to save my sister, I had to do exactly what Preston said. I had to be myself.

Rolling my shoulders back, I stood up straight and demanded, "Where. Is. My. Sister?"

Preston's nostrils flared as he growled, "There she is."

That's right, asshole. The real Marnie is here, and she's ready to play.

"All right." His head tipped in a slight nod. "Someone you care about is in this house. I will admit that."

"I want to see her."

"I didn't say it was a 'her.' "

My eyes rolled. Whatever. I'd play his little game. "Fine, I want to see *them.*"

"Don't get snarky with me." Preston tsked while wagging his finger. "You, of all people, should know how important a proper vocabulary is. It's so easy to misconstrue things. Take the scars we hide. One might think that would apply to physical marks. But not all scars are visible, are they, Little Bird?"

"A scar is defined by a mark left on the skin or within the body tissue where a wound, burn, or sore has not healed."

"Body tissue includes the mind," he argued. "And your's has been scarred for a long time, hasn't it?"

I pushed back the voices threatening to haunt my thoughts and crossed my arms. "Are you going to take me to see my sister or waste my time with a philosophical debate?"

"I told you, your sister left."

Not this again.

"Fine then, the person I care about."

Preston cocked a brow as if he was the one waiting for something.

"Are you just going to stand there?"

"You know how this works." He lifted his hand to drag a finger down one of the bars circling me. "Nothing is given for free."

I should've known.

"What do you want?"

I was tempted to jerk away when he grabbed my chin, but I liked how his thumb swept over my bottom lip.

"I want your mouth, Little Bird."

What? He didn't mean...

Preston leaned in and growled, "I want to see tears stream down your face while you choke on my cock."

That should not have sounded as enticing as it did.

"And if I refuse?"

"I guess you don't want to see your loved one that much."

It was his vagueness that made me curious. Preston was very careful not to use a name or a pronoun. "I could always bite your dick off."

"You could." He shrugged. "I could also go downstairs, slit your loved one's throat, and fuck your face anyway. Either way, I get what I want."

This son of a bitch.

I couldn't believe he was actually going to make me do this. Well, I could, but normally I could figure out an alternative. This time, however, there seemed to be no other option. If I wanted to see Trina, I'd have to bend to his will—this time.

As much as it pained me to do so, I slowly sunk to my knees, making sure Preston could see the contempt on my face the entire time. I hated him. Sometimes, I wondered if I loathed anyone more, but then my father's voice would enter my mind. If I had to save one of them, it wouldn't be my genetic relation.

What did that say about me?

My knees landed on the soft cushion as a huff pushed past my lips. Maybe my father was right, and there was something evil inside me. Why else would my core tingle when I looked at Preston? Sure, he was handsome with his angular jawline and a light dusting of whiskers on his face that gave him a five o'clock shadow, but he was a bad person who did horrible things.

Mind you, he was protective of his family, and he did push me away from a raging Parker. My tailbone still hurt from that. Chairs weren't meant for soft landings. But the way he looked at me yesterday...my entire body lit up when he touched me, and his masculine scent seemed to linger everywhere I went.

He wasn't empty and void. There was life inside him. I'd seen it. I might be the only person who had.

"Come, Little Bird. I don't have all day."

Didn't realize I had a time limit.

All right, I could do this. How hard could it be? Just stick his dick in my mouth and suck. It seemed simple enough, but the size of the bulge in his pants made me pause. How was that going to fit in my mouth? And was it wrong that I was curious to find out?

Preparing for the inevitable, I stretched my jaw and reached through the bars, but that was as far as I got. Preston slapped my hand away before I could do more than graze my fingers over his belt.

"On second thought, let's just go."

Was he fucking with me? He had to be.

"But you wanted—"

"I changed my mind."

Changed his mind? Preston didn't change his mind.

When he opened the cage and led me out of the room, I tried to let it go and considered myself lucky. I was getting to see my sister, and I didn't have to do anything for it.

Or did I...this wasn't sitting right with me.

The thought continued picking at my brain until I couldn't take it anymore. "Why did you stop me?"

Preston pulled me around a corner. "It doesn't matter."

He obviously had something up his sleeve. "If you think I'm going to do something worse later...."

"You'll do whatever I tell you to do."

"Yes, and you told me to suck your dick."

"Then I changed my mind."

There was that phrase again. "You don't change your mind."

"I did this time."

"Exactly my point!" My heart was pounding so hard I felt it in my temples.

I was onto his game, and I was not going to play it. There would be no favors for him to call in later. Fuck that. Preston wanted his dick sucked, and goddamnit, that was what was going to happen.

"All right, fine," Preston sighed. "You want the truth?"

"I thought you didn't lie," I spat back.

"There's a difference between lying and omittance."

Look at him playing with words. I could do that too.

"Avoidance doesn't equate to omittance."

We walked past the kitchen and down a hallway before he stopped and looked at me. "I didn't think you could do it."

The insult caused my jaw to drop.

Who the hell did he think he was? There wasn't a test out there that I couldn't ace with my eyes closed. My IQ would make the members of MENSA jealous, and he thought I couldn't suck a dick! That didn't even take any brain power.

Preston Whitley was not going to belittle me.

"I could so do it! In fact, I'd probably suck your dick better than anyone else." I bet I could make him come in under four minutes.

"I doubt that."

My jaw dropped more.

"But it's cute that you think so."

He did not just call me cute.

My hand sliced through the air. "That's it, take your pants off."

We were going to do this shit right here.

As if he didn't hear me, Preston turned his back to me and began typing a code into a pad on the wall.

He wasn't getting away that easy.

"Fine, if you won't take them off, I will."

I tugged on his belt, and Preston sighed before once again pushing my hand away. "I don't have time to teach you how to suck cock, Little Bird."

The fact that he thought I needed to be taught something so basic was ludicrous. "How hard can it be? I just put it in my mouth and suck."

I grabbed his hand and wrapped my lips around his finger to emphasize my point. Shadows danced across his face, darkening the lust I could see in his eyes. I realized how ridiculous I must look, yet I couldn't stop my tongue from swirling over his skin.

"Marnie?"

I froze. It couldn't be.

"Oh my god, Marnie, tell me you're okay."

That voice sent chills up my spine, but it was nothing compared to the way my blood froze when I looked into the now-open room.

"Tico?" I muttered around the finger in my mouth.

Preston leaned in and whispered, "Still want to suck my cock?"

Chapter 30
Marnie

Tico was alive.

My knees wobbled against the shock of seeing those warm brown eyes.

Clutching onto the doorframe, I closed my eyes and shook my head. This couldn't be real. It was just another trick my mind was playing. For months after he was gone, I saw Tico everywhere. He would be smiling at me in a crowd, sleeping on the couch at the Causegrove, and waving for me to follow when I walked down the beach. But every time I reached out to touch him, the haunted image faded away.

"Marnie."

"No." I shook my head, denying the familiar tone ringing through my ears. "It's not real."

I'd dreamt about this moment a thousand times and wanted nothing more than to wrap my arms around him. But I knew what would happen if I did. I would not give in to this illusion.

A hand touched my shoulder, and for a fleeting moment, I thought maybe I wasn't crazy. But it wasn't my beloved friend touching me. It was Preston.

"Open your eyes, Little Bird, and talk to your friend."

Him!

This was all his fault. Mr. Mindfuck just upped his game. I was wrong. There was no life inside him. I couldn't believe I ever thought that. Preston Whitley wasn't human, and he never would be.

I blinked open my lids and glared at him, not caring about the tears burning a trail down my face. "This is cruel, even for you."

At that moment, I swore to myself that I would watch Preston die one way or another.

"Tell me something Little Bird." His brow arched. "How exactly am I making you see someone? Do you think I have secret holographic technology?"

He had a point. Preston wasn't a moron. It took some serious intelligence to get away with the things he had, but inventing something that didn't exist was unlikely. Still...Tico couldn't be here.

Could he?

My eyes shifted back to the room, where Tico tipped his head and smiled. "It's really me."

That was when a familiar scent hit my nostrils—a mixture of mint and citrus that I hadn't smelled in almost a year.

Oh my god, it was him!

So many emotions rolled through me. Happiness had me rushing over to wrap my arms around Tico. Relief pulled more tears from my eyes, and shock hit me when I realized I could actually feel him. Then finally, anger rolled through me. I was so confused that I didn't know whether I wanted to beat him to death or hold onto him forever.

So, I did both.

One hand swung through the air, slapping Tico. "I thought you were dead."

Then, I pulled him into a hug. I was afraid that if I let him go, he'd disappear.

"I'm sorry, Marnie."

Sorry? That was all he had to say.

"Fuck you, Tico," I said. Too angry to hold onto him anymore, I shoved him away. "Do you have any idea what you put me through? What you put everyone through...."

Trina, Shelby, Riley, and even Star spent days if not months crying over his loss. We were broken and cursed the world for taking him away. And the entire time, he was here, right under our noses.

"I didn't want to hurt you." A tear trickled down Tico's face, and I could see the guilt burning in his eyes.

I wanted to forgive him. I really, really did. But the grave I spent too many nights with sucked away whatever innocence I had left. The Marnie he knew died that day.

We all died that day.

"Riley got a gun, Tico. Riley!"

Micha didn't know about it, but she told me. Riley was so scared that something would happen to someone else she loved that she drove to New Haven—a place where the addicts and degenerates of the world went to die—and bought a pistol from some random guy.

"I-I..." he stuttered. "I didn't know."

"Did you know she got drunk the night of your funeral? Shelby had to take her keys because she was going to drive, Tico."

A part of me wanted to comfort him and wipe the wet streaks off his face. Instead, I scrubbed my own tears away.

Tico reached out for me, but I jerked back. "You broke her, Tico."

He broke all of us.

"Don't get mad at him, Little Bird," Preston piped in. "He didn't have a choice."

My fists balled against the rage boiling in my veins. This was all Preston's fault. He took him away from me. He took everything away, my sister, my friends, and my life. I cursed the day I met him.

"What did you do to him?"

"Nothing," Preston said. "I'm protecting him."

"From what? The people who loved him?"

Tico was the one to answer. "My family will kill me if they know I'm alive."

"Your dad is dead!"

Silas killed him when Star went over there. She was worried because Tico was missing. Star put herself in danger and confronted a known abuser…for him.

"I'm not talking about my dad." I felt the weight of his sigh. "There's stuff you don't know about me, Marnie. But if you give me a chance, I promise I'll try and explain."

Guilt tore through my chest like a bullet through paper. He wasn't the only one hiding something. My entire being was a lie. The "Marnie" Tico thought he knew—didn't exist. She was nothing more than aI wall I put up to protect myself. I was worse than he was. The least I could do was hear him out.

Letting my fists unfurl, I blew out a breath and nodded. "Okay, let's talk."

I supposed there were a few explanations I owed him as well.

Preston left us alone. He locked the door behind him, and Tico and I sat down to talk.

He told me about his mother's cartel ties and how he helped Preston locate a person of interest. I should've been mad at Preston. Mafia and secret societies were terrible, but the cartel…didn't care about age or innocence. They would eliminate an entire family line, including friends, friends of friends, and anyone who talked to them. The cartel wasn't just bad news. They were evil. That alone was enough reason for Tico to stay "dead." I couldn't fault him for it. He was protecting himself, and the other people in his life.

However, it was Preston's actions that threw me for a loop.

Preston didn't just hide Tico, he took care of him. Carried him to bathroom, fed him, and made sure Tico was comfortable while he healed. His room was nothing like the dungeon I'd seen Lillianna in. There was nice furniture, a soft blanket on a king-size bed, a table with two chairs, a big bay window, and a large flatscreen in front of a beige loveseat. Aside from the lock on the door preventing him from leaving, Tico's suite was better than most high-end apartments.

I was kind of jealous. I woke up in a cage with no natural light whatsoever while Tico was down here.

It was nice being next to him again, so much so that once my mouth opened, I couldn't stop the secrets from coming out. I told him many things, like how I didn't need glasses, about drugging Chase Akerman, and cutting Stephen Hamilton's brake lines. I didn't realize how much I was carrying around until the weight lifted off my shoulders.

I felt lighter and a bit free. For the first time in my life, I let someone see the real me, and he didn't reject or judge me. Tico just held my hand while I talked. Then we got to the stuff about Preston, and he wasn't too happy.

"So he kidnapped you?"

"And killed someone," I reminded him.

Was Brian's body found? I hoped so. He seemed like a decent guy, and his family deserved closure.

"How can you be so calm about this?"

My shoulder lifted in a small shrug. "What good would freaking out do?"

All that would get me was buried in a hole so deep that I couldn't climb out.

"Besides, you can't tell me you haven't seen Preston kill someone."

"I have not," Tico said. "I'm not allowed out of this room."

I knew that feeling, but he'd been here for a year. "You must've seen something."

This was Preston's house. Walking away innocent wasn't an option.

Tico shook his head. "Nope. In fact, I think he goes out of his way to make sure I don't see anything."

That didn't make sense. Preston was right about one thing: he didn't lie, hide, or deny his actions. What you saw was what you got, plain and simple.

"Okay, maybe you didn't see anything, but I'm sure you heard about it."

Tico rolled his eyes. "Preston's not exactly the chatty type."

"Really? Cause I can't get him to shut up."

He was constantly using stupid logic to argue with me. 'Welcome to my parlor said the spider to the fly.' What the hell was that?

Resting his palms on the bed behind him, Tico leaned back and eyed me. He didn't say anything, just watched me. It was seriously annoying.

"What?" I snapped.

"Nothing," he sang in a way that told me it wasn't nothing.

"Whatever," I grumbled and stood up.

The sunlight streaming through the bay window was calling to me. I was intent on enjoying as much of it as I could. Except when I sat down on the pillowed bench and looked outside, the sun wasn't the only thing I saw. Preston was out there sandbagging. I watched him hoist two up on his shoulder, then walk over to the right side and place them on a barrier he was building.

"What is he doing?" Tico muttered from behind me.

I had no idea, but I did know that every time he shifted a sandbag, the muscles in his forearms bulged out in the most enticing way. His sandy hair was damp from the sweat on his forehead, and I swore I could hear him grunt.

Tico was just as entranced as I was. He plopped down on the bench beside me, propped his chin up with his hand, and followed Preston as he sauntered over to pick up a bottle of water.

"It should be against the law for someone to look that good."

"He's okay,." If okay meant 'so damn hot, I wanted him to pour that water over his head.'

Preston twisted the cap off the bottle as a monologue started in my head.

Dump it on your head.

You can do it.

Just a little drizzle.

Then damnit, when the bottle touched his lips....

Watching his Adam's apple bob while he swallowed was pretty damn sexy.

Wait. Why was I thinking about this?

Yeah, sure. Preston was good-looking, but he was cruel, evil, and rough.

And hard in all the right places.

My head tipped as he ran his fingers through his hair. I bet he smelled great right now. All masculine and covered in sweat.

Tico let out a longing sigh. "I wonder if he fucks like his dad?"

"What?" Where the hell did that question come from? Hold on... "Did you fuck his dad?"

A smirk spread across his face. "More like he fucked me."

Oh my god. "Dean Whitley? Really?"

Not that Dean wasn't nice to look at, but he was weird, always smiling and acting like the perfect dad. I couldn't imagine him in a sexual way or even being turned on.

"Was he...rough?"

"Let's just say he likes to be in control."

That made me snort. "Must be a Whitley trait."

I realized my mistake when Tico's eyes swung my way. "So Preston has fucked you?"

"Fucking implies consent," I argued with a finger point. "Which he didn't have."

"Uh-huh?" Tico huffed, making me roll my eyes.

"Can we *not* talk about this." I wasn't comfortable talking about sex with anyone.

"Whatever you say, Babe, but just so you know...." He leaned over to playfully shoulder-bump me. "It's okay to like it."

Hold up...

"I never said anything about liking it."

"Says the girl gawking out the window."

I was not gawking. "It's called observing thy enemy."

And watching how his muscles moved with every step he took.

"Do you always drool when observing your enemy?"

"Okay, first of all...."

Preston reached over his shoulder to peel his shirt off, and I completely forgot what I was saying. The term washboard abs wasn't good enough to describe the sight before me. Preston was so chiseled I wouldn't be surprised if my hand got cut touching that tanned skin. Apparently, Tico agreed.

"Fuck me," he growled. "I wouldn't mind staring at that while sucking his cock."

My eyes narrowed. "What's that supposed to mean?"

Tico's brow arched in response.

Stupid Preston, pushing me away. He changed his mind, my ass.

"I'm perfectly capable of sucking a dick."

Chapter 31
Preston

Fuck, fuck, fuck.

It never failed. Things were going great, but then some asshole came along and threw a wrench in my plans. My denial tactic was working perfectly. Not only had Marnie switched the conversation back to her inability to give a blow job, but she spent all night tossing and turning because

I didn't lay a finger on her when I climbed into bed. She was on the verge of breaking. I should be with her at home chipping away at that crack, not wasting my time here.

My jaw clenched as I glared through my windshield at the ruins of Manning Keep. Why was I here? Because my secret admirer didn't handle rejection well. Yesterday, I got another request to meet at Devil's Peak and a second video. This time it was of my brother's nanny being cut up. Meaning Ned didn't shoot up Parker's house. Mr. Ace of Spades did.

This morning, I was woken up by Nikolai.

An open hit had gone out on a network I was a part of, and the targets were every single member of The Order, including my nephew Weston and Marnie Dupire. There was a million-dollar target on everyone's head. Prick even threw Chase's club on the list. My guess was to keep the Lost Souls out of town. The pay for a member was only five grand, but it was enough to put a target on their backs. Needless to say, Snake wasn't too happy, and I wasn't sure if it was because of the extra hassle or the smaller payout.

So, I was forced to call an emergency meeting. Listening to Lou and the other Kings argue about shit they didn't understand was not my idea of fun. Mr. Ace of Spades wanted my attention. Well, now he had it. Every second I had to spend away from Marnie would be an hour of torture for him.

A Corvette swerved around the corner and skidded to a stop, causing rocks to ping off my door. The driver's green eyes twinkled as a smile spread across his face.

Fucking Mason. Who the hell gave him his license back?

He opened his door and stepped out. "Hey man, why are you still out here?"

"I'm plotting a murder."

And avoiding the frustration waiting for me inside.

I knew exactly what was going to happen when I walked in there. Micha and Logan would be freaking out about their girls. Parker would be pacing back and forth while Lou yelled at everyone to shut up. Because god forbid the King of Kings didn't have a handle on something. This wasn't a business deal gone wrong or open warfare.

This situation was underhanded, sneaky espionage in which someone would have poison slipped into their drink or were shot from a mile away. Hitmen from around the world were about to converge on Ashen Springs, and no matter what Louis thought, he wouldn't see them coming. The only hope they had was if they listened to me.

Mason slapped his hand down on the hood of my car. "Well, come on. You're the one that called this shit, so let's go inside, head honcho."

If I waited five more minutes, someone might take him out.

Fuck it. The sooner this shit was done, the sooner I could get back to fucking with Marnie.

Sighing, I got out of the car and walked past Mason to the center pillar.

"So, what's up?" The fucker was skipping behind me.

I unclipped my watch, held up my tattoo for the scanner, and arched a brow at him. "You mean, besides the million-dollar price on your head?"

His eyes widened. "Seriously?"

"I don't joke."

"One mill, huh?" He said as the entrance door slid open. "Cool."

Idiot.

Once we hit the bottom of the stairs, voices hit my ears. They were already arguing. No surprise there.

Mason slapped his hand on my back. "Looks like the party started without us."

'Don't shoot him, don't shoot him,' I silently chanted while heading toward the meeting room. And just as I suspected, everything I thought would be happening...was.

Micha and Logan were bitching about what to do with Riley and Shelby. Parker was on the far side, pacing a clean trail in the dust on the floor, and Lou was banging his mug on the table, trying to quiet everyone. The only people who weren't losing their minds were the Creswells and my dad. He was sitting in his seat, sporting a large smile.

Mason nodded at Silas and headed in that direction while I pulled out my gun and fired a shot into the roof. That shut everyone up.

"What the fuck, Preston!"

Well, everyone except Logan.

"Don't waste bullets. At least shoot someone."

"I could shoot you?"

"Let's do it, man." In true Logan Hudson style, he jumped out of his chair and smacked his chest. "Right fucking here. I can take it."

I looked down at my Desert Eagle and then back at him. "Yeah, all right."

When I raised my arm to aim, Lou interjected, "Whoa, no one is shooting anyone."

"A million buys a lot of bullets," I pointed out.

Lou rolled his eyes. "It's not as serious as you're making it out to be."

Not as serious?

"Tell me something, Lou." I dropped my hand and took a few steps in his direction. "How exactly are you planning to spot the sniper from five thousand yards away?"

Lou's face remained straight. "We're perfectly safe here. This is our town."

That didn't mean shit to these assassins.

"Three thousand, two hundred, and seven."

His brow rose. "Pardon me?"

"That's how many times I could've put one between your eyes." However, one of those was questionable. If he'd moved at the last second, Micha would've gotten it instead.

"All right, Preston," Martin piped in. "Maybe you should calm down."

I thought I was pretty calm, considering. The only thing that was pissing me off was having to take time away from my Bird.

"I don't think you understand the situation—"

"That's why you're here," Martin interrupted. "So, why don't you do your fucking job and tell us."

My eyes landed on the feminine face beside him. "Says the guy who brought his wife."

Wives weren't allowed in the meeting room. Was I surprised Martin brought her? No. For some reason, he thought he was above the rest of us.

His eyes narrowed. "I don't hide things from my wife. She knows what happens in here."

"She also knows what my dick tastes like, but you don't see me inviting her to dinner. Do you?"

Logan and Mason snorted while Silas joined his dad in the death-glare stare down.

"None of the girls are on the hit list." It was stupid to bring her.

"Does that mean they're not in danger?" Micha asked.

"No," I said, stomping on his hope. "That's why Nikolai is sending his men to pick them up."

And just like that, the ruckus started again.

"What!" Micha growled.

"I am not letting a bunch of horny Russians around Shelby," Logan said.

"Relax." Silas rolled his eyes. "No one wants to fuck your girl."

Mason held up his hand. "I'd tap that."

"See," Logan said, waving at Mason. "By the way, I totally tried to fuck Harper junior year."

Mason bolted out of his chair. "That's it, motherfucker."

"You want to go?" Logan jumped up on the table and puffed his chest out. "Bring it, bitch."

"Oh, it's on." Mason stormed over and glared up at Logan.

Logan glared down at him.

The tension lasted about three seconds.

Just when I thought one of them would take a swing, Mason waved his hand. "It's cool, man. I tried to fuck Shelby, too."

"Call it even?"

"Yeah." Mason nodded, and they both sat back down.

I scrubbed a hand down my face. How anything ever got done with those two around, I had no idea.

"There's one girl on that list." Lou's brown eyes rolled my way. "Marnie Dupire?"

Based on the look he was giving me, I'd say he knew who Marnie was and what she had on him.

"Recognize the name, Lou?"

His jaw twitched. "What I want to know is how you know the name, Preston?"

Both Micha and Logan looked at me, but my old man spoke.

"She's his girlfriend," he proclaimed proudly. "Very nice girl."

Nice wasn't the word I'd use.

325

"Wait, wait, wait." Mason held up his hands. "Preston has a girl-friend? And she's still alive?"

Micha tipped his head in a nod. "I thought he ate her at one point."

"My son is on that list!" Parker bellowed out of the blue. "So, if you all could take this shit seriously, I'd appreciate it."

I could've kissed my brother for the change of subject. Finally, the room fell silent. It wasn't all fun and games anymore, not when a child was involved.

Silas and Micha exchanged a look.

"I asked Nikolai to take them as well," I said, answering their silent question. Finn and Junior were both on that list, too.

The Bratva boss already had his men grab Lana and the babies from Boston. There was no way he would risk his one and only heir, but there was only so much he could do. Lou would never let the Russians invade his town. Plus, they'd be safer on his home turf. The criminal underworld had its own rules, and Miami belonged to Nikolai.

Unfortunately, no matter how much I argued, I couldn't stop the divide from happening. My generation wanted to do what I suggested and call in people experienced with shit like this. But the older generation was used to handling things themselves and didn't want to involve anyone else. As far as they were concerned, we were at the top of the food chain. I never thought the day would come when I'd miss my grandfather. Micha and Mason ran them out of town.

Lou did have a few valid points. Silas's grandfather would be fine. Politicians weren't easy targets to take out. That didn't mean his family was out of danger, which was a significant point of contention between Martin and me.

The end result of the meeting was not what I wanted, but there wasn't much I could do about it. Louis and Martin were too stubborn to listen. They wouldn't have a choice when things went south. I'd just have to wait until then.

We all left at the same time, but Lou dropped back and followed me.

"I need to talk to you."

I was sure he did.

"I don't think I'm the one you should be talking to." I nodded toward the front of the crowd where Micha and Logan were walking.

"So you know?"

"I assume you're talking about the pills you gave your wife to drive her crazy?" I stopped a few feet away from my BMW. "Or is it about one of the other things Marnie has in that file?"

"Look, Preston." His chest rose with a heavy breath. "Things are going on that no one knows about."

"I don't care, Lou. But Micha will, and if someone else tells him, he'll never forgive you."

"I know." He sighed. "He's my son. I don't want to hurt him."

"You once said the same thing about Mason, and look how that turned out."

His eyes drifted from one son to the other.

Boom!

The ground rocked. My first thought was that the hurricane had arrived early until I saw the pillar of fire coming from what was once Martin Creswell's car. The only thing left of Silas's parents were the bloody pieces scattered on the ground.

A car bomb.

Shit was happening quicker than I expected. Someone just earned themselves a payday.

I leaned closer to Lou and said, "Shall I call that back up now."

Chapter 32
Preston

*D*espite the oncoming storm and what happened yesterday, it was fairly nice out. The sun was shining brightly in the clear blue sky. The wind had picked up a bit, and I could see clouds off in the distance, but it was still pleasant. Or was it a mockery of what was to come?

I guess it depended on who you were and how you looked at it.

Personally, I thought the world was better off without Martin Creswell in it. I doubted Silas would agree. He was pretty broken up when I last saw him. His grandfather had picked up Finn and him this morning.

Mason didn't want to leave Silas alone, so he took Harper and went with them. That was four less people to worry about and protect. Like I said, it wasn't easy to get close to a politician. Plus, if I knew the governor, he probably already had someone grab Star from her college in New York as well.

I was curious to see how they were going to handle this. "Actress Sharon Monroe Dies by a Car Bomb" would make a great headline for the media. The questions that came with that might just give Lou a heart attack. Due to the Creswells' political ties, I imagined the story would be spun as a tragic accident that took the couple's life. Soon, there'd be a cheesy Hallmark movie about their perfect marriage. That would probably be when Silas picked up a nasty habit like alcohol or drugs.

For right now, it was quiet.

The calm before the storm. In this case, the storm wasn't necessarily a raging hail of rain and wind. Something was brewing, and it was only a matter of time before more death came to this town. That was why I called in backup. I could protect Marnie and myself. My reputation alone would be enough to keep most away. Everyone else was a different story.

Thankfully, I'd made some connections over the years. One of whom happened to be the leader of an organization called The Righteous—a group of well-trained former soldiers who weren't opposed to taking a life when justice failed. Not exactly in the same field as I was, but no one was better prepared to handle this situation.

Plus, it would free me up to care for more important things like the girl locked in my room. Marnie was pissed. She did not like being ignored for two days. The fact that I managed to restrain myself and not touch her for that long was a goddamn miracle. But nothing worthwhile came easy, and Marnie was worth every second of my time.

Longing pulled me toward my bedroom door, but duty had me typing a number into my phone.

"This is Anderson."

Here we go. "Trev, it's Preston Whitley."

"The same Preston Whitley recently listed on Loni's Shortbread?"

God, I hated that name, but everything in my world was in code. A dark website called The Hit List would probably be watched.

"So, you know why I'm calling?" That saved me time.

"Three are headed your way. We require half payment—"

I cut him off. "It's already sent. Check your account."

"Any additional problems we should be aware of?"

Yeah. "Louis Kessler doesn't like to take orders."

"Psychiatrists rarely do."

Was I surprised that he'd looked into our backgrounds? Not in the least. The Righteous probably had a file on every single member of The Order. Taking care of guys like us was kind of in their wheelhouse.

"Good job taking care of the Reapers. I certainly hope this Marnie Dupire wasn't fallout from that incident."

That was his polite way of letting me know his suspicions. If Trev knew she was locked up in my bedroom, protecting the people on the hit list wouldn't be their only agenda.

"She's not."

"That's good to hear. I certainly hope it stays that way," Trev said, then hung up.

I appreciated the short and to-the-point conversation. I still eyed my phone to make sure the call had disconnected.

My eyes automatically fell on the closed door beside me. Fuck, I was hard. For two days, I'd been smelling her with no satisfaction. It was getting harder and harder to deny myself some relief, but there was a method to my madness. Yes, I could go in there and fuck her. And yes, she would like it, but she still wouldn't admit she wanted it. That final break would come later today. In the meantime, I had one more call to make.

Unfortunately, this one wouldn't be simple and short.

"Goddamnit," I grumbled while tapping on one of the names in my contacts.

My sister answered on the second ring.

"Dominic's House of Cards, you stack 'em, and we'll rack 'em."

That didn't even make sense. What did a house of cards have to do with stacking and racking? You know what, I didn't want to know. "Ava, it's your brother."

"I know," Ava sang. "Your name popped up on my phone with a picture of Tenderheart."

"You have Tenderheart for my picture?"

"Yes, because you're kind and loving and like to give hugs."

Who did she grow up with? "It's Preston, Ava, not Parker."

"Pfft," she snorted. "I know. Parker is Grumpy Bear."

Pretty sure she got those two mixed up.

"Listen, Ava. Something's happened, and I need you to get somewhere safe."

She wasn't on the list, but she could still be used to get to one of us. Since Nikolai's men and Snake flat out refused to look after her, warning her was my only option. Can't say I blamed Snake or the others. The last time I asked someone to look after her, he lost a testicle while she went fishing in the ocean with a paddle boat.

It was quiet for a second before she whispered, "Did the bushes start attacking again?"

"Sure." Let's go with that. "The bushes are attacking."

"I knew this was going to happen."

I heard some rustling from the other end. She was probably packing a bag.

"Don't worry, Pressy. I got this. Dragons burn bushes."

And just like that, she was gone, leaving me to wonder who or what my sister considered a dragon. I just hoped she didn't burn Miami down to the ground.

GOING for a drive didn't help my Bird's mood any. Since we'd left the house, she hadn't stopped snorting out huffs or shooting me dirty looks. However, I was thoroughly enjoying our outing. Watching the storm brewing in her pretty little head was my new favorite hobby. But the best part was knowing that some part of her was mad that I hadn't given her any attention.

"Something wrong, Little Bird? You seem a tad frustrated."

When her eyes snapped my way, I would've happily suffocated in the fire blazing within those beautiful aqua depths.

"I'm fine."

'Fine' was girl-code for, 'I want to rip your balls off.' Hence she was not fine, which ironically was fine with me. Teetering on the edge of a complete breakdown was precisely where I wanted her. Emotions tended to override logic, making someone act impulsively instead of thinking things through. When you did that to someone like Marnie, who wasn't used to acting impulsively, all kinds of things came out.

Last night, I caught her spouting off things about her father, like when and how she got some of her scars and the lessons he taught her. This morning, Marnie tried to seduce me. Not well, but she still tried because I told her I didn't think she could suck a dick. Now, she had something to prove.

I wasn't lying when I said that. She was inexperienced, but it didn't matter. All she'd have to do was look up at me while her lips were wrapped around my cock, and I'd blow my load down her throat, which was precisely why I kept poking at her. That image needed to become a reality, but I wanted her to beg for it.

"You sure, Little Bird? 'Cause, you seem a little pent up?"

"You're the one that's pent up." She was trying really hard not to look at my dick. "Got blue balls yet?"

If blue balls meant being hard for two days straight, then yes. My cock was aching to sink inside her, but that was what hands were for and why she smelled like me when she woke up.

Marnie huffed and yanked on the chain, attaching her to the door. "Why did you bring me with you if you're going to keep me hand-cuffed to the car?"

"I could put you in the truck if you prefer?"

I could fuck her in there. It would be a tight fit, but we'd get it done.

"Pfft," she snorted. "At least then, I wouldn't have to smell you."

Someone was extra testy today.

Not only had I ignored her for days, but I didn't so much as give her a second glance when I climbed into bed and closed my eyes. My dick hated me for that choice.

Marnie Dupire's biggest downfall was her arrogance. She thought she could do anything, and when someone told her she couldn't...well...

"Not everyone in this car had a restful night's sleep."

She couldn't let it go.

"Sounds like a personal problem," I said while holding back the smirk threatening to curl the corner of my mouth.

I'd never get enough of that confused yet pissed-the-fuck-off look she kept shooting my way. The way her nose scrunched up while her eyes dripped with venom was utterly intoxicating. If anyone was begging to be corrupted, it was my Bird. She was a pristine little morsel that became more delicious with every bite. One snide comment or angry glare was enough to test my resolve.

"You could've left me at home."

The fact that she'd just referred to my house as 'home' told me my plan was working.

"Aww, Little Bird." I shot her a fake frown. "Did I take away your planning time?"

Her eyes narrowed into slits. "I don't need to plan an escape."

"Ah." I nodded. "I forgot, you're great at everything."

That one got to her.

"You wouldn't know, would you."

"I know you didn't run away last night."

"How could I...." The words died on her lips as realization hit her.

She wasn't bound to my bed last night. I didn't even close the bedroom door. Poor thing was so wrapped up in being denied that she didn't notice my test.

I cocked a brow at her and teased, "Something wrong, Little Bird?"

"No," she snarled while shifting in her seat. "I'm just uncomfortable."

I bet she was.

My nostrils had been soaking up the scent of her frustration all morning. So pent up with no release, I understood that. I just had better control than she did—a fact proven when a sweet smile washed over her face.

"I'm not wearing any panties."

Fuck me.

I pushed down the urge to slide my hand under that gray knee-length skirt she was wearing and keep my focus on the road. "Sounds like another personal problem."

She had the option. I laid out everything she needed, including underwear and the tights she usually paired with that skirt. It wasn't my fault she didn't put them on.

Sighing, Marnie dropped her head back on the seat. "Well, if I'm going to be stuck in this car...."

Sly little minx slid her hand up over her knee.

"I guess I'll have to entertain myself." Her hand slipped under the material covering her thighs, and I damn near pulled over.

She was getting good at this game, but not as good as me.

My shoulder lifted with a shrug. "Whatever floats your boat."

What started as a battle of wills for her was now a predicament. If she didn't follow through, she would lose. If she did, then I'd get to watch her come all over my seat. Neither of which would get me to touch her. She would have to ask for that. One of us was going to break today, and it wouldn't be me.

A thought that I reconsidered when her lips parted with the sexiest moan I'd ever heard. Then she lifted her foot up onto the dash, making her skirt slide down her leg just enough to see her wrist moving and nothing else.

I never hated an article of clothing more. Then again, there was always a way around things.

"That was a cute moan. Trying to convince yourself that you're turned on?"

Anger twisted across her face. "I am turned on."

"If you say so." I shifted my gaze her way. "It's okay. Not everyone can get themselves off."

She had the skirt pulled up to her waist before I could blink.

"See," she hissed while sliding her finger through her folds. "I wouldn't be wet if I wasn't turned on."

Oh, and she was wet. The evidence was glistening on her inner thighs. Seeing her finger work her pussy was tantalizing but nowhere near enough. I wanted to see that delicate pink flesh.

"Looks like a pussy to me."

Her jaw dropped for half a second before she twisted around to prop her other foot up on the center console, spreading her legs wide enough to give me a perfect view.

"Does it still look like just a pussy?"

Fuck no. It looked like the best goddamn pussy on the planet.

"It looks like you're taking the easy way out."

Her face dropped. "What?"

"The clitoris is a bundle of nerves," I explained while nodding at her finger that had stopped moving. "It's the easiest way to get a girl off."

I wasn't lying. Anyone could stumble around that bundle of nerves and end with pleasure. True talent came from achieving an internal orgasm.

"You think I don't know my own body?"

Not in the fucking least.

" 'Cause I can make myself come."

"If you say so."

"I do say so," she snapped. "I'll do it right now."

Do it. Finger fuck that tight little cunt.

I shrugged again. "Go ahead."

She rose to the challenge and dipped her finger in her tight opening. It was adorable watching her fumble around like a teenage boy discovering his first cunt. It was also fucking hot, especially when frustration etched across her face.

"Need some help?" I asked.

To which she hissed, "No. I got this."

No, she didn't. She wasn't anywhere close to getting it. The only thing Marnie was accomplishing was winding herself up more.

I turned down a small road and headed for the building at the end. Marnie's attempt at figuring out her body came to a grinding halt when I pulled into the parking lot.

She sat there with her legs spread and her finger in her cunt while staring at the building. "Why are we here?"

"I told you, it's my job to ensure all evacuation points are ready. Your father's church is on that list."

Her eyes swung from me to the building and back.

It was show time.

"Now, would you like to keep fingering yourself?" I held up a set of keys and jingled them. "Or would you like to join me inside?"

This was where her wall was built and was where I'd tear it down.

Chapter 33

Marnie

$\mathcal{T}$he white cross standing on the black roof should be comforting. My family ran this church, and I should be excited at the possibility of escape. But I hated this place.

If I were given a choice to destroy one building in Ashen Springs, this would be the place. I wouldn't even care if people were inside when I lit the match. God didn't rule here. Corruption did.

I learned that lesson when I was eight, and my father whipped me in front of the entire congregation. Not one single person said anything. They just sat there, chanting their holy prayers while I pleaded for mercy.

"Now, would you like to keep fingering yourself, or would you like to join me inside?"

Shit.

Stopping my attempt at self-ministrations, I quickly smoothed my skirt back into place. As much as I wanted to forget this church existed, I couldn't stop mortification from burning down my neck as guilt welled up in my chest. The word 'dirty' chanted through my thoughts, mingling with my father's voice.

'The deeds of the flesh are immoral and impure.'

'Cursed is she who lies with a tainted soul.'

'Pray for salvation.'

The only thing that quieted my mind was Preston's body leaning over me to unlock the cuff around my wrist. I stared at his back, watching his jean jacket move with his shoulders, and another voice rang through my head.

'That's a pretty dress, Marnie.'

I don't know why or what changed, but disgust made me squirm away. Every time I looked at that jacket, my stomach churned. The miscolored patch near the top of the right arm and the black spot on the cuff disturbed me. Hang on...

A hand reaching out...

Fingers curling around the strap of my dress...

And a denim cuff with a black spot...

My breath hitched. "It's his jacket."

That was why it bothered me because it came from Nash. It had to. What were the odds of two jackets having the exact same stain?

Preston sat up and cocked a brow. "What?"

Did that mean that Preston killed him? Nash's family died in a fire, or so we were told. That, of course, didn't mean anything. The amount of fake news out there was astounding. And Nash was one of the men responsible for breaking Ava, so it wouldn't be surprising if Preston did something to him.

"If I asked you something, would you answer it?"

"Depends on what you ask."

That was fair. If I were being honest, I'd tell myself to shut up. The less I knew, the better, but a fire was too easy of an out for someone like Nash. I needed to hear that he suffered. I wanted all the details of his screams and pain, how he begged for his life and died in the same hell that he cast his victims in.

I needed it so badly that I couldn't stop the words from coming out. "Did you kill Nash?"

"Define kill," Preston asked back.

I thought that word was pretty self-explanatory. "Is he dead?"

"That would depend on your definition of dead."

"Is he still breathing?" I growled out of frustration. Did everything have to be a vague answer?

Preston sat back and rolled his eyes over my face. "Why the sudden interest in Nash?"

"You're wearing his jacket." It was a half lie. Preston was wearing his jacket, but he didn't need to know how I knew that. Or what happened the day I became tainted in my father's eyes.

Unfortunately, I neglected to take into account my opponent's intelligence. If there was one thing Preston Whitley was good at, it was reading people.

"How do you know it's his jacket?"

I never thought my father would be my saving grace, but when his car pulled up beside us, I was happy for the distraction. Seeing him, however...

He climbed out of his car and stared at me with the same look of disappointment I'd seen every day of my life. I could feel the weight of it pressing down on me as Preston got out and walked around the car to open my door.

It wasn't fresh air that smacked me in the face. It was the putrid stench of Old Spice and judgment that made me want to gag.

Preston held his hand out for me. "Come on, Little Bird?"

"Little Bird," my father snorted.

He thought nicknames were the devil's work.

I slid my palm into Preston's and stepped out while he turned his attention to my father. "Is there a problem, Pastor?"

"I have many problems, young man."

No, he didn't. He had just one. Me.

"Marnie." He nodded at me.

"Daddy," I said back.

For some reason, when his eyes landed on my bare legs, I found myself tucking in closer to Preston.

"I see college hasn't helped your sense of decency."

341

Preston's grip tightened on my hand. For a second, I thought he was going to punch my father in the face.

"Let's just get this over with," Preston said.

"Very well." My father spun around and headed for the church entrance.

Preston pulled me to follow, but not before leaning in to growl a warning. "Call him daddy again, and I'll slit his fucking throat."

"That's what he is." What else did he expect me to call him?

"Not anymore."

"That's ridiculous." I rolled my eyes. "You can't opt someone out of parenthood."

It didn't work that way. Blood was blood. There was nothing you could do to change DNA.

"Tell yourself that when you see your back in the mirror."

I chose to ignore that comment and marched into the church.

My father led us to a back room where Preston began ticking things off a list. Supplies, I assumed, based on the crates of water. After that, blankets and pews were cataloged where beds would be set up. Then into my father's office, where Preston checked the evacuation map for neighborhoods delegated to this point.

The entire time we walked around, one thing picked at the back of my brain. Why wasn't my father surprised to see me? As far as he knew, I was across the country. So, why didn't he say anything when I showed up with Preston Whitley, of all people? Did he really not care about me?

There were pictures of Trina everywhere in this room, but not a single one of me. Even the one on his desk was gone. Was I that much of a disappointment that he washed his hands of his daughter the second I was no longer his responsibility?

That was when it hit me.

"You knew."

Both Preston and my father stopped looking at the map on his desk and turned their heads my way.

"You knew he was going to take me?"

Preston was the one who answered. "He signed a contract last year."

What the hell was Preston talking about?

"What kind of contract?"

"The kind that gives you to me." He said it like it was a normal thing.

"What!" I shrieked. "You gave me away? To him."

My father had done many things to me, but this hurt more than any of the scars marring my skin.

As if he was bored, my father sighed. "You made your bed, Marnie. Now, you can lay in it."

"I'm your daughter." I stomped my foot on the ground, attempting to hold back the tears burning in my eyes.

"You stopped being my daughter the instant you let another man touch you."

That raised Preston's brow, but I was too upset to care what he heard or knew.

"I was seven. You were supposed to protect me, not throw me to the wolves."

"I knew you weren't right from the moment you were born and tried to take your mother's life." My father stood up and straightened his shoulders. "Quite frankly, I'm glad to have your taint out of my house."

Was that all I was to him? The tainted child he was cursed with raising?

"Did you ever love me?"

Not even a flicker of emotion flashed across his face. "It's not a father's job to love his children."

But he loved Trina. Evidence of that was all through my childhood.

The damn holding back my pain broke. I let all the years of agony and rage pour down my face in fat, salty drops. The truth of what I'd always known was too much to bear. Trina was the daughter he wanted. I was nothing more than a burden. He didn't even care how hurt I was.

But Preston did.

He marched across the room and cupped my face in his hands. "He doesn't deserve your pain."

"But he's my—"

"No, he's not." He cut me off. "He's just the man that brought you to me."

I don't know what came over me, but when I stared up into those gray pools, all I could see was that spark I'd seen in the woods. The next thing I knew, my arms were around Preston's neck, and my mouth was on his. I kissed him without restraint or holding back my pain.

Every tear I'd shed was poured into that kiss. I didn't care that my father was in the room or about the people Preston Whitley hurt. I clung to the monster who took me and kissed him with everything I had.

My father muttered something and stormed out, but I didn't care. Everything I needed was right here. My fucked up relationship with Preston was the only real thing in my life. That spark of life that he only gave to me was the best, most demented version of love.

I'm not sure when we wound up in the main chapel or how my hand got around his cock, but for once, I wasn't thinking about what I was doing. Logic held no credence here. All that existed in this place was pure animal instinct. For the first time in my life, I was free. And it felt fantastic.

A whimper escaped when Preston twisted his hand in my hair and tore his mouth away.

"Look at you, all needy and begging to be taken." He yanked my head back, causing my pussy to clench. "Tell me what you want, Little Bird."

This was it. The moment I'd been waiting for. I could either fight him, run out the door or break and admit defeat. The options warred in my mind, but the words that came out of my mouth sealed my fate.

"I want you."

The next thing I knew, I was flipped around and slammed face down on the altar, right next to a crisp, clean bible I hated with every fiber of my being. I barely had time to suck in a breath before his cock was forced inside me.

I moaned at the stretch pouring through my core. Defeat never felt so good.

"How many times were you down there on your knees while your father stood up here preaching his righteous bullshit?" He grunted, slamming in so deep my feet lifted off the ground and folded over me. "But you weren't praying to his god, were you, Little Bird?"

A powerful thrust stole my breath as he growled in my ear, "You were praying to mine."

I'd pray to whatever god he wanted me to as long as he kept doing that, which he didn't. Why would Preston Whitley make anything easy?

He slowed down his movements to an agonizing speed. I could feel every piercing and ridge of his cock drag along my inner walls. It was nowhere near what I needed. I tried egging him on by looking back and grinding my hips.

That didn't work. Preston just slammed my face back down and continued his torment. I swear, he got off on torturing me. And that was exactly what this was. Torture.

I couldn't take it anymore. "Are you going to keep teasing me?"

"Hasn't anyone ever told you to be careful what you wish for?" Preston snickered.

Lifting my head, I glared over my shoulder and snarled, "How about you just shut up and fuck me."

If I thought Preston fucked me before, I was wrong. He slammed into me, tearing an orgasm from my very soul. I came while staring at my father's cursed bible. Then again, in the choir room, my father's office, and propped up on numerous pews.

By the time we left, we had christened every inch of my father's church with our ecstasy.

Chapter 34
Preston

The Ashen Springs Sheriff's Office looked the same today as when I was a kid. Naturally, there were some upgrades: new computers, an updated security system, a few more parking spots, and some patches on the building's roof. The average person wouldn't notice these changes, but I wasn't the average person.

I'd spent some time within these white walls, specifically behind the barred walls in the back. That was the most time I spent with Mason Kessler. It was also the night I decided where my loyalties would lie.

Up until that point, I hadn't taken The Order seriously. That was my father's thing. But as I sat there all night comforting a broken-hearted Mason, the Ravens' mantra played through my thoughts.

The ravens stand strong,
Through credence and time,
My brother is my bond,
His family is mine.

347

Mason Kessler wasn't related by blood, but he was still family. They all were, and I was their older brother. That may sound cheesy to some. Hell, I wanted to slap myself for thinking that way, but bonds forged in misery were powerful. The six of us survived a childhood that would've destroyed others. Since I was the only one unphased by what happened to us, I would be the one to take care of the other five —their watchdog in the dark.

Half the shit I'd done, none of them knew about. They didn't need to know. I could live a normal life after Ryker Hudson—the benefits of not having a conscience—but the rest of them couldn't. Trauma bred insanity, and if I could organize that chaos, Ryker and Nash would never win. We would.

This hit list was another version of that—just another time, the watchdog in the dark would have to attack an intruder. So far, I had a perfect record, minus Micha getting shot. That one was on Chase. And I was not about to let that record get marred.

That was why I was standing outside the Ashen Springs Sheriff's Office with Derek Adams, waiting for help from an organization I would avoid under normal circumstances. If they knew Marnie was with me against her will, we'd have a problem.

This was precisely why the meeting wasn't happening at my house. My Bird finally broke yesterday, but there was a high probability that she was back to hating me. I may have left her unsatisfied and locked in my room. In my defense, the temptation to leave her on the verge of an orgasm was too strong to ignore. Plus, I enjoyed watching her squirm.

Derek's blue eyes rolled my way as I leaned back against the wall. "They're late."

"Your watch is fast." According to mine, they had another ten minutes.

"I have things to do, Preston. Do you have any idea how much manpower it takes to do evacuations?"

Nope, and I didn't care. "Feel free to leave anytime. Bringing you in on this, was a courtesy."

I didn't have to tell Derek shit, but I figured things might run smoother if the sheriff knew what was happening. There would be more deaths. I was sure of that, and explaining them away might become a hassle.

That was credit I'd give to Derek Adams. When he took up the position, he'd cleaned up the department. Any people we had on our payroll were fired. Well, the ones he could prove. Hence, the contention in The Order when he took the position. His daughter solved some of those problems but not all. Occasionally, he could be convinced to look the other way, but not every time. He actually believed in upholding the law. While I thought there were better ways to get justice, I admired his conviction.

Marnie was the only other person I knew who couldn't be bought. Needless to say, I wasn't surprised when I found out they were working together.

Their teaming-up stopped the day Micha claimed Riley. It didn't matter how much conviction someone had when their weak spot was pressed. The good Sheriff still managed to keep his distance from The Order. He wanted nothing to do with us.

This situation, however, he couldn't stay out of. Hitmen were coming to Ashen Springs, and whether I liked it or not, his department would come in handy.

Derek huffed and crossed his arms. "Are you sure they're coming?"

"Don't ask stupid questions, Derek."

Of course, I was sure. I wouldn't be here if I weren't.

"Okay." He clicked his tongue and cocked a brow. "Here's a better question for you, Preston. How exactly do you know about a hit list?"

I tipped my head in his direction. "You really want me to answer that?"

He did. There was no denying the suspicion written across his face. He'd been itching for a reason to lock us up and throw away the key for years. His precious morals wouldn't allow him to look the other way, but he wouldn't pry because that would require hurting his daughter. Can't imagine Riley would be too happy if her old man threw her fiancé in jail before the wedding.

Speaking of fiancé...

My eyes narrowed on a familiar Jeep pulling into the parking lot.

What the fuck was Micha doing here? Last I heard, he was arguing with Riley when Nikolai's men came to get her and Shelby. Based on his scowl when he stepped out and headed our way, I'd say his mood hadn't improved any.

"Something wrong?"

His dark eyes locked on mine. "Don't get me started."

Aww, did Riley give him a hard time? Was he really surprised? That girl was a pain in the ass from the moment she was born.

"You didn't have to come." I'd prefer it if he didn't.

"You think I'm going to leave this shit up to you?"

Yes, I did.

Micha was too much like his old man.

I spent three hours on the phone with Lou before coming here. He was not happy about the situation. Guess what? No one was happy about the situation. Lou wasn't special or in charge, as much as he liked to think he was.

I wouldn't be surprised if he put the idea of coming down here in Micha's head. Ah well, it was one less person I'd have to introduce. I might not have to introduce anyone now. Micha could take them to meet Logan, and I could go home to play with my Bird.

"Derek." Micha eyed Derek, who returned his look with one of his own.

"Micha. Has Riley called you yet?"

"Of course," Micha growled. "Why did she forget to call you?"

A smug grin spread across Derek's face. "I heard from her as soon as she got there."

I was tempted to grab them and knock their heads together when Micha's eyes darkened. It amazed me how often Riley Adams fucked with my plans. Last month when she got in a fight with Micha, he had me track her ass down. And here I was again, stuck in the middle of some juvenile pissing contest because of her. She was lucky I was busy and couldn't drive down to Nikolai's to slap the shit out of her.

"I think we have bigger things to worry about."

"Fine." Derek huffed.

"Whatever you say," Micha growled.

Five and a half seconds. That was all I got before Micha's grumpy voice rang through my ears.

"Are these asshole's coming or what?"

Derek muttered, "That's what I said."

Why did I get stuck with the two most impatient pricks on the planet? If there were a god up there, he'd have a sniper hiding somewhere. I wouldn't even care if he shot me so long as I was taken out of my misery.

That prayer was answered when a train of three hummers turned down the road.

I nodded at them and grumbled, "Here they are."

Thank fucking God.

Micha immediately began sizing them up, eyes narrowed and suspicious while he straightened his shoulders.

Derek resumed his arms crossed and serious position.

I felt like shaking my head at their alpha macho bullshit.

Instead, I kicked off the wall and prepared to greet our guests.

The first one to step out was black-haired and amber-eyed. The second was a blonde with a glimmer in his blue eyes that reminded me of Logan. I assumed that one was Trev's brother, Arek. He'd warned me about him.

But it was the third that made my eyes roll.

A familiar man with absolutely no expression on his face appeared, and I groaned.

Fucking Wilder.

Why in the hell did they bring him? Go figure that prick worked with a group like The Righteous. Don't get me wrong. The guy had skills. I watched him sneak onto a trafficker's boat and kill mother fuckers like he was performing a goddamn dance. But he was the last person I wanted to deal with. I didn't have a conscience, but Wilder didn't have emotions, period. What he did have was total focus, which given the circumstances, probably wasn't a bad thing.

The dark-haired guy tipped his chin at me. "You Preston?"

"You must be Kes," I responded.

He nodded and walked up, which was when Derek decided to step forward. "You can't park there."

Oh man, my trigger finger was getting itchy.

"That spot is for police cruisers only."

"Derek." I sighed while pinching the bridge of my nose. "Shut the fuck up."

"I'm just saying," he muttered.

"Say it to someone else," Micha barked. "No one fucking cares where your cruisers park."

Kes's brows rose as he looked at the Sheriff, Micha, then me. "I can see you three are friends."

"Not really. I'd kind of like to kill them both right now," I said, making both Derek and Micha shoot me a glare.

"You're the one that thought strangers could protect us better than our own men."

That was Micha's old man shining through his son's eyes.

"Aaaaand there's the warm welcome Trev was talking about," Kes sang. "Pleased to meet you. Please tell me how I can further ruin your day."

"I don't know what you're talking about." The one I assumed to be Arek sauntered up and slapped his hand on Kes's back. "Look at this fabulous greeting party we have."

Kes shot him a glare that I couldn't help but agree with.

Micha was grinding his teeth beside me, the sheriff couldn't look more unimpressed, and I didn't want to be here—some greeting party.

I shook my head and returned to the matter at hand. "I assume you've been briefed on the situation?"

"My brother filled us in," the blonde answered, confirming my suspicions about who he was.

"And why the fuck should we listen to you?" Micha growled, "I don't know your fucking brother."

I was about to slap him in the back of the head when Arek popped his bottom lip out in a fake frown.

"Aww, that's too bad. Because I'm pretty sure he has the same stick shoved up his ass that you do."

Even I chuckled a touch at that one.

"Why would anyone shove a stick up their ass?"

All eyes turned to Wilder.

What the fuck? He genuinely looked perplexed by this.

"It's a figure of speech," Kes explained. "No one has an actual stick shoved up their ass."

The fact that Kes had to explain that made me pity any poor fucker Wilder called friend.

"Then why say it?

Would the robot care if I shot him?

Kes repeated, "Because it's a figure of speech."

Wilder stared blankly at him as if waiting for more of an explanation.

A few awkward moments of silence passed before Arek chimed in with, "And this is Wilder, our newest member."

"We've met," I muttered as an idea came to me. "He would be perfect to put on Louis."

If there was anyone suited to protect Louis Kessler, it was a psychopath. He wouldn't be able to get under Wilder's skin or chase him away. The only thing Wilder would care about was the task he was given. Not to mention the amusement I would get from knowing how pissed off Lou would be. I kind of wanted to see that shit go down.

"He's the one you warned Trev about?" I nodded.

"Let's just say he won't be too keen on taking orders."

Micha snorted. "That's an understatement."

He was one to talk.

Wilder suddenly perked up.

"I have a solution for that." He strutted over to his Hummer, opened the trunk, and pulled out a bundle of black rope. "The object of my affection didn't like taking orders at first either."

Kes and Arek cocked a brow as Wilder walked back over and held up the rope.

"This helped. She's much better now."

There was so much I could say here. Who in their right mind

would fuck you? Was it possible for Wilder to show affection? But I decided to see where this was going with his supposed coworkers who were against kidnapping and raping women.

I was a tad disappointed when Arek just pointed at him and said, "We're going to have a talk about that later."

Wilder's brows knit, "I hear that a lot."

I bet he did.

"Anyway," Kes rolled his eyes back to me. "What are we looking at?"

I gave them the rundown of how many of us were still in town, possible targets that might get hit, and supplies they had at their disposal. Eventually, Micha and Derek gave in and became helpful. Twenty minutes later, we had a solid plan. That was when I saw the red dot marking Micha's chest. And I wasn't the only one.

Arek yelled, "Get down." While Kes moved in and Wilder searched the horizon.

I sprang forward to knock Micha out of the way, but Derek got there first.

The sharp slice of a bullet cut through the air as the sheriff plowed into Micha, and they both tumbled to the ground. All hell broke out after that.

Someone called out, "Sweet Delilah, scan for hostiles."

A bench was flipped over to provide cover as cops, who were outside, ran in our direction. It all happened so fast that Micha had no clue what was going on. At least, that was what I assumed by the way he blinked his eyes up at me and growled, "What the fuck Derek?"

I stared down at the bright red soaking into the sheriff's shirt, "I don't think he's going to answer you."

Derek Adams wasn't going to answer anyone ever again.

Chapter 35

Preston

For the first time in my life, I was conflicted about opening a door. Not because I didn't want to see my Bird. I did. Adrenaline was pumping through my system, and I'd like nothing more than to spend the rest of the day buried in her tight cunt.

I didn't want to open the door because I didn't want to break her heart, which in itself was a fucked up feeling for me to have. I had to tell her that Derek was dead, and while he wasn't her father, she did grow up with him in her life. She probably wouldn't take it well.

My hand reached out to grab the doorknob, but I couldn't turn it. It was starting to get annoying. I'd been out here for ten minutes now, getting nothing accomplished. At one point, I thought about it like ripping a band-aid off. Just do it and move on. Then, I imagined the frown on her face and couldn't open the door.

This was fucking ridiculous. Why was I hesitating? So what? Derek died. Who the fuck cared?

She would.

A strange cool sensation rolled through my chest, further pissing me off.

Fuck this.

I threw the door open and stormed in.

Marnie was sitting on the bed reading a magazine. She looked sweet and tantalizing with her legs crossed and dark hair flowing down her back. I couldn't help but suck back a breath at the perfection before me. I wanted to grab her and bury my face between her thighs until she couldn't tell the difference between breathing and coming.

So what if she was upset? I could make her forget. It wasn't like Derek was important. He was just her friend's dad.

"Welcome back," she hissed, flipping a page.

Ooo, she was pissed. Fuck me. I wanted to play with that anger.

"I hope your meeting went well."

No, she didn't. If I walked over there right now, there was a chance she would grab the knife she'd stashed under her pillow and stab me, which wasn't helping my situation. One minute in this room, and I was already hard as fuck.

"It went fine," I grunted and readjusted my cock.

'Fine' was a slight overstatement, but I could always wait to explain later.

When Marnie lifted her head, the sight of those bright aqua depths was like a punch in the gut.

"Well, I hope you're not...." She stopped and narrowed her gaze. "Is that blood on your shirt?"

Goddamnit. Fucking white shirt. I never wore white.

"Yes," I said, not wanting to explain further.

When her eyes widened, I damn near fucked her right then and there.

"It's not mine." I felt pride like never before at that moment. Marnie Dupire was still worried about me despite her anger and hatred.

Then she ruined it. "Who's blood is it?"

Fuck. Just do it, Preston.

I sucked in a deep breath and said, "Derek Adams."

She straightened up, and I didn't like the expression etched on her face. It pulled at my gut and pissed me off. The only person she should be concerned about was me. I didn't want to share that with anyone, let alone Derek.

"Is he okay?"

The look I gave her said it all. Tears brimmed in her eyes as the corner of her mouth dipped down, and I stood there asking myself why I couldn't just say the words, 'He's dead.' It wasn't a hard task. I didn't give a shit about him, but I did give a shit about her. Was this what love felt like?

Fuck me.

"How?"

That one whispered word tore a hole of rage through me.

Suddenly, I wanted to hunt down the fucker that did this and make him suffer. Peel his skin back while Marnie watched, and then fuck her over his corpse.

"He took a bullet for Micha."

Why did I say it like that? Instead of a nice, simple, and to the point, 'He was shot.'

"Of course he did. Derek's a good man...." She stopped to take a breath. "He was a good man."

He was alright. A little uptight and stubborn as hell, but alright. I didn't have anything against him.

"Micha should've been the one who got shot."

I doubted Riley would agree, but okay.

"But why would the world start being fair now?"

Fairness was a matter of perspective.

"The world doesn't give a shit about you, Little Bird, or what you think is fair." It was time for her to emerge from her self-imposed cloud of safety. It was an illusion. "You'll die waiting for the world to bend to your will. If you want something, you have to take it."

I saw the breakdown starting, the quiver in Marnie's bottom lip, and her shoulders slumped. But it was the glimmer of something else that caught my eye. It gave me an idea.

Back at the church, Marnie said something about Nash and my jacket. I didn't put it together until I heard her say 'I was seven' to her father. He didn't fuck her, that much I knew, but Nash did something to her.

"Come with me." I held my hand out. "I want to show you something."

It wasn't a request, nor did I wait for a response. I grabbed Marnie's hand and pulled her out of the room.

"Preston, I'm not in the mood."

"But you're pissed off, right?"

"Damn right, I'm pissed off!" She stomped her foot and tried to yank out of my grip when I led her around a corner. "Now let me go back and wallow in my misery."

"What has misery ever gotten you?" I asked while opening the door to the basement, or as Marnie liked to call it, the dungeon. "Has misery ever comforted you when you were crying and alone? Did misery ever make you feel better the next morning? No. The only thing misery does is drag you down."

Now anger...that was an entirely different beast.

"What would you know about misery?" She snapped in a way that had my hand twitching to smack her ass. "You don't care about anything."

"I care about you."

Marnie wasn't the only one stunned. She stopped and stared at me while I wondered why I said that.

"What?"

Fuck. What the hell was I supposed to say now? I didn't like lying to her, but I didn't want to tell her the truth either. I was having a hard enough time admitting it to myself.

But the words came out anyway. "It's called love, Little Bird."

A fucked up and twisted version, but love was there, sinking its claws into my chest.

"This isn't love Preston."

"Then what would you call it?"

Her forehead creased as she thought for a second. "Dark, painful, and wrong?"

"What do you think love is?"

"Not this!"

"You watch too many Hallmark movies."

I stopped in front of the room at the end of the hall. "You want to see what love is?"

Punching in a code, I pushed the door open and pulled Marnie inside.

Her eyes widened at the sight of the naked, emaciated man huddled in the corner.

"What did you…." She took a few steps closer, then stopped dead as her face paled. "Is that Nash?"

"No, Marnie," I said, nodding at him. "That's what love is. It isn't rainbows and sunshine. It's messy, feral, and broken. It makes you do things you never thought you would and drives you crazy. Love doesn't heal your soul. It shatters it into a thousand pieces." I grabbed my knife out of my pocket and held it out for her. "Then bonds it together with blood and tears."

Her eyes landed on the hilt and then trailed back over to Nash. "He's already dead."

"Does it matter?"

Still, she hesitated.

"It's time to make a choice, Little Bird. You can keep hiding from who you really are, or you can take this knife and be free for the first time in your life."

"I'm not like you."

"No, you're not." I grabbed her hand and slapped the knife down into her palm. "But you have the same urges."

Her first few steps were tentative. Those quickly morphed into firmer strides until she charged across the room with the blade held high.

Nash didn't fight back when her wrath rained down on him. He barely even blinked. I think whatever part of his humanity remained was happy to have an end.

Watching my Bird vent herself in a shower of blood and pain was the most beautiful thing I'd ever seen. My cock was out and in my hand before she could deliver the third strike.

I stood back and jerked myself while she delivered blow after blow and screamed, "I hate you."

"Die!"

And...

"You ruined everything."

I saw the beast rise from inside her. I watched its sharp teeth gnash about, but I snapped when she turned around to look at me, all covered in blood.

I marched across the room and pushed down on her shoulders.

"Suck my fucking cock, Little Bird."

She peeked up at me through her lashes and smirked as she wrapped her perfect pink lips around the head of my cock. The sexy little minx didn't stop there. She worked her way up my length and swallowed me down.

A loud groan rumbled through my chest as her throat muscles constricted around my cock. Fuck me. She really was good at everything.

I wrapped my fist in her hair and fucked her face until she was gagging, and tears streamed down her face. When that wasn't enough, I pushed her back into the pool of blood beside Nash's body and tore her pants off.

She gave as good as she got. Marnie raked her nails up my back when I plowed into her and let out a long and heady moan. There was nothing sweet or tender about what we were doing. Rough would've been a step up from the brutal and messy way we were using each other.

When I bit her, she scratched me.

When I fucked her, she fucked me back just as hard.

And when I choked her, she snarled at me to do it harder.

I painted her with Nash's blood while her pussy spasmed, and she arched her back.

It was the best game of 'push and pull' I'd ever played.

This was the real Marnie Dupire. Not the timid little thing that walked around town with her head hung. She was the woman bouncing on my cock with no hesitation or thought. This was whom I saw glimmering in those eyes. This was my soulmate, my beautiful, messy, and broken soulmate.

I came so hard that it felt like my heart stopped.

Afterward, we lay there, out of breath, covered in blood, holding each other.

It was perfect until Marnie asked, "Did you get the guy that killed Derek?"

I sighed.

Fuck.

"About that…" I tightened my arm around her shoulders, pressing her harder against me. "There's a hit out on a few people in town."

"What!" She tried to lift her head off my chest, but I pushed her back down.

"There's no need to worry. I've got it handled."

"Was Derek on the list?"

I shook my head. "No, he was just a casualty."

Marnie was getting angry again. Good, I could go again. My dick was already hard when I felt her muscles tense. My eyes slid over the curve of her hip as my palm smacked down on her ass. Fuck, I loved the way she squealed when I did that.

"Stop it." She returned my hit with a tiny slap of her own on my chest. "I'm trying to have a serious conversation with you."

Well, I seriously wanted another taste of that pussy.

Ignoring her objections, I yanked Marnie's leg over my hip and slid my cock back inside her. My eyes rolled in the back of my head as her warmth enveloped me.

"Preston," she softly gritted out. "Who exactly is on this list?"

Who cared?

My hands gripped her hips, holding her in place as I ground my cock deep inside her tight cunt.

"Oh my god," she breathed out and threw her head back.

I liked the way she looked, all sweaty and on the verge of an orgasm, so I did it again. This time my reward was a long, groaned-out moan.

"Can you stop doing that and answer my question?"

There was no way in hell I was going to stop.

"What was your question?" I said while thrusting up so I could watch her pert little tits bounce.

Her hips started to move as she repeated, "Who is on that list?"

"Pretty much everyone I hang out with."

She slammed down on me, making me grunt, "Fuck. Do that again."

"Everyone you hang out with?"

"Yes," I growled and picked up the pace.

This slow shit had to go. I wanted to hear her scream while she rode my cock like a fucking champ. I had her moving in a solid rhythm when Marnie suddenly stopped.

"Wait..." She cocked a brow down at me. "Does that mean I'm on the list?"

"Yes." I speared my fingers into her hair and pulled her down for a kiss. "But I got you covered."

The euphoric blend of her sweetness, combined with blood, had barely touched my tongue before she tore her mouth away.

"I'm not worried about me, Preston! I'm worried about my sister."

Trina? "Why? She's not on the list."

"But she looks just like me."

Yeah, I could see how that might be a problem.

I could feel Marnie's fear pulsing through her pussy. I was so tempted to keep going, and I might've if she hadn't moved to jump off me.

"We need to go!" She shrieked when I grabbed her and pulled her back.

"You need to take a breath and calm down."

"Don't tell me what to do!" The snarl that curled her lip was not helping her cause any. "We need to get to my sister now!"

"Okay, but we kind of look like we just stepped out of a horror movie," I pointed out, making her stop and look down at all the blood.

"So, we could go now or have a quick shower." Where I could finish fucking her. "And then head to your parent's house right after."

I could see the urgency on her face, but logic was also there, which was what won.

"A shower might be a good idea."

Chapter 36

Marnie

$\mathcal{I}$ don't think I'd ever cursed shampoo as much as I did while trying to have the world's quickest shower. Blood did not wash out easily. I gave up after the third wash and rinse.

It probably would've helped if Preston stopped sticking his cock in me. When this was over, I was going to kick his ass. If I wasn't in such a hurry to get to my sister, I might've done more than smack him, which only spurred him on.

When we were dressed and ready to go, I practically flew out of the door.

"Roll up your window. You're gonna get sick."

I didn't care if I got sick or how cold it was. The only thing that mattered was getting to my sister. The sense of urgency wasn't getting any better. I was bouncing in my seat three minutes into the drive.

"Can you hurry up?"

"I would, Little Bird. But in case you haven't noticed, we're in the middle of a hurricane," Preston said as something large and brown blew across the road. "Speeding probably isn't the best idea."

I understood where he was coming from, but it was just a hurricane. They weren't uncommon in Florida. "We need to get to Trina."

"You won't be much help if you're dead."

As if to reiterate his point, something banged off the passenger door.

I stuck my head out the window and into the torrential downpour, trying to see any damage. My already wet hair whipping across my eyes prevented that from happening. Okay, so Preston might have a point about the window.

I pulled my head back in and hit the button to bring the pane of glass back up. That didn't do anything to dull down the sound of wind whistling past. If this were any other time, I might be concerned about being out in this weather, but this wasn't any other time. Trina's life was in danger, and that superseded any storm. A bigger car would've been nice, though.

Preston's BMW was fighting against the wind.

Every little jerk it made brought new images of horror to my mind, like finding my sister in a pool of blood…or staring into her empty eyes as she collapsed on the cold, hard ground. What if we were too late? Someone could've gotten to her already and been doing horrible things to her.

I smacked the dash. "Come on!"

Preston grumbled something under his breath. The only thing I caught was 'fucking.' I was too busy reading the street signs to listen to his random muttering. He should be happy I let him put on a shirt before pulling him out the door.

Third street.

Two more blocks, a left turn, and we'd be there.

Those last few minutes of travel dragged on. My body couldn't decide what to do. Anxiety had me bouncing in my seat, shuffling around, and rocking back and forth. I wasn't entirely sure if the car stopped before I threw open the door and ran for the house.

I rushed into my parent's house and gave the brown couch and matching chair in the living room a quick scan. They were here. I knew that because my father's and sister's cars were in the driveway. Yet, I saw and heard no one. It was quiet and calm.

Too calm.

That was when a sound coming from my sister's room caused my ear to twitch.

On the way here, I imagined finding Trina in all kinds of scenarios, bleeding, already dead, and perfectly fine. What I opened the door to didn't come close to any of the horrific images that had floated through my mind.

It was so much worse.

My feet became glued to the floor as I stood there watching a bare-ass move—my father's bare ass. Trina was under him, staring dully up at the ceiling. I couldn't 'be seeing' what I thought I was. Trina was the good one. The daughter, our father, decided to love.

My father grunted, causing a wave of nausea to roll through my stomach.

He was fucking my sister. His own daughter. Suddenly everything made sense. The special treatment he'd given Trina, her acting out, and the way he punished me. Everything clicked into place. After everything I endured to protect my sister, he still got his hands on her.

I was going to be sick.

The first time I saw fear take over my father's face was the moment he turned his head and saw me standing there.

"Marnie, this isn't what it looks like."

His pathetic dick was still inside her, and he was trying to deny it?

A silent message passed between Trina and me when our eyes locked.

Without a second thought, I snatched a belt off her dresser and jumped onto the bed, where I wrapped it around my father's neck. He bucked and shot up, trying to knock me off his back, but Trina stopped him. She wrapped her legs around him and seized fistfuls of his hair, yanking his neck down into the pressure of the belt.

All the pain and sadness I'd felt through the years came out in a scream. All the times, I had to sleep on my stomach because my back hurt too much—the lectures and holy taunts and the grains of rice

369

that dug into my knees were now coming out in coughs and sputters. He was going to choke on every second I cried myself to sleep.

My arms burned from the exertion, but I refused to stop. Hell was waiting for its next victim, and I hoped his righteous ass burned all the way down.

When my father finally went limp, I still couldn't stop. I held that belt up high and brought it down on his back, over and over and over again. Every single strike wiped a quote from my mind.

'Desire is the devil's sin.'

Smack.

'I will not let you taint and corrupt your sister.'

Thwack.

'Pray for salvation, Marnie.'

"You pray for salvation, motherfucker!"

I rained down a fury that the god of wrath would be envious of, and when I couldn't do that anymore, I grabbed the first sharp object I could find and started carving him up. Revenge was all I could taste. It clouded my vision in a bright red curtain of rage.

"Marnie."

Trina. My sweet sister's voice was right there. She was supposed to make it out clean. I could endure the abuse because she was safe.

"Marnie, stop."

But it was all a lie. Everything was a lie, and I was going to keep digging into his corpse until I found the truth.

"That's enough, Little Bird."

It would never be enough. Not as long as his eyes were still here.

But it wasn't his eyes I was staring into—his eyes weren't gray...

Preston?

His hands were cupping my cheeks, and he was talking. "He's dead. You can stop now."

Who's dead?

My eyes trickled over my arms. They were slick with a thick red substance. Blood? We showered before we came, didn't we? That was when I noticed the torn flesh around my wrists. My hands were buried in my father's stomach. I killed him. I murdered my father because he was raping my sister!

"You, son of a bitch!" I ripped my hands out of his stomach and slapped my father across the face. "I'm going to kill you!"

"Yeah, you already did that." With a grunt, Preston lifted me off the bed and carried me across the room.

I screamed and kicked out, trying to reach back for the bloody mess on Trina's bed. "I'm not finished."

"Yes, you are."

Preston sat me down on the dresser and gave my cheek a light slap.

"Look at me." I did, even though I didn't want to. "You're freaking your sister out."

Shit, Trina.

She was staring at me from the corner of the room with wide eyes. One look at the sheet she was covering herself with had me jumping off the dresser to throw my arms around her.

"Trina, I'm so sorry."

"Oh, Marnie," she cried back. "I never wanted you to see that."

We held each other for what seemed like forever, yet it didn't feel long enough. I wanted to hold her until she knew everything was going to be okay. That her suffering was over, and she was safe now. But I also wanted to know...

"Why didn't you tell me?" I pulled out of my sister's embrace and gazed into her eyes. There was a dullness behind that vibrant glimmer that I hadn't noticed. Maybe I wasn't looking hard enough. "I could've helped you."

I was so caught up in what was happening to me that I didn't think about what could be happening to her. I'd never forgive myself for being so blind.

Despite everything that just occurred, Trina still smiled. "No, you couldn't, Marnie. I know what happened with Nash."

She did? How? I never told her.

"I saw the look on your face that day. Nash broke you, and I couldn't let our father do the same. So when I saw him watching you sleep, I convinced him that more was taken from you that day." Trina glared over at what was left of our father. "Sick bastard had a thing for purity. As long as you weren't pure, he wouldn't touch you."

All this time, I thought I was protecting her. "Trina—"

She cut me off. "It's okay, Marnie. It's done."

"It's not okay." It would never be okay.

My sister pinched my chin like she used to when we were little. "You're fine, so yes, it is."

My response was interrupted by shattering glass. The next thing I knew, smoke was billowing into the room so quickly that I lost sight of everything else. The room faded away into a thick, suffocating cloud.

"Marnie, get down," Preston called out, followed by what sounded like gunfire.

I fell to my hands and knees and crawled in the direction I thought he was. It was so chaotic. Crashes, bangs, and yelling flooded my ears until I was lying on the floor, praying for it to end.

A familiar hand suddenly shot out of the madness and lifted me off the floor. I'd never been happier to see Preston than when he carried me out of the smoke-filled room.

Then I remembered. "Trina's in there."

I reached over his shoulder, desperately grasping for the cloud my sister was trapped in.

"No, she's not." Preston shook his head. "He took her."

Chapter 37
Marnie

A rift had grown between Trina and me during our teenage years. I assumed it was because we were so different. Trina liked to party, and I preferred being left alone. As it turned out, we were more similar than I thought.

We both experienced traumas, but we handled them very differently. At least I had my sister to lean on, but she had no one. Trina suffered in silence, and now, she was alone again.

I'd just gotten my sister back, only to have her taken away. It was the worst feeling in the world.

My brow rose when Preston pulled into the outlook on the bluffs.

He said he knew where they were going, but this place?

The storm dampened the geysers' roar, but the winds splashed their tinted spray across the ground. It looked like a river of blood was bubbling up through the earth. Some people in town said this place was cursed. Many had ended their lives by jumping off the edge, and even more had thought about it, including Chase. Dread hung in the air here. It painted the rocky surface with the souls it claimed.

This was the last place for a rescue mission.

"All right, Little Bird, since you insisted on coming with me, I need you to listen and listen well."

Preston wanted to drop me off at Micha's. I refused. Trina was not going to slip through my fingers. Not again. I wouldn't make the same mistake I did in childhood. This time, I would save her. No matter what it took.

"This prick wants me, not you." Preston grabbed my chin and forced me to look at him. "So no matter how much you want to run out there, you will stay behind me. Understand?"

I swallowed and nodded my head. "What if he hurts you?"

Preston rolled his eyes. "He's not that good."

He was awfully sure of himself. "He was good enough to put a hit out on everyone."

"Anyone with a computer could've done that."

That was a valid point, but still…

"How long has he been here without you knowing?"

Preston filled me in on whom he suspected this guy was, which I'd have a word with Micha about later. You didn't hire a kid to kill someone, and it didn't matter if he was a kid too.

"Exactly my point. This asshole had plenty of time to take me out, yet he didn't." Preston cocked a brow at me. "Do you know why?"

"No. Why would I know that? I'm not a…." I glanced down at the blood staining my skin. "Okay, I'm not a cold-hearted killer."

"That frat boy was pretty cold, but that's a discussion for another time." Preston nodded at something through the windshield. "Show time."

My heart stopped. Standing out on the edge of the bluff was Trina with a gun pressed to her temple. He was going to shoot her. My sister's blood would be added to the countless others that died here. This place really was cursed.

I didn't notice I was standing outside until I heard Preston grumble, "Fuck sakes."

He could be mad all he wanted, but my sole focus was on my sister and the sheet wrapped around her. It was flapping in the wind like a hand waving me over, and I followed the beckoning and stepped over the railing onto the rocky ridge.

"Marnie!" Preston yelled, or at least I thought he did. I could hear his footsteps coming up behind me, but I couldn't stop myself from moving forward.

I needed to get to Trina and the sweet smile spreading across her face.

"Marnie," she sighed. "You shouldn't have come."

"I had to come."

"No," she said. "You didn't."

"Preston." The guy holding her called out through the rain pouring down around us. "Put it down."

"Bite me, dickhead."

I felt a finger dig into my shoulder, followed by a growl. "I told you to stay behind me."

It was Preston. I knew what his touch felt like. As much as I wanted to look back and seek comfort in his face, I couldn't take my eyes off Trina.

The smile I thought was sweet...wasn't sweet at all. It was small and sad. She was so close, yet seemed so far.

"Trina..."

I reached out for her, but Preston pulled me back and cocked his gun. My heart instantly picked up.

"No." I grabbed his hand.

If he took the shot, Trina would go over the edge with him.

Preston wasn't happy with my response.

He jerked his hand and glared down at me. "Let go, Little Bird."

"No," I repeated. "He's still got her."

That's when the other man tipped his head at me. "This is the one you care about?"

The gun pulled away from Trina and aimed at me.

"Drop your gun, or I'll shoot her."

"Not before I get a shot off, asshole," Preston barked back.

I shook my head and searched his eyes, praying he'd see my plea.

He didn't, or he didn't care. He refused to drop his weapon.

"Preston," I tried again.

"Sorry, Little Bird." His eyes rolled back to his opponent. "I won't let you get hurt."

"This will hurt me."

Time slowed down as I anxiously glanced from Preston to my sister. I was terrified that everything was going to crumble. I needed Trina, and she needed me. We were two halves of the same soul.

"It'll be okay," I reassured her.

Preston would figure out something. He always did.

Not this time.

I felt a gut-wrenching pain when Trina tipped her head and whispered, "It's okay, Marnie." My soul began tearing apart, and there she was, smiling at me like when we were kids, and I skinned my knee.

Flashes and images flew through my mind. We were playing at the park with Riley and Shelby, hiding out in our secret fort in the woods, and there were other happy games. The song Trina sang while brushing my hair and the reassuring smile she gave me when we started a new school. Trina was my rock. It was my turn to be her's, but something flashed across her face, something that went beyond defeat and pain. There wasn't any fight left in those bright eyes because she'd given up.

My hand reached out desperately, trying to stretch a little closer.

"You have everything you need." Trina looked over my shoulder at Preston as the man holding her pulled back the hammer on his revolver. "And that's all that matters."

She kicked her feet off the ground, sending them both careening over the edge.

"No!" I screamed and rushed forward, prepared to go over the edge with her.

But Preston knocked me to the ground.

"Let me go. I have to save her!"

I wanted to hate him. I wanted to blame him for everything, but all I could do was cling to him and cry. "We have to save her."

"She's gone, Marnie." He kissed the top of my head. "She's been gone for a long time."

Epilogue
Preston

THREE MONTHS LATER

The hits disappeared the second the man who put them up did. It took a few weeks to make sure there was no one in town still looking to cash in, but that was handled quickly. Micha and Riley put their wedding off for a couple of months. She needed time to deal with her father's death. Pretty much everything else was back to normal.

My Bird had a hard time adjusting to the loss of her sister, but she was strong and kept her sorrow hidden from everyone but me. During the day, she put on a straight face and took charge of planning the funeral and ensuring her sister's requests were met.

I didn't think her mother would ever get over the way Marnie walked right by her without saying so much as a word. Bitch deserved worse as far as I was concerned. But there was something to be said about being left completely alone. Not even Marnie's grandmother would acknowledge her daughter's existence. Pastor Dupire's widow had no one, while the daughter she didn't protect, had me.

At night, Marnie curled into my arms for comfort, and I gave it to her. I gave her everything she could possibly need. Whether that was having me holding her all night or taking her anger out on a couple of the hitmen Kes and Arek caught. They were the new additions to my dungeon. It took a while, but Marnie came around.

She realized that she could not only survive, but she could be happy.

And I could, too.

Never thought I'd be the guy who would lay down his life for a chick. But I would. Marnie's face was the first thing I wanted to see in the morning and the last before I closed my eyes at night. I felt complete when she was around even though she still battled her urges, but that acceptance would come. She just needed a little training, which I was more than happy to help with.

It was her stubbornness that needed the most work. My Little Bird did not like to give up control. Not that I was complaining. I rather enjoyed taking it from her, and there was nothing wrong with handing her a little taste of power, which was why I'd brought her here.

"Preston." Marnie sighed as I led her through the doors of Mallum. "The wedding is a week away. I don't have time to play."

"There's always time to play."

I thought I'd get all of Marnie's time when Tico left. I called in a favor with an acquaintance. Jasper would keep Tico safe and ensure he remained that way. But Riley had her running around like crazy. It was fucking annoying. I didn't like sharing my shit, but I understood it. They'd both lost someone and had bonded over it. That didn't mean I approved of her spending so much time with someone else—especially someone who tried to talk her out of dating me when she found out about us.

Too bad for Riley—we were already married. We eloped last week, and there wasn't a motherfucker out there strong enough to take the ring off my wife's finger.

"Would you change your mind if I told you I had a present for you?" she said.

"No."

"Come on," Marnie sang. "It's something you'll want to know. I promise."

"Is it that you're pregnant?"

Her jaw dropped. "How did you know?"

"You're a week and a half late."

"Your knowledge of my cycle is seriously disturbing. Most guys don't even want to talk about that stuff."

I shrugged. "I'm not most guys."

I didn't understand what the big deal was. A period was just a little blood, which would not stop me from fucking her. We'd made worse messes with icing and sugar. That was a good cake.

Marnie huffed and followed me to the back room. "You should've said something."

"I figured you'd tell me when you wanted to."

"You know? Sometimes I really hate you."

I twisted my neck to shoot her a smirk. "No, you don't."

Her eyes narrowed. "There's a fine line between love and hate."

"Not that fine." I leaned in to growl in her ear, "And I didn't hear you complaining last night."

I'd never be tired of the pink tint flowing down her neck.

"I told you I'd only do it once."

"Oh yeah." I pushed her back against the wall and wrapped her legs around my waist. "What did you like more, Little Bird? My cock in your ass or my gun in your cunt?"

Fuck me, that was hot. I got hard just thinking about the way her perfect little pussy swallowed the barrel of my Desert Eagle while I rammed into her ass. She was starting to like anal. Moaning like a little whore while she came again and again.

Her mouth quirked up at the corner. "It might've been a little fun."

A little? I snorted.

"Wait 'til you see what I've got waiting for you in there."

Intrigue shone in her eyes as she looked over at the door next to us. I'd arranged a little surprise in Lou's dirty, dark playroom. Something I knew she was curious about.

"Well, are you going to show me or fuck me in the hall?"

I was tempted to do both, which I showed her by grinding my hips to press my cock up against her. But…sometimes the wait was better.

Setting Marnie back on her feet, I wrapped my hand around the doorknob. "You ready Little Bird?"

"Always."

That's my girl.

I swung the door open and motioned for her to enter.

The brunette lying on the bed in the center of the room sat up and smiled when we walked in.

"Marnie, this is Amy." I waved my hand, motioning at the other girl. "Amy, this is Marnie."

Amy's eyes lit up as she soaked in my gorgeous Little Bird. "She's cute."

Marnie wasn't so eager.

"Preston, what is this?"

"This is playtime," I explained. "I get to tell you what to do." I would always tell her what to do. "But you…." I wrapped my arms around her waist and whispered in her ear, "You get to tell her what to do."

Now, that news piqued her interest.

Prisoner of the Angry Russian

Hey there, Spitfire. I hope everything is going well for you in that Bratva camp. Know what I did last night? I went to a red carpet show with the governor and his grandson. I know, I know. It's tough living life with a politician, but you gotta do what you gotta do.

Anyway, I heard about your old man and wanted to say I'm sorry. I know you loved him and that he was a good man. It sucks being locked up for our safety, but I'm here for you, Spitfire. Sitting on the beach, under the sun, enjoying my freedom while my girl sucks my cock. But if you give me the word, I'll break out of this hell and come to your rescue. I love you, soon-to-be sister, and I'll always have your back.

P.S. Harper said I should send you flowers, but I thought that was a little boring. So enjoy the singing dandelions.

Your knight in
shining armor
Mason

Dear soon-to-be-dead-brother in-law

I thoroughly enjoyed your letter. It gave me something to burn while I contemplated your death. But the barbershop quartet dressed up like dandelions...now, that shit was funny. I've never seen so many confused mobsters. It's okay to call them mobsters, right? I mean, that's what they are, but try and tell them that, and it turns into this grand argument about the differences between Italian and Russian.

Thank you for the kind words about my father, which you could've said LAST WEEK at the funeral. But I'd hate to pull you away from your political duties. By the way, I'm glad Harper enjoys your dick. Maybe she can give you some tips to prevent choking when I rip it off and shove it down your throat. Please send Silas my condolences. I hope he and Finn are doing well. If THEY need anything, please reach out.

I guess I'll see you all at the wedding. Yes, Mason, that includes you. If you're not there, I will hunt your ass down. Don't mess with me. I'm pregnant and have a gun.

Your well-armed
soon to be sister
Riley

MRS. GRIER

Mrs. Grier
Six Years Later

I closed my eyes and enjoyed the warm sun on my face. The atmosphere in town was fresh and extra crisp as if new life had been breathed into Ashen Springs. And in a way, I supposed it had.

A child's laughter carried through the air, bringing a smile to my lips. All my children were here. Pride filled my heart as I looked at each one of their faces.

Micha Kessler was over by the picnic table holding his two-year-old on his hip so his wife could get something to eat. I remember how he walked down the hall with his nose in the air like he didn't have a care or worry in the world. But look at him now. The way he stared at Riley, one might think the sun and moon shone from her eyes.

He even went into the gallery business for her. Though, I suspected Riley was happy running her uncle's tattoo parlor. That girl never put much stock in money, which was how I knew she was a perfect fit for Micha. She taught him humility, and he taught her to trust herself.

"Stay away from me!" A little girl with the same black hair and navy eyes as her mother sprinted across the grass.

"Don't be such a crybaby, Verity." A little blond boy, who was the same age, chased after her. "It was just a kiss."

Verity spun around to give him the same glare Riley used to give her father. When he was close enough, her leg shot out and promptly kicked him in the dingleberries.

The little boy dropped with a groan.

"Shake it off, Colton," Logan Hudson called out. "You gotta be tougher than that when chasing stubborn pussy."

"Hey, asshole," Micha growled. "That's my daughter."

"Right." Logan slapped him on the chest, then yelled, "Don't forget to buy her flowers after."

I shook my head. Some people never changed. He had matured some because he had to take over his father's company.

"Logan, knock it off. They're only five."

Now, his wife, I liked. Her mother and Louis moved out of town last year for a quieter life. Shelby reminded me of her. She was a beautiful woman who was kind, generous, and glowing with that baby girl in her arms.

"It's never too early to start, Baby." Logan quickly rushed over to scoop the baby out of her arms. "Who's my little Cherry Tart?"

"Good lord, Logan." Shelby rolled her eyes. "Poor Pippa is going to think that's her name. Can you please find something else to call her?"

"Nope," he sang. "You're a pie, and she's a tart."

"Tarts are gone in two bites." Mason Kessler leaned over and shot Shelby a wink. "I'd rather have the pie."

"Will you stop flirting with me?"

"Sorry," he tsked. "Can't do it. I'm a perpetual flirt. It's part of my personality. Isn't that right, Edith?"

I rolled my eyes. "I'm not above giving you detention, Mr. Kessler."

"I love it when you talk dirty to me."

For as much of a hassle as he was, Mason Kessler was my favorite.

I always knew that boy had potential. He just needed a push in the right direction. He was in the last year of his Master's program for psychology, and his wife was about to publish her third book. Not too bad for the class screw-up and outcast.

"Hey!" Mason raised his hand to point at identical twin boys. One held a stick in the air, while the other had a garbage can draped over him. "How many times do I have to tell you, put your back into your swings."

His children may need the same push, except for his daughter. She was the quieter one of the triplets. Always had her nose buried in a book like her mother.

The boy holding the stick raised his thumb.

"Okay, dad," he said, then swung, clacking it off the garbage can.

Mason gave him a thumbs up in return. "Good job, Asher."

"I'm Archer."

"I knew that." Mason rolled his eyes and muttered, "I'm gonna start writing their names on their foreheads."

"Better make sure you write the right one," Silas grumbled.

"Shouldn't you be on tour somewhere?"

"Even rockstars have vacations." Silas's last album went platinum.

"Wanna see a rockstar get punched in the face?" Mason shot back.

"Wanna see a shrink get drowned in the bathtub?"

Mason's mouth fell open with an overly dramatic gasp. "That term is derogatory. London! Your husband is making fun of my chosen career path again."

Star rolled her eyes over her shoulder and sighed, "I'm sure you'll survive."

She was sitting with their son, Oliver, next to Harper and Lana.

Parker was off to the side, playing with Winslow and Mika. Mika was Harper and Mason's daughter. His son, Weston, was up in the treehouse, watching everyone. He reminded me of his uncle.

"Grandma, can I get you anything?"

My beautiful Marnie. There was a time I thought Preston Whitley was a lost cause, but he saved my girl from herself. She'd never smiled like this, not even as a child.

"No, dear, I'm fine." My eyes fell down to her swollen belly. "How's little Trina doing today?"

I missed my other granddaughter so much.

"Oof." Marnie blew out a breath and rubbed her belly. "She's kicking up a storm."

"She's like her namesake, then." I smiled.

It was good to know my granddaughter would live on in some way. The only thing I was sad about was that I wouldn't get to meet her when she was born.

"You go on now." I waved her off. "Go and get something to eat."

Marnie's husband was over by the grill, teaching their son King to cook.

My granddaughter walked away, and it warmed my heart to see how Preston looked at her.

A hand squeezed my shoulder. "Are you going to tell them?"

Greta and her husband had become dear friends. They knew why I'd arranged this get-together.

"No." I reached back and squeezed her hand. "Let them enjoy the day."

I sat for a while and watched. The love and smiles spread across my backyard. Every moment was a treasure to behold. They were going to be okay. My children had grown into amazing adults and didn't need me anymore.

When the sun started to set, I excused myself to go and lay down. Seeing all of their faces helped to set me at peace.

I headed into the house and walked up the stairs to my room but was interrupted before I could lie down.

"Gama." King stood in the doorway with his head tipped to the side. "Do you have to go now?"

He was so intuitive.

"Yes, my sweet boy. It's time for me to go and be with your grandpa."

His face screwed up, and for a moment, I thought he was going to cry.

"Will you tell him about me?"

I couldn't stop the smile from curling my lips. "Yes, King, I will tell him all about you."

"Okay." He nodded. "Have a good sleep, Gama."

"You too, sweet boy."

I watched him walk away as another voice whispered in my ear. A voice I hadn't heard in six years.

"Come on, grandma. Grandpa's waiting for us."

AFTERWORD

Thank you for reading Panic-Button

Marnie and Preston tested me at every turn and I hope you enjoyed their journey. This marks the end of The Order Of Ravens And Wolves, and because I can't seem to let them go just yet keep your eye out for an upcoming novella. All of this started with Micha and Riley and it only seems fitting to end it with their wedding.

I would like to thank my beta readers, you guys are great and I'd totally forget stuff if it wasn't for you. You keep me going when writing gets exhausting.

And to my work wives, who are always inspiring me to keep going, I love you guys.

If you'd like to know what happens with Tico you can find him in MF Adele's No Name.

If we reach 100 reviews I will release the scene with Tico and Dean.

If we get to 150 I'll release the scene with Amy, Marnie, and Preston.

Thank you for coming on this amazing ride with me. I can't wait to start the next one.

Also by T.L. Hodel

The Order Of Ravens And Wolves:
Aftereffect
Scartissue
Happenstance
Accident-Prone
Relapse
Panic-Button

Deviant House:
Innocence
Innocence corrupted (coming soon)

The Lost Souls:
Adversaries
Frenemies

Brothers Of Shadow And Death:
Backfire
Backstab (coming soon)

The Seven Sins Series:
Pride

The Buchanan Brothers
Twisted Abel
Twisting Tallon (Coming soon)

ABOUT THE AUTHOR

T.L. Hodel is a Canadian author, poet and artist. Through coming up from a difficult childhood she excelled at writing, having her first poem published in junior high. When not writing she occupies herself with numerous crafts, hobbies and is an avid gamer and horror movie fan. She lives in Calgary with her kids and cat, (who is a complete asshat), and may have a slight weakness for true crime shows.

Connect with T.L. Hodel online:
www.facebook.com/groups/272402970612789/?ref=share
www.instagram.com/tarahodel
www.facebook.com/Author-TL-Hodel-102923044775313/

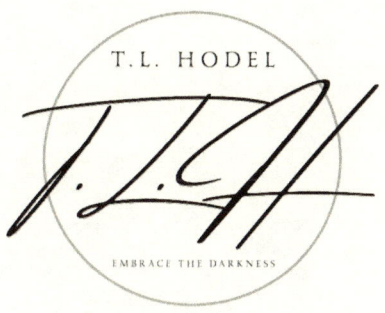